THE BARON OF MALEPERDUYS

First Calliope Press paperback edition published 2012

THE BARON OF MALEPERDUYS. Copyright 2012 by David R. Witanowski. All rights reserved. No part of this book may be used or reproduced in any matter whatsoever without written permission except in cases of brief quotation embodied in critical articles and reviews.

This book is a work of fiction. The characters, incidents, and dialogue are drawn from the author's imagination and are not to be construed as real. Any resemblance to actual events or persons, living or dead, is entirely coincidental.

Manufactured in the United States of America.

THE BARON OF MALEPERDUYS
ISBN 978-0-578-10962-6

THE BARON OF MALEPERDUYS

by

David R. Witanowski

<u>CALLIOPE PRESS</u>

"Ah, love, let us be true
To one another! For the world, which seems
To lie before us like a land of dreams,
So various, so beautiful, so new,
Hath really neither joy, nor love, nor light,
Nor certitude, nor peace, nor help for pain;
And we are here as on a darkling plain
Swept with confused alarms of struggle and flight,
Where ignorant armies clash by night."

      - Matthew Arnold

THE BARON OF MALEPERDUYS

I

The girl ran and Martin followed.

She was tall and lanky, almost awkward, her hair done up in tails that swung wildly as she ran. Her name was Rukenaw, and she lived on the far end of the village, near the north woods, and Martin was in love with her.

"Where shall we hide?" he asked her when they were far enough away from the others to stop for breath. "The stables?"

"Too easy," she replied, panting.

"Under the mill?"

Her nose, ruddy in the crisp air, wrinkled up with distaste. "It smells under there."

"And you are afraid of spiders," Martin added.

"I am not," Rukenaw protested, quietly though so as not to give away their position. "Besides, it will be the first place she'll look."

Martin poked his head around the haystack that they had chosen for a temporary hiding spot, his eyes scanning the village for signs of pursuit. But Aelcrotte was still hunched over the side of the town's well, her face pressed against the greenish stones and her arms draped over her head.

"Ah, piss," Martin spat suddenly.

"What is it?"

"Quanteskieve is under the footbridge."

She snorted, and clambered over him to get a look for herself. "Is Brunel with her?"

"I think so," Martin said, squinting for effect, suddenly aware of the soft pressure of the girl's breast against the back of his arm. "I thought I saw them go off together earlier."

"She should have picked a better spot," Rukenaw giggled, and she rolled off him, her hands brushing at the hay that clung to her simple dress. "They won't be alone very long."

"At least they have a place to hide," Martin muttered darkly. "We're going to be caught out in the open if we don't decide soon."

"Well," Rukenaw sniffed, "If you think I'm stupid enough to lurk under the footbridge with you, Martin, then perhaps I'd better look for my own place to hide."

"And just what is wrong with the footbridge?" Martin demanded.

"Well-" Rukenaw hesitated. "Well, for one thing it's far too damp."

"And?"

"I saw a snake under there once."

"Hydra's Teeth," Martin swore.

"It was a big snake," she added.

"Forget it," he said, shaking his head. "Aelcrotte's stopped counting. We might as well give up, unless you want to hide in the open pasture. Or are you afraid of sheep, too?"

Her eyes flashed hot with anger, and for a moment Martin actually thought that she might strike him, but when at last she moved she merely got to her feet and began walking towards the tall grass beyond the hayfield, and the dark eaves of the Wild Wood.

"Where are you going?" Martin asked when he had caught up with her.

"To hide, stupid."

"But-" Martin stammered. "That's not fair. The others won't find us in there."

"That's the point of the game isn't it?" Rukenaw drawled, and quickened her pace.

When she noticed that Martin was not following her she turned, her mouth curled into a fierce grin.

"You know we aren't supposed to," he said lamely. "My father says there are chimera in the woods."

"Chimera don't frighten me," she said, and parted a thick set of branches that the village priests had hung with fetishes carved into the shape of the Firebird.

Somewhere above them a trio of crows burst into flight, startled by the intrusion.

"But what if-"

"What's wrong, Martin? Don't you want to kiss me?"

Before he could answer she had disappeared into the wood.

A moment later he followed.

The air was thick and heavy under the trees of the forest, and it was so dark that Martin nearly stumbled into Rukenaw without seeing her.

"You're very brave," she said and pressed her lips against his. Slowly, he slid an arm around her waist and, when she did not protest, pulled her closer.

"It tickles," she said suddenly.

"I'm sorry," he said, releasing her.

"No, I like it," she said and took one of his hands. "I like you."

"I like you, too," he managed.

"Martin?" she said, hesitating a little. "Can you keep a secret?"

"Of course," he said, and sealed his promise with a kiss on her cheek. "What is it?"

"I want to show you something," she said, giving his hand a good tug.

"What is it?" he asked again, his voice betraying only a hint of how nervous he was. He had not forgotten where they were.

"You'll see," she said with a crooked smile and led him by the hand deeper into the woods.

* * * * * * *

"It's getting late," said Martin, as nonchalantly as he could manage. They had been walking for some time, and if Rukenaw was following a path through the old twisted trees of the wood, he could not make it out. "The others will have stopped looking for us by now."

"Just a little farther," she said. "I promise."

"How do you even know where you are going?" Martin said, wincing as a dead branch snapped loudly beneath one of his feet. He could not shake the feeling that there was something watching them, just beyond sight.

"I come here sometimes," Rukenaw answered. "When I want to be alone."

Martin did not press the girl further. He knew the reputation of the man that Rukenaw's mother had married after her husband fell victim to the Red Death.

So they walked in silence until, after passing through a tree-choked gully that led directly to a massive deposit of sandstone, Rukenaw came to a halt.

"This is it," she said.

Martin peered around the girl expectantly, but saw nothing save for a jumbled pile of mossy stones that centuries of rain had dislodged from the escarpment, having fallen against each other in such a way as to create a natural enclosure.

"What?" he said.

"Look closer," Rukenaw pleaded.

Martin sighed and crossed over to the stones. "I don't see any-"

Martin's next words caught in his throat, and he instinctively took a step backwards. There was a face glaring at him from the shadows. He thought at first that it was a man, until he could make out a pair of elongated eyes, and see that the thing's brow was crowned with a pair of curling horns.

"A faun!" Martin cried out, and cast about for a thick branch with which to defend himself. "Rukenaw, run!"

"Calm down," the girl giggled, placing a firm hand on Martin's arm to stop him. "It can't hurt you! Look."

Before he could stop her, Rukenaw had slipped between two of the fallen stones.

"Wait!" he said, alarmed, and ran in after her.

There was, of course, no faun awaiting Martin within the cramped confines of those ancient stones, though what he saw did little to ease his discomfort. What he had taken for the head of a chimera was in fact a weathered stone carving that hung, sentinel-like, over an arched passage that was too smooth to be natural. And, as his eyes adjusted to the light, he could see that the fallen rocks were actually the ancient fragments of columns, across which danced curling pictograms.

"Isn't it wonderful?" Rukenaw said, tracing her fingers along the faint lines that encircled one of the columns. "There is writing too, but I can't read it."

"Where does it go?" Martin asked in a hushed voice, staring into whatever black gulf lay beneath the solid rock.

"I don't know," the girl replied.

"Alright," Martin said, "Where do you *think* it goes?"

"Maybe it leads to a dragon's nest," the girl replied, excited, "Full of gold and jewels. Or maybe it's a tunnel, and on the other side there's a high castle where a sorcerer lives."

"It's probably just an old mine," Martin said, only half believing it himself.

"Oh, come on, Martin! Let's find out where it goes!"

"But there could be anything in there," Martin objected, "How do you know it's safe?"

"I don't," she said, and, kneeling down by the base of one of the broken columns, uncovered a basket that contained one of the bird-shaped candle lanterns that the village priest made. "But now I have my brave Martin with me."

"How did you get that?"

"I borrowed it."

"Stole it, you mean."

"I'll give it back," she fussed as she struck a few shards of flint together over a small bundle of tinder, and Martin realized that she must have stolen these items as well. "Now are you going to come with me or not?"

"Maybe I should go first," Martin offered, when she had gotten the lantern lit. "In case something happens."

"My brave Martin," Rukenaw cooed and gave his shaking hand a squeeze before passing the lantern to him.

"Who built this place?" Martin asked as he took the first few steps into the passage, his feet scattering loose pebbles that sent echoes jumping into the darkness ahead of them.

"Maybe these can tell us," Rukenaw said, peering at the walls that, like the columns at the entrance, were decorated with odd carvings.

The lantern did not provide much light, but Martin could make out a series of panels filled with human-like figures astride creatures that he might have taken for horses before noticing the curling horns that grew from their heads. Before them they drove great herds of unidentifiable beasts, some of whom they had pierced with shafts. These hunting scenes continued for some time, until they came to a great panel, far larger than the rest, which depicted seven great stars streaking across the night sky, and a great mass of figures with their arms raised towards them.

"Look at this one," he said, taking a step towards the carving. Then he felt something brittle collapse under the weight of his foot with a dull crack.

"What was that?" Rukenaw asked, her voice trembling somewhat.

Martin lowered the lantern, and when he saw that his foot was lodged in the ribcage of a massive skeleton he was so startled that he dropped the lantern, which promptly went out.

By the time the boy and girl had stopped running and collapsed panting into the thick brush that grew around the entrance to the ruin, Rukenaw's screams of terror had turned to peals of laughter that shook the young girl's body.

"It isn't funny!" Martin protested.

"Yes it is," she managed, "You should have heard yourself scream!"

"As I recall, you were screaming just as much I was."

"Well," she said, growing more sober. "At least *I* didn't drop the lantern. Now we're going to have to go back in there and get it."

"What do you mean, 'we?' I'm not going back in there! At least," he added, when he saw the disappointment etched across the girl's face, "Not without another light."

"Fine," she said, and sighed. "It's getting late anyway, and we can always come back tomorrow."

"I have chores to do tomorrow."

"The next day then?"

Martin hesitated, but said, "The next day."

He did love her, after all.

* * * * * * *

Perched high in the trees, a male shrike with a brilliant red breast shifted from foot to foot, its glittering black eyes studying the noisy pair below as they crashed clumsily through the underbrush.

"Man-fools," it chirruped as it spread its wings and launched itself into the air, heading north.

* * * * * * *

It was the month of Sowing and, as Martin was now old enough to work with the men, he spent a good deal of the next morning wielding a hoe in the spring fields. After the midday meal he was sent to collect firewood from the southern woods, which lay across the little river that ran through the village, and marked one of the ancient boundaries of the Wild Wood.

It was for this reason that Martin was the first person in the village to see the Calvarians.

He had been snapping the larger branches off a fallen limb when he heard a sort of low rumble that he took for thunder, though the skies had been clear that day and the air was not heavy the way it sometimes is before a storm. Still, as he did not want to be caught out in the open, the boy gathered up his bundle, slipped his father's hatchet into his belt, and began to make his way home.

He was fortunate that the weight of the wood on his back slowed his pace, for without it he would certainly have burst from the trees and been sighted by one of the two dozen white-skinned men riding up the eastern road. One might have taken them for a hunting party, for they rode sleek geldings, wore lacquered bows over their backs, and were accompanied by a number of fearsome lupine hounds. But though Martin had never seen a Calvarian before and could not read the runes on their caps and collars that marked them as scouts of the Fourteenth Regiment, he knew that these men were Northern soldiers.

And Calvarians never took prisoners.

Martin froze in his tracks, his heart thudding wildly in his chest, sure that at any moment one of the fearsome pack hounds would pick up his scent and lead its brothers to him with their teeth bared. But, whether the wind favored him or the beasts were too distracted at the moment to take notice, the scouting party rode by.

He paused a moment and then, shrugging off the straps of his bundle and letting the firewood clatter across the forest floor, he cut across the road and ran north.

I can warn them if I am fast enough, he thought to himself desperately as he ran, *if I can get there before they do–*

Martin might as well have tried to outrun a flood, for by the time he came to the village, his breath ragged and his gut cold, the Calvarians were already at their work. The bodies of those who had not been quick enough to run lay scattered across the southern fields and pastures, cut down by arrows where they stood. Others were being herded like sheep by the fierce dogs, whose masters had dismounted in order to more easily dispatch their prey.

But perhaps the most chilling thing was the calm of the Northerners as they methodically advanced across the village, showing mercy only to the glassy-eyed livestock that gazed on their former keepers' destruction with indifference.

There was only one place the Calvarians had not yet reached, and that was the north field, where Martin could make out a line of little figures streaming into the Wild Wood, the villagers' fear of that forest having apparently been overcome by the threat of certain death at the end of a Northern blade.

And, amongst them, he could see Rukenaw.

He did not know whether or not his father, mother, or either of his two brothers had been slain, but the sight of Rukenaw, her blue skirt and white apron tripping up her legs as she dragged another figure, her younger sister Eme, across the hayfield, put a sort of madness into Martin, and though it would likely mean his death, he broke from the relative safety of the trees and ran to join her.

He was halfway across the northern field when one of the Calvarian hounds barreled into Eme, tearing the smaller girl out of her sister's grip. The dog took hold of the girl by the neck and began to shake her about furiously, ignoring the protestations of Rukenaw, who beat her fists against the thing in vain. Within a few seconds Eme went still, and the dog then turned on the stunned older girl, knocking her to the ground with its forepaws.

Martin screamed as he closed the final distance, and before he realized what he was doing he had buried the head of his father's hatchet into the hound's skull.

The dog stumbled forward, whining in the back of its throat, and then collapsed on its side. Beneath it was Rukenaw, who, though bleeding from a set of bites on her face, was still alive.

"Eme," she said as Martin hauled her to her feet.

"She's- Rukenaw, she's-"

"Eme!" the girl shouted at the body of her sister, as if she might wake her.

"We have to go!" Martin said, and took hold of one of the girl's wrists.

"I can't leave Eme!"

"She's dead, Rukenaw!" Martin screamed, and yanked on her as hard as he could without hurting her. "Do you want to die too?"

Whether she did or not, Rukenaw did not say, but she let Martin lead her into the Wild Wood, and after awhile it was she who led the way.

* * * * * * *

Though they could still hear the distant baying of the hounds behind them, and occasionally a fierce voice crying out in the strange tongue of the Northerners, exhaustion forced them to halt at the mouth of the old ruin in the hillside.

For a while they huddled together beneath the ancient stones, breathing hard, the girl resting her head on Martin's chest, her arms and legs curled up protectively around her.

When she recovered some of her wind she began to weep, and as he held her he wept too.

"Maybe they won't find us," Martin said at last, more for the girl's sake than his own, but Rukenaw did not answer. She had not, in fact, said anything since they had entered the woods, though he had not needed to ask her where they were going. Rukenaw had led them to her secret place the way that metal is drawn to lodestone, and he knew what she intended.

"We don't know where it goes," Martin pointed out as the girl, wiping her eyes, got to her feet and took a few steps into the blackness of the tunnel. "And we don't have the lamp."

Rukenaw motioned for Martin to pick up the box of flint and tinder, and then disappeared into the dark.

And Martin followed.

For a while he could see her in the darkness ahead, her slight outline lit by the light that was rapidly diminishing behind him, but soon there was nothing but darkness. He stopped for a moment, groping with his free hand until he could feel the smooth stone under his fingers. He continued on, hugging the wall and casting about with his foot as he went.

Suddenly he felt the toe of his boot brush against something lying in the middle of the hallway.

"Rukenaw?" he called out, feeling terribly alone. "Please, say something. Where are you?"

"I'm here," he heard the girl's voice say, and felt her hand brush softly against his chest. "Take my hand."

Martin placed his hand over hers, and squeezed it.

"I think I found the lantern," he said.

"Hand me the tinder," she replied.

As Rukenaw began to work with the flint, Martin felt around blindly, his hand recoiling only slightly at the touch of what must have been a smooth and slender bone. Then he felt cold metal under his grip, and-

"Ah!" he cried, feeling something sharp and pointed pierce his palm.

"Martin?"

"I cut my hand," he replied, and sucked in his breath between gritted teeth as the first waves of pain began to throb up his arm. "The glass must have broken when I dropped it."

"Is it very deep?"

"I can't tell."

A flame flickered into life as the bit of dry straw that Rukenaw used for tinder caught, illuminating the girl's tear-streaked face. Lowering the fire she lit the tallow within the broken lantern.

Martin gazed at his hand. The cut was not deep, but it was bleeding badly, and the very sight of the wound seemed to intensify the pain that he felt.

"Don't panic," she said, and with a single motion she tore off a strip of her blouse and began wrapping it tightly around the wound. As she worked he saw that what he had taken for the bones of a giant was nothing more than the skeleton of a wild stag that must have wandered into this dark place to die.

"There," she said as she finished the makeshift tourniquet. "We should go now."

Martin nodded. Even from within the passage he could hear the sounds of their pursuers growing louder by the moment. He did not know if the Calvarians would follow them into the dark, but he did not intend to linger long enough to find out.

"What are you doing?" Rukenaw asked him as he snatched up one of the stag's loose femurs and tore off one of his sleeves.

"We need more light," he explained as he wrapped fabric around the head of the bone, until it resembled a torch.

"It will burn too fast," she said as he set fire to the bundled up shreds of cloth.

"Then we should hurry," he replied and broke into a trot.

Had the circumstances been different, Martin and Rukenaw might have marveled at the things they saw as they fled, for it seemed to them that they had entered a world made up of winding passages and pillared chambers that housed rows of great stone chests. Many of their lids had been carved into the shapes of women and men whose arms were folded neatly over their breasts, or sometimes clutching at swords or slender rods. Others were decorated with figures similar to those that covered the walls; hunters and warriors at battle with beasts and monsters, or prosaic women armed with sickles harvesting grain.

How long they ran through that lightless place Martin could not say. The way they followed was not straight, and sometimes the passages curled until they bent backwards upon themselves, leading them back to places where they could see their own tracks in the thick dust that carpeted the tiled floor.

When Martin's makeshift torch went out their pace slowed, but they could not stop. There were dogs with them in the tunnels now, the sounds of their cries echoing weirdly through the passages.

So on they went, until they reached a chamber from which there was no exit.

"Let's rest here," Martin said grimly. "Just for a while."

The girl nodded, and they lowered themselves wearily to the floor, their backs pressed up against the far wall of the chamber, and there they sat for a time listening as the clatter of boots rose above the howling of the dogs.

Soon Martin could see light in the passageway.

"Why won't they give up?" Rukenaw asked in a small voice. "Why are we so important to them?"

"I don't know," Martin replied, "But when they come, stay behind me."

"No," she said, and took his hand. "We'll stand together."

"Alright," Martin said, rising, but as he pressed his good hand against one of the carvings on the wall in order to support himself, he felt something shift underneath his palm.

Then, with a terrific squeal, the wall swung inwards.

A moment later he and the girl were lying in a heap in a narrow passage, staring at a circular flight of steps slick with slime. The secret door was already swinging back into place, its ancient hinges protesting mightily as it slammed shut with a reverberating boom.

They lay there in the dark, their lantern left behind on the other side of the wall, and listened as the chamber beyond was filled with the furious voices of both man and dog.

"Come on," Martin heard Rukenaw urge, and when he had righted himself he began to crawl up the stairs after her, though his injured hand slowed him considerably.

The Calvarians were already tapping on the walls below.

"Hydra's Teeth!" he heard the girl swear somewhere in the dark ahead of him.

"What is it?"

"It doesn't go any further!" she said, and Martin could hear her hands smacking against stone.

"Is there a latch?" he asked, his hand coming into contact with one of her slippers. "Or a lock?"

"I'm looking!"

Martin climbed up beside her and felt along the slick walls desperately, but could find nothing that indicated how to open the way.

"Wait, I think-" she said, and then Martin could hear the girl grunting as she apparently strained against some immovable force.

"Help me!" she panted.

"I don't know what-"

"Push up!" she yelled.

Martin stood as high as he was able in the cramped stairwell and pressed his back against the stone above, and when he and the girl pushed together the ceiling itself began to move, until they could see thin cracks of light peeking through the gap.

"Just a little farther," Martin groaned, and with one last push they felt the stone above them fall to one side with a crash. At nearly the same instant the false wall below them swung open, and a number of Calvarian war dogs began to speed up the stairs after them.

"*Inwitscear!*" Martin heard one of the Calvarians below shout up at them as he scrambled over the stone lip, and found himself tumbling out of a stone casket that resembled the dozen or so others that filled the low ceilinged chamber where they now found themselves. Daylight streamed into the room from a broad stairway, which they began to climb without delay.

As Martin's eyes adjusted to the sudden brightness, he saw that they were in an exposed ruin, an ancient fane- roofless and given over to moss and ivy. Across from him a trio of women fashioned out of marble stood back to back, their proud limbs and upraised faces blackened by whatever fire had razed this place.

On they ran, not daring to stop, passing underneath an archway that opened onto a weed-choked courtyard ringed by mortared walls that time had crumbled. Great white-leafed willows swayed gently in the wind that the gaps in the stonework admitted, standing sentinel over a stagnant fountain overflowing with dead leaves and branches.

And across the court, its broken parapets jagged against the sky, was the castle.

"You were right," Martin said to the girl, his pace slowing somewhat as they approached the pale door that yawned wide to accept them. "There was a castle after all."

Rukenaw shrieked, and a moment later Martin saw the cause of her distress.

A Calvarian stood in their way.

He was tall, easily twice Martin's height, and was clothed from head to toe in black, save for the hint of red at his throat. He wore a sword at his side, but more worrying to Martin were his icy blue eyes.

They were the staring eyes of a predator.

Trapped! Martin cursed inwardly as he scooped up a loose piece of masonry. *How could they get in front of us so quickly?*

The Calvarian stepped gingerly forward, his head tilting as if examining them.

"Well?" Martin cried out, hefting the stone awkwardly in his uninjured hand. "What are you waiting for?"

The first of the Calvarian hounds burst into the courtyard, skidding slightly as it rushed to bring down its helpless prey. At the same instant the Calvarian leapt towards them, his sword ringing as it slid from its sheath.

Martin charged to meet the Northerner, shouting out what he assumed would be his last cry of defiance and praying to Fenix for a swift death.

Then his legs seemed to give out from under him, and he collapsed into a clump of wild brush, shutting his eyes as he waited to feel the jaws of a dog close around his throat, or the sharp bite of steel in his back.

When neither of these things occurred, Martin turned around.

There was the Northerner, his blade now red with blood, standing directly between Rukenaw and the still form of the dog, whose severed head lay some distance away.

"Stay behind me," he said to the girl as the rest of the pack, howling triumphantly, erupted out of the ruin. She did not argue.

If he had not seen it, Martin would never have believed that one man, even armed with such an elegant blade, would have been able to fight off so many, but there the pale man was, his whirling sword cutting through the pack as they leapt at him, until he stood at the center of a ring of canine bodies.

The hounds' masters were not far behind, and as the man in black finished off one of the suffering beasts ten Calvarian raiders stepped out of the shadows of the ruined temple, their own swords drawn.

One of the them, their leader Martin assumed, pointed his blade at the newcomer and snarled, "*Hwa eart ge?*"

"*Ic hatte Isengrim,*" the man replied. "*Blod-scield ac hlafordswica.*"

Whatever the man in black's response had been, it seemed to send a visible shock through the Calvarian reavers, many of whom took a cautious step backward. Only their captain was unmoved.

"*Ou scealt yfelum deade sweltan,*" the man said, saluting the stranger with his sword. "*Hlafordswica.*"

"*Seo sculan,*" the stranger replied, returning the salute.

The captain advanced, sword raised, and when the man in black did not move he lunged forward. Once, twice, three times their blades met, and then the Calvarian officer dropped his sword, turned, and fell, his mouth foaming with blood. Martin had not even seen the fatal cut.

The other men had used this opportunity to spread out, and now two of them rushed in, their quick deaths giving several of their companions just enough time to sheath their blades and pull their slender bows from their backs.

"*Sceotan*," one of them barked, and promptly collapsed, a wicked-looking dagger embedded in the back of his neck. A moment later another pair of bowmen dropped, their breasts pierced by red-fletched shafts.

Of the ten men that had entered the courtyard, only four now stood, their heads craned towards the walls above, where Martin could see a score of dark figures training crossbows on the men below. The predators had become the prey.

"Tell them we will spare their lives," a voice echoed through the courtyard. "If they will throw down their weapons."

The man in black nodded, and spoke soft words to the men who stood opposite him.

"Calvaria!" one of them cried when Isengrim had finished, charging. His companions, not to be outdone, leapt forward with raised blades.

A moment later, all four Northerners were dead, and the men on the wall had vanished.

The man in black wiped his blade clean with an oiled cloth, sheathed his weapon, and turned towards Rukenaw, who was quivering with shock.

"Are you hurt?" he said, and offered her his hand.

"Stay away from her, you white-faced demon!" Martin shouted, stumbling to his feet and rushing to the girl's side. "If you touch her I'll kill you!"

"I wouldn't if I were you," a voice said.

Startled, the boy whipped around and found that another man, olive-skinned and dark-haired like himself, now stood by his side.

He was short, not much taller than the boy was, poised, and wiry of frame. From his dress Martin might have taken him for a gentleman of quality, for his scarlet doublet and breeches were of fine make, until he noticed that they were patched, worn, and as stained with mud as his boots. Finer though than his clothes was the basket-hilted sword he wore at his side, and the violet gemstone that Martin could see winking at him from under the man's open doublet.

"You are very brave, Martin," the man said with a tilt of his head. "But if you had been paying attention just now, you might have noticed that this 'demon' just saved your life, as well as that of the girl."

"How-" the boy sputtered. "How did you know my name?"

The man smiled, but did not answer.

"Any trouble?" the man asked the Calvarian, nodding towards the bodies that littered the courtyard.

"Their *prafost* had some skill."

"Hirsent will not be happy."

"Hirsent is not here."

Other men, Arcasians all of them, were entering the court now. They were all armed.

Brigands, Martin thought.

"Wulf! They are stubborn," spat a lean man wearing a bandolier of knives over a breastplate as he delivered a kick to one of the corpses. "Friends of yours, Isengrim?"

"Scouts from the Fourteenth," the Calvarian replied coolly as he inspected one of the dead men's collars. "There should be at least another dozen soldiers, and half as many dogs."

"Bastards are a long way from Larsa," rumbled an enormous brute with a double-headed axe. "And you can bet they're not alone."

"I was thinking the same thing," the short man said, turning his attention to a shallow-cheeked bowman whose eyes were nearly concealed beneath a strangely peaked cap. "Who can we spare to scout out the eastern reach?"

"Geaibleu and Bavarde are strong enough now to make the flight," the man answered, his soft voice betraying a Luxian accent. "But they cannot speak as well as their mother."

"It will have to do," the short man sighed, dismissing the Southerner. "Now then, we don't have much time to waste. Tybalt!"

"You don't have to yell," the knifeman replied.

"I need you and your best men to set a snare down in the catacombs for whoever comes looking for these scouts."

"How glamorous," the man drawled as he retrieved a blade from one of the bodies. "I just happen to know the perfect spot."

"Don't engage. Just lead them to the southwest junction-"

"Where Bruin's lot will be waiting, yes, I know the drill, *Baron* Reynard."

"Good," the man in scarlet replied curtly. "As for the rest of you: get mounted up, and pack enough food and drink for three days. We might just need to run the maze."

"Hey, Tybalt," the axe wielding giant shouted as the men began to file out of the courtyard, over half of them exiting by way of the ruined temple, snatching up the torches and lanterns that the Calvarians had carried as they did so. "Make sure you don't get used up before I get my boys in place."

Tybalt flashed a vulgar pair of fingers in response and then descended into the dark.

"Bruin's men are not accustomed to close quarters combat," the Calvarian said. "Perhaps I should accompany them-"

"*Ceorl!*" a voice snapped, and Martin nearly jumped when he saw that another Calvarian, a woman in white, was now crossing the courtyard rapidly, her eyes smoldering with what appeared to be considerable anger. "What is meaning of this?"

"Hirsent," the man called Isengrim began, "This is not what it-"

"You are promising never to be doing this again," the woman fumed in broken Arcasian. "You are making promise to me."

"I was never in any real danger."

The woman's hand flew through the air to strike the man in the face, but he caught her arm by the wrist and held it there for a moment. As he released her she lapsed into the Northern tongue, making furious gestures towards the bodies heaped around them.

"Reynard," Isengrim said, his voice shaking. "Perhaps you might see to the boy and girl?"

"Of course," the other replied, and turned towards the boy and girl with an outstretched hand. "Will you come with me, please? I swear that no harm will come to either of you for as long as you remain my guests."

When they both nodded their assent the man in scarlet turned and led them to an ivy-shrouded portal in the wall that opened onto a stairwell.

"My mother," Rukenaw said as they began to climb, choking on the word. "There were others that got out of the village before- Do you know if they-"

"I wish I could tell you that they were safe," the man said, turning, his tin-flecked eyes soft for a moment. "But I fear that you and Martin are the only survivors from your village. I am sorry."

"Who are you?" the boy demanded, "What is this place?"

"My name is Reynard," he replied, "And this is my home."

The man opened a reinforced door, and when they passed through it and looked over the weathered parapet, they could see that this ancient fortress stood at the center of a bowl-shaped valley, perched on a pair of perilously steep cliffs overlooking a lake whose waters shone like turquoise.

"Welcome to Maleperduys."

II

Hermeline kept a small garden off the kitchen, which she shared with Madam Slopecade, the cook, so that one could find feverfew and valerian growing there side by side with rosemary, sage, and mint. It was a tiny place compared to the sprawling temple gardens she had tended when she lived in Calyx, but it still managed to remind her of those times, and she found comfort there, when Reynard was away.

"Martin, be a dear and fetch me some fresh water," she said to the boy, who had hardly looked up from weeding since that morning.

The boy nodded as he rose from his work, and exited the garden by way of the kitchen, where the women were busy preparing the midday meal.

"What's wrong with him?" the girl asked, once Martin was gone. "He's so quiet."

"Be patient with him," Hermeline said, setting a freshly picked bundle of herbs into the girl's lap. "He is not as strong as you are."

The girl seemed to reflect on this for a moment.

"Mistress, what will happen to us- Martin and me?"

"I'm afraid that I can never be entirely certain what Master Reynard will say or do," Hermeline answered, her lips curling into a little smile, "But I imagine that he will let you stay here with us. Would you like that?"

"Could I help you tend your garden?"

"Of course," the older woman replied. "And I could teach you to dance, and how to sing."

"And what about Martin?" the girl said, glancing towards the kitchen.

"We always need more hands here," Hermeline said. "Especially men."

"Will he learn how to fight?"

"If that is what he wishes," Hermeline replied, and stretched until her back popped with a crack. "But it will be some time before he is old enough to think of such things."

When the boy returned, Hermeline set him and Rukenaw to watering the plants, and watched them as she finished her own work.

A shadow passed fleetingly over the garden. Hermeline shielded her eyes with one hand and looked to the sky where she could just make out the winged creature circling the castle.

It was one of Tiecelin's shrikes, returning with news.

"Rukenaw," the woman said as she lifted herself to her feet, her heart pounding in her chest. "When you and Martin are done, see if Madam Slopecade has any chores for you."

"Where are you going?" the girl asked, a hint of worry creeping into her voice.

"I won't be gone for very long," Hermeline reassured her as she brushed a bit of dirt off the rear of her skirts. "I promise."

"Can I come with you?"

"I'd rather that you stayed here and worked," Hermeline said, "But if you promise me that you will do as I say and don't wander off, I suppose it will be alright."

"I promise," the girl said, setting down her watering can and latching onto Martin's hand instinctively. "And Martin too."

"I can stay," Martin said to the girl. "I want to help."

"You'll be alright by yourself?" Hermeline asked.

The boy nodded.

"Very well," Hermeline said, and stepped through the wooden gate that separated the garden from the keep's main courtyard.

Bruin was there, running several of the men through a series of exercises. There were almost a hundred men and women who lived under Reynard's protection now, almost all of whom owed him their lives. Many were like Martin and Rukenaw: innocents who had been driven into the wilds by marauding soldiers on either side of the war between Arcasia and Calvaria. Others, such as Baldwin, the castle's resident priest of the Firebird, they had picked up during the dangerous journey to the barony. Some were even the remnants of a gang of brigands that had terrorized the countryside for years before Reynard put an end to them, offering mercy to those who would swear loyalty to him.

Bruin was too busy to notice her as she and the girl crossed the courtyard, but Gaignun and Veillantif, who were standing watch on the parapet called down greetings to them, and pleaded with her to dance that evening at dinner.

"Perhaps I will," she replied. "If you men ever learn how to behave around a lady."

Normally there were not sentries manning the walls of Maleperduys for, due to the castle's remote location near the center of what the men called 'the Maze' and the constant vigilance of the shrikes, they rarely had visitors they were not expecting. But with so many of the chimera gone, it had become necessary to set a watch over the hidden valley they now called home, and so men that had spent most of their lives as trappers, wood cutters, or farmers now found themselves bedecked in brigandine and armed like proper soldiers as they went about their rounds.

They left the men behind, and approached the high tower where the shrikes roosted. It was a lonely place, generally avoided by the human inhabitants of the castle, save of course for Tiecelin, who had chosen the second floor for his own quarters. Hermeline hated it. She'd never grown used to the chimera, no matter how many times they'd proven themselves to be useful.

She breathed deeply as she approached the tower, mustering her courage as she glanced upwards at the gaping hole the chimera used to enter and exit the roost, hoping perhaps that one of them might see her and save her the trip up the winding stairs.

She sighed. None of Tiecelin's 'pets' were about.

Midnight, a fat black cat that belonged to Tybalt, was napping on the steps of the tower and as they passed its pale yellow eyes opened to a fine slit before closing again.

"Now," Hermeline said to the girl once they had reached the door, "I want you to stay here until I return- and I don't want to hear any further argument out of you. Do you understand?"

Rukenaw pulled a face, but plopped obediently onto the steps, clicking her tongue against her teeth in a vain attempt to attract the cat's attention.

Hermeline stepped into the bare room at the foot of the tower and closed the door behind her.

It was far cooler here than it had been outside, for only a high, narrow window admitted light to this place. A corridor off the main chamber housed a winding spiral staircase, and from it came the unnerving sounds of the chimera that lived above; bird-like chatter filled with half-comprehended words, and the occasional sound of wings beating furiously as one of the things flitted from perch to perch.

Hermeline climbed, and as she did so she was reminded of the fear she had felt when they had first come here, over two years past.

Before the shrikes had led them to it, the castle of Maleperduys had been uninhabited- by people at any rate. There had been no chimera, as Hermeline had feared, but the place had been infested with bats and deadly spiders that grew as big as one's hands. Worse were the caustic slimes that fed on these creatures- sightless horrors that lurked in darkened pools or clung to stone ceilings until prey passed beneath them. A liberal use of fire had burned these terrors out, but even though Reynard regularly sent patrols armed with torches down the passages that wound through the rock below the castle, Hermeline still found herself pausing to glance upward whenever she had to visit the privy after dark.

She'd reached the second story now, and rapped gently on the door that led to Tiecelin's quarters, out of instinct perhaps, for she knew that Tiecelin had gone with Reynard to lead the Calvarians astray within the tangles of the forest.

Hermeline opened the door and glanced about the neatly ordered room. She'd been there only once before, when Reynard and Isengrim had been gone for nearly a month on one of their many foraging expeditions, and waiting until supper to get fresh news from Tiecelin had finally proven to be a trial that Hermeline could no longer bear. She'd found the man sitting by the window, singing softly to one of Sharpebeck's sickly chicks, like one might to a child. When he looked up at her she could see that his eyes were rimmed red, and she guessed that he had not slept for days.

"There's something very strange about that man," Hermeline had said to Reynard when he and Isengrim finally returned.

"Oh?" Reynard had said, distantly.

"He hardly ever speaks, and he spends far too much time shut up with those- things. It isn't natural."

"He is an honest man, and loyal," he'd replied, and flashed his winning grin at her and added, "Besides, what man does not have his secrets?"

Hermeline had given in then, as she always did, but it had not made her any more comfortable around the Luxian, or his shrikes.

Hermeline climbed.

As she approached the top of the stair a foul reek filled the air, like that of meat that has spoiled in the sun, and she covered her nose with a hand in an attempt to mask the stench of it. But when she saw the open portal that led to the shrike's roost yawning ahead of her she lowered her hand, and called out,

"Greetings!"

There was silence for a moment, and then a shrill voice responded. "Whoit calls?"

"I am Hermeline, mistress of Reynard."

"Come it upwards, sowit I can spy it," it said after a pause, burbling noises that seemed to come from deep within its throat.

Hermeline steeled herself, and pressed on.

Though she knew what to expect of the shrike roost, she still had to stifle a cry when she finally saw it: a two story tall chamber, its floorboards filthy with dung, and hanging from hooks that Tiecelin had installed along the walls were the rotting bodies of the Calvarians that had pursued Martin and Rukenaw through the catacombs, as well as the dozen or so others that Tybalt and Bruin's men had ambushed.

Only one of the shrikes was present, a male. It was one of Sharpebeck's brood, Hermeline thought. Its plumage was a vibrant mixture of blues and whites, and it wore a crest of feathers on its head that bristled somewhat as it regarded her.

Hermeline could not help but notice that there was a strip of human flesh dangling from the rafter where it was perched. She had interrupted the thing's feeding.

The shrike inspected her, chirruped loudly, apparently content, and hopped down to the level of the floor so suddenly that Hermeline could not stifle a shriek.

"Speakit," the thing said, its claws clicking against the floor as it took a few hopping steps forward.

"Forgive my intrusion," she said, backing up against the jamb of the door. "But I thought that you might have news of Master Reynard-"

"Master?" the thing said, cocking its head sideways.

"Yes, Master. Master Reynard. Do you know where he is?"

"Rey-nard," the thing said, seemingly suddenly to comprehend. "Him izzit near."

"He *is* near?" she asked, wondering inwardly if the shrikes had been learning to speak Arcasian by listening to Hirsent and Isengrim fight. "He is safe?"

The shrike chirruped, and bobbed its head.

"Thank you," she said gratefully, and bowed her head as she left. "Thank you. I will leave you now."

The shrike's comb straightened, and it made clicking noises as it flew back to its perch and snatched up the rest of its meal with a pair of sharp fangs.

Hermeline nearly flew herself as she rushed down the stairs, three days and nights of worry washing from her mind with each step she took.

He is alive, she exulted, *he is coming home.*

Rukenaw was still sitting on the stairs when Hermeline exited the tower, but the girl was not alone.

Tybalt was leaning against the railing, one of his sharp knives whirling across his palm. At the sight of Hermeline the man grinned sourly.

"Look, Mistress," the girl said, turning to Hermeline with sheer delight written across her face, "He can make it dance!"

"Rukenaw, come away from that man," Hermeline said firmly as she bustled down the steps.

"What's the matter, Hermeline?" Tybalt said, flipping his knife into the air and catching it by the handle. "Can't a man talk to a pretty girl?"

"Isn't she a little young for you, Tybalt?"

"Girls age, don't they?"

Hermeline advanced on the former brigand until she stood directly between him and the girl.

"Do *not* let me catch you around her again, Tybalt, or I will tell Reynard-"

"Tell him what?" he sneered. "What could you possibly tell his lordship about me that he doesn't already know?"

When Hermeline did not respond, Tybalt chuckled and stalked off. As he went Midnight darted after him, chasing his heels and begging to be fed.

"You stay away from him," Hermeline said to the girl when he was gone.

"Why?"

"He is not a good man, and ought to know better."

"He seemed nice enough to me," the girl muttered under her breath.

* * * * * * *

Reynard returned to Maleperduys shortly after midday, along with all who had set out with him- Isengrim, of course, as well as Hirsent, Tiecelin, and a handful of men who had proven themselves to be competent horsemen. The rest of the shrikes arrived shortly thereafter, and they circled their tower lazily before swooping in to nest.

As Reynard's company clattered across the narrow causeway that separated the castle from the valley below, Hermeline rushed down from the battlements to meet them. She'd been standing there, waiting, reasoning that Slopecade could watch over the boy and girl for an hour or two.

As Hermeline pressed through the assembling crowd, she could see her lover dismount, his movements slow and weary, and she redoubled her efforts to squeeze past the men-at-arms who stood in her path.

Reynard had hardly set both feet on the ground before Hermeline was upon him, her arms wrapped tightly around his shoulders as she planted a series of kisses on his lips, much to the crowd's amusement.

"Slow down, slow down," he begged. "And be gentle with me."

"Are you hurt?"

"Only sore," he replied, and gave her a gentle push. "And I don't imagine that I smell very good either."

"We must give you a bath."

"Just as soon as I've had something to eat," he replied, and began to unsaddle his horse- a beautiful courser with a ruddy coat that Hermeline suspected he had stolen.

"Did the Calvarians kill any of Bruin or Tybalt's men?" Reynard asked.

"Yes," Hermeline nodded. "Borre and Marmorie- and one of them cut Sorrel's arm clean off. He died yesterday."

"I should have been here."

"It could not be helped," Hermeline said, and cast her eyes over Reynard's companions as they dismounted. No one appeared to have been seriously hurt, save for Tencendur, who was limping badly.

"What happened?" she asked the man.

"I caught it between a pair of roots," he responded, wincing. "Thought it was broke for certain."

"Let me see it."

"Leg is fine," Hirsent interjected loudly when she noticed the man pulling at his boot. "Will heal."

"Come and see me later," Hermeline whispered to the man once Hirsent was out of earshot. She'd long since learned not to contradict Isengrim's wife openly.

"What news?" Bruin bellowed at Reynard, the sound of his voice instantly silencing the rising din of the men and women gathering in the courtyard. "Did you outfox the bastards as usual?"

"Only by a hair," Reynard replied, "and they made a good show of it. Would have caught us near the Maidenhead if they knew the ground better."

"You lost them, though?"

Reynard shook his head. "They gave up last night, right as I was starting to consider leading them into warg-country. By this morning the shrikes couldn't find a single pale face from here to Cerynea- present company excluded," he added, nodding politely to Isengrim and Hirsent.

"Nobel is giving them some trouble, you think?" Bruin asked, scratching at his beard.

"Either that or they're massing for a fresh stab southwards. Whatever the cause, we should be thankful. It saved our skins."

"Then we are out of danger?" Hermeline asked.

"For now."

"What were they doing here?" Hermeline asked, suddenly furious. "And what kind of men are they, that kill defenseless women and children?"

"It was not done out of any malice," Isengrim replied. "By destroying farmland, along with the men and women who work it, the Calvarians hope to rob their enemies of the means to fight, while bolstering their own stores. Soldiers must eat, whether they be light-skinned or dark."

"Are there none left alive in all of Lothier?" Bruin asked.

"There are many," Reynard replied sadly. "But the Calvarians might as well have killed them, as they have no food, no homes, and no one to turn to for aid- save for the great lords who would rather jockey for position in Calyx than tend to their people."

"Is- is there nothing we can do?" Hermeline asked.

"We can survive," Reynard answered.

* * * * * * *

Baron Reynard's companions celebrated their lord's return with a grand feast, which lasted until the Firebird sank beneath the peaks of the valley.

Reynard did not dine in the great hall often, as he preferred to prepare his own food, being generally suspicious of anything that he had not cooked with his own hands. An endearing trait, Hermeline thought, perhaps left over from his youth.

But even Reynard could not entirely ignore etiquette, and when circumstance demanded he took his place at the head table, his captains at his side, and made merry. He told Slopecade to break out a cask of wine that he'd somehow managed to smuggle all the way from the March of Carabas, had Baldwin play upon his dulcimer, and eventually managed to coerce Hermeline into dancing.

So she twirled her skirts and clicked her castanets, and as the men laughed and hollered and generally made idiots out of themselves, she felt herself a priestess again.

As the Firebird set, Maugris, a ragged servant of the Watcher who'd lived in Larsa before the war had orphaned him, played on his harp and sang the tragedy of Prince Kaspar of Solothurn, who had thought himself blessed when the Watcher promised he would spare him from death if someone would stand in his place, until his beloved wife Katja stepped forward. They feasted then on fresh bread and mutton that Tybalt had plundered from the little village that had crouched in the shadow of the forest, provender that would feed the castle's inhabitants until spring came, and if Martin and Rukenaw guessed at the source of their supper they did not speak of it.

All through the feast Reynard seemed nearly as deep in his cups as Bruin, who spent the latter part of the feast singing bawdy soldiers' songs until he thankfully passed out. But after the last of the men had stumbled off to bed, or left to take their turn at watch, and Slopecade's girls had begun clearing the tables, Reynard shed his drunkard's stagger and led Hermeline up to their shared quarters on the top floor of the keep.

"Slopecade is watching the boy and girl?" he asked as he threw the latch on the door.

"Yes," she purred. "We will be alone all night."

"How are they doing?"

"They are as well as can be expected," she answered, kneeling down by the room's single hearth and fiddling with the bird-shaped lighter that Reynard kept on the mantle. "They will need time."

"Wulf, it is cold," Reynard shivered as he removed his mud-spattered doublet. He'd done his best to make the room comfortable, but it was a far cry from the luxurious quarters he'd once known, and the castle was as drafty as it was old.

Once he'd thrown on his heaviest robe Reynard opened his bureau, settled into a chair and began to draft a letter.

"Must you work tonight?" Hermeline said with a yawn.

"I will not be long," he replied, his hand stopping just long enough to dip his quill into the inkpot. "And besides, the water isn't ready yet."

"Is it very important?"

"Very."

She sighed and returned to her work, but when she had gotten the fire going, and had set a great kettle full of water over it, she came up behind Reynard and leaned over him and squinted at the odd jumble of letters that were etched across the page.

"Why," she said. "This is just nonsense."

"To you, perhaps."

"Ah," she said. "There is a trick to it?"

"Indeed."

"Show me," she said.

"Very well," Reynard said, and his quill came to a stop. "Let us say that I am away, and I wish to write you a letter-"

"A love letter?"

"What else?" Reynard quipped. "But this is a love letter that only you and I can read, because only the two of us know how to read it."

"So Tiecelin does not read it before I do?"

"Precisely," Reynard said and began to scribble on a loose scrap of parchment. "So I begin by writing your name-"

"But my name does not begin with a 'gee.'"

"Ah, but if I previously told you that 'gee' stood for an 'aitch-'"

"Oh, I see," she exclaimed, and before Reynard could stop her she'd snapped up the half-written letter from his desk and skipped closer to the fire to examine it.

Reynard turned around in his chair, a bemused smile on his face.

"But, this is still nonsense," Hermeline said at last.

"That's because it wasn't written with such simple substitution- no one would have much trouble figuring out that I'd only moved the letters one place backwards in the alphabet."

As Reynard spoke he rose from his seat and came up behind Hermeline, his hands caressing as he turned her round to face him.

"And this one you write to," Hermeline said, keeping the letter safely out of Reynard's reach as he leaned forward to kiss her lightly on the throat. "They can read it?"

"They have the key, yes."

"And where is your key?"

"Somewhere safe," Reynard replied, tapping his forehead as he pressed closer to her. "I believe that the water is ready."

"To the Watcher with it," she said, and at last released the letter from her grip. As it fell from her hand Reynard caught it in his own, and set it on one of the chairs next to the hearth.

****

"Do I still get my shave?"

"Tomorrow," Hermeline yawned. "If I did it now I would cut you to ribbons- a rather ignoble end for the Baron of Maleperduys, I think."

"It would please Nobel, at any rate," Reynard said as he pulled on his nightshirt. "If you ever grow tired of me, you might consider negotiating with him. You could probably make enough coin to build your own temple."

"Somewhere warmer I hope, and far from all of this dreary pile."

"Sailors say that Therimere is lovely this time of year- by the sea, the Firebird shining overhead, the scent of hyacinths heavy in the air-"

"It sounds lovely," Hermeline sighed. "But I doubt that I'd live long enough to enjoy it once the king and queen of ice got wind of it."

"You'd have to do them in first," Reynard said. "Slip some nightshade into their porridge."

"Might be doing them a favor," Hermeline said, "The way that they have been at each other lately."

"Hmmm."

"How are they, by the by? I did not see them at dinner."

"They're improving," Reynard replied. "A good chase through the woods with a host of enemies at their heels always seems to cheer them. Reminds them of the old days, perhaps."

"Old days," she yawned. She had not had a proper night's sleep for several days now, and her eyes were heavy.

"Do you miss them?"

"Do I miss hot baths, and fresh clothes, and good food?" she teased, running her fingers up his arm. "Who would ever miss that?"

"I am serious," he said, gently swatting her hand away.

"I do miss my garden," she said, "and all of my girls, of course. And sometimes I miss the men, if you must know."

"You wound me."

"No! I tease," she said, pressing closer. "You are a most excellent man- though I do wish you would stop wearing this cold thing to bed."

Hermeline's fingers plucked the ruby necklace from Reynard's breast and tugged at the chain.

"*Gea, laruwa*," Reynard said obediently, removing the jewel and placing it gently on the table next to the headboard. "*Ablissian?*"

"Yes," Hermeline said, and laughed. "And you?"

"Need you ask?"

"I still like to hear it."

"I do love you," he said.

"Do you?"

"Have I ever lied to you?"

"Only a thousand times, my sweet Percehaie," Hermeline said and finally closed her eyes.

Eventually she turned on her side and when Reynard heard her breathing go steady he slipped out of their shared bed and retrieved the letter. It was creased from Hermeline's grip.

Slowly, so as not to disturb his lover, he smoothed out the parchment and began to write again.

* * * * * * *

Reynard rose early the next morning, in the grayness that comes before dawn, and exited the keep by way of a wide breezeway that led to the shrike's tower.

Isengrim was waiting for him there, alone, his eyes trained on the fog-shrouded landscape below. For a moment Reynard was not certain if the man was aware of his presence, but then the Northerner turned and acknowledged him with the slightest of bows and said, "You are early."

"As are you," Reynard replied. "Should we expect Hirsent?"

"No. She is- unwell."

"The Watcher's curse?" Reynard asked.

Isengrim paused, then nodded.

"I would ask Hermeline to brew her a potion," Reynard said with sympathy, "if I thought that she would stoop to drink it."

Isengrim's mouth cracked into a faint smile.

"Shall we?" Reynard said, casually reaching for his sword.

The Northerner's black-gloved hand caught Reynard's arm before he could draw and shook his head.

"Wait until she rises," Isengrim said, releasing his grip.

"As you wish," Reynard said, and joined his old friend by the parapet to wait for the Firebird.

The sky grew brighter. The smell of the cooking fires wafted up from Madam Slopecade's kitchen. Somewhere below them a flock of waterfowl took to wing, honking as they went.

"Summer is coming," Isengrim said.

"Yes," Reynard sighed. "There will be a good harvest this season, and good hunting in the fall."

"You speak as though we will not be here to see it."

Reynard reached into his doublet and produced the letter, sealed now with wax and marked with the distinctive 'R' rune that Isengrim himself had fashioned for him.

Isengrim studied the letter for a moment. "Your informant in Calyx?"

Reynard nodded.

"So you mean to go south?"

"I have not decided what I intend to do," Reynard replied. "But our enemies will find us here eventually, be they light-skinned or dark, and we die by inches each day that we do nothing."

"*Awyrigung*," Isengrim muttered darkly under his breath.

"Do you curse?" Reynard said. "I did not think I would live to see the day that you would shrink from battle."

"It has been many years now, Reynard, since I have known the fear of my own death- a blood-guard can ill afford such weakness. But a man as worldly as yourself must know that a swordsman can win a thousand combats and still fear his wife."

"Be thankful, at least, that she does not shave you."

"When will you tell Hermeline?" Isengrim asked.

"Soon."

Isengrim reached over and patted Reynard on the shoulder, and as he did so the first shimmering rays of the Firebird appeared in the east, red against the orange sky.

"Another day," Isengrim said as he unsheathed Right-Hand from its scabbard.

"May we live to see another," Reynard added, and drew.

III

    The morning mists had burned away by the time that Rohart took flight from Maleperduys, a scroll case securely fastened to one of his legs, so that as he soared upwards he could plainly see the whole of Reynard's domain, nestled safely in the winding tracks of the forest. As he climbed higher Rohart had only to tilt his head to gaze upon the whole of western Arcasia, from the partially submerged city of Kerys to the gulf of Lorn.
    From such a lofty place one might gaze upon the horrors of war with indifference, for even the lands the Calvarians had ravaged looked peaceful and serene save for the dark plumes that rose in the east, where the terrible siege of Barca was in progress. There men rotted in the open, baking under the Firebird's uncaring gaze, while the city's vineyards, once green and lush, had been trampled beneath the Calvarian's hulking siege engines- things of iron and bronze that belched flame as they vomited forth their murderous shot at the walls. Acre upon acre of farmland lay barren and despoiled, put to the torch by the Arcasians themselves in order to deny the Northerners the fruits of their own labor, while the sluggish Vinus choked on the wreckage of ships and the bloated corpses of the slain. But even these horrors seemed no more real than the play of children with dolls, when they are seen from the heights.
    He spent that night in the eaves of an abandoned farmhouse, undisturbed by its previous inhabitants, whose burnt and twisted bodies now adorned a nearby oak. In the morning the shrike made a breakfast of their eyes, which were mercifully blind to their own fate.
    Rohart found sustenance of this kind was now common, even when he had flown far from the battlefields of Lothier and Carabas, for the countryside of Arcasia teemed with deserters and mercenaries in search of plunder, women, and food. Nor was Rohart the only chimera to be seen winging in the skies above, for shrikes native to Engadlin and Luxia had migrated north in order to feast on the bounty of war. These creatures were wild and fierce, more animal than man, and more than once Rohart

was forced to veer off course in order to avoid being torn apart by a shrieking flock rising from the trees to defend their territory. His superior size and speed allowed him to cow the shrikes native to Maleperduys, as had his more human intellect, but what his Arcasian cousins lacked in brains and brawn they more than made up for in numbers.

 Yet even with such distractions, it took the messenger shrike no more than two days to reach Calyx, and as the night was black- the skull-moon being no more than a pale sliver- Rohart used the cover of darkness to mask his approach to the capital.

 Physically, the city was little different from the one that Reynard and his companions had left behind them. War had drained the royal coffers, and besides bolstering the city's walls and expanding his personal guard, Nobel had little money to spare for the well-being of his own subjects. For though several years of peace in Engadlin had provided the king with enough bread to fill his people's bellies, it had not granted him the means to house the masses that now crowded the streets of the royal city, seeking succor of their king.

 As ever it was Low Quarter that suffered the brunt of this human press, but even in the most fashionable parts of Calyx one could see men and women living in the squalor of the streets, no roof above their head save for whatever crude shelter they could construct out of tarp and loose boards. Filth was everywhere, despite the best efforts of the priestesses of Sphinx to keep the city clean. An outbreak of the bloody flux had already felled more men, women, and children than had died in any battle with the Calvarians, and even the wealthy could be seen wearing the distinctive sores of the pox. Those who showed any signs of suffering from the dreaded Red Death were often boarded up in their own homes, or forced onto one of the hulking galleons set aside by the king for just such a purpose, where they would linger on for days before succumbing to either starvation or whatever malady afflicted them, their impassioned screams ignored.

 There was only one place in all of Calyx where one might find sanctuary from the wretched sights that assaulted the senses of whoever dared walk the city streets, and this was the island palace of the King and Queen of Arcasia, where high walls and armed men were more than capable of keeping the rabble at bay. Into this place Rohart dove, his silent descent unnoticed by sentries who had been trained to expect *human* intruders. The shrike was in the palace grounds for only a few moments before he took to the air again, the case missing from his leg, and a smugly satisfied smile breaking the symmetry of his coal-black face.

To the west of Calyx, nestled between two sharp bends of the Vinus, there is a wood that generations of the Dukes of Arcas have used for the pleasure of the hunt. Towards this place Rohart descended, eventually landing on one of the highest boughs of a Moly tree. It was a dangerous perch, for each hour he remained he risked the chance he might be discovered, and shot down by one of the King's game wardens. But Rohart would not leave- at least not until he had retrieved the answer to Reynard's letter.

Father had commanded it.

* * * * * * *

At dawn Queen Persephone was roused from her slumber by the arrival of her personal maid, Columbine, a woman no more than a year or two older than herself, who would wait dutifully as the Queen washed her hands and face in a basin of lily-scented water. When she had finished drying herself with a fresh cotton cloth Columbine would follow her into the royal boudoir, where she would assist Her Majesty as she disrobed and was bound into whatever gown and bodice had been set aside for her the night before. Next, Columbine would comb and style the Queen's hair and apply cosmetics to the queen's face as she sat in front of her vanity. Persephone was very familiar with her maid, and allowed her to gossip ceaselessly as she worked, so that the Queen had come to know even the lowliest of her servants by name, if not by face.

Passing from her boudoir to the royal parlor, the queen took her breakfast in the company of her ladies-in-waiting, daughters of the great counts and barons of the land whose close proximity to the royal presence enhanced their own influence. Their dress and manners were, of course, impeccable, their speech was often witty, and their knowledge of Aquilian poetry extensive. But, for the most part, Persephone found their forced company rather dull and artificial, and wondered what dark thoughts might lurk hidden behind their darting eyes.

After breakfast the Queen and her retinue adjourned to the audience hall, where it fell upon her to receive petitioners. These were more often than not the representatives of the country's many guilds, whose state-sponsored monopolies had been thrown into considerable disarray by the war with Calvaria, but ever so often she met with a Frisian diplomat, or settled a land dispute. Very rarely did she meet with someone who was not an individual of quality, as Count Bricemer, who was now the King's Lord High Secretary, tended to weed out any petitions that he felt were not worthy of the Queen's attention.

At midday the palace was cleared of petitioners, and the Queen presided over a formal meal attended by whichever of the King's highest ministers were present, all of whom generally used this opportunity to verbally cut each other down. A popular target was the Lord High Chancellor, Count Cherax, a mousy-haired man whose only interest outside of keeping a well-balanced ledger seemed to be a love of antiques. Easily flummoxed by the presence of women, Cherax made easy sport for the Queen's ladies-in-waiting, who teased him so mercilessly that by the time the midday feast was over he could hardly deliver his financial report to the Queen without stammering. Persephone felt great pity for the man, and only rarely laughed at Pierrot's impressions of him, no matter how accurate they might be.

Once Count Cherax had excused himself, fleeing no doubt to the safety of the Royal Mint, the Queen saw to the state of the palace, a task that entailed a series of meetings with the King's senior servants. First there was Madam Epine, who oversaw the considerable task of keeping the palace clean without being seen. Then the Queen paid a brief visit to the kitchen, where she conferred with Master Roboast, the royal cook, and approved the menu for the evening's feast. Next came the stables, for though the Queen did not enjoy the hunt, it was still her duty in the King's absence to receive reports from Master Arlequin, the Chief Groom, and to make at least a cursory inspection into the state of her husband's falcons and kennel.

It was only after she had finished with these duties that the Queen at last made her way to the south garden of the palace and, breaking from the phalanx of companions and bodyguards that had accompanied her since daybreak, took her customary seat beneath one of the Ash trees that formed a ring around a pale jade statue of Chloris the Serene and was, for a few precious moments, truly alone.

For a time Persephone did nothing but sit and breathe, savoring the thought that the silence of the grove was broken only by the sound of the wind rustling the leaves overhead. Then she would stand, and make a circuitous path around the jade maiden, her right arm outstretched so that as she passed each tree she could run her palm over the bark, her fingers probing into the hollows, feeling for the thin leather case Reynard's courier had somehow managed to place there, unseen by the palace guard.

More often than not, Persephone completed her circuit empty-handed, yet she repeated this ritual every day the weather permitted, and today, as her hand brushed against the boiled leather hide of the casing, she knew that her vigilance had been rewarded. Her pulse quickened as the familiar thrill of discovery washed over her, a feeling that was soon replaced by the anticipation of the moment when she might read the coded letter within. But for the moment she merely paused, as if taking a moment to reflect on the delicate curves of Chloris' maidenly arms and legs, and tucked the leather case into her sleeve with a deft movement of her right hand.

When she'd finished her vigil, Persephone sat down on one of the curved marble benches that encircled the goddess, an act that signaled she was ready to receive the company of her son.

It was Madam Corte who had been given the honor of seeing to the care of Prince Lionel and, though she could have been assisted by any number of younger servants, she always insisted on bearing the heir to the throne of Arcasia by herself as she promenaded across the lawn, the swaddled Prince nestled in the crook of her stick-like arm, her nose turned upwards at the sight of the Queen's retinue, whom she generally regarded as no more than glorified strumpets. The only companion she tolerated was Paquette, a painfully shy girl who had been a mere chambermaid before she had been chosen to serve as Prince Lionel's wet-nurse.

"Your Majesty," Madam Corte said as she dipped into a precarious curtsey.

"How is he today?" Persephone asked, her arms outstretched to accept her son. "Still fussy?"

"I'm afraid so Majesty," Madam Corte answered, gently handing over the Prince. "But then, so were you at his age."

"Oof, he is getting heavy," Persephone said, and gazed down at the sleepy-eyed infant in her arms. "I imagine it will not be long before he will be able to walk on his own."

"Yes, Your Majesty."

"Has he spoken?" Persephone asked, gently tickling Lionel's chin.

"Why, yes, Majesty," Madam Corte replied, casting a glance towards Paquette, who was staring intently at the grass beneath her feet. "As a matter of fact he has, just this morning. Strange that you should ask today."

"What did he say?" the Queen asked, turning her attention to the maid.

"The Queen is addressing you, Paquette," Madam Corte hissed between clenched teeth, prodding the girl with her tortoiseshell fan.

The girl's head shot up, her eyes suddenly wide with a terror she could barely restrain. Her mouth opened and closed slightly, a sight that Persephone found sadly comic.

"Please," Persephone begged, "What were my son's first words?"

"'Mama,'" the girl replied, and unable to meet the Queen's gaze any longer she lowered her head.

"Mama," the Queen said softly, and rocked her child for a while. "I should like very much to hear him say it."

"The Prince is tired, Your Majesty," Madam Corte sputtered. "You know it is almost time for him to sleep-"

"Paquette," the Queen interjected, "Come here and sit by my side."

Trembling, the maid complied. Persephone had never seen the poor girl so close.

"Take him," the Queen said, and offered Paquette her son.

The maid reached out with shaking hands, but as she took hold of the Prince and held him close to her breast her grip relaxed considerably. Lionel seemed to recognize the girl's arms, and burbled contentedly for a time before falling asleep.

"Tomorrow," the Queen said when he was silent. "Perhaps tomorrow."

The Queen's attention was so wholly focused on her child at this time that she did not notice the approach of the slender figure that was limping across the lawn, who eventually was forced to cough politely into a gloved hand in order to announce his presence.

"Count Bricemer," the Queen said, somewhat petulantly as she turned her gaze towards the Lord High Secretary, "I believe I have given explicit instructions not to be disturbed at this hour."

The Queen had never gotten along well with the man, whom the King had left behind to provide 'guidance' to his wife while he was away on campaign.

"Forgive me, Your Majesty," Bricemer said, apparently unfazed by the Queen's ire, "But I thought it prudent to inform you that the King himself is expected to arrive at any moment."

"My husband?" the Queen said, rising from her seat, her hand tugging slightly at one of her sleeves as if she had an itch. "Why was I not informed earlier?"

"I myself received word by messenger pigeon of the King's approach only an hour ago," Bricemer said, producing a scroll from his belt. "And I am afraid that the Captain of the Guard did not wish to go against your orders to be left undisturbed."

Persephone took the scroll from Bricemer's leather-gloved hand, and scanned its contents silently.

"Clever creatures, birds," Count Bricemer commented dryly. "It is unfortunate that they cannot speak, or we might use them as scouts."

"A victory against the Calvarians at Pardus," Persephone said quietly, ignoring the Count's comment. "It is hard to believe."

"Perhaps, though the King spent much of his youth studying the battles of his forefathers. And," Bricemer added, coughing slightly into a fist, "It was the King who defeated your own father at the battle of the Sicoris."

"I have not forgotten," the Queen said flatly. "But what brings the King here with such haste? Has Barca already fallen to the enemy?"

"I must confess that I know little of military matters, Your Majesty," Bricemer replied with false modesty. "I am not, after all, the Lord High Marshal. Nor would I wish to be . . . but I imagine that you will soon have the opportunity to discuss this personally with His Highness."

"My Queen," Madam Corte blurted, unable to keep her mouth shut any longer. "We must prepare for the King's arrival. The kitchen staff-"

"I trust that Master Roboast will be more than able to handle the matter," Persephone said smoothly. "Count Bricemer, when my husband arrives will you be so kind as inform him that the Queen is in the company of Prince Lionel?"

"As you wish, Your Majesty," Bricemer said as he excused himself, his prim face betraying nothing of the certain resentment he felt at being treated as a messenger by the Queen. Persephone smirked slightly, and considered the earlier remark about her slain father at least partially avenged.

The Queen returned to her seat, and tried to ignore the fidgeting of Madam Corte as she waited for her husband to arrive. She knew it would not be long, for even behind the walls of the island palace she could hear the growing roar of the city welcoming its King's return. The din grew loud enough to awaken the Prince, who complained loudly despite Paquette's best efforts to calm him.

"Your Majesty," Madam Corte nagged at last, "The Prince should return to his quarters. It is not seemly."

"Let him stay awhile longer," the Queen replied. "His father will be glad of the sight of him."

Madam Corte, defeated, curtsied wobbily and retired to the rear of the grove.

The sharp retort of soldiers' voices echoed across the garden then, and between the eaves of the Ash trees Persephone could see that armed men wearing the purple tunics of the King's personal bodyguard were scurrying out of the palace at the double-step. When they had formed a perimeter around the garden a figure appeared at the garden gate: Nobel, resplendent in a suit of polished Arcasian plate that gleamed magnificently as he stepped into the reddish light of the afternoon.

Servants and courtiers alike bowed their heads low as the King approached, his violet cloak trailing behind him like the plumage of some exotic Frisian bird. He carried his aquiline helmet in the crook of his arm, and as the Queen stepped out of the cool shadows of the grove to greet her husband he handed it to one of his bodyguards so he might take his wife's hand.

"My Queen," he said, bending slightly as he kissed the back of Persephone's palm.

"Your Majesty," she replied, bowing her head as he straightened to his full height. "I had scarcely thought I would see you before Summer's End."

"Indeed," Nobel chuckled, "I had hoped my early arrival might catch you by surprise."

"You are looking well," the Queen said, examining the King's face, which had become quite tan since she had seen him last. He also had grown a fulsome beard, and wore it in the curling style of old Aquilia. "War seems to agree with you."

"And you are as beautiful as ever, my Queen," Nobel replied, and raising a gauntleted hand he brushed Persephone's cheek. "But come! Count Bricemer told me that you were in the company of the Prince, and I would see my son before supper."

At a motion from the Queen, Paquette stepped forward with the sleeping Prince in her arms, her head hung low to avoid the King's gaze.

Nobel's angular features seemed to soften somewhat as he took the child into his mailed arms, and tickled him gently with a cold metal finger. Prince Lionel awoke with a start and, staring up at the gleaming figure that loomed over him, immediately began to weep piteously.

"You should not frighten him so!"

Nobel laughed, and said: "Ah! But look how he struggles! He will make a mighty King, one day."

"Perhaps," Persephone said, lifting the Prince out of the King's hands and soothing him as best she could. "But will he be a just one?"

"He will be- that is, if he follows the example set for him by his mother."

"And what of his father?"

"When the war is over, and I have driven the last of the Calvarians into the sea, I will see to it that he is not deprived of an education befitting a King."

"Let that day come soon," the Queen sighed, and returned the Prince to Madam Corte, who retreated from the royal pair with Paquette close behind her. "Lest your children be full grown before knowing their father's face."

"Fear not," the King said, and retrieved his helm as he began to lead the way back to the palace. "For we have won a great victory on the plain of Pardus. It may have cost us dearly, but the Calvarians will never match our strength in numbers."

"Is there no hope for peace?"

"None."

"You dismiss the notion too quickly, I think," the Queen chided. "Is there not peace between Arcas and Luxia?"

"You were not at Pardus," Nobel replied curtly. "Not a single Calvarian fled once the tide of the battle had turned against them, and they would not quit fighting even after we had outflanked them entirely. I have never seen such a thing before, and I have witnessed many battles. They are worthy foes, and I guess that they will not quit this war unless utterly destroyed."

"In a week's time I and all of my court will leave for Gadwall," Nobel continued, raising his voice so that the assembled nobles could easily make out his words. "And there I will muster the greatest army that Arcasia has ever known- a force so mighty that the Lioness herself will shake beneath its tread! For let it be known throughout the realm that the King of Arcasia summons all of his nobles to his side- and that any who refuse this call will be branded as traitors, their titles stripped from them and their lands forfeit. Death and dishonor shall be their lot . . . but for those that are loyal and true, rich rewards and glory await! Long live Arcasia!"

"Long live Arcasia!" the King's Guard echoed, unsheathing their blades. "Long live the King!"

The Queen was silent as the fever of war took hold of the courtyard, the nobles drawing their weapons and shouting out oaths of loyalty to the King and Queen of Arcasia. But once she and her husband had passed underneath the gate that led to the palace she halted and, adopting a more demure attitude than was customary, begged leave to retire to the privacy of her quarters so that she might refresh herself before the inevitable banquet that would be held in honor of Nobel's victory over the foreign invaders.

It was a kind of torture for the Queen not to be able to run as she made her way through the palace, followed as she always was by a train of guards and servants, but a lifetime of courtly discipline helped her keep her steps even and stately, her face betraying nothing of the urgency that coursed through her.

Only when she had shut herself within her bedchamber did she drop the act, nearly tearing the coded letter as she unfolded it with shaking hands.

She had only enough time to read it once, and when she had finished, the Queen clutched the parchment to her breast and with eyes closed she quietly breathed the name, "Reynard."

She dared not keep his letters, for their discovery had the potential to reignite the war between Luxia and Arcas, but as she could not bring herself to destroy them, the Queen wrote her own messages to Reynard on the reverse of the letters she received. And so, regretting that she must hurry through one of the few acts that brought her any true joy, Queen Persephone flattened the letter onto her writing desk, and began to scratch out her response with an ink quill.

* * * * * * *

The lake beneath Maleperduys was very still that morning, its waters as smooth as a polished mirror. For a long time the only sound Martin could hear came from the creaking of the timbers below him, and the gentle lapping of the waves against the little boat that carried him and his master.

Suddenly the boat listed, and there was a desperate splash that he had come to know very well.

"My lord," he said, "Your line."

Reynard, who was sitting directly across from the boy, opened a single eye and peered at the fishing rod he had balanced against the side of their boat. Its back was as bent as an old man's, and the line that hung from it was darting about like a thing alive.

With a yawn Reynard pushed his weathered hat out of his face and took hold of the rod.

"It's a shame," Reynard said wistfully as he pulled in his catch, "I was having the nicest dream."

"Forgive me, my lord."

"I will, if you will refrain from calling me 'my lord' in the future," Reynard said, and with a grunt he dragged a glittering fish out of the water and, removing the barbed hook from its mouth, dropped it into a bucket.

"But," Martin protested, "You are a great lord, a Baron of the King, and I- I am just a peasant."

"That may be, but that does not make me a better man than you. Who can say what you may achieve one day? Perhaps you will be Count of Lothier, and I a mere Baron."

"That is unlikely," Martin said. "For I am not brave or clever like you are. I would not have gone into Calvaria, nor Vulp Vora either."

"That is very wise," Reynard said, remembering for a moment the cruel fate that had befallen Cointereau, Moire, and the others of the Quicksilver in that nightmarish place. "And you should know that I did not choose that path willingly- it was thrust upon me by Nobel and his minions."

"But, the stories-"

"The stories lie," Reynard said, cutting the boy off more harshly perhaps than he had intended. "They are pretty tales that mask the ugliness of what really happened."

"Then, you did not strike down the King of the Calvarians, and set their city alight with demon fire- or escape from Dis riding atop the back of a warg?"

"Not exactly," Reynard chuckled.

"What about the city of demons, the leviathan beneath the mountains, or the naga that sing men to their deaths-"

Reynard raised up his palms in surrender, and said, "I will tell you all about our 'adventures,' if that is what you wish, over supper, and the others may have more to tell than I for I am weary of the tale. But for the moment I beg of you some peace. You are scaring off the fish."

"Forgive me, my-" the boy began to say before catching himself. "Forgive me, Master Reynard. I will be silent."

Reynard nodded, and leaned back against the boat's prow before pulling his hat back over his face. But he'd been still for only a few moments before he sat back up, and let out a low sigh.

"What is it?" Martin asked.

"You think very loudly," Reynard replied, and shifted forward so he might take hold of the oars. "And we've caught enough fish for one day."

Reynard did not make for the shore, but instead directed the boat towards the massive crag that supported the fortress above them, guiding them towards a jagged gap in the cliff-face just wide enough to admit a vessel such as theirs.

"Master Reynard," Martin said as they approached the dark fissure, "Who was it built this place?"

"That I cannot answer with any certainty," Reynard answered, slowing the pace of his strokes considerably to avoid colliding with the walls of the cave, which were decorated with the same curling pictograms Martin and Rukenaw had discovered at the entrance to the catacombs. "But the servants of the Watcher tell us that all of Arcasia was once home to the golden-skinned Telchines, whom our own ancestors hunted down nearly to extinction. This may have been one of their fortresses, a safe and secret place too deep within this forest for any enemy to find."

"But if that was true, then why are there no Telchines here today?"

"Who can say? A plague could have wiped them out, or famine may have forced them to abandon this place. They may have bred with the chimera of the woods for so long that they forgot they were once men, and took to living like beasts in the wild. Or perhaps the men of old Aquilia finally discovered one of the secret paths that lead to the citadel, and what the Telchines had intended to be a sanctuary became a trap of their own creation."

"What were they like, the Telchines?"

"I wish that Hermeline were here to hear you rattle on so," Reynard said, pausing to push their boat away from the wall. "She tells me you've hardly spoken a word for the past week, and now you are full of nothing but questions!"

"I- I didn't mean to bother you."

"It is nothing to apologize for," Reynard said. "It is good to hear you talk, and I don't mind answering . . . though I imagine Master Maugris might be able to tell you more than I, who was only a servant of the Watcher long enough to learn how to read and play the fiddle."

The boy's eyes widened. "You were a servant of the Watcher?"

"By Hydra's Teeth! One story at a time! Now, do you want to hear about the Telchines, or don't you?"

"Yes, please."

"Then light a torch, will you? I can hardly see my own hands in front of my face."

"Yes, Master Reynard."

"Now then," Reynard said once the boy had done as he'd asked. "The Telchines were an ancient race, who lived long before the rule of the demons. It is said that they knew nothing of horses until the arrival of the Aquilians, and instead went about on great riding stags, or atop the backs of chimera, with whom they have often been allies . . ."

As Reynard told Martin all that he knew of the Telchines, they approached the dimly-lit grotto where the boat was normally moored- a seemingly unremarkable place that Reynard had supplied with enough nautical detritus to make it appear as an abandoned smuggler's hideout.

A dark figure stood on the shoreline, outlined by the light of a blazing torch sconce, and as they drew nearer Martin could see it was one of Reynard's lieutenants- the quiet one with the peaked cap that the others called Tiecelin. He was smoking, and the air was thick with the cloying scent of Frisian tobacco.

"Reynard," Tiecelin said, emptying his clay pipe against the heel of his boot as the boat reached the shore. "Rohart has returned."

"Sooner than I had expected," Reynard said as he stepped out of the boat and took the letter, his fresh catch forgotten as his eyes flicked over its contents.

"Master Tiecelin," Reynard said at last, stuffing the hastily composed note into his coat pocket. "When the Firebird is at her zenith I want all of the men and women gathered in the great hall."

Tiecelin nodded without comment and exited the grotto by way of the secret stair that led to the castle's undercroft, snatching up a lantern as he did.

"What does it say?" Martin asked when he had gained the courage to speak. He did not know why, but there was something unsettling about the way Reynard had not moved since dismissing his chief scout.

"You will know soon enough," Reynard answered, his voice distant. "For now you may take our catch up to Madam Slopecade."

"Aren't you coming?"

"Leave me," Reynard said, his tin-flecked eyes glimmering in the torchlight, "I must think."

Martin did as he was asked, and as he left, the darkness his sputtering torch had kept at bay swept over Reynard like a black tide.

* * * * * * *

True to his orders, Tiecelin had assembled the inhabitants of the fortress by midday, though as Reynard entered the great hall a few of the men and women who had been planting the spring harvest were still filing through the doors.

"Reynard," Hermeline said as he reached the head of the table, her brows knit with worry. "What's wrong?"

"A letter arrived," he replied. "From Calyx."

"Martin told me. What did it say?"

"It should wait until everyone is here," he answered softly, and perhaps due to the look in his eyes she acquiesced.

The last to arrive were Tybalt and his men, who had been hunting for game in the forest before Sharpebeck and her children had been dispatched to find them.

"So, Reynard," Tybalt said loudly as he took his customary seat, his mud-caked riding boots soiling the freshly washed tablecloth as he rested his feet on the table. "What is it that's so important that it can't wait until supper? Expecting another tussle with our pale-faced friends?"

"I am," Reynard answered, waiting a moment for the whispered oaths of those present to die down before adding, "And though it is not a battle that I would choose, I have long readied myself for its coming."

"Speak plainly, Reynard," Bruin said. "What battle? Where?"

Reynard did not answer at first, but scanned the crowd until his gaze met with the icy blue eyes of Isengrim. And, though his old friend's face did not show the slightest flicker of emotion, Reynard could tell that the Northerner already knew what he was going to say.

"This morning," he began, "I received word from Calyx- where, as some of you are already aware, a party friendly to our cause has kept me informed of the war raging beyond this hidden valley."

"Are the Calvarians marching on Maleperduys?" Bruin asked, using the words that no one else was bold enough to utter.

"No," Reynard answered. "Rather it is King Nobel who, having apparently won a minor victory near Nemea, now plans a fresh campaign to retake the northlands from the invaders and has called for all of his lords to muster at Gadwall within the next fortnight."

"*All* of his lords?" Tybalt said, his interest suddenly piqued.

"All," Reynard answered, and the hall filled then with the buzz of a hundred throats.

"Surely, though," Hermeline said, her voice tight, "you do not mean to go?"

"I do," he replied, not turning from the open accusation he saw written across her face. "And if I am to reach Gadwall in time, I must leave within the hour."

"We are with you, Baron!" one of the men cried from the back of the crowd, a cry soon taken up by most of the men assembled. The women, however, were silent- and in the ensuing din Hermeline turned from Reynard and swept up the stairwell like an ascending thundercloud.

"Peace!" Bruin roared at last, quieting the men with his customary bluster. "Let us hear what Reynard has to say!"

"My thanks, Master Bruin," Reynard said with a nod. "And to you, my bold companions- you show a courage more worthy than that of the King's own guard. But I do not ask any man to accompany me unless they wish it. For I am sure that my presence alone will satisfy Nobel's thirst for blood."

"I at least will go," Bruin rumbled. "Along with any of my lads that feel the inclination."

"As will I," Tiecelin added.

"You can count me in as well," Tybalt joined in, getting to his feet. "If it pleases your lordship."

"You, Tybalt?" Reynard said, honestly surprised by the show of support from the habitually contrary brigand. "I had not expected you to take up my cause so willingly."

"What can I say?" Tybalt said with a shrug. "The prospect of plunder, loose women, and a chance to cut down a few white-faced pricks is just too good for me to pass up."

"I too will go," said Maugris. "So that my lord's great deeds may be known by any whom we meet."

"And I," Baldwin said with considerably less enthusiasm than his grimmer counterpart. "If it pleases you, my lord." Baldwin was a fairly competent farrier, and could mend a broken blade, but he was far too meek to make an effective warrior.

"That will not be necessary," Reynard said to the priest of the Firebird. "And if, Baldwin, you are willing to remain here in my absence, I would ask that you, Hermeline, and any others who choose to do so watch over this place as proof against marauders- for I will not take anyone with me who is unsuited for war, and I would have them kept safe."

As he spoke these words Reynard cast a meaningful glance towards Martin, who had stepped forward with the other men.

"Please, my lord," the boy begged, his promise to not address Reynard in that manner forgotten in his urgency. "Do not send me from your side!"

"If I am truly your lord," Reynard answered, "Then you will do as I command and stay here to protect Rukenaw and the others. Will you do this?"

The boy's face fell as he realized that he could not contradict Reynard's words, and he nodded before slinking back into the crowd, his head hung low.

"Who says I need protecting?" Rukenaw muttered as Martin joined her, and some of the women laughed approvingly.

Out of all of Reynard's original companions, only two remained who had not spoken their peace, and Reynard approached them now.

"And you, Isengrim," Reynard said, addressing the man who had stood by his side since they had walked into the heart of Dis. "Can I count on my strong right-arm?"

"I will go," the Calvarian replied, "If that is your wish."

Reynard paused. There was hesitation in the Calvarian's voice, the same as he had heard on the battlements just six-days past.

"This is not a command," Reynard said. "And if you choose to stay I will feel safer leaving Hermeline behind."

Isengrim's eyes flicked towards Hirsent, who was standing just to his left. She too had kept her peace, and her own gaze was locked on Reynard.

"I will be going with," she said, and took a step forward, her jaw set. "You will be needing me."

Isengrim shifted, his brow darkening, and opened his mouth to object.

"I am speaking for myself," she barked, silencing her husband before turning back to Reynard. "Now say that I may be going."

Reynard looked to his old friend, and saw something buried behind the Northerner's cold eyes he had never thought possible of the man: fear.

"I cannot stop you from going," Reynard said, somewhat lamely, "But it will be dangerous for you."

"Because I am being a woman?" Hirsent said, and laughed. She knew as well as he that she was the equal of any man present in battle, save for her lover.

"No," Reynard replied. "It is because you are a Calvarian. We of the South fear your people more than any chimera or giant, and may attack you before anyone can explain that you are not their enemy."

"And it is not being dangerous for Isengrim?" she huffed.

"He has more experience hiding amongst us, and as a man he will not stand out as much as a woman might, for our women do not normally go to war as yours do," Reynard explained before adding, "And Isengrim speaks our language far better than you can."

"Then I will not be speaking, and I will wear cape and- *grima*," she said, using the Calvarian word for helmet. "One that will be covering my face- and I will cut my hair the way a man is wearing it so they are not knowing I am woman."

"Do you desire so much to go with us?"

"I do."

"Very well then. You may go."

"Good," she said, delivering a curt bow before brushing past her husband. "I will be making ready to leave."

The tension in the room seemed to lessen somewhat as Hirsent left it, and soon the men who would follow Reynard into battle had filed out of the hall with their wives or lovers in tow, hurrying off to whatever private place they might find for a farewell tryst.

"Reynard," Isengrim said quietly, taking a meaningful step towards the smaller man.

"Do not worry," Reynard said, anticipating his friend's anxiety. "I will not put her in any more danger than is absolutely necessary. She will be safe."

"For your sake," Isengrim replied softly, "I hope that you are right."

* * * * * * *

"How long?" Hermeline asked from her seat by the window, her voice flat.

"A month or two at least," Reynard answered, his back to the hearth, where a damp log hissed and cracked as it burned. "But- it may be longer."

"I see."

Reynard crossed the distance between them, and gently placed a hand on her shoulder.

"Don't," she said, shying away from his touch.

"Hermeline-"

"Do you know I actually believed you when you said that you would stay this time?" she said with a chuckle, the bitterness in her voice as sharp as steel. "I should have known better."

"You know I don't have any choice."

"No choice? No choice?" she said, suddenly furious. "Oh, Reynard, I thought I'd heard the worst of your lies, but that one trumps all!"

"It is not a lie. If I ignore the King's summons-"

"Then what?" she shot back, rising from her chair. "He'll strip you of lands and titles that mean nothing to you? Or maybe he'll start sending better assassins after us than the ones he's sent already? When have you ever given a shit about what Nobel commands, Reynard? When have you ever done anything you haven't already planned from the start?"

She had been advancing on him as she hurled her scornful words and with her last words she took up a ceramic basin, a beautiful thing that Reynard had brought back from one of his forays, and pitched it at him. It sailed past him, and shattered against the hearth noisily.

"And what would you have me do?" Reynard asked. "Skulk here in this rat hole until my enemies find me?"

"No!" she said. "We've escaped from Nobel once already. Let us leave this place and sail to Frisia- Solothurn- even to the jungles of Tyris if we must! I don't care where you lead us, Reynard! Just don't leave me here alone!"

"And have you thought about how many might die Hermeline?" he asked, his voice calm. "Because *I* have. I have to, now that they all count on me. Even if we could take them all with us, and bring enough to feed them, how many would survive the journey? Could you live with the knowledge that you'd led someone to their deaths, when you could have stopped it?"

"No," she said finally. "No, I couldn't."

"Then you understand why I must go."

"Reynard," she said, grabbing hold of him. "Nobel is King now. If you go he will surely kill you."

"He cannot kill me openly," Reynard replied with a weak smile. "At least, not without a reason. The same laws that bind me to him also tie his hands as well- and once I arrive at Gadwall I will have fulfilled my obligation to him. I need only fight."

"But the Calvarians- What if you are slain? What will become of us if-"

"I promise you that I will not let myself be killed," Reynard said, kissing her cheek to seal his words. "I promise you, Hermeline."

"Then," she said, her grip tightening considerably. "Take me with you. Don't leave me here alone. I cannot bear the thought of it."

"I'm sorry," he said, shaking his head. "It will be too dangerous for you, and I will need you here to manage things for me. After all, I can hardly count on Baldwin to keep this place standing."

"But if any of you are hurt," she breathed. "Who will look after you?"

"Hirsent can take care of us."

Hermeline's brow darkened.

"You are taking her but not me?"

"Hirsent can watch out for herself," he replied simply. "She is a warrior, and a decent healer, though her bedside manner leaves something to be desired."

"And how would you know anything about that?" Hermeline asked, and Reynard could tell that she was only half-joking.

"Because we have been having an affair," he replied, raising a finger to his lips. "Don't tell Isengrim."

In spite of her anger, she laughed.

"Have I ever told you that you're very pretty when you are jealous?"

"Have I ever told you that you're a bastard?"

"Once or twice," he said and took her in his arms.

"You will write," she said. It was not a request.

IV

In the end, Reynard left Maleperduys in the company of thirty of his best warriors. He might have taken more, but his stables held only some fifty odd steeds fit enough for the long journey, and as he did not wish to strip the fortress completely of horse, he chose only to accept the most talented of his men as companions. None of them were equal in skill when compared to the likes of Tybalt, Bruin, or Tiecelin, but they had all proven themselves to be resilient fighters, and Reynard was glad to have their company- as well as that of Tiecelin's shrikes, who would prove invaluable as scouts.

They had, in point of fact, only been traveling for an hour when the youngest of the shrikes, a tan-feathered female whose tail feathers were the color of burnt umber (Reynard constantly marveled at the wild diversity of shape and color amongst Sharpebeck's children- who were only one generation removed from the nearly human shrike Tybalt had killed in Vulp Vora) swooped down through a gap in the foliage and lit on an overhanging tree branch. The chimera chirruped several garbled words to Tiecelin before erupting back into flight.

"We are being followed," Tiecelin said, bringing his steed alongside Reynard's.

"Chimera?"

The Luxian shook his head. "A horse bearing two riders, Rossignol says."

Reynard groaned. He could easily guess who might be following them, and they were already too deep in the tangled depths of the forest to send a pair of children back to Maleperduys unescorted.

"Go on ahead without me," Reynard said to the others, slowing his own horse to a trot. "I will handle this and then catch up with you at the Maidenhead."

"It is dangerous for one to be alone in these woods," Isengrim said, beginning to rein in his own black stallion.

"Fear not," Reynard said, patting his mount's well-muscled neck. "I will have Bayard to keep me safe. There is not warg nor faun alive that could outrun this horse."

"You are certain?"

"Aye," Reynard answered.

Isengrim nodded and rode on with the others, who soon disappeared from sight, the sounds of their passing swallowed up by the boughs of ancient trees.

The forest creaked ominously in the wind and small unseen creatures rustled in the underbrush. Bayard snorted impatiently, and Reynard was inclined to agree with him. It had been some time since he had gone alone into the forest, and he little liked the way the shadows between the trees played tricks on the eye, so that there always seemed to be something moving just out of sight.

"Easy, there," he said. "We'll be on our way soon enough."

Shortly Reynard could hear the telltale sound of horse hooves beating against the trail that led back to the castle, and above it the high-pitched voices of a young man and woman arguing- and though he was angry he could not help but smile as he listened to them.

"But how can you be sure this is even their trail?" Martin was saying, "I saw dozens of tracks back at the last crosspath!"

"These are fresher," Rukenaw replied. "Look how the earth is torn up."

"I suppose you fancy yourself a tracker now?"

"Anyone can tell fresh tracks from old, Martin!"

"And what if you're wrong? We're in the middle of the Wild Woods- there's no telling what could be out here."

"Oh, you worry as much as an old woman," the girl grumbled. "Master Tybalt has gone out hunting in the forest every day this past week and he's come back safe."

"That's because he goes hunting with at least ten men to back him up if he runs into any trouble. And besides, Baron Reynard told me that the woods are full of faun- and wargs too."

"Baron Reynard," the girl said, mocking Martin's reverential tone, "Baron Reynard! Is that all you can ever talk about?"

"He is a great man," Martin replied hotly, "Better than Master Tybalt, I can tell you that."

"You're just jealous."

"And you're blind if you can't see what a rat Tybalt is!"

Reynard could see them now, the girl riding behind the boy, who had twisted around in the saddle to argue with her. They were astride a packhorse, an older mare that Reynard recalled as belonging to Baldwin, and both had equipped themselves with swords and ill-fitting mail. So preoccupied were they with their own fight that they did not notice the rider standing in their path until they were nearly right on top of him, at which point Martin tugged sharply on the mare's reins and came to an abrupt halt.

"What do you think you are doing?" Reynard asked, arching one of his eyebrows. "Do you realize how dangerous it is in these woods? How deep they are? What might happen to the both of you if you lost our path?"

"We didn't-" Martin sputtered. "I mean Rukenaw, she-"

"Please, don't be mad at him," the girl said, mercifully cutting the boy off. "It wasn't his idea to follow you. It was mine."

"Is that so?"

The girl nodded.

"You said that I should protect her," Martin added sheepishly. "And when I couldn't convince her to stay, I felt that I should go too."

"And just what were you planning to do? Shadow us all the way to Gadwall with what can't be more than three or four days worth of food?"

"We wanted to go with you," the girl replied, "and fight the Calvarians, and I thought that if we could stay on your trail long enough it would be too late to turn us back."

"Then it's lucky for you that I caught you before we left the forest! As it stands there's just enough time for me to get you back to Hermeline, and give you a sound whipping before I rejoin the others."

"No," the girl said. "I won't go back there. I want to fight- and kill some of the same folk as killed my sister, my mother, and Martin's kin too! They took everything! Everything! Everything I ever had, except- except for Martin."

The girl was crying now, freely, unashamed of her sorrow, and Martin's eyes too were wet with his own tears.

"I understand your pain," Reynard said softly, "And the rage you both must be feeling right now- but what I need you to understand is that you are *not* ready for this. You're not warriors. When you are older, and you still feel that this is something you must do, then I promise you that I will be at your side. But until that day comes you need to be young, to learn, to enjoy the time you have before you lose it forever. Revenge can always wait."

"Seal your promise," Rukenaw said, fiercely.

Reynard nodded and, leaning over in his saddle so that his face hung between that of boy and girl, he gave each a quick peck on the cheek.

"Now then," Reynard said as he straightened himself, "Will you let me take you back home?"

"Alright," Rukenaw said, wiping her eyes with her sleeve.

"Yes, please," Martin added.

"Good," Reynard said, and smiled. "Now then, I suppose I shouldn't mention it, seeing as you've given me such trouble, but if you are very careful maybe you can return what you've stolen and sneak back into the castle without Hermeline noticing. How does that sound-"

Reynard's last word froze in his throat, half-spoken.

"What's-" Martin began to say, but Reynard cut him off with an upraised palm.

The forest had gone utterly quiet.

Reynard's eyes flitted left and right, scanning each darkened gap between the trees, his hand coming to rest on the hilt of his sword as he did so.

Then the wind picked up, rustling the red leaves so that they hissed like an adder, and a pair of dark shapes erupted out of the underbrush.

Reynard drew, but his blade had hardly left its sheath before the lithe figures- a pair of white-bellied does- were gone, having already leapt over the path and vanished back into the wood.

"What was it?" Rukenaw said, lifting her head up from behind Martin's shoulder.

"Only a pair of deer," Martin said, and began to laugh. "For a moment there I thought-"

"Hush!" Reynard hissed, but it was too late. A throaty growl ripped menacingly through the air, and then a trio of lean creatures stalked out of the shadows.

Their gray pelts were dark, in some places nearly black. Their bodies were, for the most part, wolf-shaped, but their long and muscular forearms ended in almost human digits tipped with claws, and they were far larger than their natural counterparts, standing nearly the height of a man.

Even Martin and Rukenaw, who had never seen such things before, had no doubt that the creatures that stood before them were wargs.

"Tresspasserrr," the biggest of the things snarled, its upper lip curled back to reveal yellowed fangs. This one bore a distinctive mark on its right shoulder- a row of evenly spaced scars that were nearly identical to ones that Reynard had seen before on the body of a dead warg, though whether it was a mark of honor or shame, or a way to differentiate between members of rival tribes he could not say.

"We want no fight with you, chimera," Reynard said, making certain that the creatures could see his naked blade. "Let us pass, and continue your hunt in peace."

"Grrrl," the beast growled, casting a glance towards the shaking young woman. "Give-issus grrrl and you go."

"No," Reynard replied, his mouth suddenly dry, "I have meat that I can offer you, but the girl and the boy stay with me."

"You die then, and we take grrrl anyway!"

"We shall see."

The big warg began to pace back and forth, its eyes narrowing with rage as the two smaller chimera moved to encircle them.

Baldwin's mare whinnied with terror, her eyes rolling in their sockets. Reynard knew that at any moment she might bolt.

"Martin," Reynard said, keeping his eyes on the wargs. "Can you get back to the castle without my help?"

"I think," the boy answered. "But what about you?"

"Just do it!" he shouted and slapped the flat of his blade on the mare's rump.

Baldwin's steed started into a wild gallop, nearly colliding with one of the two smaller wargs as they leapt after it in pursuit. The largest of the chimera pounced at Reynard, who only just managed to twist around in time to slash at the beast as it raked its filthy claws across Bayard's flank.

A normal horse might have panicked then, but Bayard had been trained for the chaos of battle. He began to turn and buck with his deadly hooves, and with a sharp kick he managed to throw the slavering creature into the underbrush.

And by the time the injured warg had recovered its footing, Reynard and his steed were already gone, having joined the chase down the narrow pathways of the forest.

Bayard was swift, and was more accustomed to the forest than the mount that carried Martin and Rukenaw, so that it was not long before Reynard could make out the form of the desperate horse and its riders through the trees. The wargs were right on their heels, though they appeared to be waiting for the older beast to slow before closing in for the kill.

Reynard goaded Bayard with his heels, and the bay put on fresh speed, until they were within ten feet of the chimera.

Ahead the path split. The left hand way led to Maleperduys, while the right would wind backwards through the forest for mile upon mile.

Reynard could see Martin pulling desperately on the reins of Baldwin's mare, but the fear-maddened beast could not be guided, and plunged down the wrong path. As they did, one of the wargs veered off into the trees, while the other turned and, using a rising embankment as a stepping-stone, launched itself at Reynard.

The chimera collided with him head-on, throwing him from Bayard's back and knocking his sword from his hand as they tumbled wildly into the brush. It was on top of him then, its jaws snapping wildly as it lunged for his unprotected throat. Reynard thrust his right arm into its mouth, feeling the cruel pinch of its unnatural bite even through his vambraces, and with his other hand he freed his dagger from its sheath and plunged it as deep as he was able into the warg's shoulder.

The warg howled in agony, and as it momentarily released its grip on him he grabbed the beast by the muzzle and shifted his blade to stab at its exposed jugular. But he had not the chance to strike before the chimera had caught his hand in one of its own and began to squeeze both it and the dagger together with vice-like strength.

Screaming now, Reynard beat his armored forearm repeatedly against the warg's face, but the chimera merely continued to increase the intensity of its grip until, with a series of dull pops, Reynard's fingers snapped out of their joints.

Reynard felt suddenly woozy, and realized that he might pass out from the pain that was coursing through him. The chimera, perhaps sensing this, released his foe's mangled hand and delivered a fierce punch to Reynard's stomach.

Reynard reeled from the blow, and went limp.

The warg roared in triumph, but as it dipped its head to tear out his throat Reynard grabbed the thing by the face and plunged his thumb into its eye.

The warg whipped its head back and forth, but still Reynard held on, until at last the thing released its hold on him and danced away- its left eye a bloody ruin.

Reynard stumbled to his feet, and scrambled for something that he could see lying in the bushes nearby.

"Killlll youuuu!" the warg cried, rising on its hind legs until it stood nearly as tall as Isengrim.

Reynard turned, and as the thing loped wildly forward, he opened its throat with a single swipe of his recovered sword.

The warg staggered and, after it had collapsed to the forest floor, Reynard buried his blade in its back.

When the chimera had finally stopped breathing, Reynard forced himself to look at his wounded left hand. His normally graceful fingers were bent and twisted, and his glove had grown dark with the stain of his own blood, but the damage was not as great as he had feared.

Somewhere nearby another warg howled, and Reynard forgot his pain.

"The children," he said, and half-ran, half-stumbled back onto the path.

Reynard was relieved to find that Bayard had not gone far once his master had been unseated.

"Some help you are," he said to the bay as he picked up the reins

Bayard snorted, as if in indignation, but nuzzled his long nose against his master's face and bent his knees so that Reynard could more easily climb onto his back.

"Speed, my friend," Reynard whispered, kicking his heels, and they were off.

* * * * * * *

"Get back!" Martin shouted, pushing Rukenaw behind him as he slashed at the advancing chimera.

They stood near the bottom of a jagged ravine, its walls far too steep for a human to easily climb. Their horse lay dead nearby- her throat rent open by tooth and claw. The warg had killed her first. It had jumped down at them from the escarpment above, its superior knowledge of the terrain having allowed it to get far enough ahead of them to lay an ambush.

The warg was, for now, keeping its distance, swiping at Martin almost playfully, as if prolonging the moment when it would slay him and carry the young girl off to whatever den such beasts might keep.

Shuddering at the thought, Martin let out a desperate cry, and charged- receiving an openhanded blow across the face that knocked the wind out of him as he fell face first onto the ground.

"Too slllow," the thing chuckled, and advanced then on Rukenaw, who had buried her face into the chalky soil of the embankment. She raised her sword to defend herself, but the warg slapped it out of her hands as one might disarm a child with a stick.

Rukenaw felt the hot blast of its breath as it leaned over her, leering as its human-like hands tore open the front of her leather jack.

"Please," she said, not knowing what else to say. "Please."

"Get off of her!" she heard Martin cry, and the warg turned to face the boy, who had regained his feet and was advancing towards the chimera.

"Martin, no!" Rukenaw screamed. "He's too strong!"

But Martin did not listen, and charged again. This time the warg was not so gentle- with its claws it ripped open the boy's shoulder, the force of the swipe whipping him around like a ragdoll before knocking him to the ground.

Shakily, Martin began to rise again, but as he did so the warg's jaws closed around his skull.

"Good nighhht, Martinnn," the warg sneered at him through its gritted teeth, each syllable serving to grind the beast's fangs deeper into his flesh.

The boy struggled wildly, panic overtaking him as he realized that he had failed to protect Rukenaw, and that these moments would be his last. The world seemed spitefully alive to him in that moment- the merry whistling of birds, the cool touch of crushed wildflowers under the palm of his hand- even the beating of his heart seemed to pound in his chest like the sound of a galloping stallion.

Strangely, Martin felt the warg's hold on him slacken, and then he was free of its jaws. The violent cry of a horse split the air and, wiping his own blood out of his eyes, he looked up just in time to see one of Bayard's steel-capped hooves come crashing down onto the chimera's skull.

Several strikes later, the beast was dead.

"Are you badly hurt?" Reynard asked the boy as he leapt from Bayard's back.

"Don't worry about me," Martin replied shakily. "But, Rukenaw- is she-"

"I'm fine," the girl said, tearing a strip of cloth from her already ruined chemise and binding it around Martin's shoulder the way that Hermeline had shown her. As she pulled the tourniquet tight the boy cried out, and fainted.

"Will he die?" the girl asked, softly.

"I think not- though he has lost a lot of blood," Reynard said, lifting the boy as best he could. "Help me get him onto Bayard."

"Oh, your hand," Rukenaw sighed, wincing at the sight of his mangled digits.

"It will have to wait until I have you both safely home. Now, help me."

They eventually managed to hoist Martin awkwardly onto Bayard's back, and then the girl climbed into the saddle to hold him steady. Reynard took hold of the reins, and began to lead the way on foot.

They had nearly climbed to the summit of the ravine when Reynard stopped. Rukenaw opened her mouth to ask what was wrong, but then she too saw the dark figures that blocked their path, and words were lost to her.

Perched in the rocks ahead of them were at least six or seven wargs.

The largest of them- still bleeding from the cut that Reynard had recently given him- curled his canine lips into the semblance of a sneer and barked out the order to attack.

"Hold onto Martin!" Reynard shouted to Rukenaw as the wargs leapt from the rocks. Then he pulled himself into the saddle and, whispering a quick apology to his horse for the extra weight, he brought Bayard around so that they might run for their lives.

Bayard flew down the path, kicking up rocks and pebbles as his hooves tore into the soil, and leapt with expert skill over the corpse of Baldwin's mare as they passed the place where Rukenaw and Martin had been unhorsed. Reynard risked a glance backwards, faintly hoping that the wargs might cease their pursuit at the sight of a fresh meal that would not fight back, but the chimera did not even pause to inspect the body of their slain pack-mate as they passed it. The injury done to their tribe, Reynard guessed, was a slight that could not be forgiven.

The wargs would chase them, Reynard knew, until either they or the chimera were dead.

Bayard shot out of the ravine and back into the shadows of the forest. The trail was faint here- little more than a narrow line that looped this way and that- but the trees were thinner as well, and there was little in the way of underbrush, so that Bayard could easily pass between their trunks.

Reynard steered Bayard off the path. He feared losing their way, for who knew how deep these woods might stretch or what other den of chimera they might stumble upon, but all that would matter little if the wargs caught them.

The wargs followed, zigzagging between the trees while widening the line of their pursuit. They even appeared to be slowing somewhat, as though they were certain of the chase's outcome and did not wish to overexert themselves.

The reason for this soon became evident, for the forest suddenly gave way to a rocky-soiled clearing, beyond which yawned a sharp-edged canyon, and as Bayard sharply turned to avoid plunging over the edge of this precipice, Reynard could see that they had allowed themselves to be herded onto an ever narrowing spur of earth from which there was no exit save the way they had come.

So, with only two choices before him, and the first of them being to turn and face the wargs that were even now fanning out to prevent their escape, Reynard urged Bayard towards the narrowest point of the promontory- a frightfully thin strip of land that pointed finger-like over the chasm, almost bridging the distance between this cliff and the opposite.

Perhaps guessing what Reynard intended to do, the wargs quickened their pace, their jaws slavering as they raced to cut him off. One of them, a female with a wild streak of white in its coat, got close enough to snap at Bayard's legs before the deadly swipe of Reynard's blade forced it to back off.

Reynard need hardly have bothered, however, for there was now hardly enough room for Bayard alone to gallop. Ahead of them loomed the ragged tip of spur, and the long drop into the dry riverbed below.

Rukenaw's grip around Reynard's waist tightened, and he could feel the girl burying her head into the small of his back as Bayard tensed for the attempt across the gorge.

Bayard reached the edge, and jumped.

For a terrible moment Reynard could almost feel the gulf below them, and his stomach rose into his throat at the thought of the long drop, and the horror of the thought that the fall might not serve to kill them.

Then he felt Bayard's hooves touch onto solid ground, and after they had gone some little way along this side of the cliff Reynard was forced to accept that somehow, even with a trio of riders weighing him down, Bayard had made the seemingly impossible jump.

Only one of the wargs had been foolhardy enough to follow Bayard over the cliff's edge- the former leader of the pack, whose broken form now lay quivering at the bottom of the canyon.

The other chimera stood along the cliff-side, staring after their escaped prey with a look etched into their canine features that hovered somewhere between rage and respect- and as Reynard and the others disappeared into the trees that lined the opposite side of the chasm, they turned and slunk back into the darkness of the forest.

* * * * * * *

For some time they wandered through the forest, Reynard leading the way with Bayard's reins in hand, pressing eastward until they left the trees and returned to one of the wood's natural pathways.

They had gone a little ways along this path when Reynard came to a halt and groaned.

"What is it?" Rukenaw asked.

"Do you see that?" Reynard replied, pointing towards a large oak by the side of the trail.

Rukenaw squinted, and saw that a simple rune had been carved into the tree's ashy trunk.

"What is it?"

"One of Tiecelin's blaze markers. They serve as signposts through the wood, for those who can read them."

"Is that not a good thing?"

"Normally, yes, for we would likely be lost without it," Reynard said. "But this one tells me that we are far from Maleperduys- and I must reunite with the others by nightfall."

"Then, you mean-"

"Yes," Reynard sighed, "It appears that you and Martin will be joining us, though it stands against my better judgment."

"Oh, Martin," Rukenaw said, giving the boy a good shake, "Did you hear? We will go to Gadwall!"

"Wake me when we get there," the boy moaned.

****

The Maidenhead was a verdant grove that lay between the confluence of the rocky streams that formed the source of the River Course. Hidden from plain sight by thick ferns and gnarled roots, this refuge had often served Reynard and his companions as a temporary hiding place from the Calvarian patrols that occasionally ventured into the forest of Maleperduys.

It was near on towards midnight by the time that Reynard, Martin, and Rukenaw came to that hidden place- but even in the dim light Reynard could plainly see the distinct forms of the sentries waiting in the trees, and he silently made a note to himself to have words with Bruin concerning the need for subtlety on their journey. They had miles upon miles of territory to cross before they reached Gadwall, and would not last long unless they could pass through undetected.

"Who goes?" a voice cried out suddenly. It belonged to Jacquet, one of Tybalt's men.

"It is only I," Reynard answered back, "You may lower your crossbow."

Two men stepped from the trees, clearly relieved by the sight of Reynard. One was Jacquet and the other was Maugris, who had traded his harp for a sharp-edged spear.

"How came these two to join you?" the priest of the Watcher asked, glowering at the youths sitting astride Bayard.

"It is a long story," Reynard answered. "But, quickly now, take us to Hirsent. The boy is wounded- and I as well."

Both men turned sharply and proceeded to lead them through a shallow cleft in the hillside, and then down into the coombe below, where Reynard's companions had set their tents around a crackling bonfire that stood near the water's edge.

The tent Isengrim and Hirsent shared was a rather plain thing compared to the multi-colored shelters that surrounded it, though it was far more spacious as they did not share their quarters with anyone but themselves.

The tent's flaps were closed, so as they approached Maugris called out, "Madam Hirsent, you are needed!"

Reynard could hear rustling within the tent, the metallic clink of a belt being buckled, and then Hirsent appeared. Reynard could not help but notice that she did not resemble her usual self: the front of her uniform was undone, and her eyes were rimmed red.

"Who is hurt?" she asked, reflexively buttoning up her chalk-white jacket as she settled her eyes on Reynard and the others.

"Martin," Maugris replied.

"Young boy?" she queried, craning her neck out of the tent flap. "And girl too I see. Is hurt as well?"

"Only the boy," Reynard answered, gingerly helping Rukenaw lower Martin out of the saddle. The boy was pale and silent, the tourniquet tied round his shoulder soaked through with blood.

"Sit him down," Hirsent said, indicating a nearby tree stump. "And boil water! I must be fetching my tools."

At a glance from Reynard, Jacquet ran off to find a pan.

"Where are Isengrim and the others?" Reynard asked Maugris as Hirsent rummaged through her saddlebags, for he noticed that half of the men's horses were missing, including Isengrim's black palfrey.

"When you did not show up, Tiecelin sent the shrikes out to look for you- and when they could not find you, Isengrim insisted on mounting a search party."

Reynard sat down on a nearby rock, his head suddenly dizzy.

"Are you alright, my lord?" Maugris asked.

"It is nothing," he said, ignoring the waves of pain that were climbing up his left arm. "Did Tiecelin leave any of the bird-chimera behind in case I returned on my own?"

"Aye," Maugris replied, pointing towards one of the trees, where Reynard could make out the outline of two of the odd creatures roosting in its branches.

"Have them find the search party before it gets too dark," Reynard said, rubbing his bicep. "I would have us gone by sunrise, and men and shrike alike will need to rest."

The priest made his obeisance and left on his errand without complaint- though Reynard noted the hesitation in his step as he went, and felt some pity for him. A servant of the Watcher Maugris might be, but he was still not as accustomed to the presence of the chimera as the men who had gone with Reynard through Vulp Vora and back.

Hirsent, meanwhile, had retrieved the black leather case that the men had taken to calling the 'butcher's bag,' and had begun to unravel the blood-soaked bandages that covered Martin's shoulder.

"Tourniquet is good," the Calvarian woman commented, and glanced upwards at Reynard. "Is yours?"

"Hers," Reynard replied, and gestured to Rukenaw, who had been standing nearby with a stony expression on her face.

"Is good work," Hirsent said, smiling at the girl. "But perhaps I show you how to do it better?"

"Hermeline taught me how to do it," Rukenaw answered back hotly. "I don't want your help."

Hirsent's smile disappeared, and without another word she returned to her work.

"What give him these wounds?" she asked, prodding Martin's ragged shoulder until the boy hissed with pain. "Wolf?"

"Warg," Reynard replied.

"Warg?"

"Warg."

"Hmm," she hummed, as if only marginally impressed, and went back to work.

"Is he going to be alright?" Reynard asked, his tongue suddenly thick in his mouth.

"*Gea*," she replied. "Wounds are not very deep- but they must be washed and then I must stitch. Is water being ready?"

"I will check," Reynard offered, unsteadily rising to his feet.

"Reynard," Hirsent said, her brow suddenly knit with genuine concern. "You are looking very pale."

"Am I?" he said, and collapsed.

* * * * * * *

Reynard was awoken by the sound of screams- and a moment later he realized that they were his own.

He was on his back. Hirsent hovered over him, his mangled hand caught in her powerful grip. Maugris and Jacquet were holding him down, and Hirsent had lodged a bit of leather between his teeth in order to keep him from biting through his own tongue. The remnants of his glove lay nearby, smeared with blood.

"One more," Hirsent said, "You are understanding?"

"Wait," he panted, knowing all too well what she meant. "Just give me a moment to-"

Hirsent's fingers wrapped around one of his dislocated digits and forced it back into place with a savage yank.

"Ahhhhhhh!" Reynard screamed again, before adding: "By Wulf, I told you to wait!"

"You are being fortunate that bones were not broken," Hirsent replied with a faint smile. "Pain then being much worse. I will be applying splints now."

"Will it hurt?"

"Only a little," she said and began to tie two of the splints together with a fresh piece of cloth. The pain was nowhere near as great as what he had felt before, but it was still excruciating. He did not, however, scream.

He did not want to give her the satisfaction.

When Hirsent had tied the last pair of splints into place she began to wrap his entire hand up with linen, until his left arm resembled that of a Glyconese corpse.

"You may be letting go now," Hirsent said, and at once the two men holding Reynard down released their grip on him. A moment later they were gone, glad perhaps to be away from that place.

"Why did you wait to show me hand?" Hirsent asked.

"I was worried about the boy," he answered. "How is he?"

"Boy is fine. Girl is fine. You- not so fine."

"How long?" Reynard asked Hirsent as he examined his bandaged arm.

"Bandages are coming off in fourteen nights," she replied, returning some of her tools to her case.

"I meant, how long until I can use it?"

"Month- maybe longer."

"Hydra's Teeth," he cursed, and started to rise.

Hirsent placed her palm on his chest, and firmly pushed him back down to the ground. He found that he was too weak to resist.

"You are not to be moving," she said. "Not until morning."

"I have my own bedroll-"

"You are *not* to be moving," she repeated, dangling a finger in his face for emphasis. "Not until it is being morning."

Reynard glanced about the tent. There was only one bedroll.

"And where will you be sleeping?"

"I will be sleeping outside," she huffed, a little color flushing into her cheeks as she stalked out of the tent and threw closed the flaps. "Now, be trying to sleep!"

Reynard chuckled and decided to follow Hirsent's advice.

* * * * * * *

"Reynard," said a familiar voice. "It is nearly dawn."

Reynard opened his eyes blearily, wondering how he could have slept through the racket that the men were making as they broke camp.

Isengrim stood in the doorway of the tent.

"I take it that you got my message," Reynard said, rising to his feet. The pain in his hand had dulled somewhat, though he still longed for one of Hermeline's herbal brews to take the edge off.

"The children say that you fought a warg," Isengrim said.

"It wasn't very big," he replied as nonchalantly as he was able. "And the fight nearly cost me a hand."

"Still, there are few men who can say they have faced a warg and lived to tell of it. I am impressed."

The Calvarian bowed lower than Reynard had ever seen him do so before- it was an extremely rare show of respect.

"Did Martin mention that there were actually three wargs?" Reynard added once the Calvarian had straightened to his full height. "Because I wouldn't mind seeing you bow again."

For a moment Isengrim stared at Reynard, his cold eyes fixed and dangerous. Then he laughed and, clapping a hand on Reynard's shoulder he said, "When you slay another warg, perhaps I will. But for now I have a tent to strike, and you are in my way."

Reynard stayed awhile longer, helping Isengrim as well as he could with only one hand. When they had gotten the tent down Hirsent joined them, handing Reynard a bowl of cold porridge.

"Eat," she said simply, and then took over his share of the work.

"*Where have you been?*" Isengrim asked her, quietly and in their own tongue, his neutral tone belying his obvious concern.

"*Sick,*" she replied. "*Something I ate, perhaps.*"

"*Do you wish to take some rest?*"

"*No, I want to help,*" she replied, kissing him on the cheek before adding, "*But thank you for asking.*"

So, Reynard ate his breakfast and watched as Isengrim and Hirsent neatly folded up their tent, continuing to chat in Calvarian as they worked, and for the first time in a long while he was reminded of the days when they had just discovered Maleperduys, and the two Calvarians had been as young lovers are when their love is a thing new and glorious to them.

"I should see to the children," Reynard said, excusing himself.

He washed out his bowl in the nearby pool and returned to the main camp, where most of the men were already mounted.

"I hear that you outran a pack of overgrown wolves," Tybalt said as he approached, adding, "I expect that Maugris is already adding it to the catalogue of your exploits."

"I must admit that Bayard did most of the work," Reynard replied, and patted his mount on the rump affectionately. At some point during the night someone had tended to the bay's wounds, and had groomed the animal's coat 'til it shone.

"Who's taken such care of you, my friend?" Reynard asked the horse as he checked his hooves for loose stones and found none.

"I have, Master Reynard," Martin beamed, stepping out of the press of men. He looked a good deal healthier than he had the day before, despite the wounds that covered his face. "I know how to groom an animal. I used to take care of my father's horse, before-"

The boy's voice faltered.

"Yes," Reynard said, mercifully, "I can see that you know quite a lot about horses- certainly more than I did at your age. And, as you and Rukenaw will be traveling with us to Gadwall, I wonder if you might care to play the part of my page?"

"Your page?" the boy replied with a puzzled expression. "What is that?"

"It means that you will be my attendant," Reynard replied, "And see to the care of my horse and armor-"

"And polish the Baron's boots when he can't be bothered to do so himself," Bruin added, and the men laughed.

"But most important of all, Martin," Reynard went on, "Is that you will obey my word- and if I command you to stay behind and out of danger you will do so without complaint. Do you understand?"

Martin sank to one knee. "Whatever you command, Master Reynard, it will be done."

"Then rise, and lend me one of your hands."

So, with Martin's help, Reynard climbed back into his saddle and once he was comfortable, he offered his own hand to the boy.

"We will ride together," he said, and pulled Martin up so that the boy sat behind him. "At least until I can find a steed fit for my page."

"But as for you," Reynard continued, turning towards Rukenaw, "You must ride with another- for I would not overburden Bayard more than I already have on this journey."

"The girl can ride with me," Tybalt offered, guiding his gelding to come up alongside her. "She can sit in front of me if she likes."

"Filthy dog," Martin growled under his breath.

"What's that, boy?" Tybalt said, his eyes dangerous. "Did you say something?"

"I think, Tybalt," Reynard cut in, "That it might be more suitable if Madam Rukenaw rode with someone who could keep their hands to themselves."

"She may be riding with me," Hirsent said, stepping forward. "If she is being willing."

The girl did not answer, but shook her head 'no.' If Hirsent took offense, she did not show it, but merely returned to the task of inspecting her own steed.

"I will take her," Tiecelin said, and when the girl did not complain the dark-eyed man lifted her onto the back of his gray courser.

"Now let us quit this place," Reynard said, "We have a long journey ahead of us, and have already wasted enough time on my account."

"And mine," Rukenaw grumbled.

"You are certain that you wish to bring these children with us?" Isengrim asked from the saddle of his own horse.

"I would send them back if I could spare either the time or the men," Reynard answered. "But I fear that with the wargs riled up it would take all of us to return to Maleperduys safely."

"All the same," he said, pulling a sheaf of parchment from his saddlebag "I would not worry Hermeline, who by now must imagine that these two have been eaten whole by giants."

Once he had found ink and quill, Reynard scratched out a note that explained the children's absence, warned Hermeline to keep the men out of the forest until he returned, and promised to keep himself out of harm's way- all the while adorning it with enough personal endearments to choke an ox.

When he was done he turned to Tiecelin and asked: "Can you spare one of your children for this errand?"

"Sharpebeck!" the Luxian called out, and with a wild flutter of wings the plum-feathered shrike lit on the ground next to him.

"You wishit something, Father?" Sharpebeck said. She was not as human as her mother had been, being smaller and more avian in form, but though she was only three years old she already had the face, and the voice, of a grown woman.

Tiecelin knelt down so that he could speak to the shrike face to face.

"Master Reynard has a letter for Madam Hermeline. Can you deliver it to her and return to me by midday?"

Sharpebeck yawned, but nodded her ascent all the same. She, like her brother, was fiercely loyal to the man that she called 'Father.' Reynard wondered if that would be the case should she ever discover the truth of her parentage.

"Then go, and return safely," Tiecelin said, tying Reynard's letter to one of the shrike's scaly legs before planting a pair of kisses on her downy cheeks.

"I will, Father," she replied, and was gone, her brilliant wings catching the first light of day.

Within moments Reynard's band was off, leaving no trace of their camp save for the droppings of their steeds. And as they thundered out of the forest, Martin turned round long enough to catch a glimpse of Sharpebeck soaring westward on the wind, towards home.

V

Tiecelin's boot stamping out the fire was the only warning Reynard had before he knew that they were in danger.

It was dusk, and they were camped on a wooded shelf somewhere along the edge of the mountainous Erycinian Highlands, through which the shrikes had led them so as to avoid the open plains of Barca. They'd made good time despite the terrain, and had found the isolated villages of the mountainous plateau more than happy to refill their packs with fresh food and water- especially once they were told that they were playing host to the retinue of the illustrious Baron Reynard- though Reynard suspected that they might have been just as accommodating to any large group of armed men that did not resort to violence to get what they wanted.

Reynard was reclining on a broad stone, his face turned southward, where Mount Mulciber smoked fitfully amongst black peaks, his uninjured hand tucked under his coat and fiddling with the gem that hung always near his heart.

"What is it?" Martin managed to blurt out before Bruin clapped one of his enormous hands over the boy's mouth. The others were already kicking loose bits of dirt over the smoking embers of the fire pit, or loosening their swords from their scabbards.

Reynard gained his feet smoothly despite his injury, and looked to Tiecelin, who was crouching low, his head cocked to the side like one of his 'children.' A moment later the scout straightened and motioned for Reynard and Isengrim to follow.

As they went to comply, Hirsent made as if to join them. Reynard halted her with an upraised palm, and pointed to his eyes before stabbing his fingers towards Martin and Rukenaw.

Scowling, Hirsent laid a gloved hand on her hip and gestured to the dozen or so armed men who were surrounding the two youngsters. Reynard sighed quietly and motioned for her to join them.

Tiecelin led them along uneven ground, and it took careful footing not to dislodge any of the tiny pebbles that were strewn about the rocks. At one point one of Isengrim's boots scuffed noisily against a bit of gravel, an act that froze Tiecelin in his tracks until he was certain that they had not been heard.

Eventually they came to a thick jumble of man-sized stones where they found Tybalt, who had been on patrol, hunkering down behind cover.

"Wondered when you'd all be along," Tybalt breathed as they crouched down beside them, ignoring the fierce look that Tiecelin gave him. "I think we've got some company."

"Calvarians?" Reynard whispered.

"Take a look for yourself, your lordship."

Reynard and the others peered over the rocks, gazing down at an old footpath that lay between the escarpment where they were perched and a tree-crowned drumlin opposite their position. Moving slowly through this pass was a squadron of Calvarian soldiers astride sleek horses whose gray coats almost matched those of their riders.

"Another long patrol," Isengrim said.

"Raiders?" Hirsent asked.

Reynard shook his head. "We're leagues from any settlement I know of."

"Well, I count only ten of the bastards," Tybalt added, silently slipping one of his knives out of his bandolier. "And it's a lovely spot for an ambush . . ."

"Stay your hand a moment," Reynard said suddenly. "I have the odd feeling that these boys aren't alone."

Tybalt rolled his eyes, but was still.

The Calvarians were riding at a steady canter, and before long they rounded the drumlin and disappeared from sight.

"Well, there's that opportunity gone," Tybalt said as he returned his knife to its sheath. "'Course, we might have had them if Tiecelin's pets had given us some warning. Where are those overgrown buzzards of yours, anyhow?"

"Geaibleau and Bavarde are scouting to the south," Tiecelin answered coolly, "And the others must rest sometime . . ."

"What's wrong?" Reynard asked.

"I hear-" the Luxian began, before hissing, "Get down!"

Reynard was so used to Tiecelin's keen senses that he immediately sank to the ground, and pressed against the nearest stone, which was still warm from the heat of the Firebird. Looking about he saw that the others had done the same.

A moment later Reynard could hear the unmistakable tramp of boots marching in grim staccato, echoing off the walls of the valley below them.

As the echoes rose to a cacophony, Tiecelin peered through a crack made by a pair of the larger stones.

"Doom," Tiecelin said quietly before ducking back behind cover.

"That bad?" Reynard asked, finding himself somewhat shaken by the uncharacteristic look of concern plastered across the Luxian's face.

Tiecelin merely nodded and moved aside so that Reynard might see for himself.

Reynard leaned forward and pressed his face against the gap between the two stones. At once his vision was filled by the sight of mail-clad Calvarians marching in serried ranks, the tips of their steely javelins swaying above them like wheat-stalks. A hundred men passed them by, and then a hundred more, and yet still more came trudging through the pass, until Reynard was certain that he'd seen near on to a thousand soldiers march past their position.

When the column of foot finally petered out, a new group of figures riding Calvarian warhorses came into view. The foremost amongst them was a stony-faced man with hair as gray as a storm cloud wearing a rather elaborate fur-lined coat over his armor. Behind him rode a thick-necked blond holding aloft a standard on which was depicted the image of a snarling wolf crushing a blazing sun-disc between its jaws, and with them a trio of black uniformed Blood-Guards.

"Isengrim," Reynard said, waving the Northerner forward, "Any of this lot look familiar to you?"

"The Blood-Guards I do not recognize," Isengrim said when he finally leaned back. "But there are few Calvarians alive who would not know the banner of the Seventeenth."

"*Seofontene?*" Hirsent said, her eyes widening considerably. "Then their *Latteowa* is being-"

"Yes," Isengrim replied. "It is Drauglir."

"*Awyrigung*," Hirsent cursed, her face turning a shade paler than Reynard might have thought possible.

"Drauglir?" Reynard said, taking another look through the rocks just in time to see the severe Calvarian and his retinue disappear from view, only to be replaced by the head of yet another column of heavy infantry. "You know the man?"

"*Latteowa* Drauglir is widely considered amongst my people to be one of the finest military commanders that ever came out of the *inburg-campraeden*," Isengrim answered. "His veterans have seen battle across the breadth of the North- from Brobdingang to the islands of the Hesperides. I can not imagine a more dangerous foe."

"Excellent," Tybalt drawled, and began chewing on his thumbnail.

By now the sky had gone blue with the onset of twilight, and though he found it impossible to relax completely, Reynard settled himself against one of the rocks and listened to the rumble of the passing Calvarian army. Occasionally he would lean forward and catch a glimpse of strange Calvarian war machines being hauled forward by teams of enormous Northern steeds, or a host of cavalrymen cantering in tight formation around a thick knot of white and tan-uniformed civilians leading pack mules laden with supplies.

Finally, the last column of soldiers disappeared behind the drumlin, and within a few moments the air was full of nothing but the low twittering of the first nightjars of the evening, looking for mates.

"They are gone," Tiecelin said, one of his knees popping sharply as he stood to his full height.

"I think, perhaps, that we should be going as well," Reynard added. "I'd feel a lot more comfortable with a few leagues distance between us and the Calvarians . . . I imagine we may not be as lucky the next time a patrol stumbles upon us."

"I agree," Isengrim said, beginning to make his way back. "We will be meeting *Latteowa* Drauglir soon enough as it is."

* * * * * * *

Traveling by the light of the stars, they rode until they came to a place where the course of the river called the Samara had dug a sheer-edged ravine straight through the limestone that made up the eastern thrust of the Erycinian Highlands. There they made a second camp, though Reynard ordered that no fire be lit, and they ate their rations cold.

The next morning they carefully led the horses down one of the many treacherous paths from the heights, and began to follow the course of the Samara east into the heart of Gadwall, which had mostly been cleared for the purposes of agriculture- though the freshly tilled fields appeared to have been abandoned by their tenants, and they saw only a handful of Arcasians as they tore across the countryside.

"Where are they all?" Martin asked Reynard when they had slowed long enough for him to speak without fear of biting off his own tongue.

"Hiding, I expect," Reynard answered.

"From the Calvarians?"

"From us!" Reynard answered laughingly, and the boy nodded, perhaps finding it odd that only a month before it might have been him cowering at the sight of so many armed men.

As they rode, the sky turned gray and shortly after midday a heavy rain began to fall. The recently ploughed fields of Gadwall quickly turned to a morass of cake-like mud that made riding extremely difficult, and even the shrikes were forced to seek shelter beneath a dense copse that stood between the farmland and the Samara.

"What do your children see, Tiecelin?" Reynard said, shaking a bit of water out of his hat as he approached the Luxian and his menagerie of chimera. "How much further is Nobel's muster?"

"Only a few leagues- they are camped along the northern bank of the river."

"And the Calvarians?"

"They, too, are close."

"Then we cannot afford to wait for the rain to pass," Reynard concluded as he turned to the others. "Take what food and drink you can. We're pressing on as soon as I get back."

"Where are you going?" Bruin asked.

"To take a piss," Reynard answered, and disappeared into the brush.

"Are you cold?" Martin asked Rukenaw, putting an arm around her rain-soaked shoulders.

"No," she shivered and nestled closer to him.

"Aren't adventures fun?" Tybalt said, carving a thick slice of bread from a tough loaf he'd pulled out of his pack. "Aren't you both glad you came?"

"I am," Rukenaw answered back. "I think it's exciting."

"So do I," Martin nodded.

Tybalt chuckled darkly, and tossed the remainder of the loaf to Martin before offering him his knife, adding: "See to it that you don't cut yourself, boy."

Martin scowled, but took the offered blade.

"It was like this before the battle of Moulinsart," Bruin said, turning to stare out at the rain. "There were pools of water on the field so deep a man could have drowned in them- I saw it happen too, to some fat chevalier who'd been knocked off his horse. A lot of men went to meet the Watcher that day."

"This time may be being different," Hirsent offered.

"Yeah," Tybalt said in between bites. "And I'm the Prince of Therimere."

Hirsent opened her mouth to reply, but her words seemed to catch in her throat before she could get them out. Her brow furrowed, and she pressed a gloved palm against the small of her back.

"What is it?" Isengrim said, reaching for her.

"Nothing," Hirsent replied, shying away from his touch as she moved deeper into the copse.

"The curse?" Bruin asked softly, offering Isengrim his wineskin.

"I do not think so," Isengrim said, refusing the wine with a polite wave of his hand. "She has been sick too long."

"Could be flux," Bruin said, "Could be anything- but then I guess she hasn't been to see Hermeline ever since . . ."

Bruin stopped talking. A pall fell over the copse as the other men, too, ceased their banter and turned their gazes towards Isengrim, whose own eyes had gone hard and cold.

"Forgive me," the big man said, backing up slightly. "I forgot-"

"Pay it no mind," Isengrim said suddenly, and made his away across the camp, the others avoiding his gaze as he passed.

"Thank you Fenix for your mercy," Bruin exhaled before taking a huge swig from his wineskin.

"What was that?" Martin said.

"What was what?" Tybalt answered dryly, stretching out an open palm towards the boy.

Martin blinked, confused by the gesture.

"My knife?" Tybalt offered in his kindest tone.

Martin returned the blade, his attention still fixed on the tall Calvarian, who had begun grooming his black charger.

"Let me give you a bit of advice," Tybalt said to the boy in a low voice. "You want to grow up to be a man?"

Martin frowned, but nodded.

"Then don't pry into Isengrim's business."

"It's alright, Tybalt," said Reynard, whose sudden appearance behind them made Martin and Rukenaw gasp. "I'll handle this."

"Your funeral," the dark-eyed brigand said, and went to tend to his own steed.

Reynard beckoned the two youths closer, and the three of them knelt down on a bed of ferns.

Reynard took a deep breath and began.

"The two of you have probably noticed by now that, despite the fact they are lovers, Isengrim and Hirsent do not have any children, yes?"

Rukenaw and Martin nodded, the boy adding: "But she had a child once, long ago, that the Calvarians killed. I remember that, from the songs."

"Ah," Reynard sighed. "But what you do not know is that they had a second child- or they would have, if it had not been stillborn."

"Why did it die?" Rukenaw asked.

"Who can say, save the Watcher?" Reynard answered, shaking his head. "Hermeline would know more than I. She was there when it happened, after all, and that is why-"

Reynard's words ground to a halt as Hirsent stepped out of the brush, the signs of her ailment having appeared to pass. If she had heard a word of what Reynard had said, she showed no sign, but went to her husband's side and took his arm in her own.

"Ever since then," Reynard went on quietly, "Things have been . . . difficult between her and Hermeline."

"But it wasn't her fault!" Rukenaw said, perhaps a little louder than she had meant to. "Was it?"

"I do not think so- but do *not* think of trying to explain that to Hirsent, nor speak of what I have told you within earshot of Isengrim."

"I understand," Martin said, "But I still don't get why she and Isengrim fight so much."

"That is far more complicated a matter than I have time to explain," Reynard said, getting to his feet. "But I tend to believe that it is because they love each other."

* * * * * *

"Gods, I hate rain," Reynard grumbled as Bayard slogged across yet another pasture. The storm had finally passed as the day had grown long, but that did little to comfort Reynard's band, whose clothes and gear were totally soaked through.

It was in this fashion- wet, cold, and generally miserable- that they came within sight of Nobel's camp- if camp was the proper word to describe the sprawling city of multi-hued tents that haphazardly stretched before them. It certainly dwarfed any village that they had come across in their travels, and they slowed to a trot to take in the full spectacle of Nobel's muster. Even from this distance the smell of the place was incredible, the savory scent of a thousand cook pots and wood fires mixing with the fetid odor of manure and sweat.

"I didn't know there were so many people in the world!" Rukenaw said from her seat behind Tiecelin.

"This is nothing," Reynard said. "They say there are over a hundred thousand men, women, and children living in Calyx alone- and those are just the ones that the tax-collectors know about."

"It's twice the size of any muster I've ever seen," Bruin rumbled. "What say you, Tiecelin?"

"Indeed," the Luxian replied, his flinty eyes scanning the row upon row of tents. "If I had to guess I'd say there were thirty thousand men here- maybe even more."

"Well, at least we ought to have numbers on our side," Tybalt said. "That should count for something."

"Nobel may have mustered more men," Isengrim said with his usual candor. "But I wonder how many of them are truly soldiers."

"What do you mean?"

"Calvarian warriors do not spend their summers planting crops or threshing grain- they devote their every waking hour to the maintenance of body and mind."

"You almost sound like you admire them," Tybalt sneered.

"I find it hard not to admire excellence."

"We'll see how excellent your old friends are with a good blade stuck between their ribs."

"Enough, both of you," Reynard said, his voice tired. "We should be on- before Nobel's sentries mistake us for Calvarian scouts and riddle us full of crossbow bolts!"

The muster was arrayed upon a wide low hill, around which a forest of sharpened stakes had been driven into the earth, their points facing outwards to deter a direct attack. Crude watchtowers had been erected along the perimeter as well, and as they approached one of the few breaks in the fortifications, they could see that Reynard had been perfectly correct in his estimation of the mood of the soldiers posted about the king's encampment- by the time they slowed to a halt there were over a hundred crossbows trained on them.

"Halt!" a voice called out from one of the nearest towers. It belonged to a haughty-looking fellow with an enormous nose- and an even bigger mustache- whose glimmering breastplate bore the emblem of a chimera with an eagle's head on a lion's body. "Name yourselves!"

"I am Reynard, Baron of Maleperduys," Reynard shouted back, "And I have come here with my captains to answer the summons of the King of Arcasia!"

A murmur ran through the ranks of the soldiers gazing at them from behind the fortifications, and the crossbowmen wavered slightly.

"You have heard of us, then?" Reynard asked.

"There are few in Arcasia that haven't," the man replied. "But what proof can you offer us that you are indeed who you say you are?"

Reynard didn't blame the man's skepticism. In their current state he and his retinue hardly looked like men of great renown.

"I know of few Arcasians who travel in the company of Calvarians," Reynard said, giving a nod to Isengrim, who pulled back his cloak so that the men above could see his face. Then Reynard held aloft the violet ruby he wore at his neck. "And look! Here is the gem that the Queen Persephone herself gifted to me. Are these proof enough?"

The man paused, as if considering, but answered: "They are. You and your company have my leave to enter, Lord Reynard."

As Reynard had expected, they had no sooner passed through the break in the palisade when they were surrounded by a crowd of curious soldiers, each of whom attempted to push his way forward for a closer look at the men who had stolen the gem of Zosia out of Calvaria and had lived to tell of it. And, after a few moments of being jostled and slapped heartily by men wearing mailed gauntlets, Reynard began to find himself longing for his old days of anonymity. Even Isengrim who, despite looking fearsome astride his great black stallion, was no exception to the mob's attention, and Reynard chuckled a bit at the man's discomfort at being gawked at and jabbered over- to say the least of his obvious concern for Hirsent, who had slunk so low in her saddle that she nearly seemed hunchbacked.

At last the officer who had hailed them from the tower forced his way through the throng, bellowing at the men to return to their posts and using a thick riding crop to motivate any who were slow to obey. And, as the crowd broke up, Reynard realized that he recognized him: he was the Baron Cygne, captain of Nobel's bodyguard. He had been a man with a bad reputation in Calyx despite his position, for he was a notorious braggart with a fiery temper to match, and had killed more than his share of men whom he felt had insulted his honor. Reynard had never met him personally, but he had seen him often enough slumming it at The Slaughter Prince in River Quarter, ready to skewer any dockyard thug who dared to speak ill of the nobility in his presence.

One might have thought the Baron would have been a likely target of that famed cat burglar The Fox, but there were reasons that the younger Reynard had chosen to spare Cygne the humiliation of one of his larcenous visits.

The first- and infinitely more practical- reason was that the Baron's apartments were located within the confines of Nobel's palace, where Reynard had not dared venture until the sight of the Countess Persephone had made the prospect of such an incursion irresistible.

The second was that he had a certain amount of admiration for the man, grudging though it was. Even he had to admit that, unlike the old Duke, Cygne had always fought his own duels, and he traversed the dangerous streets that led from the palace to River Quarter without the security of an armed escort. He might have named such behavior bravery, if he did not also consider it more than a touch suicidal.

"My greetings, Lord Cygne," Reynard said with a sweep of his hat. "Forgive me that I did not recognize you until now, and forgive also our appearance- we have ridden hard to answer King Nobel's summons, and have want of food, fire and shelter."

"I accept your apology, Lord Reynard, unnecessary though it is- you will find far filthier men within this camp, and none that have traveled from as far flung a place as Maleperduys!"

"I'm afraid our journey had its costs," Reynard said, indicating his injured hand. "I do hope we are not late."

Cygne's moustache twitched. "You are indeed fortunate to have arrived when you did, for even now His Majesty sits in counsel with his vassals, and your immediate presence is required."

"I had hoped to have a moment to refresh myself, but if there is no time . . ."

"Come! I myself will escort you to the King's tent."

"You do me great honor my Lord," Reynard said, bowing again.

"My horse!" Cygne called out, and a groom began to untether a large courser from a nearby corral.

As he waited for his steed to be saddled, the Baron cast his eyes upon Reynard's companions, his gaze lingering the longest on Hirsent who had declined to cover her head with either helmet or hooded cape. The Calvarian woman returned the Baron's stare fiercely.

"I'm afraid that your . . . soldiers may not accompany us. One of my men will find them a suitable place to encamp."

Reynard felt Martin's body grow suddenly tense against him.

"May I bring my page?" Reynard asked, nodding his head towards the boy. "My steed will need looking after."

Cygne regarded Martin with considerable disregard, but nodded his acquiescence.

"I too will accompany the Baron," Isengrim said flatly as Cygne lifted himself into his saddle, a statement that nearly caused the man to miss his step.

"You expect me to bring a Calvarian before His Majesty?" the man said, blanching. "Surely you jest?"

"The Baron goes nowhere without an escort," Isengrim replied with finality, locking eyes with the outraged nobleman- whose hand was now resting on his sword, and who was breathing so heavily that the whiskers of his moustache seemed to be caught in the wind. For a moment Reynard thought that he might even draw on Isengrim, an act that, while spelling certain doom for Baron Cygne, would prove disastrous for them all.

"*If* you must accompany us," Cygne said at last, perhaps having remembered one of the many tales of Isengrim's efficacy with a blade, "Then you will do so divested of your sword, or any other weapon on your person."

"As you wish," Isengrim replied, and began to unbuckle Right-Hand from his belt.

Reynard tried to suppress a smirk as the words that Isengrim had spoken to him years past echoed in his head: *Do you truly believe that the outcome of the fight will be different because you have a sword?*

Isengrim handed Right-Hand to Hirsent, who said, "You always are finding a way to escape me."

"*We will return soon*," he replied sharply in his own tongue.

"Hirsent," Reynard said, hoping to diffuse the situation before it grew worse, "You will be in command in my absence. See that the men are properly quartered and fed, and refrain from getting into trouble. I trust you will not disappoint me?"

"I-" Hirsent stammered uncharacteristically. "I will not."

"Good. Now then, my Lord Cygne, shall we be off?"

"Hrrraf!" the chevalier snorted, and whipped his horse into a canter.

Reynard, Isengrim, and Martin followed.

The muster was even larger than Reynard had taken it to be from a distance- a virtual maze of tents, wagons, and makeshift corrals broken only by pathways that had turned to mud. If there was any logic behind its layout Reynard could not discern it, though he guessed that the chevalier and men-at-arms of each great lord of Arcasia had simply raised their tents wherever they could find room. Here and there campfires punctuated the place, and as it was nearing dusk there were all manner of folk about- for besides professional soldiers the army was made up of an almost equal number of petty laborers, laundresses, children, and guildsmen of all types working at their crafts. Servants of the gods there were too: priests of Fenix working at anvils and forges and, of course, the priestesses of Sphinx who, besides providing comfort to the men, were also useful in tending to those suffering of the flux- who seemed to be everywhere, laid flat on their backs amidst the mud and filth.

"You didn't have to come with me, you know," Reynard said to Isengrim as Baron Cygne led them closer to the center of the camp, where ten great tents ringed an enormous marquee.

"I did not think you would mind the company," Isengrim replied, and Reynard smiled, feeling considerably relieved that he would not be traveling into the lion's den alone.

Not surprisingly, the tents of the nobility had been raised on a hillock above the common rabble, a position that afforded them a clear view of the surrounding countryside, and as Baron Cygne slowed his steed to a trot, Reynard found himself glancing northward, where even now he could discern the glimmer of what was undoubtedly the enemy camp. A quick thrill of fear ran through him, the likes of which he had not felt for many years, and then they had passed into the inner circle of tents, and the sight of the distant host was replaced by the majesty of the banners of the Counts of Arcasia. Each of these great lords had traveled to the muster with all manner of liveried servants and minor nobles in their wake, as well as racing steeds, hunting dogs, falcons, and even musicians. Strangest of all was the occasional glimpse of noble ladies, strolling about in gowns of such finery that Reynard might have thought he had stumbled upon a royal ball of some sort, far removed from fear and death.

Baron Cygne led them round an immense marquee, over which several dozen formidably armored figures wearing Nobel's heraldry stood watch. Then they reached a place where the wide flaps of the tent had been tied open, and their guide brought his horse to a halt.

"I will announce your presence to the King," Cygne said rather brusquely as he dismounted, his mail jingling brightly as he strode past the guards and into the marquee, from which emanated the susurrus of a dozen or so quarreling voices.

"Stay with Bayard," Reynard said to Martin as he helped the boy climb off of the horse's powerful back.

"Yes," Martin said, still gawking at the splendor around him. Reynard did not blame him, guessing correctly that the boy had never seen such riches.

After a moment the voices within the King's tent grew silent. Then Cygne reappeared and beckoned for Reynard- and Isengrim- to enter.

"Reynard, Baron of Maleperduys!" Cygne boomed as they entered the tent, and a sea of heads swiveled towards them.

The interior of the marquee was so richly adorned that it might have been mistaken for one of the rooms in Nobel's palace were it not for the tent poles that kept the sloping ceiling in place, for it was hung with tapestries and a series of thick carpets concealed the grassy turf beneath them. The center of the room was dominated by an immense vellum map, on which an army of toy-sized soldiers carved out of wood was arrayed. Around this scene loomed scores of noblemen, the most important of whom had been provided with seats, and on a low dais sat King Nobel, his mailed fingers wrapped tightly around a swagger stick.

To Nobel's right sat Count Bricemer, who at the sight of Reynard lurched to his feet with the aid of an ivory cane. To Nobel's left Reynard recognized the former rebel Count Corvino of Luxia, uncle to the Queen, and next to him the timid Count Cherax, Nobel's treasurer, who looked incredibly uncomfortable in his heavy plate, as well as Lord Gallopin, whom the King had named Count of Engadlin and whose wife Reynard had once seduced in the guise of the rake Malebranche. The others were strangers to him, but he knew some by their heraldry if not by face.

"Sit down," Nobel hissed to Bricemer, who- suddenly remembering himself- gingerly returned to his seat.

"Your Majesty," Reynard said, bowing to the King with as much dignity as he could muster considering his appearance.

"Well," Nobel hummed, "What have we here? I had expected the Lord of Maleperduys, not a pair of beggars, come in from the rain. You smell like a wet dog."

"Forgive me Your Majesty. I and my men have just arrived, and the road has been long and dangerous."

"What do you make of them, Pierrot?" Nobel addressed a diminutive figure who lounged near his feet. "Do we have lords or dogs amongst us?"

The man- a servant of the Watcher, Reynard guessed from the lute he cradled in his arms and his odd, bleached white garments- cocked his head to one side and regarded Reynard and Isengrim with wide, unblinking eyes.

"There once was a blind shepherd," the man said, "Who knew every animal merely by touch. One day, thinking to trick him, somebody handed him a fox-cub. He felt it and was unsure, but said: 'I don't know if it be the whelp of a wolf or a fox, but what I do know is that it should not be put amongst the sheep.'"

"Wise words," Nobel said, and rose to his feet, motioning for his vassals to keep their seats as he stepped heavily off of the dais. "So, Lord Reynard, I might have guessed that you would answer my summons- despite the fact that your Baronial seat is so deep within the forest of Maleperduys that even my own messengers cannot find you."

"I fear that such precautions are necessary, Your Majesty," Reynard replied pointedly. Both men knew what sort of 'messengers' of Nobel's had been looking for Reynard's hidden valley. "But I have managed to keep myself informed of Your Majesty's wishes all the same."

"Then perhaps you also know, *Lord* Reynard, that I expect my Barons to levy men in times of war. I see you have brought the mighty Isengrim with you . . . no doubt you have several of the other great heroes of Arcasia riding in your wake?"

"Indeed, Your Majesty."

"But tell me Lord Reynard, besides these worthies, how many soldiers have you brought me?"

"Thirty, Your Majesty, all of them good men and true."

"Surely, Lord Reynard, this is one of your jests," Nobel retorted darkly. "Why even the lowest of my nobles can boast of a retinue twice the size of your own- and from the description Baron Cygne has supplied I guess that most of them are nothing more than mounted irregulars. Am I correct?"

"I brought only my best, Your Majesty."

"Your best!" Nobel said, and laughed. "Do you hear the Baron, gentlemen? He has brought us a handful of his *best*! No chevalier, no footmen, no heavy armor, and he is injured to boot- but he brings us his best! We must consider carefully, gentlemen, how to deploy such mighty warriors!"

The assembly chuckled heartily, and Reynard felt his ears grow hot with anger, but he kept his peace. He'd not come this far, and survived so many attempts on his life to be baited so easily.

"You may have answered my summons, Lord Reynard," Nobel said, wagging his mailed finger, "but it is a pity that in all of the years that have passed since you last graced us with your presence you did not take a moment to learn something of the art of war. Perhaps- later- I can educate you regarding such matters, but for now you and your . . . *watch-hound* may take your place amongst the retinue of Count Bricemer."

"As you wish, Your Majesty," Reynard said, and made his way over to the Count, Isengrim following silently in his tow.

"Lord Reynard," Bricemer said under his breath as Reynard passed him, his eyes narrowing into tiny slits.

"Your Excellency," Reynard said with a nod, and found himself sidling next to Count Gallopin. The former Lord of Barca sniffed with derision and attempted as best as he could to stand at a distance from the mud-encrusted pair.

"My Lords, let us continue," Nobel said, motioning to the map, and punctuating each of his remarks with the tip of his swagger stick. "Given our present position, the Calvarians no doubt intend to engage us here, on a low ridge between the Forest of Jennet and the Samara, where the narrow topography will limit our overwhelming numerical superiority."

"Might we not outflank them, Your Majesty?" suggested a languid-looking nobleman wearing a leopard pelt as a cloak. "Move a part of our army through the Jennet, and attack on two fronts?"

"I had considered that stratagem, Firapel," Nobel replied, "But these woods are dense and rocky, and dangerous to move an army through. Rather we must draw them to us, and meet them on our own terms."

"The Calvarians will not give up their position lightly, Your Majesty," Bricemer said, his fingers lightly tapping against his ivory cane.

"Calvarian battle tactics, Bricemer- though effective- are simple to predict," Nobel responded. "They will rely on their archers to thin our ranks before sending in the heavy infantry to smash directly through our center. In anticipation of this, I have divided our order of battle into three ranks."

"The first will be made up entirely of light infantry. Ten companies of Mandrossian crossbowmen have been raised to form the center of this force, and arrayed on either flank will be our own skirmishers."

Here Nobel turned his gaze back to Reynard.

"And since, Lord Reynard, you have brought me nothing *but* skirmishers, I am afraid I have no choice but to add you to their numbers. Fear not for your prestige, however- I am certain a suitable place of honor can be found for you amongst the mercenaries and peasants."

"You honor me, Your Majesty," Reynard replied as the aristocrats once again chuckled at his expense.

"To continue," Nobel said, drawing an imaginary line along the length of the map, "the first wave will advance until they are within one hundred yards of the enemy, harassing them as the second wave, composed of ten thousand pikemen, moves into position behind them. Once the men-at-arms are in place, the skirmishers will withdraw to the rear."

As the King spoke a number of his bodyguards stepped from their places around the perimeter of the tent and maneuvered the wooden soldiers until a thick block of purple manikins was face to face with the dull gray ranks of their enemies.

"As the Calvarians press forward, our own forces will gradually give ground, drawing them from their position on the ridge . . . and when the moment is right, our cavalry will outflank the enemy and attack them from the rear, catching them- as it were- between the hammer and the anvil."

With those words Nobel tipped over a mounted figure that Reynard took to be the Calvarian general.

"This is all sound strategy," Count Corvino mused, stroking his cheek absently. "But what of their own cavalry?"

"If you had been at Pardus, Corvino, you would know that their horsemen are little more than mounted scouts . . . all the same, I have split our chevalier into two separate forces. Should those on the right flank find themselves occupied with the enemy horse, the ones on the left will be more than able to serve their purpose."

"And who will command the right flank?" Corvino asked. Reynard guessed from his tone that he already knew the answer.

"I will," Nobel replied bluntly. "And you will command the left."

Several of the Counts shifted uncomfortably at the King's words.

"Your Majesty," a gray-haired noble said, rising to his feet. "If you will forgive my words, this is outrageous! The command of the left flank has long been held by the Counts of Poictesme. How have I offended Your Majesty, that you give it now to this rebel?"

"How dare you!" one of the younger lords in the Luxian retinue barked. "You speak of the Queen's uncle!"

"Peace, Tancrede," Count Corvino said, gesturing for his man to step back as he turned his attention to his peers. "We are all Arcasians now, Lord Peryton. I can assure you there are no rebels here. At least, none that I know of."

"Forgive me," the Count of Poictesme said, returning to his seat. "I spoke out of turn, and I imagine that the Count of Luxia has far more experience commanding the forces of Genova and Tarsus than any amongst us."

"Well spoken," Nobel said. "And do not fear, for to you Count Peryton I grant command of the center, and the combined forces of Engadlin, Osca, and Astolat."

No sooner had Nobel said these words than half the room erupted with protest, as the Counts of those fiefs gained their feet. What followed was the longest display of outrage, bluster, and rattling of blades that Reynard had ever witnessed, and it went on so long that he found himself growing drowsy. It seemed as though every petty jealousy or old rivalry between the nobles had to be addressed, and it struck Reynard that if the great lords of Arcasia fought the Calvarians with as much vigor as they quarreled with each other for a place of honor on the field then they would have little to fear from the enemy.

It was during this tumult that Reynard noticed a flutter of movement behind Nobel's dais, where a thick curtain formed a barrier between the makeshift council chamber and what Reynard guessed to be the King's personal quarters. There was a slight gap between two of the great sheets of cloth and, though he could not see any hint of light through the crack, a pair of delicate silken slippers peeking out from underneath the curtain confirmed the fact that there was someone behind it.

"Then, if all are satisfied?" the distinctive timbre of Nobel's voice brought Reynard quickly back to the matter at hand- the order of battle seemed finally to have been settled upon.

The King's gaze swept over the room, challenging the men assembled there to speak. He was greeted by silence. He nodded, pleased, and said, "Then let us adjourn. I must have counsel with the Captain of the mercenaries, and would review the men I am to lead tomorrow. Let us feast tonight on the banks of the Samara, and tomorrow in the ruins of Calvaria!"

"Long live the King!" the chorus of nobles shouted. "Long live Arcasia!"

With that the assembled lords made to depart, their retinues trailing close behind them, but as Count Bricemer lifted himself from his seat, Nobel turned to him and said, "A moment, Bricemer. Your other vassals may go, but I would have a private word with the Baron of Maleperduys."

Bricemer nodded and stood to one side as the last of the nobles exited, until there were none left in the King's tent with them save for Nobel, Bricemer, two dozen of the King's Guard, and the strange servant of the Watcher who was still reclining on the dais, propped up by his skinny elbows and smiling.

"A spider's web is a beautiful thing," Pierrot said to no one in particular. "Provided you are not a fly."

VI

"You wish something more of me, Your Majesty?" Reynard said coolly, his mind calculating how many of the guards Isengrim could bring down before they were overwhelmed.

"Let us drop the formalities," Nobel said. "We all know you for what you really are."

"Then you *know* I am the Princess Zara of Beria?" Reynard replied, fluttering his lashes. "Why, Nobel, whatever gave me away?"

"You insolent cur!" Count Bricemer snarled under his breath, but otherwise kept his peace. He did not look eager to be any closer to Reynard, or the deadly man who stood by his side.

"You must forgive the Lord High Secretary," Nobel said with a cluck of his tongue. "I'm afraid your continued existence troubles him greatly. And given the outcome of your last encounter I can hardly blame him. For you have been in my thoughts as well, Lord Reynard. I have spent many nights wondering what was to be done about the troublesome Baron of Maleperduys . . . would you care for some wine?"

Nobel did not wait for a response, and snapped his mailed fingers. At once Pierrot hoisted himself up from the floor and, retrieving a bottle from a nearby cabinet, filled a pair of silver goblets before offering one of them to Reynard.

"Your health," Nobel said, and drained his cup.

Reynard returned the gesture without hesitation and handed his empty goblet back to Pierrot, who proceeded to pour himself a draught.

"So," Nobel went on, "after all these years you simply walk into my grasp. Had I known that you would do so, I might have saved myself the trouble of hiring men to hunt you down."

"They have been a persistent lot," Reynard said, stifling a yawn. "What *was* the name of that last one? Chacal? He was good, wasn't he?"

Reynard directed this last question to Isengrim, who replied with a curt nod.

"Spare me your bravado," Nobel said. "A hundred of my personal guard stand watch outside this tent- you know as I do that, even with your pet Calvarian by your side, I could crush you like an ant if I so chose."

"On what grounds?" Reynard asked coolly. "Surely you are not in the habit of murdering your own vassals?"

"Loyal ones?" Nobel replied, "No. But a traitor- perhaps one who has grown to sympathize with our Northern foes, and plans my death- that is a different matter all together."

"The great heroes of Arcasia return from the wilderness only to betray their King on the eve of battle?" Reynard mused, nibbling momentarily on his thumb. "I suppose there *is* a certain drama to it . . . but I can't imagine that it will be very good for your army's morale."

"I think," Nobel retorted, his lips pursing, "that you overestimate your influence."

"Do I?"

Nobel paused, the supercilious look on his face drooping ever so slightly. Reynard wondered if, in addition to describing the shabbiness of his men, the Baron Cygne had told him of the reception they had received upon entering the muster.

"You may be popular with the common folk, Reynard, and I know that you do not fear me," Nobel said, holding out his goblet for Pierrot to refill. "I have known that ever since the day I put a pear-of-anguish in your mouth. But there is something else about you that I learned that day."

"And that is?"

"Lord Cygne," Nobel said, turning to the Captain of his guards. "Tell me again of Reynard's soldiers."

"There are just over thirty of them, Your Majesty, all of them irregulars on horseback, and two of them women- the Calvarian and another, no more than a girl."

"Thank you, Lord Cygne," Nobel said, "So, Reynard, you may not fear death, but I am still the King of Arcasia, and if I wished it, I could ensure that you and *all* of your followers would have the distinct honor of being in the vanguard of the army . . . unless, clever man, you can offer me a reason to grant you my clemency?"

"Perhaps," Reynard replied smoothly, "Your Majesty might accept a gift?"

"What manner of gift?"

"If you will accompany me to my horse, Your Majesty, you may see for yourself."

One of Nobel's fingers tapped against the silver filigree of his wine goblet.

"Very well," Nobel said, resting his goblet on the arm of his throne. "We will see this gift of yours. You may lead the way."

Reynard bowed deferentially and, flashing Isengrim a toothy grin, made for the exit. The King followed, Bricemer and Cygne falling into his train along with the sentries that ringed the tent.

"Your Majesty," Bricemer whispered, a hint of alarm creeping into his voice. "Are you certain that this is wise?"

Now it was Reynard's turn to laugh.

"Come now, Your Excellency," he chuckled as the guards at the marquee's entrance parted for him. "Do you forget the company of men that await us outside? Surely they will provide adequate protection for His Majesty . . . and yourself."

Bricemer nodded slowly, and followed Reynard and Isengrim out into the deepening dusk, but as he did so his gaze flitted towards the heavens- as though expecting a murderous flock of shrikes to descend upon them. Reynard laughed again, and called out for Martin to bring him his horse.

The boy, who was busy brushing Bayard's coat, seemed nearly to swoon as he turned to face the sight of Reynard standing almost side by side with the King and his guards. He took the great steed by the reins, his hand trembling visibly, and guided him towards the tent.

"A fine horse," Nobel said to Reynard approvingly. "He is yours?"

"He is now," Reynard replied.

"What is his name?"

"I call him Bayard. And this is my page."

Nobel cast a fleeting glance at the dirty-looking boy in mismatched armor.

"He suits you."

"Martin," Reynard said. "Bring me my saddlebag."

The boy bowed and, when he had finally managed to untie the satchel from Bayard's saddle, took a few tentative steps towards Reynard and the King.

"Halt, boy," Cygne commanded, stopping Martin in his tracks. The guard captain motioned one of his men forward to take the saddlebag out of the boy's hands.

"Dump it out," Cygne ordered.

The guard did so, scattering Reynard's personal effects across the trampled grass.

"That was hardly necessary," Reynard sniffed. "But what you are looking for is there. Open it, if you like."

He pointed to a large drawstring bag.

"Captain?" The guard said, looking to Cygne for orders.

"Do as he says."

The man bowed his head and undid the drawstring.

"Gods," the bodyguard blurted suddenly, his eyes gone wide.

"What is it?" Cygne asked, his hand suddenly on his sword.

The man thrust his gloved hand deep into the bag and when he pulled it out his palm glittered. It was full of precious gems. Polished emeralds and sapphires lay amongst milky pearls and engraved purple amethysts.

"There's more, Captain," the man said, scooping up another handful to prove his point. "The whole bag is full of them."

A hushed muttering arose from the assembled guards and servants.

"They are real, I trust?" Nobel said coolly.

"You may have Count Cherax examine them, if you must," Reynard said. "But, yes, I assure you, they are real. Maleperduys may be a poor barony when it comes to farmland, but its wild woods are rife with the ruins of the Telchines . . . whose custom it was to bury their dead along with all of their worldly possessions."

"So," Reynard continued, "will these suffice to please Your Highness? I know it is not gold or silver, but I have had to travel lightly. And, besides, I seem to recall that you have a passing interest in gems."

All eyes turned to Nobel, but the King was silent.

"There once was a Fox that had never seen a Lion," Pierrot began, but a fierce look from the King shut him up before he could continue.

"This is," the King said, "A suitable gift, Lord Reynard. But you forget that I am not some cheap watchman that you may bribe with a handful of coins. Keep your baubles . . . and gift to me instead your horse."

"Bayard?" Reynard could not help but blanche, though he regretted it immediately. The look on Nobel's face told him that he'd seen his mask slip.

"Your Majesty has unparalleled taste," he said, attempting to seem nonchalant, "but would you deprive me of my mount? How will I ride into battle?"

"Unlike some men I could name, Master Reynard, I am not a thief," Nobel said. "I will see to it that you are provided with a horse as befits a man of your pedigree."

"Bayard is worth ten horses."

"Then you shall have ten," Nobel said, and smiled. He knew that he had won. "After the battle."

"As it pleases Your Majesty," Reynard said, gritting his teeth. "The horse is yours."

"Excellent," Nobel said. "Where is my groom?"

"Here, Your Majesty," a dark-skinned servant in a checkered coat called out, striding over from a nearby corral.

"Arlequin, have this animal quartered with the rest of my steeds, and see that he is cleaned properly."

"Yes, Your Majesty," the man said, and moved to carry out the King's order.

"No!" Martin cried as the King's groom approached. "Bayard is Baron Reynard's horse."

"Not anymore, boy," Arlequin said, and gave Martin a shove that knocked him on his rear. Bayard snorted darkly, and pawed at the ground with one of his great steel-shod hooves.

Reynard instinctively took a step forward, but then Isengrim's hand was on his arm, and he forced himself to relax.

"He's a beauty, Your Highness!" the groom said, waiting for Bayard to calm somewhat before approaching him. "Truly fit for a King!"

"Indeed," Nobel said. "And, so, Lord Reynard, I thank you for your gift. Dispose of your troops as you see fit, and remain the Baron of Maleperduys . . . for one day more at the very least."

"Your Majesty is too generous," Reynard replied.

"Perhaps I am," Nobel mused, and swept past Reynard towards a fine gray gelding, which he mounted with the aid of two liveried youths.

Count Bricemer hoisted himself onto a sleek-looking mare, wincing no doubt at the pain in his knee.

"Until tomorrow, Lord Reynard," the King said once he was comfortably seated. "Lord Cygne, see that the Baron of Maleperduys safely finds his way back to his men."

"I will, Your Highness."

With that Nobel flicked the gelding's reins, and cantered off, Bricemer and twenty mounted King's Guards following in his wake.

"He's *your* horse," Martin began to say as Reynard helped him to his feet, but Reynard shushed him, and set him to gathering up his possessions from the ground.

"Goodbye, my friend," Reynard said, stroking Bayard's neck to calm him. "And take care."

"He will be well provided for, your lordship," the groom said, offering the animal a bit of sugar. "His Majesty knows the value of a good horse."

Bayard sniffed at the groom's hand, took the offered sugar, and before long he was being led off as though he had always been Nobel's steed. Reynard was not surprised. The horse had belonged to a Calvarian soldier before Reynard had opened the man's throat with his rapier, and he'd accepted his former master's killer quickly enough.

* * * * * * *

It was full dark by the time that they left the King's pavilion, Reynard and Martin riding on a borrowed horse, and the Baron Cygne and a dozen of his men leading the way. They rode to the edge of the muster, where men had encamped amongst the brush.

"Here we are," the captain said, bringing his horse to a halt. "I'm afraid there was no room for you, save amongst the mercenaries. I'm certain one of their captains can direct you better than I."

"My thanks, Baron Cygne," Reynard started to say, but the man had no sooner turned his horse around than he was gone, his escort following suit.

"You know," Reynard said as Martin dismounted, "I sometimes get the impression that I am not very well-liked at court."

"You shouldn't have let them take Bayard," Martin sulked. "He was your horse."

"It was a price I had to pay," Reynard said, "Now help me down, and let's find the others."

The mercenaries' camp was far more colorful than that of the main army, each company having pitched their canvas tents around those of their captains, and at every camp hard-looking men from Mandross and Therimere busied themselves caring for their armor, sparring with sword, spear, and mace, or honing their skills with the crossbow against straw targets. The foreigners had brought their own camp followers with them, as well as their own taste in food; the air was rich with the savory scents of dishes flavored with Hivan chili and sauces made from groundnut. Everywhere there were strange sights to see: Mandrossian warrior priests whose long beards had been dyed bright red, great Tyrisian jungle cats kept as pets, and slender Telchine prostitutes of both sexes hawking their wares. Reynard even caught a brief glimpse of a true giant, a coppery-skinned hulk who would have put Bruin to shame, but when he turned to point the thing out to Martin he saw that the boy was barely keeping up with them, his eyes heavy and his tread slow. He'd forgotten that the boy had not rested since they had sheltered in the copse.

"Why don't you ride for awhile?" Reynard said, and Martin made no complaint, even when Isengrim lifted him into the air and placed him on his black stallion. Soon he was asleep, his head resting against the horse's powerful neck.

"You have been very quiet," Reynard said to Isengrim once he was sure that the boy slumbered.

"I have been listening."

"And?" Reynard prompted. "Do you believe Nobel can defeat Drauglir?"

"His strategy is sound, but simple," Isengrim said, considering. "I fear *Latteowa* Drauglir will not be taken so easily."

"The best plans are often simple," Reynard said, smiling as he remembered older days. "Besides, if Tiecelin's count is even remotely accurate we outnumber them three to one."

"True," Isengrim replied. "But numbers do not win battles, and Drauglir has one great advantage."

"And that is?"

"He commands but a single army. Nobel must contend with twelve."

Reynard nodded. The nobles of Arcasia had hardly seemed a unified group.

"Still," Reynard said. "Nobel is cleverer than most. Look at how he dealt with us; we may all still die in tomorrow's battle, and, even if we do not, he has humiliated us all the same."

"Perhaps," Isengrim said. "But it is too late now to worry about our honor."

"I agree," Reynard said quietly, coming to a halt.

Isengrim looked back at him. "You are not coming?"

Reynard shook his head. "Return to camp. Have Tiecelin send his 'children' out to scout the battlefield. I would at least know the lay of the land I may die upon."

Isengrim nodded.

"And, provided he's not already drunk, give Tybalt a few of the smaller gems and tell him to see what kind of arms and armor he can gather for us- we'll need more than leather jacks and bucklers if we're going to be marching into battle."

"And you?"

"I have some private business to attend to."

* * * * * * *

"Your Majesty will be late for supper," Columbine urged the Queen, bustling after her mistress with a heap of clothing tossed over one arm. "Majesty must choose."

Persephone paused in front of a mannequin wearing a square-necked gown of red velvet with fur-lined sleeves. "Have I worn this before?" she asked. "I do not recognize it."

"Your Majesty wore it at the Midwinter Festival."

"Ah, yes," she said, stroking one of the sleeves. "Pretty."

"Does Majesty wish to try it on?"

"No," Persephone said, walking to the next mannequin. "Perhaps something more floral?"

Columbine groaned, and followed.

The King and Queen's private chamber was nowhere near as spacious as Persephone's palace boudoir, but it was still large enough to contain more wigs, hats, and gowns than a guild master's wife and daughters could ever hope to acquire- not to mention the numerous pairs of gloves, shoes, and gauzy undergarments that filled the numerous chests and drawers that stood like sentinels along the walls. The finest of the Queen's outfits, however, were worn by a host of mannequins that had been set in a great circle about the room.

"The brocade?" the maid offered.

"Too gloomy."

"The Frisian gold?"

"It's a bit much."

"This one is new, your Majesty," Columbine said, motioning to a slender dress of light silvery silk. "A gift from your cousin, Lady Celia Corvino."

"Hmmm. Best have the house guards check it for poison needles."

Columbine tittered, but Persephone was only half-joking. Celia was her junior by only a year, and served as one of her honored ladies-in-waiting, but she was her uncle's daughter, and ambitious. Had Persephone not become Queen, Celia might have sat at Nobel's side, and the knowledge of that no doubt rankled the younger woman.

"What about this one?" Persephone said, tapping a dress made of green damask. The collar was lined with gold, and the damask had been woven so finely as to make it iridescent. "Too gaudy?"

"Hardly, your Majesty," the maid shook her head. "And the color will bring out your eyes."

"Very well." Persephone nodded. "If Madam will assist me?"

Considerably relieved, Columbine helped Persephone dress. The maid's plump fingers were surprisingly nimble, and before long she was pinning the Queen's ebony locks to a matching Luxian hood, and fastening a thin golden choker around her throat.

"Majesty looks most beautiful," Columbine said, holding up a mirror. "Shall I tell Master Arlequin to saddle your horse?"

"Do not trouble him," the Queen said.

"Surely Majesty does not intend to walk?"

"Majesty does not intend anything." Persephone took the mirror from Columbine's hands. "Leave me, and inform my ladies-in-waiting that they may attend this evening's feast without me."

"But Majesty," Columbine pouted. "The whole court is assembled- the King will be expecting you. What will I say?"

"Tell them," Persephone said, closing her eyes for a moment, "I do not wish to be disturbed. Tell them that I am unwell."

"Even though Majesty is *not* unwell?"

"Do as I say, Columbine," the Queen said. "Please."

"As Majesty wishes," Columbine grumbled, and began to make her way towards the far end of the tent. "But if Majesty is hungry in the middle of the night, do not call for Columbine to bring her soup."

Persephone smiled at the woman's cheek as the maid slipped into the adjoining chamber, and listened for awhile as the woman grumbled her way across the now empty council room.

Finally, the Queen was alone.

A carafe of wine and a pair of silver goblets stood on a bedside table- Nobel having balked at the thought of his Queen doing without a single piece of her personal furniture- and Persephone went to it now, noticing only as she poured herself a glass that her hand was shaking. She closed her eyes and drew in a slow deep breath, exhaled, and then took another.

When she was finally still she took her first sip of the wine. It was a sweet Oscan white, and she let it dance on her tongue before swallowing.

The King's marquee was made of thick canvas several layers deep, but even so Persephone could hear the din of the royal feast, and as she drank she could picture it: great dishes laden with roasted fowl, suckled pig and fried eel, a thousand drunken chevalier swearing and boasting, dreamy-eyed Pierrot walking upon his hands and speaking in his clever metaphors, the inevitable duel over a lady's honor, and her husband, the King, sitting with an empty seat at his side.

She put down her empty cup, took up her mirror, and looked into it. Her face was still youthful, though it was no longer that of a girl's and her hair had lightened ever so slightly, but her eyes- her hazel eyes- were unchanged.

"You're acting like a fool," she said quietly, and began to lower the mirror when she saw the dark figure standing amongst her mannequins.

She whirled around, letting out a stifled gasp as she dropped the mirror. It fell to the carpet beneath her with a thump.

"We have to stop meeting like this," Reynard said as he stepped out of the shadows.

"Reynard," she said, her voice no more than a whisper. "How long have you been there?"

"I didn't watch you change, if that's what you're asking." He flashed his lopsided grin, and took a step closer. He appeared to have traded his mud-encrusted traveling gear for a gray-buttoned jerkin and breeches over a red doublet. His face looked freshly washed.

"We are alone?" he asked.

"Yes," she said.

"No house guard? No chaperone in the next room armed with a candelabra?"

"Madam Corte has her own tent," Persephone said, "With my son."

Reynard blinked, and his smile faded.

"I had a room like this, once," he said, stepping over to one of the mannequins and stroking the fine material with the back of his hand. "In Calyx. I wish- I wish that I could have shown it to you."

"You're hurt," she said suddenly, noticing his bandaged hand.

"It's nothing," he said, drawing closer to her, until he stood close enough to touch. "You look lovely."

"You look," she said and paused, uncertain of what to say.

"Clean?" he offered. "I saw you watching me. Or was that one of your maids?"

"No," she replied. "It was I. I- I knew that you would come."

"I too am an Arcasian," Reynard said simply. "Besides, your husband's invitation was so compelling- what was it again? My titles stripped, my name dishonored, and death if I didn't answer his summons?"

"That's- that's not what I meant."

"I know," he said. He reached forward then, and took one of her hands in his own, and lifted it to his lips and kissed it.

"Reynard," she said, trembling. "You know how dangerous this is."

"I know," he said again, and released her hand, "You are the King's wife, and to touch you is death for us both. So in spite of my desires I will never hold you in my arms, never feel the beat of your heart beside mine, and never will I do this . . ."

He leaned forward and kissed her, his good hand wrapping around her waist, and then her own hands were stroking his cheek, his hair, his strong neck.

"Come with me," he said at last, still holding her, his grip firm but gentle.

"Reynard," she said, softly.

"Come with me," he said again. "My men are here, and Nobel has his battle to fight. We will be leagues away by the time he-"

"Reynard," she said, her throat tightening as she spoke. "I- you know that I cannot."

"It's you I should have stolen that night. I know that now. We could-"

"Don't," she said. "Please. This is not easy for me either."

Reynard's hand slipped from her.

"Do you love him?" he asked, his voice low.

"He is my husband. He is the father of my child."

"Do you love him?"

"He's brought peace-"

"You have a strange definition of the word 'peace.'" Reynard said hotly. "Do you really think Nobel will be content with defeating the Calvarians? He thinks he's Aquilia reborn, heir to the old empire, and Solothurn and Frisia will have to be brought to heel before he's satisfied."

"He ended the war between Arcas and Luxia," she said, her cheeks flushed.

"Yes," Reynard said. "By killing your father, and bedding you."

She felt the tears running down her face before she knew that she was crying.

"Please go," she said, her hand resting on her bedside. "Please."

"Persephone," he said, all of the anger drained from his voice. "Persephone, I'm sorry. Don't cry. I didn't mean-"

"*Go*," she said. "Leave me, leave here, leave the muster. Go back to your Hermeline. She loves you, does she not? Write me your letters if you must, but leave. If you stay you'll die. He'll kill you, I know it."

"I won't leave," he said. "Not without you."

"I cannot," she said, her voice nearly breaking. "Please, I couldn't bear it, Reynard, please, is there nothing I can say?"

"Tell me that you love him, and I will go."

She looked into his eyes, his brilliant tin-flecked eyes, and opened her mouth to speak . . . and then the jingle of mail and the rattle of sword against armor made her heart leap in her chest. She turned towards the tent flaps just as they parted, revealing her husband and two of his personal squires- Acteon, Bricemer's heir, and Lanolin, youngest son of the Count of Tarsus- but when she turned back towards Reynard she saw that he was gone, until she noticed a single booted foot disappear underneath the royal bed.

"My Queen," Nobel said with concern. "Your ladies-in-waiting have informed me that you are unwell."

"A chill," she said, wiping at her eyes. "It has passed."

"I see you have dressed."

"Yes, I thought I might join the feast."

"The feast is over," Nobel said.

Had it been so long? She could not say, the wine had made her head light.

"My armor," the King said, and his squires were at his side at once, their gloved fingers as nimble as Columbine's as they began to strip Nobel's plate from him, setting each piece aside with the greatest of care. When they had finished he stood only in his arming doublet and hose.

"Leave us," he said then, and the two youths bowed and removed themselves to the audience chamber, closing the tent flaps behind them.

All the while Persephone had stood by the bed, not daring to move, her heart pounding in her throat.

"Will you have some wine?" Nobel said, pouring himself a cup.

"If it would please Your Majesty," she replied, and he poured her a cup as well. She took it, but did not drink.

"It has often been said that there is no city more devoted to the Firebird than Luxia," Nobel said, swallowing a mouthful of the wine. "Luxia, 'the city of lights' they call it, do they not?"

Persephone nodded and did not drink.

"In the north we too worship the Firebird, but my father told me when I was young that the Dukes of Arcas are the beloved of Sphinx, and that it is the Lioness and not the Firebird that has made my family strong, for a Lioness needs be strong to protect her cubs."

"That is why you bear a lion as your emblem," Persephone said, nodding slightly. She'd heard the same stories herself when she was young, though Madame Corte had also said that that was why the Arcasians were so wicked, and overly fond of their prostitutes.

"My own cub needs protecting now, as well as my lovely wife," he said, setting down his cup. "On the morrow I may die. Tonight, let us make another lion- a brother for our son, or a sister, as beautiful as her mother. They say the Lioness will bless such a union."

No, she thought, *oh gods please no. Not now, not here, not with him here*, but all she could say was, "Your Majesty, I am- tired. The chill-"

"It will not take long," Nobel said, taking the cup from her hand. "You are so very beautiful."

He leaned slightly to kiss her- he was so much taller than Reynard- and his mouth tasted of the sweet Oscan wine, and then his hands were lifting the hem of her dress, and *no, no, no*, she thought and he lifted her up and placed her on the edge of the bed like a child's doll, and *no* she thought, *no not now-* and in spite of that, *in spite of that* she was ready for him, so ready for him, and she could not hold back a gasp as he entered her and she undid one of the ties of his doublet and ran her hand across his chest- he was so lean, lean as one of his racing hounds. His eyes were closed- he always closed his eyes, so she closed hers and she thought of different eyes and different hands, and *oh* she thought and *oh* she gasped *oh oh ohhhhhhh*.

A moment she lay there, simply breathing. There were tears on her cheeks again.

"Did I hurt you?" Nobel said, and he was her husband then, and she pitied him, and hated him, and loved him.

"Tears of joy, husband," she said. "The Lioness will give us a child, I know it."

He smiled, a strange sight, and kissed at her tears, and then her mouth, and said, "I love you My Queen."

"And I you," she said, and a fresh set of tears sprang from her eyes.

He kissed her again, and got to his feet and re-tied his doublet, and called for his squires, and as they entered they seemed to bring the King back with them, and her husband vanished beneath mail.

"I must go," the King said. "May we meet again, My Queen."

"May we meet again," she said and then he was gone.

For awhile all she could do was to bury her face in a pillow and weep, and she waited for Reynard- waited for him to touch her, to shout at her, to strike her even, but Reynard did not come. At last she brought herself to peer under the bed.

Reynard was not there.

* * * * * * *

Tybalt was sitting atop a wagon when Reynard found him, holding court over a troupe of mercenaries and prostitutes. He had a bottle of Old Dusty in one of his hands and a doe-eyed woman in the other.

"Black bird, black bird, sitting in a tree," he sang, and took a swig of wine. "Why, oh black bird, don't you sing for me?"

"Perhaps I'll not sing prettily enough, my lord," Tybalt's woman replied, smiling. Her teeth were very crooked, but still fairly healthy.

Tybalt pulled her closer and purred, "Black bird, black bird, why don't you sing? Do you wait to see what the night will bring?"

"Tybalt," Reynard said, pushing past two of the sellswords.

Tybalt regarded Reynard merrily. "Gentlemen, ladies, behold his highness, the Baron of Maleperduys!"

Some of the drunker men cheered, and the prostitutes laughed, but others did not- they saw the gem that hung from Reynard's neck, and the look on his face.

"Did Isengrim speak with you?" Reynard said.

"He did!" Tybalt replied. "Fear not, *Baron*, the job is done. We have more arms and plate than you'll know what to do with."

Reynard nodded, and turned to leave- then he turned back.

"I'll give you a crown for that bottle," he said.

Tybalt raised an eyebrow. "A crown for Old Dusty? You've gone mad, Reynard- though even this was hard enough to come by."

"A diamond then," Reynard said and produced one out of the air.

"You have gone mad," Tybalt said, corking the bottle and tossing it down to him. Reynard threw the bandit the diamond. Tybalt caught it easily, chuckled, and lifted a fresh bottle from the wagon.

"Wounded bird with broken wing," Tybalt sang as Reynard walked away, the laughter of whores ringing in his ears, "Why is that you make me sing?"

He walked aimlessly for a while, pulling on the bottle. The wine was as dry as it was sour, but he didn't care: it was almost better that way.

When the bottle was empty he bought another, this time for only a pair of coppers. He'd drunk enough that the quality no longer mattered, and by the time he finally stumbled upon his own camp he could barely walk in a straight line.

"Reynard," he heard Tiecelin say, "My children have scouted the enemy camp, and they report-"

"Later," he said, and sat down heavily. "Tomorrow."

"As you wish," the Luxian said, and left him in peace.

He sat there for a long time, near the fire, and stared at the half-empty bottle clutched in his fingers. It was late, he realized, and only Tiecelin and Gaignun were still awake, standing watch over them in case Nobel's men came for them during the night.

They won't, Reynard thought bitterly. *He's won.*

Sleep, he told himself. *Sleep and in the morning you'll know what to do. You'll twist and turn and lie and cheat and win. You always find a way to win in the end.*

He got up from the fire and leaned against the side of one of the tents, and closed his eyes.

He'd almost drifted off when a very familiar sound filled his ears, and he realized whose tent it was that he was resting on.

"*All I ask*," Isengrim was saying, "*Is that you stay in camp and watch over the children. Is that so terrible?*"

"*I have told you before*," Hirsent replied. "*Wherever you go, I will follow.*"

Perhaps if I drink enough, Reynard mused as he took another swig of Old Dusty, *I will forget how to speak Calvarian.*

"*Hirsent, please, I only want for you to be safe.*"

"*And what of your own safety?*" Hirsent shot back. "*What will become of me if you are slain, alone amongst these- these- these barbarians?*"

"*Reynard will take care of you*," Isengrim replied.

"*Reynard is not my husband. Isengrim is.*"

"*I know.*"

"*Then why must you go?*"

There was silence in the tent for a moment.

"*For*," Isengrim said quietly, "*Reynard.*"

"*Reynard, Reynard, always Reynard!*" Hirsent fumed. "*I grow so tired of hearing that name! Are you Reynard's servant now?*"

"*I owe him my life,*" Isengrim replied.

"*And how long must you repay that debt? Until you lie cold and dead on some battlefield?*"

"*You do not understand . . . you are not a blood-guard.*"

"*Neither are you!*" Hirsent shouted. "*Or have you forgotten that as well?*"

There was silence again, and then the tent flaps flew open and Isengrim stalked out into the night.

Reynard found him not far from the camp, staring grimly across the black waters of the Samara. He turned at the sound of Reynard's approach, his hand on his sword hilt.

"Do you want a drink?" Reynard said, offering the Northerner the bottle.

"A blood-guard does not-" Isengrim began to say.

Then he took the bottle.

VII

Reynard awoke with a start and found that he was in his tent, tangled within the folds of his traveling cloak. Whether he had crawled into it during the night or if Isengrim had carried him there he could not say. His guts roiled and there was an ache between his eyes when he moved.

He threw the cloak from his legs and staggered outside. It was false dawn, and Nobel's host was still slumbering fitfully around them. Isengrim was sitting by the fire sharpening his sword- from the look of his eyes Reynard guessed that he hadn't slept a wink.

The Northerner looked up as Reynard took a few shaky steps forward.

"This water is fairly clean," he said, and handed Reynard a canteen.

Reynard took a few draughts and returned the bottle with a hoarse, "Thank you."

"I sent Bruin out to scavenge for eggs," Isengrim went on. "He should return soon."

Reynard nodded and walked towards the crude latrine that one of his men had dug some distance from the camp. After he'd relieved himself, and washed himself with the water from the Samara he felt somewhat sprightlier, and by the time he'd returned to camp one would be hard pressed to notice that he was hung over.

Gradually the sky turned gray, and his companions rose from their own tents. Bruin returned with a big jar of pickled eggs under one of his massive arms. Reynard's stomach turned somewhat as he took a few bites of one, but he forced it all down and drank more water, and then Tiecelin was by his side skinning a fat rabbit that one of the shrikes had caught and roasting it over the fire. The smell of cooking meat roused the others, and soon they were all gathered. Tybalt looked even worse for wear than Reynard, and snarled at Martin to shut up as he waited for a kettle of Hivan coffee to boil. Hirsent sat down next to her husband, and took his hand.

"Tell me of the enemy," Reynard said finally, addressing his Luxian scout.

"Rohart is the last of my children to have returned," Tiecelin said. "He tells me that they are already breaking camp- half of the infantry and all of their horse have formed a battle line between their baggage train and us, while the other half are busy filling in pits and pulling up stakes."

"How many are they?"

"Hard to say," Tiecelin admitted. "Rohart cannot count as well as I might. But if the numbers we saw ourselves are accurate, I'd say there are at least seven thousand of them- give or take."

Reynard considered for a moment and then said: "Take two of the men and bring this news to the King. He may already know of it, but I doubt any of his scouts can fly."

Tiecelin nodded curtly, mounted, and rode off, taking Sautperdu and Passecerf with him.

"Dawn is coming," Reynard said, turning to Isengrim. "We should arm ourselves. You know your people's ways better than any of us- what do you recommend?"

"Shields," Isengrim replied immediately. "Helmets and breastplates as well, especially as we will be in the vanguard."

"I can hardly use a shield," Reynard said. "I only have one arm free, and I will need that for my sword."

"At least wear one upon your back," the Northerner replied. "You can always toss it aside should we find ourselves in direct contact with the enemy."

"Direct contact with the enemy," Tybalt repeated in a low mocking voice. Isengrim ignored him.

"And weapons?" Reynard asked.

"Swords will do for close quarters, though I wish we had more bows."

"We've got plenty of crossbows," Bruin said, motioning towards the tarp that protected their weapons and armor from the moisture in the air.

"Their front line will likely be a shield wall," Isengrim said in response. "We will have to take very careful aim to find our marks, and crossbows take longer than bows to reload."

"Don't worry about whether or not we find our marks," Reynard said, turning to address the others. "We're only supposed to soften the enemy up until the pikemen get into position, and then withdraw to form the rearguard. That's all that Nobel expects of us, thank the gods, so do your best to stay alive and we'll live to see the morrow."

Reynard's companions nodded silently.

"Now then," Reynard said, "We must decide who will stay behind to watch over Martin and Rukenaw."

"But-" Martin started to complain, but Rukenaw jabbed him in the side and he was silent.

"I'll stay," Tybalt offered with a sour grin. "If I'd known your *plan* was going to involve walking into direct arrow fire I might have stayed home."

"And miss the chance to 'cut down a few white-faced pricks?'" Reynard said unsmiling.

"Ah, piss off," Tybalt said, and sipped at his coffee.

"Tencendur," Reynard said, turning to the curly-haired man. "How is your leg?"

"It pains me when I walk," the man replied. "But I can still ride well enough, as my lord already knows."

"I believe that Nobel intends for us to advance on foot- so it seems as though you are the man for this task."

"As my lord wishes," Tencendur said, the relief on his face written as clear as day.

"I would leave others if I thought we could spare the men," Reynard said, getting to his feet. "But I remind all here that I ask no man to come with me unwillingly. If anyone wishes to stay, speak now, and I will not think less of him."

His men were silent, even Tybalt. Isengrim cast a glance towards Hirsent, but she was still.

"Very well then," he said. "Let us arm ourselves."

Jacquet and Blanc uncovered the arms and armor that Tybalt had collected the night before and the men gathered around, taking up helmets, breastplates, and shields of Mandrossian make. For himself, Reynard picked a darkened steel breastplate and a thick wooden shield.

As he began to remove his jerkin to don his armor Tencendur caught him by his good arm and said, "Reynard, what do I do if . . ."

"If we do not come back," Reynard said, handing the man the purse full of diamonds, "You put them both on horses and ride as hard as you can."

"To Maleperduys?"

"Anywhere but here."

****

Tiecelin returned from his errand with a 'gift' from Nobel: a boar spear with a wild fox impaled upon it. "He intends that we should use it as a standard."

It was a mock, Reynard knew, but something about it felt right, so he gave the spear to Maugris and told him to bear it proudly.

As they dressed for battle the songs of morning birds disappeared beneath the din of an army bestirring itself; underneath the steady beat of war drums were hundreds upon hundreds of captains shouting orders, men bellowing songs and praying, the priests of Fenix hammering madly at rivets, and the neighing of steeds as they were saddled and armored. The smell of funeral pyres wafted through the air, for those whom the flux and fever had carried away during the night were now being burned by the river.

Reynard opened his pack and took out his writing kit, and flattened a sheet of parchment against his newly acquired shield. He did not have much time, so he made his message brief.

Hermeline, he wrote with a steady hand. *The time has come for us to go to battle. If I do not return to you, my love, you will find a loose tile within the undercroft that hides enough gold to bring you wherever you might choose to go. Take any that you trust.*

Know that I love you, and that the children are safe.

Reynard

Reynard found Tiecelin speaking to his own 'children,' who had huddled around him like ducklings.

"Do not fear," the Luxian was saying. "Father will return. Father will return and keep you safe."

The shrikes cooed and twittered, and Sharpebeck nuzzled her girlish face against Tiecelin's gloved hand.

"I need to deliver a letter," Reynard said, and the chimera turned to regard him with their cold pupil-less eyes.

"To Hermeline?" the scout asked.

"To Hermeline."

"Bavarde will take it," he said stroking the eldest of Sharpebeck's brood.

"Take it," Bavarde repeated, eagerly. "Take it take it take it."

Reynard handed the man the letter, and no sooner had he done so than the drums began to beat.

BOOM BOOM BOOM, they cried, a hundred strong. BOOM BOOM BOOM.

"To arms!" Bruin bellowed, donning his helmet. The men did the same, some of them fiddling with this strap or that as they made their final preparations.

"Your shield," Isengrim said to Reynard, and helped him strap it onto his back.

The Northerner had donned a suit of blackened armor with a fearsome warg-shaped helm that made him look like something out of a child's nightmare. Hirsent had attempted to do the same but the Mandrossian armor was ill-suited to her womanly frame, and so she'd cobbled what she could from several suits.

Reynard felt uncomfortable himself in his plate. He'd never worn armor so heavy, and with only one free arm he felt clumsy and slow. *Still*, he thought, *better to be slow than dead*.

BOOM BOOM BOOM, the drums cried again, more insistent than before.

"Well, I suppose there's nothing for it," Reynard sighed, and turned to his men to say, "Follow me."

****

It took most of the morning for Nobel's host to assemble, but the mercenaries were ready long before the foot and horse, and so Reynard and his companions found their place amongst them quickly enough. As Reynard had suspected he might, Nobel had ordered the captain of the mercenaries to place them in the direct center of the skirmish line, between two companies of Mandrossian crossbowmen. The captain, a stout keg of a man with graying sideburns, had complained and groused about the integrity of his battle line, but orders were orders and so room was made for them, and now the Mandrossians were casting odd glances towards the men (and woman) who stood beneath Reynard's grisly banner.

Behind them the drums were still beating, BOOM BOOM BOOM, and rank after rank of pikemen were forming into squares, a great swaying mass of men punctuated by the banners of their lords. Closest to them flew the chimera of Poictesme, a hunting bird with a stag's head, and beside it clustered the black otter of Osca, the blue maiden of Astolat, and the red flower of Engadlin. Peering down the line, Reynard could make out the stag of Lothier, the boar of Carabas, and the leopard of Lorn beneath the great white lion of Arcas, while on the left flank the black raven of the Count of Luxia was attended by the golden ram of Tarsus and the balanced scales of Genova. And though he could not see them, he knew that somewhere behind the pikemen the chevalier were mounting their steeds, a host of squires helping to affix shields and barding as the horsemen took up their lances.

He turned to face the enemy. As Nobel had predicted, they had arrayed themselves along a stretch of high ground between the river and the dense woods of the Jennet. From this distance they seemed nothing more than a dull unbroken gray line, but Reynard could still make out the banner that he had glimpsed from the rocks of the Erycinian Highlands: a wolf with the Firebird in its jaws.

He commands but a single army, Isengrim's words echoed in his head.

The field that lay before them had been farmland once, Reynard could tell that from how flat the soil was, but it had clearly lain fallow for quite some time and weeds and scrub grass grew where grain or vegetables might. On their left the Samara flowed, swollen from yesterday's rain, and on the right the branches of the Jennet swayed. Every now and then a wild shrike would rise croaking into the air from the woods; Tiecelin's own brood were far from the only ones present. He'd heard countless soldiers' tales over the years, and they all said that a shrike could smell a battle coming the way a hog could sniff out truffles. Even now a few of them circled above, waiting for the coming feast.

Reynard's legs were beginning to tire when the drums grew suddenly silent. The host was assembled.

"Bruin," Reynard said. "You served in the army. You understand the cadences, do you not?"

"Cadences?" Bruin replied.

"The drums."

"Oh, aye, Reynard," Bruin said then.

"Then call out the commands. I have not had time to learn them all."

"Aye, Reynard," Bruin said.

It was quiet for a time, save for the whinnying of horses and the cries of the shrikes above them. Then Reynard could hear a voice crying out from the pikemen behind them. It was Count Peryton he guessed, or possibly even Nobel, attempting to inspire his men. A moment later the captain of the mercenaries rode past them on a courser.

"Gods be with you," he grunted as he passed.

"Guess the sellswords don't need as much encouragement as the footmen," Tybalt said, and spat into the grass.

"Hur," Bruin laughed. "The sellswords are being paid."

"That's more than I can say for us," Tybalt grumbled.

"Tybalt," Reynard said. "If the two of us get back to Maleperduys alive, I'll give you a bag full of gold. Now shut up."

"A bag of gold, eh?" Tybalt said, and was silent.

A great cheer rose from the pikemen then, and Reynard heard cries of 'Arcasia! Arcasia!' and 'The King! The King!'

A moment later the drums beat to beat again, steadily. Reynard did not need to be told what they were saying.

"Forward!" Bruin roared, his voice mingling with the other officers shouting around them. "At the steady!"

Reynard led the way, Isengrim and Hirsent on his right, Maugris and the standard on his left. Bruin and Tybalt's men clustered around their captains, while Tiecelin took up the rear, his keen eyes fixed upon the enemy.

In spite of their armor they were still faster than the Mandrossian crossbowmen, who were carrying nearly man-sized wooden shields on their backs, and Reynard was forced to slow his pace to avoid drawing too far ahead of the skirmish line. Still they made good time, and before long Reynard could start to distinguish the Calvarians from each other. Companies stood side by side, each armed with a steel-tipped javelin, and close enough to his or her neighbor that they appeared nothing more than a long line of intersecting shields.

They'd nearly halved the distance between themselves and the enemy when a horn sounded, and the Calvarian host began to advance.

My gods, Reynard thought, his mouth suddenly dry as bone. *They're coming right for us.*

Quickly the drum cadence changed, and then stopped.

"Halt!" Bruin called out.

Bomitty-bomitty-bomitty-bom.

"Prepare to fire!" Bruin ordered. The men began loading their crossbows. Tiecelin strung his bow. The mercenaries planted their shields into the soft ground beneath their feet.

Reynard kept his eyes on the enemy. As the Calvarians marched forward he could see a second, smaller gray line behind the first. Another horn blared, and the second line broke into three pieces, two of them rushing around the bulk of the host.

"Their archers are forming on the flanks," Tiecelin said matter-of-factly. Reynard envied his calm.

"What are they doing?" Reynard asked Isengrim. "Nobel's horse will run them down for certain."

"I do not know," the Northerner responded, and readied his own bow, a red-lacquered one that he'd stripped from one of the scouts back in Maleperduys. "I am not *Latteowa* Drauglir."

BOOM BOOM BOOM, the drums beat behind them.

"Here come the footmen," Bruin said, and Reynard turned to catch a glance at the great mass of men that was marching up to meet the enemy. He could see the chevalier now, two great wedges of flashing steel and horse bringing up the rear.

"C'mon, c'mon," Tybalt snarled, his hand tightening and un-tightening around the butt of his crossbow. "They must be within range by now!"

"Not yet," Tiecelin said. "They're still- shields!"

Reynard immediately scrambled to bring his shield up, and as he did so he could hear the unmistakable 'swoosh' of a flight of arrows and watched as a black cloud of shafts rose from the Calvarian archers high into the air before plummeting into the skirmish line.

One of the arrowheads struck his shield, another ricocheted off of Bruin's thick armor, and a third plunged directly into Climborin's thigh.

Cries began to fill the air, and curses.

The Calvarians came on. Another flight of arrows rose and fell, but Reynard's men were ready this time and none found their mark. Climborin broke the shaft that had pierced him, and screamed as he pulled both ends free.

"They are holding back," Isengrim said, notching an arrow of his own and sending into the air with a 'twang.' It fell somewhere amongst the main body of the enemy.

"Perhaps they're saving their arrows for the main host," Reynard said, pulling the arrow out of his shield with a grunt.

"Perhaps," Isengrim said, and loosed another arrow.

The Calvarians came on, so close that Reynard could make out faces. Then the drums beat out *bomitty-bom*, and Bruin yelled, "Fire!"

Reynard's men let loose their quarrels nearly in tandem with the Mandrossians. They streaked towards the enemy, who with a single motion knelt, the second and third ranks pressing forward to add their own shields to the wall. There was a sound like a rain of pebbles clattering against a tiled roof, and then the Calvarians were up and marching again.

Bomitty-bomitty-bomitty-bom.

"Reload!"

"Reload!" the Captain of the mercenaries repeated as he rode past on his courser.

As the men began to rewind their crossbows, the Mandrossians ducking behind their great wooden shields, the Calvarian archers sent another flight of arrows into their ranks. One of them landed so close to Reynard's foot that for a moment he thought he might have lost a toe. Another struck Veillantif right below the eye, killing him almost instantly.

The men were still reloading when Tiecelin began to open fire, loosing arrows as fast as he could draw. Most of them disappeared into the fourth or fifth ranks of the enemy, but he saw one of them dive straight through a gap in the shield wall, and then one of the Calvarians staggered out of step, a red-fletched arrow protruding from his neck. The man collapsed forward, and then disappeared beneath the boots of his brothers.

Bomitty-bom.

"Fire!"

Again the Calvarian ranks closed up, and the majority of the quarrels bounced harmlessly off of Northern steel.

They came on. Reynard could see the flash of their eyes beneath their gleaming helms.

BOOM BOOM, the drums called, sounding something like a heartbeat, *BOOM BOOM*.

"Withdraw!" Bruin shouted, taking up his shield. "Withdraw!"

The mercenaries immediately ripped up their shields and strapped them to their backs. His men were doing the same with their crossbows, and then the skirmish line split and they were sprinting towards the river- on their right, the enemy, and on their left, a sea of outstretched pikes was advancing rapidly.

We'll be caught between them, Reynard thought redoubling his step, desperately trying to keep his eyes on the backs of the mercenaries ahead of them. *We'll be caught between them and we'll die.*

"Wait!" Climborin called out then. He was falling behind due to his leg wound.

Reynard slowed instinctively, but then Isengrim's mailed hand was on his arm, urging him on.

"There is nothing you can do," the Northerner said and Reynard nodded, but try as he might he could not seem to drown out the man's cries for them to stop.

Arrows swooped out of the sky above them, threatening death, but they had not been intended for them and fell amongst the pikemen instead, who had naught but a round buckler and breastplate for defense. A hundred men screamed out, or simply fell over dead.

"They are still holding back," Isengrim noted. Reynard did not argue.

"*Blood and honor!*" a deep Calvarian voice cried to his right.

"*Blood and honor!*" the Calvarian host repeated, and broke into a sprint.

"Luxia!" bellowed some Southern captain. "Tarsus!"

"LUXIA!" the troops called back, setting their pikes into the ground, "LUXIA! LUXIA!"

It was a close thing, but finally the mercenaries in front of them wheeled and they were running along the muddy bank of the Samara. Reynard risked a look backwards, and as he did so the Calvarians launched their javelins at the front ranks of the pikemen. Two of them struck Climborin, who spun around like a dancing priestess before collapsing into the mud. Then the Northerners drew their swords, and the battle was joined.

****

Reynard was panting by the time they reached the rear, as were most of his men, the rush of battle leaving them as quickly as it had come. He was so dazed that he nearly ran into one of the Mandrossians, who had come to a halt and were seeing to their wounded.

"Is anyone hurt?" he asked.

"None," Isengrim said. "Save for Veillantif and Climborin."

Reynard shook his head, and rubbed at his temples.

"Coulda been a lot worse," Bruin said, clapping a giant hand on Reynard's shoulder. "Believe me."

"I believe you," Reynard said.

Once he'd gotten his bearing he saw that they'd reformed on an incline that afforded an excellent view of the field below. The chevalier were massed on the wings, the Southerners so close that Reynard could hear them sniggering at the sight of his standard. Each rider had his own emblem besides that of his lord, and many personalized their armor to resemble birds and beasts, though none more spectacularly than the Count of Luxia, whose raven-shaped helm used rubies to suggest gleaming red eyes.

Slightly above them the war priests of Fenix had assembled with their drums and pennons bearing the Firebird, and near them too sat Count Bricemer, surrounded by bodyguards, his eyes trained on the battle below them. As Reynard watched, a messenger in powder blue tore up the hill on a horse and handed the Count a scroll. Nobel's seneschal scanned its contents, said something, raised his gloved palm, and lowered it.

BOOM. BOOM.

"Give ground," Bruin explained, though he needn't have- the great host below was already moving.

It was strange, Reynard thought, watching the battle from here. It did not seem entirely real. Certainly he could still hear the sound of steel on steel, the war cries and the screams of the dying, but it was as if he were one of Tiecelin's shrikes, looking down from the heights with their black uncaring eyes.

Bricemer raised his hand and lowered it.

BOOM BOOM BOOM.

"Reform," Bruin said. The Arcasian foot halted and held their ground as best as they were able.

Another messenger rode past them, this one headed for the wedge of chevalier. He dismounted before his horse had come to a halt, trotted over to the cavalry, and bowed before Count Corvino.

"Your Excellency," the messenger said. "The King orders you to advance!"

The Count of Luxia nodded, lowered his beaked helm over his eyes, and gave a wave of his hand.

"Cavalry!" one of the chevalier close to the Count shouted. "Forward!"

"For the Queen!" another chevalier cried as they broke into a trot. "Luxia and the Queen!"

"Luxia and the Queen!" a chevalier answered.

"Engadlin!" yelled another.

"Tarsus!" cried a third, and then they had passed them, and were picking up speed as they continued downhill.

Reynard's eyes flicked to the right. The horse commanded by Nobel were advancing as well.

The Arcasian horse had not gotten far when the Calvarian trumpets began to bray, and the rear guard of the Calvarian host began to move.

"Tiecelin," he said, squinting. "What do you see?"

"Their reserves are moving to the flanks," the scout replied. "Their archers are advancing as if to meet our horse . . . and there's something coming over the ridge. Wagons, I think."

The chevalier were picking up speed, their advance heralded by the steady beat of hooves. Great clods of black earth were being kicked up by their steeds, and those closest to the river seemed to be gliding through a spray of sea foam as they say Lady Morgen did when she escaped from the sack of Kerys.

"Their archers are withdrawing now," Tiecelin went on. Reynard could make them out too, rushing back to their own line. "They're throwing something behind them."

"Caltrops," Isengrim said. Reynard nodded. He'd used them enough himself on the Calvarians to know how effective they were at slowing horse.

"And the wagons?" Reynard asked.

"They're pulling them to the flanks."

Stop, he wanted to shout. *Turn back*. But there was nothing he could do but watch as the horse broke into a full charge.

When the Calvarian archers reached their own flank they came to a halt, turned, and opened fire just as the first of the chevalier reached the caltrops.

Reynard suddenly understood what Isengrim had meant about them 'holding back.'

No sooner had the first flight of arrows landed amongst the clustered chevalier than another was in the air. Reynard counted between shots and guessed they were getting a flight off at every count of ten. True, he'd seen Tiecelin shoot faster, but there was only one of Tiecelin, not hundreds.

"Gods," Tybalt said, his voice quiet as the wedge began to break apart- even at this distance the screams of horses and men dying seemed deafening. Still, though, the chevalier advanced, their lances lowering for the final impact.

They had nearly reached the archers when the Calvarian ranks split to reveal the wagons that Tiecelin had seen. For a moment he could make out the hulking war machines that sat astride the wagons, and then there was a sound like a series of thunderclaps and the Calvarian flanks disappeared behind thick plumes of smoke.

The entire front line of horse seemed to wither, as if a giant invisible fist had slammed into them, the impact sending some riders whirling madly through the air as their steeds fell beneath them. The chevalier wheeled, reformed, and charged on. A second retort echoed across the field and more chevalier fell. Then the riders disappeared into the haze of the smoke, shrieking out battle cries.

The east wind blew the smoke towards them. It had an acrid smell, reminding Reynard of the explosive powder that the priests of Fenix used in their ceremonies. And as it cleared, Reynard could see the survivors.

At least five hundred chevalier had ridden with Count Corvino. Now they were less than a hundred. The few that still had their horses were beating a hasty retreat towards them. Others were slogging through the mud, their heavy armor sucking them down with each step. Some crawled. As they got closer he could see the Count of Luxia himself, being steadied between two bloodied men. His helm had broken off, and Reynard could not tell if he was alive or dead.

A riderless horse galloped past them, seemingly untouched. A horn sounded.

"Gods," Tybalt said again.

"Nobel," Bruin said to no one in particular. "You think he . . ."

"Look!" Tybalt cried, pointing towards the battle that was still raging below them. "They're pushing them back!"

He was right. The entire right flank of the Calvarian host was giving ground. The archers and war machines were withdrawing as well, and the reserves were streaming back towards the center of their line.

"LUXIA!" the Southern pikemen cried and pressed the attack. "CORVINO! LUXIA!"

BOOM BOOM BOOM, the drums beat. BOOM BOOM BOOM, but the Luxian pikemen kept pushing until they'd nearly passed the men that formed the Arcasian right.

"Reform!" Reynard could hear Bricemer screaming as the drums continued to beat out their commands. "Hold your ground!"

It was too late. The entire left flank had split from the rest of the army, and into that gap roared the Calvarian reserve, led by their horse. The pikemen in the rear began to turn to face them, but they were too slow, and then the enemy cavalry crashed into them. The Calvarian foot charged into the left flank of the Arcasian center.

They will all die, Reynard realized as rank after rank of pikemen began to buckle. *They will all die unless . . .*

The mercenaries were muttering darkly to their right. Reynard turned back to Bricemer- the man was sitting stock still on his horse.

"Your Excellency!" the captain of the mercenaries yelled as he rode up on his own steed. "What are your orders?"

"I-" Bricemer sputtered. "The King. I must speak with the King . . ."

"My lord, there is no time! What are your orders?"

"We must find the King," Bricemer said, and turning his mount he and his bodyguards rode off towards the right flank.

"What do we do?" Bruin said, turning to Reynard.

"We fight," he heard himself say as he drew his sword and began walking towards the battle. "Forward!"

"Forward!" Bruin repeated.

"Arcasia!" Reynard shouted as his men joined him. "Arcasia!"

The mercenaries did not move, but a company of Arcasian irregulars began to advance as well, and then another, and another, and then a thousand or so men were marching, all of them crying out "Arcasia! Arcasia" and suddenly a man cried out, "The Fox!" and soon they were all crying it, even the chevalier who'd joined with them. "THE FOX! THE FOX! THE FOX!"

They were running now, racing across the trampled grass. Ahead of them the Calvarians were cutting a swath through the pikemen, their steel swords flashing red in the sun as they sheared through flesh and bone. A horn cried out and some of the Calvarians turned to face them, beginning to lock their shields.

But it was too late.

Maugris plunged his boar spear into one man's face as they met, and then Isengrim's sword slashed straight through a Calavarian's sword arm. Reynard sent his rapier directly into another man's eye, and pressed on.

A Calvarian soldier swung his sword at him, but Reynard ducked under the blow and thrust upwards. His blade sheared through the man's neck and toppled the helmet from his head as it came out of the back of his skull. Soon he was trading blows with a new opponent, a man nearly twice his size, until Bruin's axe whistled through the air and separated the Northerner's head from his shoulders.

"Thanks," Reynard breathed. Bruin merely grunted as he pressed forward, his axe dripping with gore.

A fresh knot of enemies rushed to face them, shorter than the others. It wasn't until after Reynard had slashed one's neck open and heard her shriek that he realized they were women.

You've killed women before, he thought, remembering the way that Pinch's girls had screamed as the flames devoured the Anthill tenement, but it still made him feel sick. Then another female warrior slammed her shield into him and knocked him to the ground. She brought her sword down so quickly that he only just parried it. She kicked viciously at his feet, so he rolled to the left- wincing at the pain in his hand as he crushed it- and got to one knee.

"*Southern dog!*" the woman yelled, bringing her sword down again and again.

"*Northern bitch!*" he replied, and when the woman hesitated he knocked her sword aside with his and smashed his helmeted head into hers as he rose. She staggered backwards, cursing, her nose broken and bleeding. Reynard finished her off with a thrust to the jugular.

There were friends and foes all around them now. The pikemen had dropped their polearms and were fighting with their short swords. A chevalier and a Calvarian were wrestling in the mud, fighting for a dagger. Dozens of dead and wounded Arcasians littered the ground, pierced by shaft and blade, and Reynard nearly tripped over one of them as he looked for any sign of his companions.

When he looked down he saw that it was Maugris. A Calvarian sword had cut through his belly, and his guts were strewn on the ground beside him.

How many others? Reynard wondered. *How many others will die because I brought them here?*

Reynard heard the sound of hooves and turned just as a Calvarian on horseback charged past him, his longsword glancing off of his helmet with a metallic 'clang.' The force of the blow sent his head reeling for a moment, just long enough for the man to wheel his horse around for a second pass.

Reynard brought up his sword, his head still swimming, but he knew it was futile. The man on the horse was charging straight at him now. He'd be trampled if nothing else.

Then a blade cut through the horse's left front leg. The animal screamed as it fell, and the rider howled as the horse crushed him beneath its weight.

Isengrim looked down at the man for a moment, and then he put an end to him.

"Where is Hirsent?" Reynard asked, stepping forward.

"I do not know," Isengrim replied quietly. "I had thought she might be with you."

"We will find her," Reynard said, and then they were in the thick of it again, and any who stood against them died.

They found Hirsent surrounded by a half dozen Arcasian foot- they had clearly taken her for an enemy. Her helmet had been knocked from her head, and her sandy locks and fair skin were plain to see. One of the men charged at her hopelessly, but as she knocked him down a second came up behind her and kicked her in the back of the knee. She went down hard, and the others moved to finish her off with their swords.

Isengrim made a noise deep in his throat, and then he was amongst them.

When he was done he knelt down and gently helped her to her feet.

"*I am uninjured*," she said in her own tongue.

"*If I had not been here-*" Isengrim began to say, but there was no time for words. More Calvarians were pressing their attack, and soon Reynard, Isengrim, and Hirsent were standing nearly back-to-back as they fought to stay alive.

Reynard had just dispatched an opponent when he heard the drums. They seemed so far off, but he heard them all the same.

BOOM BOOM, they beat. BOOM BOOM.

"No," Reynard said, but there was nothing he could do. Men were already turning from the enemy, some throwing down their weapons as they did so, panic spreading through the ranks like wild fire as men ran, and begged for mercy, and died.

Retreat! the drums sounded again. *Retreat! Retreat!*

There was no time to argue. Reynard sheathed his rapier, pointed to what he could only guess was west and yelled, "Follow me!" and then they were running, Hirsent at his side and Isengrim bringing up the rear.

The Calvarians were coming up behind them fast, many of them on horseback, and they were cutting down men left and right. Reynard felt his heart pounding in his chest, and his sides ached, but he did not slow. To slow was to die.

Then he noticed that the soil beneath his feet had turned to mud, and saw the Samara in front of him, and he realized that they were running in the wrong direction. He veered left, as did the men behind them, but ahead he could only see a thick mass of Arcasian foot slogging slowly through the mud, slowed by caltrops, slain horses, and the bodies of hundreds of dead and dying chevalier.

That way lies death, Reynard thought, but there was nothing for it. The only other option was to turn and face the Calvarians.

Ride to the left, lose your horse, Grymbart had said in the Gate of Tears. *Ride to the right, lose your head.*

As they joined the crowd, several dozen other men pressed in behind them, and soon Reynard could hardly see a foot in front of his face. Men were shouting and cursing, and then they were screaming as the Calvarians slammed into their rear. A big chevalier in armor lurched into Reynard and he nearly fell, but Hirsent grabbed onto his arm and steadied him.

Somehow Reynard managed to draw his dagger, and he sawed at his sling until his left arm was free.

"Take my arm!" he shouted at Hirsent, and she did so. It felt as though a thousand pins were stabbing his arm at once, and he grimaced, but he did not pull away. He needed at least one good arm.

They lurched again, wildly, and Reynard found himself standing in a foot of water. It was faster than it looked and it seemed to tug at his legs like an insistent child. A man near him fell, and was trampled into the mud.

"Your armor!" he yelled at Hirsent, tossing aside his helmet and shield. "Take off your armor!"

Reynard cut free the straps of his breastplate and began to do the same for Hirsent. He could tell that another push was coming and tried to plant his feet, but he might as well have tried to steady himself in a tub full of butter, and when the man next to him leaned against him with the weight of all of the men behind him, he fell. Hirsent tried to stop him, but the weight of the press knocked her over as well. They fell into the Samara together, and then the river had them.

"Hirsent!" Isengrim cried out, his arm outstretched towards them both, and then the crowd closed in around him and he was gone, a man amongst the hundreds that were struggling alongside the river.

The water was shockingly cold and it filled his boots and soaked his small clothes, and threatened to drag him under. He saw Hirsent's head bob up madly for air, and then his own head was underwater.

She is too heavy, he thought, *she will drown us both,* but he curled his injured hand around her wrist and did not let go. Agony shot up his arm, but he did not let go.

Somehow he got his head above the surface and took a breath. Something tugged heavily at his shoulder, and he went down again. He lashed out with his dagger and felt it connect with something. The blade jumped out of his hand, but whatever had grabbed him let go, and then he was pumping his arms and legs and he surfaced with a gasp.

He twisted in the water and took Hirsent with his right hand, his good hand, and freed his left. Her fingers wrapped around his wrist and squeezed.

Then he saw the branch.

A cluster of trees grew close to the river here, and a thick bough had partially snapped off of one of them and fallen into the Samara. If Hirsent could grab it . . . but Hirsent could barely keep her head above the water. He didn't even know if she'd noticed the branch.

And they were only going to get one chance, he knew.

Hirsent passed underneath the branch, and disappeared beneath the river. Her fingers squeezed his wrist fiercely.

He reached up with his left hand and grabbed the branch.

The Samara tugged at them madly, unwilling to let go. His shoulder screamed with pain as Hirsent's weight nearly pulled it out of its socket. He was screaming too, the pain in his hand threatening to knock him out, but he held on.

Oh gods, he thought as he felt his grip begin to loosen, *I can't. I can't I can't I can't. Forgive me, Hirsent, I can't hold on.*

Then Hirsent's other hand took hold of his arm, and she was climbing up him. Her face burst from the river above him and she choked and sputtered, but she took hold of the branch and put her other arm around him and told him to hold onto her. He clutched at her with his right hand and she pulled him to the shore and collapsed into the grass.

VIII

Hirsent was woken by the flutter of wings.

She did not remember having fallen asleep, but she must have for the sun was in the west now, and the shadows of the trees around them had lengthened.

Stupid, she cursed herself, and sat up. Her clothes were still wet from the river, and Reynard still lay beside her, his eyes closed and his breathing troubled.

Something moved in one of the trees above them- a shrike, she saw. For a moment she took it for one of Tiecelin's- Rohart perhaps for its feathers were black- and she made to speak to it, but then she saw that it was far too small, and its face was more bird than man. It quorked at her, tilting its head quizzically as it shuffled across a tree branch.

"*Go away*," she said and, finding a stone, flung it at the thing. It cawed angrily and went to look for easier prey.

Reynard was whimpering in his sleep. She couldn't blame him- his left hand had swollen up like a bladder, and had turned purple. *Broken, most likely*, Hirsent thought, wishing that she'd had her surgical kit with her, but she had left it in her tent.

How far did the river take us? she wondered as she began unbuttoning her coat. It had seemed as though they had spent an eternity in the river, the cold water pressing in around her like a thing alive, but she could not rightly say. Her coat off, she tore off one of her sleeves, and began to redress Reynard's hand as best she could.

As she worked Reynard awoke with a cry. "Shhh," she hushed, and put a pair of fingers over his mouth. "Enemies may still being near."

"Where are we?" he said, wincing as she bound up his fingers.

"I am not knowing."

"How- how long was I-"

"Shhh," she said again. "Rest. I will be seeing what there is to be seeing."

Reynard nodded and laid his head on it's side, but he did not go back to sleep. *Perhaps that is best*, she reasoned, thinking of the shrike. *There are bound to be more of them.*

She dared not go west, so she followed the course of the river for a while, her sword naked in her hand. It had belonged to one of the prafosts her husband had cut down on the dam, the night before she had escaped from Dis, and Reynard had named it *Harrower*. A silly thing, she thought, to name a sword, but she was grateful that she had not lost it in the river, as she had her breastplate, and one of her vambraces, though she could not remember how.

She had not gone far when she came to a place where the thicket gave way to freshly-tilled soil. A great willow had come down here sometime ago, having fallen partially into the river, and its skeletal boughs were hung with the bodies of dead Southerners. A pair of shrikes were feeding on them, but at her approach they burst into flight and glided to the other side of the river.

If only we had wings to fly. The terrain beyond the copse was little but open field, and unfamiliar to her.

The Samara had swept them past Nobel's muster.

"Camp of Nobel is west," she said when she'd returned to Reynard. "Isengrim may be being there. And others."

"The same could be said for Drauglir," Reynard responded. "Whatever the case, we cannot stay here."

Hirsent nodded. The Seventeenth's scouts would no doubt be combing the river looking for stragglers.

"Woods are being in the north," she said. "We might be hiding there until armies have gone."

"It will make it harder for our friends to find us as well," he said, getting shakily to his feet. "But I can't think of a better plan . . . at least, not at the moment."

"You walk?" she asked.

He took a few steps, and nodded.

"Here," she said, handing him a sword that she'd taken from one of the corpses. Only then did he seem to notice that his own blade was missing. "You may be naming it if you like."

"Give me some time to think on it," he said, and smiled faintly.

* * * * * * *

Reynard put on a good show, but Hirsent could tell that he was exhausted, and in a great deal of pain besides. She wished that she could let him rest, even for a moment, but she knew they could not stop as they crossed the farmland between the river and the forest that the Southerners called the Jennet.

She could see the hillock that had served as the center of Nobel's camp now, and the great plumes of black smoke that were rising from it, and at any moment she expected to see riders bearing down on them, exposed in the open with no place to hide. When Reynard stumbled she caught him and helped him stagger towards the tree line.

They'd nearly reached the woods when she heard distant shouts, and when she turned she saw at least a score of men running across the field- Southerners, she could tell, even from this distance.

For a moment she thought she might call out to them, but then she remembered the pikemen that had surrounded her once she'd lost her helmet. *Slut*, they'd called her as they'd tried to kill her, *whore*, they'd screamed and *bitch*. She'd heard the words muttered enough by some of Reynard's men to understand what they meant.

These men will be the same, she thought, these men would only see the color of her skin and hair, and so she stayed her tongue and half dragged Reynard into the forest.

Suddenly the riders she had so greatly feared appeared, breaking out of the thicket that she had Reynard had wisely left behind and streaking across the field to intercept the Southerners.

"We must go," she said, tugging at Reynard.

"A moment," he breathed, doubling over. "Just a moment."

"Now," she said, and scooped the man up into her arms.

He is lighter than he looks, she thought as they pushed deeper into the woods, the sounds of dying men fading behind them.

The Jennet was not like the forest of Maleperduys- for one thing it was far less dense, its foliage little more than ferns and the shoots of young trees. The sun shining through the boughs and the calls of songbirds made it seem a cheery place, but Hirsent did not slow until her arms began to shake with exertion, and even then she merely laid Reynard down for a time, feeding him little sips of water from her canteen before taking him up again and resuming her march.

As the day wore on it began to rain again. The woods protected them from the worst of it, but their clothes were still wet and it wasn't long before they were both as soaked as before. Reynard began to shiver in her arms, and his teeth chattered. She laid him down again and, removing one of her gloves, pressed her palm to his forehead.

It was not yet a fever, but it soon would be if they did not stop to find some shelter. How far had they traveled, she wondered. A league? Two? Three? She could not tell, but it would have to be enough.

She found the largest tree she could and laid Reynard against it, and sat down beside him. It was only then that she realized how hungry she was, and she unfastened the pouch at her belt and pulled a few strips of salted mutton from it, as well as a soggy hunk of bread. She couldn't remember the last time food had tasted so good.

"Cold," Reynard whispered at her side. He'd pulled his legs up to his chest and was hugging them with his right hand.

"Here," she said, offering him a piece of jerky. "Eat."

Reynard took what was offered and chewed on it slowly before swallowing. *Good*, she thought. She did not know what she would do if he could not eat.

"I'm cold," he said again, and shivered. "A fire-"

"No fire," Hirsent said. She wasn't certain she could even make one, given the rain, but even if she could, "Fire will be bringing enemies."

Reynard nodded slowly, but continued to quake. Hirsent watched him for a moment and then stood.

Forgive me, my love, she thought as she took off her belt. *There is no other way.*

She was topless by the time that Reynard noticed what she was doing.

"Hirsent, don't," he said, and tried to stand. His good arm couldn't support his weight and he sat back down. "This isn't-"

"You are being *fisicien*?" she asked, slipping out of her breeches. "Be taking off your *loda*."

"Hirsent," he said again, but his fingers began to fumble at the buttons of his doublet.

"Stop," she said, pushing his shaking hand aside, and undid it herself.

When she'd stripped Reynard she draped their clothes over a nearby branch and then spread his thick cloak across the forest floor. She laid him down on it, and then she lay on top of him- favoring his good side- and pulled the cloak tight around them both.

His body was both like and unlike Isengrim's- his muscles were hard, yet lean, and his skin was soft to the touch, a thick little tuft of hair growing on his chest. His beard tickled the skin at her neck, but she curled her leg around him to warm him better, and after awhile his shivering lessened.

Eventually she felt him stiffen beneath her, and he tried to turn away, but she held him close with her strong arms. She knew as well as he did that it was the best way for them to stay warm.

"I'm sorry," he said, hoarse. "I- I can't help it."

"*Shut your eyes,*" she said. "*And sleep.*"

* * * * * * *

The next morning she was not sick.

She slipped out of their makeshift bedroll, re-covering Reynard when he did not wake, made water in the woods behind a tree and waited for the nausea to come, and when it did not she surprised herself by crying.

Be quiet, she told herself. *Be still. Do you want him to hear? Haven't you cried enough?*

She had cried for a year when they'd taken her first child, her and Isengrim's nameless son. The blood-guard had expected her to do the honorable thing then, and take her own life, but she hadn't. *Fuck their honor*, she'd thought, *let them be shamed by me*, and that was when she'd started to compete in the arena.

By Calvarian law, the arenas were the only place where men and women of any class could associate freely, and then only in competition. She suffered bruises and injuries, and insults from the crowds, but she did not give up. For ten years she struggled in the fighting pits, whenever her duties did not require her elsewhere, and every time she triumphed over a prafost or heafodcarl she knew how much it tormented them- all of them.

Every night she went to sleep cherishing that thought, caressing it in her mind the way she had once caressed Isengrim.

Then Isengrim had returned, and Reynard with him, and she knew a year of joy. The Southern lands had seemed so exotic then, so wild and free, and they fought brigand and chimera in the wild woods . . . and then her second child had quickened in her belly, and for nine months she had cried tears of happiness as she waited for it to come.

And then the child had come- a girl, and stillborn. A moon-calf the Southerners called it, a child of Wulf. She remembered the way she'd screamed at Hermeline, the words she'd spoken.

It is not her fault, Isengrim had said.

I know, she'd wanted to scream back at him, *I know, don't you think I know?*

She knew whose fault it was.

Maleperduys would never again be beautiful to her, she knew, and the little garden that Hermeline had made would only serve to remind her of the babe that she had buried there, a round stone the only marker of the grave.

It was then that she'd stopped learning the Southern tongue, and for a long time afterwards, she would not let Isengrim touch her. He had never complained, but sometimes, when he thought that she was not looking, she could see the sadness in his eyes, and he began to spend more and more time at his forge, beating farmer's plowshares into blades and spearheads, until she could not stand it anymore and she went to him, and lay with him . . . and afterwards she always cursed herself for a weakling.

Isengrim, she would whisper, *Isengrim, my love, how weak you make me.*

If she had not been proud, she knew, the third child would never have come. There were plants, she knew, whose leaves or resin could have aided her, the blood-guard grew them during the summer in lands set aside for such a purpose, but she was a combat surgeon, not a blood-guard, nor a Southern priestess, and she simply could not bring herself to go to Hermeline. To do so would have been weakness.

To do so would be to admit that she had failed.

And now she had lost her Isengrim for a second time, and he might never know what she carried in her belly. She wondered if she had looked as he had, arm outstretched, her eyes pleading as he plummeted into the abyss.

"*I will find you,*" she whispered to the woods. "*Alive or dead, I will find you.*"

She wiped her eyes as best she could, pulled on her damp clothes, and went to rouse Reynard.

He was already awake, propped up slightly on his side, his injured hand lying limp across his lap.

"Good morning," he said, his voice raw.

"Water," she said, tossing him her canteen. She checked her pouch- only a single strip of jerky remained. She tore it in two, and offered him half.

He took it and smiled at her, sadly. "You're not fooling anyone, you know."

"What are you meaning?" she said.

"Well, Bruin maybe," Reynard went on. He sounded very tired. "He's never been very bright. But otherwise I'd bet even Martin can tell that you're pregnant."

How did he know? she wondered.

"It's been all over your face for a month now," he said, as if he'd known what she'd been thinking. "And the signs are rather obvious."

"Is-" she stammered, and cursed herself. "Is Isengrim knowing?"

"Isengrim isn't stupid," he said. "And I imagine that part of a blood-guard's training must entail knowing how to tell when a woman is with child."

He is right. She knew he was right, only she'd been too proud to see it.

"Why then is he saying nothing?" she asked.

"Because he is waiting for you to tell him," Reynard answered.

"*I cannot tell him,*" she replied, reverting to her own tongue.

"You are a coward then."

"*Who are you to call me coward?*" she shouted at him. "*Who are you to call me weak? You never lost a child! How can you know what that is like?*"

"I cannot."

"*I am no coward,*" she said, drawing her sword. "*And I will kill you if you call me such again.*"

"Then kill me," he said.

She stood over him, her breathing hard, but she lowered her sword.

"Do you want the child?" he asked.

"*Yes,*" she answered.

"Then tell Isengrim the truth."

"*And what if it dies?*" she said, her voice suddenly small.

"What if?" Reynard replied with a shrug. "The child may *live*, Hirsent."

"*But if it dies,*" she said, fighting back her tears, "*If it dies then Isengrim will- he will-*"

"Isengrim *loves* you," Reynard said firmly. "He will love you if the child dies, and he will love you if the child lives. He will always love you."

Hirsent could not stem the flow of tears any longer, and she sat down and cried.

"*Stupid,*" she said, sobbing. "*Weak, stupid.*"

Reynard was holding her then, in his good arm.

"Tears do not make you weak, Hirsent," he said. "Love does not make you weak."

She clutched at him, and cried into his neck, and when she was done he kissed her on the forehead and rose to his feet slowly.

She blinked at his nakedness, and turned away blushing.

"Reynard," she said. "*Thank you. For saving me.*"

"Don't mention it," Reynard said as he clumsily stepped into his britches. "In fact you can repay me by not mentioning any of this to Isengrim."

"*If he lives.*"

"If he lives."

* * * * * * *

Reynard seemed stronger to Hirsent- he could walk on his own, though not as fast as she might have liked, and he seemed less flushed, but it was not his head that was worrying her.

It was his hand.

She had insisted on checking it before they set out, and she did not like what she saw- it was still bruised, and she did not doubt that he'd broken a bone or two, but it had also begun to turn an angry shade of red. Broken bones she could mend, but there was only one sure way that she knew how to prevent blood poisoning.

"Is it bad?" he had asked.

She knew he would know if she lied to him.

"Is bad."

He stared at his hand as she bandaged it back up, but said nothing, and then they were off.

"We need to find a way out of these woods," he said as they continued to push north. "Find a village or a town."

"It will be more danger," she replied.

"It might be more *dangerous*," he said, laughing, "But we won't last long without food and water."

She couldn't argue. She was so hungry that she might have happily eaten her boots and belt, if they'd had anything to cook with. She found a nice round stone and kept it in her hand, in case she saw a likely bird or tree rat in one of the branches, and as they walked she turned it in her fist. There was something calming about it.

Hirsent led them east, or as east as she could tell- neither she nor Reynard were as skilled woodsmen as Tiecelin or Tybalt- and before midday she brought a lean-looking gray rodent down with a well-placed throw. She broke the things neck neatly and contemplated eating it raw, but thought the better of it and placed it in her pack.

"At least we'll have supper," Reynard jested, but he was not smiling.

"You are having much pain?" she asked.

"I can take it," he said, and resumed walking, dead twigs snapping loudly under his feet as he went.

He is very sick, she thought. *The old Reynard would not have made a sound.*

They walked and walked, sometimes circling around places where fallen trees made the going impossible, other times passing through open glens where bell-shaped little white flowers grew, and delicate trees with brilliant pink leaves. Berries there were, as well, and had Hermeline been with them she might have been able to distinguish between the harmless and the lethal, but she was not, and so she left them be.

Reynard was beginning to stagger again when the woods finally broke. Beyond the trees wheat fields stretched from north to south, and farther on she could make out a settlement of some kind just beyond a slow-flowing creek. A village, she decided- there were no defensive walls and it was far too small to be a town. On the northern side of the water a large stone building loomed, the seat of some petty Southern lord perhaps, but it was roofless now and its windows were broken.

"What are you thinking?" Hirsent asked.

"I think we should have a closer look."

They pushed into the wheat field, which was clearly ready to be harvested. *Perhaps there will be a mill,* Hirsent thought. *We might grind some of it up and bake some bread.*

They came upon the ruin first. Its stones had clearly been scorched by fire, and where there might have been a grand archway there was only a great hole, as if a giant had kicked the whole edifice in.

"Drauglir?" Reynard said.

"Drauglir," she replied.

She glanced inside the structure- it was a blackened shell, full of nothing but fallen stones and burnt support beams.

They left the destroyed manor behind them and headed towards the place where a stone bridge forded the stream. Sure enough, a stone mill sat astride the river here, its waterwheel green with algae. Beyond, the villagers had partially dammed the creek to create an artificial pond. *There might still be fish in there,* she thought, her stomach growling. She doubted that the Seventeenth had left much else.

"Hirsent," Reynard said, touching her lightly on the shoulder. "Look."

He pointed to an enormous oak that grew beside the mill. There were three naked men hanging from its boughs, nooses around their necks.

They were Calvarians.

"They've not been hanging here long," Reynard remarked. "The shrikes have not been at them yet. Who were they, do you think?"

"*They must have lain with Southern women,*" she said, thinking it more likely that two had held one woman down as the third had done his business. "*Amongst our people, the punishment for this is death.*"

"How can you tell?" Reynard asked.

"*They have been stripped of their weapons, their armor, their uniforms. They were not worthy of them.*"

"That's some justice, I suppose."

"*It was not done out of kindness,*" Hirsent said, pointing to a freshly dug pit nearby. Reynard peered into it grimly. Hirsent did not need to be told what had been thrown into it and left to rot.

"*A Calvarian who gives his strength to our enemies is a traitor,*" Hirsent said. "*And a woman who carries that strength within her is an enemy to be slain, whether she be warrior or not.*"

"Let's search the village," Reynard said, sounding very tired as he turned his back on the pit. "If anything, we might find some firewood to cook up that squirrel."

Hirsent nodded, smiling in spite of herself. She had forgotten that the Southerner name for tree rat was 'squirrel.'

They crossed the bridge. The rest of the village had been built out of daub and wattle, the largest example of which was a two-story building that appeared to be mostly intact. A crudely carved sign in the shape of a bat hung above the door, and some petty artist had painted it blue.

"The inn will be a good start," Reynard said, peering into one of the structure's crude glass windows. "It's not been burned down, at any rate."

Hirsent went in first, her sword drawn, and Reynard came in afterwards. The place had a sour smell, the stench of spilled beer and dried vomit depressingly familiar to her now. It was dim as well, for no fire roared in the hearth, and the lamps that hung from the rafters were dead. Along one wall the former proprietor of the inn had set up a crude bar- little more than a pair of thick planks of wood supported by empty barrels- and behind that a series of rickety looking steps provided access to the sleeping quarters above.

"This is being a rat hole," she said, covering her nose with the back of her hand. "We are not finding anything here."

"Don't be too quick to judge," Reynard said, pointing to the under side of the staircase.

Whatever else the Calvarians had plundered, they'd left behind several barrels of beer.

"That is not being food," she said.

"It's made out of grain," he said, picking up a ceramic cup that was sitting on the bar. "And I need *something* in my stomach. We both do."

"I am having *sqirrl*."

"One drink, please," he said. "I need to sit down."

She acquiesced, and took the cup he offered her.

The beer was dark and bitter to taste, but it seemed only moments before her cup was empty. Reynard sat down on a three-legged stool by the cold hearth and sipped from his own cup slowly, his eyes closed.

"Is there anything that can be done?" he said, his voice quiet.

She did not need to ask what he was referring to. It was in her mind as well.

"There is," she replied, flatly, knowing full well that he would know if she lied to him.

"If it comes to that," he said, "promise me you won't hesitate to do it."

She looked at him. He was hunched over, exhausted, his eyes red and his face smeared with grime. And he was *afraid*. She could see it in his eyes. She had never seen him bat so much as an eyelash in the face of death until now. It frightened her.

"If it comes to that," she said at last.

And then she heard the horses.

The sound of hoof beats was unmistakable- there were horses coming, and more than one.

"Out the back," Reynard said as she lifted him to his feet. They crossed the room, Reynard stumbling as he went, and passed through an ill-fitting door that led to a cramped kitchen. It had been thoroughly ransacked, the dirt floor carpeted with pots and pans, and broken clay jars. Sunlight streamed into the room through an open doorway- and beyond Hirsent could see what might have been a stable yard, and beyond that the pond.

The horses were drawing closer. And they were slowing.

Reynard kicked a kettle as they made for the door, and it clattered noisily as it spun madly across the room. She could only hope that whoever was coming had not heard. She paused for a moment as they entered the yard, letting her eyes adjust to the light.

Directly across from the inn an outhouse stood, and beyond that a short pier stretched partway into the pond. She braced Reynard with her shoulder and started to make for it, thinking that they might hide underneath it, when five men on horseback came galloping around both sides of the inn.

They were not Calvarians. Nor were they Arcasians. Their olive skin, and their curved swords and oddly-peaked helms marked them as foreigners.

Mercenaries.

When they saw Hirsent and Reynard, they pulled up their reins and brought their steeds to a halt.

"Let me do the talking," Reynard whispered to her.

She nodded and kept her sword ready.

"Who are you?" Reynard called out as the men dismounted. He'd drawn the sword that she had given him.

No one answered, and for a moment they simply stared at each other. Then Hirsent heard a crash from the kitchen, and turned to see another four armed men standing side by side.

"Well, now," one of them said, a clean-shaven man wearing a mail and plate coat. His skin was as dark as a chestnut. "A cripple and a Calvo bitch. This *is* interesting, isn't it boys?"

Some of the men chuckled.

"We saw you from the crossroads," the man went on, pointing north. "I thought you might try and slip out the backdoor. Seems I was right."

"Greetings," Reynard said, and bowed. "Whom do I have the pleasure of addressing?"

"He's got a fancy tongue," one of the others said.

"Fancier than his clothes at any rate," replied the one Hirsent could only assume was their leader. He took a step forward and bowed slightly. "Call me Pinabel."

"You have the look of Therimere," Reynard said. "Are you sellswords?"

"That we are. You look upon all that remains of the Iron Band, a free company currently without an employer."

His men laughed again.

"And you are their captain?" Reynard asked.

"Old Captain Ganelon got used up at the Samara, but I've ridden with the company longer than any of this lot. Suppose that makes me chief."

"We were at the Samara as well. I am Reynard, the Baron of Maleperduys, and this is the Lady Hirsent."

"The Fox and the She-Wolf, eh?" Pinabel said, casting a lingering glance at her. "Don't see too many Calvos off on their own . . . might be you're telling the truth."

"I am," Reynard said. "What news of the battle? Does the King live?"

"Nobel?" the man snorted. "He lives, though I'd hardly call him a King, what with half of the lords of Arcasia dead. We were raven-men ourselves until old Corvino died of his wounds."

"The Count of Luxia is dead?"

"Him and his eldest, Wulf take them both," Pinabel said, and spat. "Them and that jumped up bitch that calls herself the Countess now. Told us our 'services were no longer required.' If it weren't for her bodyguards I'd have serviced her, good and hard, and slit her throat when I was finished."

"Then you're no longer with the army?" Reynard asked, throwing Hirsent a worried glance.

"What do you think this is, a scouting party?" Pinabel said with a guffaw, and the others laughed with him. "All me and my boys want is to get out of this bleeding country . . . and maybe have a little fun along the way, eh boys?"

"Fun," one of the others repeated, grinning, and some of the other laughed.

Hirsent sometimes had a hard time understanding the subtleties of the Southern tongue, but it didn't take a translator for her to understand what the man was suggesting. She tightened her grip on her sword.

"I wouldn't recommend bedding this one," Reynard said, stepping between Hirsent and the mercenaries' leader. "She's as like to rip your throat out with her teeth than kiss you. Besides, I could easily arrange passage for all of you: provide us with safe conduct to Maleperduys and I'll pay you with gold, gems, whatever you desire."

"You say that now," the man shot back, "But so did the Count of Luxia, and look where that got us."

"I can pay you with this," Reynard said, pulling his ruby necklace out from under his doublet. "It's worth a fortune."

"No doubt," Pinabel said, smiling widely. "I'll tell you what, Baron Reynard, you give us the gem and the woman without a fight and you can walk out of here alive."

"You can have the gem," Reynard said. "But the woman stays with me."

"As you wish," Pinabel said. "Dardilhon, kill him."

One of the men brought up a crossbow to bear on Reynard, but Hirsent was ready- she shoved Reynard aside just as the man fired. The bolt thudded harmlessly into the side of the inn. When the man went for his knife Hirsent closed the distance between them and buried her sword edge into the side of his face.

"She's got a little fight in her, boys!" she heard the captain say as she kicked the wounded crossbowman away from her.

There are only eight of them, she thought as two of them came at her with sword and shield. *And they're Southerners. Isengrim could cut them all down without breaking a sweat.*

You are not Isengrim, another voice said as she danced away from the pair. *And you're hungry and tired and have a baby in your belly.*

"C'mon, drop the sword, girlie," one of them said as he circled around her, "We'll be nice, I promise."

"Yer," the other said, slashing at her with his curved blade. "If we like you maybe we'll let you keep that pretty face."

Hirsent kept dodging and weaving, and then one of them stumbled slightly over a stone. She smashed the man's sword aside with her own and slashed his side clean open.

"Calvarian whore!" the other said, bringing his sword down in an arc above his head. She parried the blow, kicked the man backwards, and then sidestepped as a third opponent armed with a steel mace nearly stove her head in. Before he could recover his footing she slashed through his spine.

She was tiring, she knew, and far too soon. Six men were still circling around her, weapons ready, while Reynard was lying facedown in the mud. She hadn't even seen him fall. She lunged at one of them and sheared a leg in two.

The one called Pinabel came at her, blocking her strikes with a beautiful cane shield with iron struts and a fat upraised boss. As her thrusts and cuts slowed he went onto the offensive, forcing her back, back, until her back was to the wall of the inn. She bulled into him then, using all of her weight, and for a moment they wrestled like lovers before the man hit the ground heavily.

She was pulling back her sword to finish him off when something struck her in the back of the head. Somehow she held onto her sword, but the world was suddenly spinning and she weaved crazily as she tried to keep her feet. A shape loomed up before her, and then her sword was torn from her fingers.

No, she thought, shaking her head to clear it. *Don't let them-*

A mailed fist smashed into her ribs, knocking the breath from her. It took only a shove to put her flat on her back, and then they were over her.

"Hold her," she heard Pinabel say, and then two of them were on top of her. One of them had her by the wrists, and the other had a leg. Pinabel had a slim ivory-handled dagger in his fist.

Two to hold her down. A third to do his business.

"We saw plenty of mates cut down by your brothers and sisters, She-Wolf," he said, and slashed open the front of her uniform. "And we're going to pay you back for each and every one of them."

"This one's still breathing, Pinabel," one of the other men said. He was turning Reynard over. "What should I do with him?"

"Wake him," the Captain said, fussing with the drawstrings of Hirsent's breeches. "We might as well give him a show before sending him to the Watcher."

"Hirsent," she heard Reynard say as he opened his eyes. "I've thought of a name for my sword: Cut-throat."

Reynard slashed upwards, straight through the man's neck. Blood poured wildly from him as he fell.

Reynard was on his feet then, and as Pinabel rushed to meet him Hirsent dared hope. But whatever last reserve he'd had was clearly spent, and the mercenary captain had only to bat Reynard's sword aside with his hand to disarm him. Reynard tried to dodge, but the captain knocked his legs out from under him and began to kick with his hobnailed boots.

"The Baron of Maleperduys," the man said, kneeling down to tear Reynard's bandages open. "You're the Baron of shit-all now."

Pinabel stomped on Reynard's left hand. Reynard screamed and screamed, and then Pinabel ground his heel into the dirt and Reynard finally passed out.

"Watch him," Pinabel said to the men holding her legs. "I can handle this bitch myself."

She kicked at him as he got back on top of her, and lunged at his face with hers, her teeth bared like an animal. He merely laughed and struck her across the mouth with one of his mailed gloves. She spat blood. He was between her legs now, the rings of his mail coat cutting into her skin as he fiddled with his breeches.

Don't cry, she thought, and leveled her gaze on the blue sky above. *They want you to cry. Don't give them the satisfaction.*

"You might just like this, Calvo," Pinabel was saying. He had taken off one of his gloves and spat into his palm. "You'll swear off Northern men for life."

There were birds circling in the sky above them. *No*, she realized. *Not birds. Shrikes. What had Bruin said? Shrikes can smell a battle coming from leagues away.* Pinabel was inside of her now, his hands gripping her hips as he grunted with exertion. *They're getting closer.*

They're-

Rohart's talons raked Pinabel's face as he collided into him, one of them plunging directly into an eye. The man tumbled off her, too stunned to scream, and as he attempted to get to his feet Sharpebeck was on him, and then Rossignol and Geaibleu. She could hardly see the man through their flapping wings and darting heads, but she could see the blood on the shrikes' faces, and when he finally started to scream it was more beautiful than a song.

The man holding her wrists was swearing, yelling for the others to help him, to kill the shrikes, to do something, anything, and then she rocked backwards and kicked him in the face.

They hadn't taken off her boots.

The man released her and she grabbed the knife that Pinabel had used to cut off her clothes. A second later she had lodged it in the man's thigh, and then in his arm, and then straight through his palm as he raised his hand to defend himself. She stabbed him again and again and again.

By the time the man died the other two were on their horses and heading south, across an open meadow. An arrow streaked out of the sky and caught one in the chest. The other suddenly wheeled his mount around and a moment later Hirsent could see why.

Isengrim's steed flew over a low rise, his master leaning forward in the saddle as he urged the beast on. The mercenary's horse was fast, but

Isengrim's was faster. Isengrim's sword flashed in the sun, and then the man tumbled off of his horse in a red spray.

The others were not far behind: Bruin, Tybalt, Tiecelin, several of Reynard's warriors, and even the children, but Hirsent had no time to be grateful.

"Hirsent," Isengrim said as he rode up, and dismounted smoothly. There were tears in his eyes as he embraced her. "*Oh my love, my love. What have they done to you?*"

"*Nothing, my love,*" she lied, and nestled her head against his chest. "*Nothing. The chimera saved me.*"

One of the mercenaries- the one she had wounded in the side- groaned piteously. Isengrim buried the tip of his sword in his breast to quiet him.

"Reynard," he said. "*Is he-*"

"*Help me carry him to the water,*" she said, cutting him off. "*We need to clean his wounds.*"

Isengrim picked up Reynard as one might a child, and followed Hirsent down to the pond.

"*Did you bring my kit?*" she asked as she stripped Reynard's jerkin and doublet off of him.

Isengrim shook his head. "*There was no time.*"

"*Give me your belt,*" she said.

He did not argue.

The others had joined them by this time, but none of them spoke.

"Be starting a fire," Hirsent said. "Bruin, you are having wine?"

"Yer," Bruin said, and pulled a skin from his saddlebag.

"Boil it."

Bruin nodded and followed Tiecelin into the inn.

They'd nearly readied the wine when Reynard came to.

"Are they-" he said, wearily, squinting up at her with his almond colored eyes.

"They are all dead," Isengrim said. The men had made certain of that, and the shrikes were already picking at them.

Reynard tried to get up, but Hirsent stopped him with a touch. Then he saw that Isengrim was sharpening his sword with his whetstone.

She opened her mouth to speak, but nothing came out.

"If it comes to that," he said, and smiled at her, weakly.

"*The shock alone could kill you,*" she said to him. "*You know that, do you not?*"

"I know," he said.

"*I will try to save as much of it as I can.*"

"Thank you."

The wine was boiling.

"*Are you ready?*" she asked.

"Yes."

"*Hold out your arm.*"

Reynard lifted his arm. His hand was nothing more than a blood-colored claw- and little veins of red were spiraling up his wrist.

Hirsent cinched the belt around his arm, just below the elbow. Isengrim raised Right-Hand above his head, two hands on the sword's hilt.

The sword hung in the air. Hirsent felt Reynard's fingers tighten around her arm.

"Do it," he said.

Isengrim brought Right-Hand down.

IX

His hand hurt.

No, Reynard thought, *I do not have a hand,* but all the same it hurt. His ghost-hand hurt.

He was sitting with his back against the old tree. There had been bodies in it when they had come, rotted beyond recognition. Reynard had had them cut down and burned, but the place still had the scent of death about it.

He'd been bedridden for a week, but Hirsent seemed to think that the worst had passed, and had given him leave to walk. There wasn't much to see: an old farmhouse, a cavernous barn, half a league of pasture, and the Jennet all around them.

The shrikes had led them here. Tiecelin said that they had often nested here on their way to deliver messages to the Queen, and they knew the countryside here nearly as well as they did Maleperduys. Every hour one of them would return with news- the Calvarians were besieging Calyx, the remnants of Nobel's army was marching towards Engadlin, and the Black Fleet was coming up the Vinus, while brigands and mercenaries and soldiers were burning and pillaging and raping in every direction.

And the Queen had gone with her King.

The contents of his saddle bag was strewn out before him. His shaving kit, his bird-shaped lighter, his quill, ink, and rolls of parchment, his wine skin, the bag of gems that Tencendur had returned to him, a whetstone, a silver plate, horn spoon, and knife, a tiny bag of salt, and, secure in a leather case, his fiddle.

He opened up the case, instinctually reaching for the fiddle with his ghost-hand, and found himself staring at the bandaged stump that now graced his left arm. He picked the thing up with his right instead.

It was an old thing- it had once belonged to Primaut, the servant of the Watcher he had once trained under, before he repaid the old man's kindness with theft. He ran his fingers over the strings and along the neck, and remembered how he'd made it sing the night he stole the Kasha violin from Lord Chanticleer.

And now he would never play again.

He grasped the fiddle by the neck and smashed it against a nearby rock. The delicate seasoned wood shattered, the strings came free, and finally the neck snapped off in his hand.

At last he threw the thing away.

"I've been waiting for this day for a long time, Reynard," he heard a voice say. "A long time."

It was Tybalt. He had one of his daggers in his hand, and several of his men were with him: Blanc, Sautperdu, and Jacquet, and the twins Gerin and Gerier. They had their armor on.

"I knew it would come," Tybalt went on. "I knew someday you'd finally get knocked down into the shit with the rest of us, and I'd be there to see it. Everyone goes down, in the end. All I had to do was wait, the way I waited for my brother to step into filth up to his knees. You remind me of him, you know? He thought he was invincible, too, but he wasn't."

Tybalt flicked the dagger. It struck the tree just beside Reynard's head, and stuck there.

"No one's invincible."

Reynard was silent.

"What?" Tybalt said, grinning like a cat. "No clever quip? No smile and witty jest?"

Reynard was silent.

"You can keep the dagger," Tybalt said. "I'd once thought to kill you with it, but I think I like this better. At any rate, I'm off. You can crawl back to your woods and your ruin and your whore, but I'm through following you, Reynard, and I'm taking the boys with me."

"Farewell," Reynard said.

"Piss on your farewell," Tybalt said, and spat in his face before turning to leave. The others followed, but none could look Reynard in the eye. They mounted their horses and broke into a canter.

"Tybalt," Reynard called out as they went. The brigand slowed his courser and turned in the saddle, still grinning.

"What is it, Baron?"

"I just wanted to thank you."

"What for?" Tybalt asked.

"For giving me a reason to go on living," Reynard answered.

Tybalt scowled and kicked his heels, and rode off.

Reynard returned his things to his saddle bag, and stood. His ghost-hand hurt, but he didn't mind. It would always remind him of this day.

"Do you want me to go after them?" Isengrim asked when he returned to the farmhouse. The others were scattered about the room, some sitting, others leaning against the polished wooden timber that made up the walls.

"No," he said. "Let them go. I'll not force any man to follow me."

He looked about the little room. There were only thirteen of them now, unless one counted the shrikes. Maugris, Climborin, Veillantif, Gramimond, Tachebrun, Malquiant- all had been slain at the Samara, and with Tybalt and his men gone that left only Isengrim and Hirsent, Tiecelin, Martin and Rukenaw, and Bruin, and Bruin's men: lame Tencendur, Gaignun, Passecerf, Grandoyne, Valdabrun, and Gringolet, who'd taken several wounds in the battle but had somehow refused to fall.

"We're still with you, Reynard" Bruin said. "You're still the best, no matter what Tybalt says."

"No," Reynard said. "Tybalt was right. I failed you. All of you. I tried to beat Nobel at his own game, and men died because of it."

He raised his stump.

"I've paid my own price, but no more. No more lies. From now on, we will be no one but ourselves."

"And who are we?" Tiecelin asked.

"Raiders," Reynard answered. "Raiders and brigands, and murderers. And thieves. From now on, we will do what we do best. From now we will fight our way."

"Then we make for Maleperduys?" Bruin asked.

Reynard squeezed his ghost-hand into a fist and felt a dull ache race up his arm.

"No," Reynard said. "We are going east to break the siege of Calyx."

****

The supply train was right on time- the Calvarians were nothing if not punctual. For the fifth time since they'd set up the ambush, Reynard checked his crossbow. It was still loaded, just as it had been a moment ago.

Three covered wagons made up the bulk of the train, and twenty two men marched in columns alongside them- ten soldiers and their *prafost* on either side. The Calvarians had brought oxen to haul the wagons- they were slower than horses but they were stronger and could more easily handle the unpaved trails of the Kingswood. Each wagon had a white-uniformed drover to help guide the oxen. It had been several days since the last rainfall and the drovers looked like they were sweltering beneath their fur shakos, but their faces were set and they did not complain. Neither did the soldiers, who must have been baking in their mail.

Good, Reynard thought. *It may make them slower.*

The train was traveling along the Vinus, the Calvarian supplies having been unloaded downriver, where the enemy engineers were still attempting to clear the way for the Black Fleet- Nobel had set fire ships loose and had scuttled cogs and barges and caravels until the river was thick with broken wrecks. It was likely the only reason that Calyx had not yet fallen to Drauglir, but every day the Calvarian fleet sunk anchor closer to the capital, and the distance between the ships and the Seventeenth shortened.

Reynard was lying face down beneath a thick leafed Moly tree- they were quite common in this part of the Kingswood- his crossbow balanced on a wooden stock that Isengrim had made for him. He was glad of it- they were outnumbered and needed to bring down as many of the enemy as they could quickly.

He could not see the others, but he knew they were there. The shrikes had given them ample warning of the train's approach, and he'd chosen all of their hiding spots himself.

Between those two rocks is Bruin, he thought, glancing at a pair of moss covered stones. *Tiecelin is sitting in that tree.*

They were close now, not more than ten yards away from where he lay. One of the drovers cracked his whip. The soldiers' mail jingled. A bird cried.

Reynard fired. His bolt went straight through the neck of the nearest *prafost*. One of Tiecelin's arrows struck the next man in line, and then one of Isengrim's struck another. They'd worked out their targets in advance. Only three shots went wild, though one of them struck one of the oxen, and it bellowed in pain.

Seven Calvarians lay dead or dying. *Still outnumbered*, Reynard thought, exchanging his crossbow for Cut-Throat.

"*Defensive formation!*" he heard the other prafost yell, just as a second shower of crossbow bolts flew into the column- he'd armed everyone but himself with a loaded spare. "*Lock shields!*"

There were only eight Calvarian soldiers left standing. Another one of Tiecelin's arrows struck the prafost, and then there were seven.

Reynard almost felt sorry for them as he and his companions burst from cover. The drovers were brave- they had only their whips, but they stood their ground. Bruin flattened one with the flat of his axe and then stove another's head in with the butt. Reynard rushed at the third, dodging as the man sent the end of his bullwhip whistling through the air. The strike might have taken out an eye, but it missed, and then his sword was at the man's throat.

"*Drop it,*" he said. The man was brave, but not stupid. His grip loosened and the whip fell to the ground.

The other Calvarians were already dead. Isengrim and Bruin finished off the dying. The shrikes landed and fed.

"Get these animals moving!" he shouted, though he needn't have. Gaignun, Tencendur, and Gringolet were already urging the huge beasts on. "We've got a lot of ground to cover before nightfall!"

"What about this one?" Bruin said, indicating the drover as he hefted his axe from fist to fist.

"He lives," Reynard said, and looked the man in the eyes.

"*Follow the river,*" Reynard said in the Northern tongue. "*Take as much food and water as you need. Do you understand me?*"

The drover nodded.

"*Good. Tell them what happened here. And that the Fox sends his regards.*"

The man took a pair of canteens and a pack full of hard tack and went. He did not look back.

"They will send out scouts after us," Isengrim said, cleaning his blade.

"Good," Reynard said. He knew just where to lead them to die.

* * * * * * *

Turpin's mother had once told him that the village of Silverbirch was named for the slender white-barked trees that grew thick around the chevalier's manor, but after the Calvarians came he wondered if their village would need a new name.

Bloodwood, men might call it, and their inn would be *The Hanged Man*. There were certainly enough bodies hanging from its rafters now, one out of every ten of them. Man, woman or child, the Calvarians did not care. They'd made them draw lots. Turpin's son and his sister, who'd married Harmel the milkman, had been picked, and when he'd pleaded with the Calvarian's translator to take him in their stead he'd merely told him that there would be no exceptions, and no substitutions.

He would have throttled the translator- a round-faced man who wore a grayish brown uniform and a peaked cap- he would have done it gladly, but he knew one of the Calvarians would kill him before he could finish the man off. Turpin was a big man, and years of working as a servant of the Firebird had made him strong as an ox, but the Calvarians were on horse, and they had steel. One of them had cut Hauteclere, their Lord's bailiff, in two. No one had resisted after that.

"This settlement is suspected of participating in or aiding banditry directed at the Seventeenth regiment," the translator had told them, once they'd been rounded up. "Accordingly, you will surrender to us as much grain, millet, and fruit as our mounts can carry, as well as all of your animals, including your pigs, goats, sheep, poultry, and milk cows. You may keep your hounds."

"Ere," Durendal had said, stupidly, "We'll starve without our animals. Leave us a quarter of em at least. We're no brigands!"

The translator repeated the man's words to the Calvarian captain, a lean man with shock-white hair. The captain said something quiet and then two of the soldiers had dragged Durendal away from the others and beheaded him.

The Captain spoke, and a moment later the translator said, "*Heafodcarl* Farbauti does not tolerate insolence. If you do not do as he asks, he promises you that he will not leave a village behind."

Farbauti spoke again.

"He will leave a graveyard."

They went to work in shifts then, some of them weeping, giving the Calvarians even their hidden stores for fear that they would be discovered and punished for it. At last they'd loaded every horse, and had surrendered up every last animal that could be of use to an army.

Then the Calvarians made them draw lots.

When the sound of hooves had finally faded, Turpin cut his son down and held him to his breast. He'd hoped the boy might be a priest himself one day, when he came of age: he'd already had a bit of his father's strength and had smiled even as a child when he'd put one of his smaller hammers in his hands. Geline, his wife, helped to clean him, and then they had burned him on a pyre, alongside his aunt, and the thirteen others who had drawn the short straws.

The funeral pyres attracted a pair of shrikes. They hung in the sky above, circling for a time, but then they wheeled north and disappeared into the trees.

The fires were dying by the time the strangers came, riding into town from the northern woods. There were only ten of them, nine men and a boy, but the women had screamed at the sound of horses, thinking perhaps that the Calvarians had changed their minds. Turpin kept his wits and rushed to his forge, taking up his largest hammers as the strangers rode towards the center of the town. Some of the other men had the same notion, and fetched pitchforks and axes. Harmel had the old sword that had belonged to his grandfather in his hands.

"Who are you?" Turpin shouted at the strangers as they brought their steeds to a halt. They were a grim-looking group, and heavily armored. Even the boy wore a mail coat.

"My name is Reynard," said one of them- a man with only one hand. "The Calvarians call me The Fox, but I mean you no harm."

"Reynard," Bruyer the miller's son said. "I know that name."

"What do you want?" Turpin shouted, not lowering his hammer. *Words are one thing, actions another.*

"I only wish to make you an offer," the man said.

"Speak then," Turpin said.

"We have food," the man said. "Enough to feed all of you, and safe quarters that the Calvarians will never find. Join us, and all I will ask in return is that you help us kill the Calvarians."

A murmur went up amongst the villagers.

"You're the bandits the Calvarians were looking for," Turpin said. "Aren't you?"

"Yes," the one-handed man replied.

"It's because of you the Calvarians came!" shrieked Anna, whose daughter had been run down by one of the Northerners' steeds. "You're the reason my Patrice is dead!"

"No," one of the others said, a huge man in a black suit of plate whose face was concealed behind a helmet shaped like a warg's head. "The Calvarians would have stolen your crops and animals and killed your daughters with or without us. If Calyx falls they will return in force and kill all of you and perhaps even build their own village over the ruins of yours."

"He's telling the truth," the armored boy said. "I used to live in the north until the Calvarians came to my village. They killed everyone except the animals. Only Rukenaw and me escaped."

"So," the man called Reynard said. "You have your choice. Stay and die, or come with me and live."

"We won't live long if we fight the Calvarians," Turpin shot back. "We're no warriors."

"Isengrim," Reynard said, turning to the giant in black. "Show them your bow."

The man dismounted and removed his helm. Turpin blanched- the man was himself a Calvarian. He untied a length of red-laquered wood from the side of his horse, and held it forth.

"This is a Calvarian longbow," the man called Isengrim said, stringing the thing. "It is crafted from a single piece of wood, and takes ten hours to properly carve. The wood comes from a tree that grows only in a forest called the Jarnvidr, along the eastern coast of the island of Thule."

Isengrim nocked an arrow.

"It takes a Calvarian archer at least five years to build up the strength to properly draw this bow, and another five to master it. They must be trained from the time they are seven years old, and practice every day, before they are considered fit for military duty."

Isengrim drew and raised the bow. Some of the villagers stepped back instinctively. He loosed, and sent the arrow screaming into the sign of the inn, a young chick newly risen from its egg. The sign spun completely around from the force of the impact.

Isengrim unstrung his bow and returned it to his saddle.

"Bruin," Reynard said. "Give Martin your crossbow."

A barrel of a man pulled a crossbow from his back and offered it to the boy.

"My Lord?" Martin said, puzzled.

"Take it," Reynard said.

The boy took the weapon.

"The crossbow is essentially a bow, mounted on a stick," Reynard said, "but a single quarrel can pierce through all but the thickest armor. Martin, have you ever fired a crossbow before?"

"No," the boy said.

"No?" Reynard said. "Very well, try and hit the sign."

The boy called Martin swallowed, nervous, but raised the weapon, squinting down the sight as he leveled it with the sign of The Hatchling. He fired.

The bolt went too high, and buried itself in the wooden siding of the inn.

"Try again," Reynard said.

Martin reloaded, clumsily, wound the weapon, aimed and fired. And missed.

"Again."

The boy reloaded, aimed, fired.

The third bolt struck the sign. And the fourth. And the fifth. The boy was reloading faster too.

"Thank you Martin," Reynard said at last and the boy grinned. "It takes the Calvarians ten years to train an archer. I can train a hundred crossbowmen in an afternoon. Give me a month, and we'll be an army. Give me a year and I'll give you the heads of every Northman that was here today. Fight for me, and I promise you, you will have your vengeance. Now what will it be? Will you fight, or will you die?"

"I'll fight," Turpin said, and lowered his hammer.

* * * * * * *

"*Do you think any of it is true?*" Gelert Secondson asked Cafall as they walked towards the mess tent. "*What they say about the Fox?*"

"*Honestly?*" Cafall Firstson replied. "*I do not believe the man exists.*"

"*But three long patrols missing?*" the younger man went on, "*It cannot be the work of mere brigands. I even hear that Drauglir's reassigned the engineers from the Tenth to hack a clearer road through the forest, and that the guard on every supply train has been tripled.*"

Cafall considered the man's words as they received their midday ration, a sort of chowder that even Gelert did not complain about. Gelert had been trained as a cook before the attack on Dis had led him to apply for reassignment to the military, and he loved to talk about food. When they'd first caught sight of the Southern continent all the man could do was began to fill the men's heads with visions of grilled pilchards and herring, until Prafost Hrungnir had heard enough of his prattle and threatened to put him on latrine duty for a month.

Cafall remembered that day well, though it was now two years past: the jagged coast of limestone cliffs and outcroppings sprinkled by odd-looking trees and scrubland. The shallows were so incredibly vibrant, in places a shade of brilliant turquoise that he could not help but find beautiful, though he had kept his thoughts to himself. His company had been sharing a boat with one of the blood-guards assigned to their regiment, and it is generally considered unwise for a Calvarian to speak too fondly of foreign things when a blood-guard is listening.

Only a few hours later he had fought in his first battle, a sea engagement whose purpose was to break the blockade of Svartgard, which the Southerners call Larsa. His company had the honor of being assigned to the Naglfar, Latteowa Hrym's flagship, and he had watched with his own eyes when Hrym had chopped off the head of the Southern admiral. He'd killed his first man that day, a queer-looking brute who had tried to strike him down with an axe. He had slain a dozen more at the battle of the river, and several score more during the sack of the vine-city, but many of those had gone unrecorded by the blood-guard. Cafall did not blame them, either. Few of the Southerners had really been warriors.

"*They say that many of the black dogs scattered after the river,*" Cafall said at last, putting down his empty bowl and reaching for his waterskin. "*It is to be expected that some of them might still lurk in the woods and hills . . . but all this the work of one man? No. I do not believe it.*"

"*Still,*" Gelert said, "*Three long patrols. It makes one wonder.*"

"*I heard some of the scouts talking about the Fox,*" a voice said. It belonged to Triath Fourthson, who had been sitting nearby.

"*I do not doubt that you have,*" Cafall said, frowning. Triath was a notorious eavesdropper, and worse still a gossip.

"*What did you hear?*" Gelert asked.

Cafall sighed.

"*They say the Southerner villages for leagues around are all empty,*" Triath said, leaning close. "*And the woods are full of abandoned campsites. They say there must be hundreds of them, maybe even thousands, hiding somewhere in the woods, but the scouts say they never find anything but fire pits and cast-off animal bones and night soil- except for the ones that disappear.*"

"*I heard that the drover told Heafodcarl Byleist that the Fox has only one hand,*" Gelert said, nodding. "*And that he had a giant and a warg that fought at his side- or was it a giant warg? He said that he could speak with shrikes. Do you think any of that was true?*"

"*I already told you what I think,*" Cafall said, getting up. "*And if that drover said half of what you just burbled, he should have been whipped out of camp. Now, be quiet, the both of you. Heartseeker is coming.*"

Heartseeker was what the men of the Seventeenth called Regin No-Father, the blood-guard that had been attached to their encampment. After the battle at the river, Latteowa Drauglir had split the Seventeenth into three equal hosts in order to properly besiege the Southerners' capital. There were always three blood-guards assigned to every regiment, and each host had been assigned one of them. Regin No-Father was theirs.

Men quieted as Heartseeker approached. He was not as young as Otr No-Father, who'd been assigned to the men under Heafodcarl Andvari, but he was still young for a blood-guard, and ill-tempered. Cafall thought that was because he was dark of hair- it being commonly thought that a Calvarian with dusky locks must have some Southern blood in his veins. Some of the older veterans claimed that Regin had killed a fellow blood-guard who had suggested such in a duel, and that that was how he had gotten his nickname, but Cafall doubted such a man would be allowed to serve Calvaria.

Still, the ways of the blood-guard were a mystery to all but the Judges- and it was whispered that only one out of every ten child in training survived to become a true member of the order. Perhaps the veterans had it right.

Triath had his own theory about Heartseeker's nickname: namely, that despite his dark hair, many women found him very attractive. Perhaps there was something to that too- Cafall had seen the way that Fisicien first class Jarnsaxa had looked at the man when she had seen to a minor wound he'd suffered during the siege of the vine-city, and all the men said that she'd been carved out of a block of ice that the Twentieth had fished out of the waters east of Nastrond.

Cafall felt a lump form in his throat as Heartseeker came to a halt in front of him.

His hair might have been dark, but Heartseeker's eyes were piercingly blue. He regarded his companions, lingering for a moment on Triath, and for a moment Cafall wondered if the gossip had finally said too much, but then the man looked him in the eye. It was like looking into the eyes of a hawk. Cafall shuddered inside, but kept his gaze level.

"*You are Cafall of the Second Company of Foot?*" the blood-guard asked.

"*I am, sir.*"

"*I have been reviewing your recent battle record, Cafall of the Second Company of Foot,*" Heartseeker said, "*And it pleases me to inform you that your recent actions on the field have qualified you to receive an additional dispensation regarding any future children you might have.*"

In truth, Heartseeker did not look at all pleased, but Cafall bowed low and said, "*Sir, you honor me, sir.*"

"*That brings your current tally up to three, Cafall of the Second Company of Foot,*" the blood-guard went on. "*Do you wish to put in a request for a suitable mate?*"

"*Not at this time, sir,*" Cafall replied, thinking of Skadi.

"*Then return to your duties,*" Heartseeker said, and strode away before Cafall had even begun to bow.

"*Three,*" Gelert said, whistling. "*And to think, I haven't even gotten my one.*"

"*We all get one,*" Triath pointed out.

"*I mean my first dispensation,*" Gelert said. "*Congratulations, Cafall!*"

"*Congratulations, Cafall,*" Triath repeated good-naturedly. He had received two dispensations himself, Cafall knew. He might be a gossip, but he was a good warrior as well.

Some of the other men that were supping with them congratulated him as well, even stony-faced Prafost Hrungir, though he grunted the words between spoonfuls of chowder.

"*Thank you,*" was all that Cafall said. He wanted to leap into the air and shout his joy to the heavens, but he didn't want to be put on night watch duty either, so he returned his mess bowl and girded himself for the afternoon's work.

* * * * * *

Cafall's company was one of the thirty or so that had been assigned to encircle the western approach to the city, their orders being to breach the wall with artillery fire and take the west bank by force. Then they would turn their engines on the strongpoint that dominated the river, and turn it into rubble.

Those had been Drauglir's orders, at any rate, but the raids on their supply lines had drawn a major flaw in the Latteowa's plan into sharp relief: namely, they could not reduce the walls without ammunition.

Personally, Cafall found the new war machines incredibly distasteful- they were not, after all, the weapons of a true warrior. They were manned by men and women of the engineers, and had been guided into battle by the servants. To think that men who wore the white and tan were being admitted to the war college rankled. Triath Fourthson even swore that a new class of warrior was being created by the Judges to classify these strange pseudo-soldiers.

If that is the case, Cafall thought to himself, shifting his weight, *they will surely be the lowest of warriors. A true warrior knows the face of the enemy he slays.*

Before the raids they'd done considerable damage to the city's walls, as they had at the vine-city, though every night the Southern defenders attempted to repair their shattered battlements. Now the Southerners were making use of the lull to erect wooden hoardings over the ruins of their walls.

Perhaps they have run out of stone, Cafall thought, chuckling to himself as the Southerners scattered under arrow fire. The archers sent a couple more shafts towards the wall, and a few of the braver Southerners shot back- but the weak Southern bows could not hope to match the range of

Calvarian Jarnwood and their arrows fell harmlessly short of their earthworks.

Truth be told, there was little for Cafall to do save lean on his javelin and watch the archers have their bit of fun. The Second Foot had been stationed almost directly in the middle of the siege line, but until the walls were down their only duty comprised of standing watch in shifts with the First and Third Foot companies. Today, theirs was the afternoon watch. He envied the men of the First, hard at training in the camp. The prafosts might be drilling them so hard that by the evening watch their legs would be weak and their arms could barely lift a spoon to their mouth, but at least they were moving.

Cafall stifled a yawn and thought of Skadi.

He had met her at Svartgard. They had been given a few days leave after their victory at sea while Drauglir conferred with Skoll, the Latteowa of the Fourteenth, and Cafall had used the days to inspect the murals of the city's still unfinished Hall-of-Knowledge. Most of his fellow soldiers enjoyed nothing more than to dine and watch the fights of the arena, but Cafall preferred art.

He had been walking through a partially-finished wing of the Hall when he saw her. She was a painter, a woman of the tan, but her hair was golden and her jaw strong. She had asked him if he approved of her work and he'd told her yes, and she had smiled. Her face lit up when she smiled, and he knew then as he knew now that he was in love with her. He had asked her if she wanted to walk with him by the water, when she was not on duty, and she had said that it was dangerous to do so, that Latteowa Skoll himself had warned the civilians that there were still Southern rebels in the city who would stop at nothing to rape and kill a Northern woman. Cafall had told her not to worry, that he would be with her, and if any Southerner dared lay a hand on her he would make a corpse of the brute with his sword, and asked her again if she would like to join him.

She had smiled again, and said yes.

She had worn her winter coat and hat, though the night was merely cool. She told him where she had been born, and how frightened she had been when she had been selected for duty in the South. She said that she had a lover once, when she had been studying at the art college, but the blood-guard had denied their application. The man had been deemed inferior. Cafall had told her that he had not yet had a lover and she had touched his arm and told him that his words surprised her.

They met again the next night and the night after that, and then his leave was over and they had marched south to the vine-city.

When the campaign was over Cafall would apply for transfer to the Fourteenth. They would be together then, and they would walk by the water, and she would smile. The blood-guard might refuse an application for their coupling, but it was a chance he had to take.

He was still thinking of Skadi when the messenger arrived. Senior Heafodcarl Byleist was in the middle of inspecting their line so Cafall heard the message along with the other men of the Second Foot.

"*The Fox has been sighted,*" the messenger had said, not bothering to dismount. "*He and a hundred raiders attempted to assault Heafodcarl Andvari's position but were repulsed. Latteowa Drauglir orders you to dispatch a third of your men to aid in the pursuit.*"

"*We have him,*" Byleist growled as the messenger rode off, and called for the assembly.

Within minutes the cavalry were prepared to ride, along with half of the scouts and six companies of foot. Cafall ached to be with them, but the Third had been roused for the duty, and so he could only watch as they marched at the quick step out of camp, heading north. Byleist himself was leading them, mounted on a black charger, the sun glinting off of his steel armor as he rode.

Cafall sighed, and turned back to watch their archers fire another volley at the walls.

They were relieved at dusk by the First, whose training had been set aside so that they might catch some rest. Cafall's legs were sore and he was hungry, and though the evening ration was merely broth with a bit of poultry in it, it tasted as good to him as food had ever tasted. Gelert spent the meal yammering on and on about the Fox, wondering if their Heafodcarl would bring back the man's head, or the warg that was said to ride with him, but Triath was mercifully supping with the scouts, probably hoping to overhear another scrap or two of news. Cafall drank down his broth, and nearly fell into his tent as he lay down on his pallet to sleep.

It was late in the night when he awoke, his eyes popping open at the sounds of the night watch yelling out that the scouts were returning. He yawned and opened his tent flap. The other men were still sleeping it seemed, and their company's campfire was nothing more than a pile of glowing embers.

He had to make water, so he strapped on his sword and made for the latrine. It was on the northern side of the camp, where the engineers had diverted part of the river to create a flowing channel, so by the time Cafall had finished with his business he was far from the gate, but he could still hear the scouts' steeds snorting and whickering as they rode into camp.

Cafall was walking back to his company's tents when he noticed that the fires around the western gate had gone out. He had taken a few steps when another set of torches along the wall seemed to gutter and die.

The scouts have returned. The words echoed in his head as he drew his sword and quickened his pace. Not the heavy cavalry or the foot. Only the scouts. Three long patrols, Gelert had said, again and again. Three long patrols, a hundred men.

A hundred men missing.

A hundred men returning.

Another set of torches flickered and died. He could see the figures now, creeping over the walls. There were hundreds of them.

"*To arms!*" Cafall yelled, breaking into a run. "*To arms! We are breached! To arms!*"

Then one of the powder stores blew.

Cafall was thrown off of his feet by the force of the blast. When he got to his feet the camp was full of fire and smoke and death. Sleeping men were stumbling from their tents, unarmored, rushing to the defenses, but it was too late. They were breached. A second blast shot through the night and Cafall could see one of the siege engines go up as well, its crew sailing up into the night sky like dolls before coming down again.

"*Form shields!*" a prafost was shouting, but Cafall had no shield. A hail of bolts tore into the knot of men that were around him, and a dozen of them fell.

He pressed on, leaving the others behind. He needed to get back to his company, he needed his armor, he needed–

A dark-skinned man in a scout's uniform nearly took his head off with a sword. He parried the man's next attack and stabbed him in the gut, his blade punching through the Southerner's own mail. The man died against him, but before he could recover a second foe drove an axe head into his shoulder. He was raising it for another strike when he suddenly crumpled to the ground, and a black shape stepped out of the night.

"*Can you fight?*" Heartseeker said, and Cafall nodded. He couldn't feel his left arm, but he still had his right.

"*Good,*" the blood-guard said and broke into a run.

He followed.

Everywhere they went they came upon scenes of slaughter. Everywhere the men of the Seventeenth lay dead, slashed open or riddled with crossbow bolts. In one camp it was obvious that nearly the entire company had been slain as they had slept.

It was the Second Foot he realized, and wondered if Gelert had had a chance to reach for his sword before his throat had been cut.

"*Keep moving,*" Heartseeker said.

They found corpses charred by fire, and men whose limbs had been torn from their bodies. They found a headless horse lying beside a dead female Southerner armed with a Calvarian blade. Everywhere they found death.

Then they found the enemy.

There were over a dozen of them, all armed with crossbows. Heartseeker ran straight at them, taking several quarrels to the chest for his efforts. Still, he did not fall, and he cut down three of them with his sword before a huge bear of a man with an axe split him open.

Cafall raised his sword, but his arm shook. He had lost more blood than he had thought.

The man with the axe said something in the Southerners' odd tongue, and then the others advanced on him with their own swords drawn.

Skadi, he thought as one of them aimed a swing at his head, and then the world was black.

* * * * * * *

"Skadi," Cafall said, awakening suddenly.

For a moment he thought that he had been fortunate, and that the Southerners had left him for dead, for a Calvarian woman in white was leaning over him, applying a poultice to his wounded shoulder.

Then he saw that her uniform was patched and faded, and that she wore no insignia on her collar. It looked as though it had been torn off.

They were somewhere in the woods. Where he could not say. For all he knew, these were not even the woods that grew north of the Southern capital. There were several others of the Seventeenth here as well, most of them wore the tan and white. All of them were bound and guarded.

And for every one of them, there were ten of the enemy.

"*You are a prisoner?*" he asked the woman in white, but she did not answer. She finished tying a bandage to hold the poultice in place and went to see to another wounded man.

Then the Fox came.

He was a small man, and as the drover had said he had only one hand. His coat was dusky red, his cloak gray as slate. The warg was at his side, a tall man in black armor. The woman in white went to him and whispered something low.

"*Greetings,*" the Fox said. He spoke their language perfectly. "*I believe you know who I am.*"

"*We do,*" another man said, one of the prafosts from the Thirteenth Foot, Cafall thought. "*You are the Black Dog of the woods.*"

"*I prefer the name Fox,*" the man said.

"*I do not care what you prefer,*" the prafost shot back. "*And I do not fear death. So do what you will to us, we will not beg for mercy!*"

"*Calvaria!*" one of the other soldiers shouted, and Cafall called out the cry as well, but the trees seemed to swallow up their shouts and the Fox merely smiled at them.

"*You are a long way from Calvaria,*" the man said. "*And when you return to Latteowa Drauglir I would appreciate it if you would explain to him that these woods belong to the Fox.*"

"*You are going to release us?*" Cafall said.

"*I am,*" Fox said. "*But, first, we are going to draw lots.*"

The Fox raised his right hand. There were straws in his fist.

"*Lots,*" a voice cawed from above. Cafall had not noticed before, but there were shrikes in the trees.

"*Lots,*" another one of the chimera repeated. "*Lots lots lots.*"

X

Of the few survivors of the raid, over half had asked permission to fall on their swords. Drauglir had refused them all.

He needed soldiers, not corpses.

Drauglir rubbed his eyes and scanned the final tally laid out before him. Eleven companies of foot had been demolished, along with a third of their artillery and two hundred scouts- three hundred if one counted the ones that the Southerners had taken in the forest. Add to that the men they had lost attempting to guard the supply caravans and it totaled over one thousand five hundred soldiers dead. That was more than twice the numbers that had fallen smashing the Southerner's petty King on the river.

They were losses he could not easily afford.

"*Prafost*," he said, setting the report aside. "*Send to the quartermaster for a pitcher of lemon water, honey too, if they have it.*"

"Yes, sir," the petty officer said, signaling to one of his soldiers to carry out the request. The soldier did not need to go far- the kitchens were directly attached to the hall that Latteowa Drauglir was currently using for his headquarters.

Lacking the numbers required to maintain the siege of the enemy capital, he had been forced to pull the Seventeenth back to the settlement the Southerners called Barca. The vine-city his own soldiers had named it, for the vineyards that had surrounded it before the Calvarians had put them to the torch. The bulk of his troops he had quartered in the walled town, and set the engineers to repairing the walls. The veterans were quartered with him, in the castle that overlooked the harbor.

He would have far preferred the simple comforts of his tent to this joke of a fortress, but there was precious little room within the city walls as it was, and his own officers had insisted that he make the castle his seat.

An ugly place, he'd thought, when he'd first set eyes on the place, *though practical enough*. It had been built atop a limestone outcrop that jutted out into the river, but the Southerners had bothered to build it out of quarried sandstone. The only room of any note was the great hall, which had been hung with some Southern lord's banner: a ridiculous thing with a trio of rabbits chasing each other in a circle. *An appropriate emblem for a coward*, Drauglir thought when his veterans had done as he had commanded and torn it down to be burned. Mosca, his Southern scribe, had informed him that the coward in question had fled long before they had even begun the siege, and had left his second behind to die in his stead.

A man like that was not a worthy foe.

He preferred enemies like the Southern chieftain that called himself 'King' Nobel. Reports said that he rode into battle at the head of his soldiers, and that he had crushed the chiefs of the far South before bending them to his will. He had most certainly defeated Latteowa Gondul and slain all the men and women of the Fourth Regiment.

A worthy foe, he'd thought, *but no Drauglir Seventhson.*

'King' Nobel had not disappointed, either. The battle at the river had been beautiful to watch from his position at the rear. It made him long for his younger days, when he would have been the one to lead the cavalry through the gap in the enemy lines, but a man must not be greedy.

The younger men were still hungry for battle, and desperate for mates and children.

Drauglir was over forty summers old and already had seven mates himself, and fifteen sons and daughters. Only the eighth had been an accident, a child of love with one of his former Heafodcarls, a fierce woman named Synmara, who had been reassigned to train soldiers at the war-college after a Vanir warrior had taken one of her eyes from her. They had chosen to give the boy to the blood-guard, and though it was forbidden for a blood-guard to know his parents, Drauglir knew that exceptions were sometimes made, especially when the parent was a senior Judge.

When I am a Judge, he had told Synmara after they had handed the newborn over to the blood-guards, *we will know our son.*

If I am ever a Judge, he thought, staring down at the next report. He had been outmaneuvered, humiliated, and forced to retreat, giving the 'King' of the South time to marshal new forces while he licked his wounds. And now, another scouting party had gone missing, this one not a league or two from Barca. He did not hold out much hope that they were still alive. He took up ink and quill and began to scratch out new orders to

Heafodcarl Farbauti, who had the command of the scouts. *No more long patrols*, Drauglir thought as he scribbled. *The scouts will man the walls and fire at any Southerner who comes within range.*

It might make them blind, but he felt blind already. No matter how many soldiers he sent out looking for the enemy, the Southerners always managed to evade or ambush them. *And no wonder*, he mused, thinking of what one of the survivors had told him of 'The Fox.' *The Southerners' scouts have wings.*

The Fox. To say that the man intrigued him would have been a gross understatement. Fafnir and Otr No-Father were reporting more and more talk of The Fox amongst the soldiers every day. Some of them were even whispering that he was a demon, Skindancer or the Ruiner reborn, but Drauglir knew that he was just a man. *But who was he?* No great lord, Mosca had said, and yet there was something nagging at Drauglir. Before the Seventeenth had left Svartgard, he vaguely remembered Latteowa Skoll grumbling about raiding parties gone missing. It had not seemed very important at the time, some losses in war were, after all, inevitable. But now . . .

The soldier returned with his lemon water. He poured himself a cup, sipped at it, and was pleased to taste the sweet bite of honey in it. *We are, at least, well provisioned.* The fleet brought in fresh supplies every day down from Svartgard, where engineers were planting crops that would bloom before the autumn came.

The next report cheered him considerably. The Second and Ninth Regiments had landed at Svartgard and would soon be moving south. Drauglir had sent for reinforcements over a month ago, in the wake of the news of the Fourth's destruction, and he had originally hoped that the Ninth might press the attack further upriver while the Second bolstered his own ranks. Now he planned to use their combined strength to destroy The Fox, though the how of it had not yet come to him.

At any rate, he looked forward to seeing Latteowa Thrivaldi again- they had fought together during his campaign to put down the rebellion of the Hesperides, and the man was an excellent sparring partner. Latteowa Thrym, the young commander of the Second, he had never met, but he had heard promising things about him from Synmara- she had even teased that she might take the man for a lover.

Any man good enough for my Synmara must be a man of worth, he thought, thinking briefly of how the patch over her left eye always made it seem as if she were winking at him.

There was only one last report that required his immediate attention. The rest were of little import- Heafodcarl Andvari, whom he had promoted to be his second, could easily handle them. He slipped the minor reports into a leather case and signaled for the prafost to have them taken away.

"*Fetch me my Southern dog,*" he said. "*And bring me the curs that Heafodcarl Byleist has caught as well. I would speak with them myself.*"

The prafost bowed and sent men to carry out Drauglir's commands.

"*Oh, what I might give up for my tent,*" he said, stretching his arms. "*It is nearly midday and it is as nearly as dark as a cavern in here. These Southerners know nothing of how to build, eh, Golden Arm?*"

Fafnir No-Father nodded curtly. The Golden Arm did not speak very often, but he did not seem to mind being spoken to, and Drauglir had long found that comforting. He had been with the Seventeenth even longer than Drauglir, and had outlived five blood-guards since then. His white hair had receded to form a sharp peak, but he was still as fit as a man half his age. Most of his men thought his nickname came from the gilt of his sword, but Drauglir knew the truth of it- the Golden Arm had likely been an artisan's unwanted son, for he loved to make things of beauty with his hands. After their first campaign together he had given Drauglir a skinning knife that would have been fit for any Southern King. After their second, a soapstone campraeden set that a Judge might have owned.

What are you making for me this time, Golden Arm? he always asked the man, usually midway through a campaign, but Fafnir No-Father never answered.

Drauglir was polishing off his lemon water when Mosca arrived. The cierran-notere was a stout man, round faced and round eyed, but he was skilled and highly efficient.

More importantly, he was obedient.

The man bowed deeply and awaited instructions.

"*I will shortly be interviewing a group of Southerners,*" Drauglir said. "*You will translate their words for me, and mine for them.*"

"*I will do as you command, master,*" the man said, bowing again. "*May you slay me if I do less.*"

Mosca took a place beside Drauglir, and kept his eyes down as they waited for Heafodcarl Byleist's prisoners to arrive.

They did not have to wait long.

When the last of the filth-ridden men had been herded into the room, and had been made to kneel, Drauglir cleared his throat and said, "*Ask them who they are.*"

"*Yes, Master,*" Mosca said, and then spoke in the low Southern tongue, his words so succinct that he almost managed to make it sound pretty.

The Southerners' response was nowhere near as eloquent-sounding. Several of them were speaking at once, and though Drauglir could hear the fear in their voices, he could not make out a word of it.

They all speak so fast, Drauglir thought to himself, frowning. *It amazes me that they can even understand each other.*

"*They call themselves goat-men, Master,*" Mosca said at last. "*I believe they refer to the emblem of one of the states of the far South. They claim to be hired swords.*"

"*Are they?*" Drauglir asked.

"*They are lying, Master,*" Mosca said. "*They are more likely deserters.*"

"*I see,*" Drauglir said. "*And their crimes?*"

Mosca spoke again, and the Southerners jabbered back.

"*They claim that they only wish to return to their homeland, Master, and wish nothing but peace with Calvaria. They claim that they found the supply wagon deserted, yet still well provisioned. These, too, are lies.*"

Drauglir refilled his cup.

"*Tell them that I offer them a single chance to show their friendship,*" Drauglir said. "*Tell them I will pardon their theft, and release them with clean clothes and provisions, and a letter that will ensure safe passage to the South, provided that they tell me all they know about the man called The Fox.*"

Mosca translated Drauglir's words.

The room was silent for a moment, save for the sound of the prisoners' anxious breathing. Then one of the men raised his head slightly, and words began to pour from him. When he was done a second man spoke, and then a third, until they had all burbled something.

"*Master,*" Mosca said, "*they say that The Fox is the lord of the forest far west of Svartgard, called Maleperduys, and that his true name is Reynard.*"

"*Reynard the Fox*," Drauglir said, his lips curling into a tight smile. *So the man has a name after all.* "What else?"

"*They say,*" Mosca paused. "*They say that he struck down the lord of Calvaria, and that he crowned the Southern 'King.' They say he has died twice, once on a gallows and once on the battlefield, but that he cannot be slain. They say he charmed a sea serpent with his voice. They say-*"

"*That he rides wargs and can pass through walls and pisses demon-fire,*" Drauglir said, cutting the scribe off. "I might as well have my own soldiers questioned. These men are useless to me. Prafost, take them out into the courtyard and execute them at once."

"Yes, sir," the prafost said, and at his command the men were hauled from the room. When they realized they were not going to be released a few of them began to weep.

"*You are dismissed,*" Drauglir said to Mosca as he got to his feet. "Golden Arm, shall we spar?"

Fafnir No-Father nodded.

* * * * * * *

The next day Drauglir's evening meal was interrupted by news that Latteowas Thrivaldi and Thrym had arrived by ship, and were disembarking at the postern gate. He put down his fork and carving knife and made to greet them.

He met them in the outer ward, the Golden Arm standing by his side and a company of his veterans standing at attention. They had ridden their horses up the causeway that led down to the river gate, Thrivaldi on a stout gelding and Thrym on a sleek mare, but as they entered the yard they dismounted, and bowed, Thrym first, as he was the junior of both of them. They had brought their own blood-guards with them as well, but if Fafnir No-Father knew either of the cold-eyed men he did not show it.

"*It is good to see you again, Latteowa Thrivaldi,*" Drauglir said, once he had bowed. "*And it is a pleasure to meet you as well, Latteowa Thrym.*"

"*You honor me, sir,*" the younger man said. He had fiery red hair and was as handsome as Synmara had described him, though half of his face was marked with a jagged white scar. "*I have long wished to meet the great Latteowa Drauglir.*"

"I trust Thrivaldi has been filling your head with exaggerated reports of our exploits during the Hesperides campaign?"

"Since we made port at Svartgard," Thrivaldi said, and smiled, mostly around his eyes. He was more than a few years younger than Drauglir, but long years serving under the Southern sun had reddened his skin and given him an almost permanent scowl.

"How long has it been since I saw you last?" Drauglir asked. "Six years?"

"Seven," Thrivaldi answered. "You have not missed much. The Vanir are still as insolent as ever. There will be war with them again, I have no doubt."

"Have either of you supped?" Drauglir asked. "The game of this land does not compare to that of Calvaria, but the cooks have prepared a roast haunch of venison that is passable."

"That sounds most agreeable," Thrivaldi said. Thrym merely nodded.

The boy is frightened of me, Drauglir mused. *He cannot have long been a Latteowa.*

"Tell me, Latteowa Thrym," he said as they walked around the inner curtain. "How did you come by your command? The last I had heard, the Second's Latteowa was Volund Thirdson."

"I served under Volund for ten years. He was a good commander," the younger man said.

"What became of him?" Drauglir asked.

"The Second had been stationed in a fortress that guarded a vital pass through the Riphean Mountains," Thrym answered. "There were reports that chimera were massing in the forests. Latteowa Volund had just sent out several long patrols to verify when they fell on us. There were thousands upon thousands of them. We lost nearly half of our officers that first night, and nearly as many the next. On the third, their chieftain slew Volund Thirdson. I was the only senior officer left, so the command fell to me. We fought all the following day and night, but in the end the horde finally broke."

"And was the chimera chieftain slain?" Drauglir asked as they passed underneath the murder holes and moved into the inner ward.

"No, he fled before we could kill him, though I have this scar to remember him by."

"He was a coward then," Drauglir said.

"What else do you expect from a mongrel?" Thrivaldi said. "What did this one call himself?"

"'The Raveler,'" Thrym answered. "The reports said that he spoke only in riddles."

"*That must have made for confusing battle orders,*" Thrivaldi said, chuckling. "*They are all so proud of the names they give themselves, are they not? What was it that last Vanir chief called himself? That one who rode a boar into battle, remember him?*"

"*Ah,*" Drauglir breathed. "'*The Dawn Sword.*'"

"'*The Dawn Sword,' yes that was it. He should have named himself the 'Brittle Blade' instead. It would have been more fitting. Ah well, I imagine we will have to contend with this 'Raveler' someday . . . but first we have this Southern rebel to deal with, this man who calls himself 'King.' What is it they call him? The Fox?*"

"*The Fox is not their king,*" Drauglir said, "*Though perhaps he should be. He is a far more dangerous foe than 'King' Nobel.*"

"*But certainly no match for the mighty Drauglir,*" Thrivaldi said. They had reached the main hall, where the evening ration was being served. A hundred men rose from their seats to stand at attention as they entered.

"*At ease,*" Drauglir said, and led the others to the head table. Golden Arm and the other blood-guards took up positions around the edges of the room. A blood-guard eats only with others of his order.

Drauglir took his seat and began to carve the venison.

"*Forgive me for asking, Latteowa Drauglir,*" Thrym said once they had all been served. "*But how can a mere bandit be more dangerous than the Southerners' chieftain?*"

"*The Fox is no ordinary bandit,*" Drauglir said, pouring himself a fresh cup of water. "*I had thought that there was something familiar about his name, and now I suspect that I am right: if our intelligence is to be believed, he has been raiding our supply lines for the past two years. Now, with only a token force, he has managed to break my siege of the Southerners' capital, and bottle up the Seventeenth in this dunghill of a city.*"

"*We have heard of such, back in Svartgard,*" Thrivaldi said, wiping his mouth with a cloth napkin, "*but the reports have been confusing to say the least- the man sounds half-chimera with all this talk of wargs and shrikes.*"

"*The warg is merely a man in a mask,*" Drauglir said. "*But the shrikes at least are real. I have not confirmed it, but I believe he may be using them as scouts. I have ordered our archers to shoot down any bird larger than a raven.*"

"*This cranberry sauce is delicious,*" Thrivaldi said, spearing another bite of the roast with his fork. "*I should have my cooks speak with yours.*"

"*Surely, though,*" Thrym said, "*With our greater numbers, this 'Fox' will be easily dealt with.*"

Drauglir shook his head. "*He refuses to engage in open battle. A handful of his men led a third of my army on a chase that covered leagues, while his main force was positioning itself to attack the weakest of our strong points.*"

"Perhaps we might play the same game," Thrivaldi said. "*Tempt him with a poorly-defended supply caravan, say, and hide our own troops in the woods.*"

"There is too much ground to cover," Drauglir said. "*And besides, I doubt that this one will fall for so simple a ruse.*"

"*You say he has only a token force, and will not face us openly,*" Thrym said then. "*What if we split our forces equally and surrounded him? If he engages any one of us, the other two will maneuver to cut off any hope of retreat.*"

Drauglir smiled.

"*Heafodcarl Synmara told me you were a good student of battle, Latteowa Thrym. As it happens, I was thinking of doing the same thing.*"

Drauglir nearly laughed out loud when Thrym blushed.

"*However, there is a problem: it is impossible to predict where he and his men will be. The scouts all report the same thing. The Fox keeps no permanent camp. Until I know where he is, I dare not move.*"

"Between the Ninth and the Second, we have nearly two thousand scouts, and several hundred tracking dogs," Thrivaldi said. "*If they ride in force they should be able to sniff out The Fox.*"

"For now," Drauglir said, nodding. "*That is our best, and only option.*"

* * * * * * *

Though the night had been cool, Drauglir woke drenched in sweat. He knew who The Fox was.

"*Prafost!*" he shouted to the man standing guard at his door. "*Wake Latteowas Thrivaldi and Thrym, and all of the senior Heafodcarls. I will meet them in my office.*"

"*Yes sir!*" the man said, saluting, and then he was barking out commands to his soldiers.

Drauglir dressed hurriedly, and made his way down a narrow stairwell to the room beneath his. It might have been a bedroom for some Southern lord once, but Drauglir had converted it into a room to store his files, reports, and books. A pair of soldiers stood guard by the door.

"*Wake one of the clerks and bring them here at once,*" he said, and one of the men ran off to the barracks. Drauglir did not wait, and getting on his hands and knees he began to rummage through a huge pile of missives.

He had been dreaming of the day that he had received the report that Dis had been infiltrated and attacked. A Southerner posing as a servant had gotten into the city, aided by a pair of traitors: one who had posed as an officer and the other a disgruntled battle surgeon. The Southerner and his companions slew one of the blood-guard, and had gone on to steal an historic artifact, strike a judge in the face, and kill over a hundred soldiers in an explosion, and then several dozen more during their escape. The shame of it had been so great, that Latteowa Garm, the commander of the First, had committed suicide.

The Twentieth had nearly caught the trio near the Gate of Tears, but they had fled into the channel, and three warships were lost during the pursuit. All had assumed that the Southerners and the traitors had perished as well, but now . . .

They say he charmed a sea serpent with his voice, Mosca had said. *They say that he struck down the lord of Calvaria.*

What a fool I have been, he thought. *It has been right in front of me this whole time.*

"*There was a woman with them,*" the prafost had said, when he had questioned the survivors of the raid. "*A Calvarian, I mean. She had a surgeon's uniform on and mended our wounds.*"

He had been stationed in Solothurn when the attack had occurred, but the Judges had recalled him as soon as they were able to grant him the supreme command of the invasion force. They did not know yet which Southern power had been responsible for this outrage, but it did not matter- one of them would surely pay in blood, and a hundred thousand Southerners would have to die before they were satisfied. They slew the servants first, their owners often glad to do the duty themselves. Drauglir had to directly intervene to keep Mosca from being lynched by his own soldiers.

Within the year Nobel had named himself 'King,' and had sent an envoy to Svartgard demanding that the Calvarians return the Southerners' cities to them. Skoll had sent the man back with his own message: *Drauglir is coming.*

Most likely the fool did not know it, but Drauglir Seventhson was the great great grandson of the man who had brought the land the Southerners called Arcasia to its knees, Tyr Thirdson. It was a monument to Tyr's victory that the Southern saboteur had defiled, and many said that Drauglir was Tyr reborn.

A stack of papers toppled over as Fafnir No-Father entered the room. Drauglir might not have called for him, but his shadow had an uncanny way of knowing where he was.

"*What are you looking for?*" the Golden Arm asked.

"*I need a copy of the full report of the attack on Dis,*" he answered. "*The full report.*"

The blood-guard's eyes flicked towards another shelf. Drauglir went to it, and found what he was looking for within minutes: a black leather dossier. He nearly ripped the binding as he thumbed through it.

Finally, he found the passage he had been looking for.

Synmara. He realized that his hands were shaking. *We will know our son.*

He waited for Thrivaldi and Thrym to arrive, and his Heafodcarls as well. Andvari came first, then Farbauti and Hervor, Managarm (the first born son of Latteowa Garm) and Byleist, who had looked drawn and pale since the raid. Last to arrive was Heafodcarl Skirnir, who had been in command of the night watch.

"*Forgive me for waking you,*" Drauglir said once all were assembled. "*But I believe this could not wait until morning.*"

"*Is that the report on the attack on Dis?*" Thrivaldi asked, his permanent scowl even more pronounced in the light that the room's solitary fireplace was casting.

"*It is,*" Drauglir answered. "*And I believe you will all find the following portion of it of great interest.*"

Drauglir cleared his throat, and read.

"*. . . It is conjectured by some that the blood-guard, Filtiarn No-Father had suspected that Hirsent Second-daughter was in league with the traitor calling himself Heafodcarl Foalan, and the Southern agent, for he made a regular practice of recording her movements, and on the same night that he was slain he had taken command of two squads of the city guard, ostensibly to arrest Hirsent Second-daughter, though evidence suggests that Filtiarn No-Father may have intended to arrest all three. According to eyewitnesses, Filtiarn No-Father encountered the pair while investigating a disturbance* *about one of the ferries bound for Dis. Strangely, his own reports say nothing of a meeting between himself and the traitor calling himself Heafodcarl Foalan, though Vargan Firstson, the ferry master, claims that he questioned him."*

Drauglir, flipped ahead a few pages, cleared his throat, and continued.

"The only other official records of the traitor calling himself Heafodcarl Foalan and the Southern agent come from the registry of a way station along the eastwatch road, and from the report of the prafost on duty when the two passed through the outer gates of Dis. The way station log states that Heafodcarl Foalan arrived after the evening meal, spent the night, and was given a place of honor on the next sleigh bound for Dis. The Southerner's presence was noted in the margin of the night ledger. The second report is much the same, only the prafost on watch, Fjalar Thirdson, requested to see official papers granting Heafodcarl Foalan permission to be accompanied by a Southerner. These documents, likely forged, appeared genuine. Prafost Fjalar Thirdson's report- his direct testimony being unavailable due to the fact that he was killed during the escape of the traitors- states that the name given for the man was **Fox.**"

Drauglir closed the dossier.

"*A Southern name*," Thrivaldi said. "*What does it mean?*"

"*Fox*," Drauglir answered.

* * * * * * *

By midmorning the main boulevard of the city was full to bursting with Southerners. Drauglir had posted troops all along the street, and placed a triple guard on the market square, but for every Calvarian there were at least ten dark-faced men and women.

"*There are so many of them*," Latteowa Thrym said, shifting in his seat. Drauglir had heard that refrain many times- first from the soldiers during the crossing, each of them eager to slay enemies and gain mates, and then again when the enemy fleet had stretched before them. He had heard it when Barca fell and he had ordered one out of every ten Southerner slain for their defiance, and again at the battle of the river, as the enemy host advanced.

There are so many of them. The words had begun to take on a darker meaning for Drauglir, but not today. Today he would have welcomed a hundred thousand more.

He and his fellow Latteowas sat atop a central platform that the engineers had constructed, an honor guard six ranks deep surrounding them, and arrayed around them were eight iron-banded chests, their lids thrown open to display their contents.

Gold.

"*But, Latteowa,*" Svartgard's chief engineer had balked once he had finished reading Drauglir's specifications. "*This gold was intended for the beautification of the city. To simply give it to Southerners-*"

"*Latteowa Drauglir gave you a command,*" Fafnir No-Father had said then, his hand resting casually on his sword hilt, and the engineer's protests ceased.

"*That one has been too long in the South,*" Drauglir had said afterwards, and the Golden Arm had nodded.

The engineers had done an excellent job copying the coin molds of the Southerners- unsurprisingly, the Calvarian-made coins were of much higher quality. When they were done Drauglir had sent out the scouts.

Each scout company had been given a hundred copies of Drauglir's pronouncement, and as they swept the land they nailed them to trees at crossroads, inns, the doors of the Southerners' temples, anywhere a Southerner might see them. Mosca had written the first of them, and the scribes had copied his script exact.

By order of Drauglir Seventhson, Latteowa of the Seventeenth Regiment, a reward of a hundred thousand gold crowns is offered to any man, woman, or child who can deliver to him the notorious bandit known as Reynard the Fox, the Baron of Maleperduys. Furthermore, safe conduct will be assured for any who wish to come forward with information regarding the aforesaid renegade, and further gold coins shall be awarded to any who prove useful. Latteowa Drauglir will personally receive those who wish to answer this summons in the marketplace of the city formerly known as Barca until Reynard the Fox is found.

"*A bounty? You are going soft, Drauglir,*" Thrivaldi had said, but he had quickly agreed that his plan would certainly produce results.

Thrym had been harder to convince. "*This man must be a great hero to the Southerners,*" he had said. "*Surely they will not give him up to us, no matter how much metal we throw in their faces.*"

"*I know Southerners,*" Drauglir had replied. "*And they are all mad for gold. Many, no doubt, will be true to their country, and to their 'Fox,' but I do not doubt that there will be more than a few who will not be able to resist the temptation.*"

Of course, he had been right. Even he was surprised by how many had come out to betray the hero of the South. In a way, it depressed him.

All morning long they listened to the informants, and would-be claimants of the gold, the process slowed considerably by the fact that no one but the cierran-noteres could understand more than a few words of the Southern tongue. Drauglir had ordered a half dozen of them brought down from Svartgard, but even with Mosca it took hours to sort through the chaff.

For the most part the information they gleaned was useless- though Drauglir was more wont to listen to the Southerners' tales of The Fox's exploits now that he thought there might be a germ of truth in them. The stories of 'Lord' Isengrim and 'Lady' Hirsent had at least confirmed his theory regarding the Fox's identity, and explained how they had been able to slay one of the blood-guard. The fallen blood-guard Isengrim No-Father had been thought dead for over ten years, but now he too would be brought to justice.

He began to regret his promise of safe conduct after the first head had been presented to him- every tenth petitioner seemed to have brought one with them. Some, he guessed, had been gathered from the mass graves that dotted the countryside, and others looked so dried and withered that they might have been relics from the siege of Svartgard. But there were fresher ones too- one man had a pickle barrel full of them, and claimed that they were the heads of not only the Fox, but his captains as well. Another brought in the head of a wolf, and claimed that the Fox had been a warg. Thrivaldi had laughed at that, but Drauglir had not.

Do they take us for fools?

Whatever the case, none of the heads belonged to The Fox- every man who had survived the raid could personally attest to that.

Soon, it was long past midday and Drauglir's back was aching. He had hardly touched the midday ration that had been brought to them, and the heat was blistering. He rubbed his eyes and looked down at the new petitioners that were standing below the platform.

There were six of them, and they were not like the others, Drauglir noted. For one thing they wore armor, and had weapons. One of them was clearly their chief- he was standing apart from the rest and wore a toothy grin on his swarthy face.

An insolent-looking cur, Drauglir thought to himself. *At least he does not appear to have brought me a head.*

"*What does this one call himself?*" he said, glancing briefly at Mosca.

His cierran-notere spoke. The man answered slowly, almost lazily.

"*He says that he is known as the 'Prince of Cats,' Latteowa.*"

"*They are proud of their names,*" Thrivaldi said, shaking his head.

"*What information does he offer?*" Drauglir said. "*Can he deliver The Fox to us?*"

Mosca translated the question. The Southerner laughed, and answered.

"*Latteowa,*" Mosca said. "*He says that he cannot deliver 'The Fox' to us, but if we give him the gold, he can lead us straight to The Fox's den.*"

XI

Hermeline had just lain down for an afternoon nap when there was a knock at her door.

If it is Baldwin again, she thought as she threw on one of her robes, *I will wring the man's neck.* The timid priest seemed to have more sicknesses and minor injuries than all of the other men and women under her care combined. Just the night before he had summoned her to his bedchamber, complaining of fever. *You've only eaten too much, you ass*, she'd grumbled as she gave him a bit of ginger to chew on. A week before he claimed to have caught the Red Death. *You are allergic to hay*, she had said, examining the angry rashes on his skin. *Stay out of the fields.*

The man was pratically driving her to distraction.

"Who is it?" she called out, cinching her belt.

"It's Russet," a muffled voice said. It belonged to one of the sentinels. "I'm sorry to bother you, Mistress Hermeline, but we've spotted riders along the edge of the lake."

The sentinel's words sent ice through her guts.

Have the Calvarians found us at last?

"What do they look like?" she asked, rushing to the door. "Friends or foes?"

"Friends," Reynard said once she'd thrown open the door. "I believe Baron Reynard has returned to Maleperduys."

For a moment she thought she might slap him, but then she was kissing him, and laughing, her arms holding him tight.

"I'm happy to see you too," he said, smiling.

"Why didn't you write?" she asked, "I could have- I might have been ready for you."

"I thought you might enjoy a surprise."

"It has been over a month," she said, forcing herself to push him away. "I thought you might have-"

"I couldn't spare the shrikes," he said. "We had to take the long route home to avoid leading the wolves straight to our door. We've been trudging through Lorn for over a month."

"Then," she said, hoping, "you mean to stay?"

"For the winter at least," he replied. "Perhaps longer. I left Tiecelin in charge of my fastest riders- he plays the part of The Fox fair enough, and Bruin and he will keep the Calvarians on their toes until the spring comes."

"And what of the others?" she asked. "Your followers I mean?"

"They are a few days march behind," Reynard answered, "Isengrim is leading them."

"They are coming here?" she said. "All of them?"

"All that wished to come. Do not worry, we've brought our own supplies with us, and there's always plenty of game in the forest."

"And plenty of wargs," she said. "We've had some problems since you've been gone."

"I remember your last letter," he said. "They've been killing the sheep?"

"And the sheep dogs," she said. "They're getting bolder every day. We're lucky they haven't attacked anyone yet."

"Well, you don't have to worry anymore," he said, "I'll put an end to them."

"You've lost weight," she said, squinting at him.

"More than I would have liked," he said, and pulled up a sleeve to reveal the stump of his left arm.

"Oh gods," she said. "I'm sorry. I had- I had forgotten."

"It's alright," he said. "You're not the one who took it from me."

"Oh, Reynard," she said and kissed him again, more deeply, and ran her hand down his chest. As she began to unlace his breeches he pulled away from her.

"Don't you miss me?" she asked, hurt.

"Of course I do," he said, and grinned his charming grin, "But there will be time enough for that later. First, though, there is someone who would like to speak with you."

He turned towards the door. Hermeline had not noticed before, but Hirsent was standing in the doorway.

Her belly had grown so big that she had half undone the buttons of her faded uniform.

"I'll leave you two alone," Reynard said. "But come down to the courtyard when you are finished. Martin and Rukenaw want to see you."

"Of course," she said, but she was only half listening. Reynard shut the door behind him as he went.

Hirsent could barely meet her gaze.

"Hirsent," Hermeline said. "It is- good to see you."

"I am being," Hirsent Hirsent seemed to be searching for her words. "No- *awyrigung*, not *being*... I *am* pregnant."

"Yes," Hermeline said, nodding. "I can see that."

"I am being very scared," the Northerner said then, tears welling in her deep blue eyes. "I would be- I am desiring very much that you help me. When baby come. Will you-"

"Of course," Hermeline said, taking Hirsent's gloved hands in hers. The woman was shaking. "Of course I will help you."

"I- I was saying words to you before," the Northerner began to sob. "When child come. Words I am now regretting. Words I am not meaning. Words that are bringing me much shame to be remembering. Can you- will you be forgiving me?"

"There is nothing to forgive," Hermeline said and held Hirsent in her arms.

* * * * * *

The courtyard was full by the time that Hermeline and Hirsent came down from her quarters. Most of the men were knotted around Reynard, rapt with attention as he spoke to them of the many battles he had won, but the women had clustered around the men that had come back with them- Gaignun and his woman were practically on top of one another, and Madam Slopecade was hanging so heavily on Tencendur that she thought the man might keel over. There were tears as well, as men and women mourned friends and lovers lost.

Some, at least, I will not mourn, Hermeline thought, thinking of Tybalt. She had been taking care of his cat while he had been away. *I Suppose Midnight belongs to me now.*

She hardly recognized Rukenaw. The girl had nearly knocked her down when she'd hugged her, and it was not until she had spoken that Hermeline realized who was kissing her.

"My Gods, you've grown!" she said, kissing the girl back. She was not much taller than she had been before, but her figure had filled out considerably.

Martin had changed less so, though he had begun to grow a wispy beard. His cheeks flushed when Hermeline pressed against him.

"You're beginning to look very handsome," she told the boy. "And Reynard tells me that he's made you his squire. The girls must all be mad for you."

"Oh," Martin said, his eyes flicking towards Rukenaw. "I suppose, I mean, no, I haven't- there hasn't been any- well, I mean, if I-"

Hermeline laughed and gave Martin a kiss.

"Spoken like a true man," she said. "Don't worry, I won't ask you any more questions about your love life. In any case, you both look strong and healthy."

"There has been plenty to eat," Rukenaw said. "I never ate so much meat before."

"Me either," Martin added. "The only pig I ever ate before was during midwinter festival, and that wasn't more than some crisp in my porridge, but now I've had a whole slice of leg, and lamb, and even a bit of beef. My father never had beef, I bet, and he was one of the richest men in our village."

"Well," Hermeline breathed. "I'm afraid we won't be having beef tonight, but we *will* need to celebrate Baron Reynard's return, and I bet there'll be some ducks that Madam Slopecade will do up savory, and fresh carrots, and onions, and apple pie, too, if we're lucky. But first you two need a bath . . . and maybe a shave for Martin?"

The boy nodded his head bashfully, and she led them both off to the bathhouse.

The feast that night was finer than even Hermeline had expected. Reynard and his men had brought back all sorts of odd delicacies with them: Luxian almonds, Lornish truffles, port from Therimere, and even a block of Hivan chocolate. Hermeline had not tasted chocolate for years, and this had been flavored with mint. The duck did not disappoint either. Its crispy skin had been made rich with drippings, and Slopcade had garnished it with Reynard's almonds as well as their own vegetables. She had to force herself to eat slowly, and washed every bite down with a sip of port.

Reynard ate sparingly, she noticed, after she had helped him cut up his meat, and he drank only a sip or two of red wine. He was quieter too, letting the men do the boasting that he might have done, and merely nodding at their praise of him. He rarely smiled.

He's changed. The thought did not surprise her. She could not imagine what it must be like, to lose one's hand. *I'd make a sad sight myself,* she mused, *if I tried to dance with only one foot.*

"Thank you for the chocolate," she said, stroking his right arm with her fingers. "And the port. Won't you have some?"

"I'd rather you had it," he said. "The duck is fine enough for me."

"The almonds are delicious as well," she said. "Did you travel so far south?"

"No. But Lorn has largely been untouched by the war, and there is little that a man with a bagful of gems cannot buy."

"Save for love," she said, and leaned over to kiss him.

"Save for love," he said as their lips parted.

He retired early. Hermeline waited as long as she could before following him.

The door to their chambers was slightly ajar. She opened it and found Reynard lying on the bed, wearing nothing but one of his nightshirts. His clothes, boots, and sword lay in a heap by the bedside.

"You do not work tonight?" she asked, undoing the front of her gown as she clambered onto him.

"Not tonight," he said, and pulled her close.

* * * * * * *

Two days later Isengrim arrived, along with the rest of Reynard's host. Martin and Rukenaw watched them arrive from the battlements, though the Firebird was nearly setting by the time the last wagon had been led through the Wild Wood to the safety of Baron Reynard's hidden valley. The forest had forced them to travel single file, and true to his words, Reynard's band had grown into a small army. They'd been recruited from the baronies of Arcas and Astolat, and from the march of Carabas to the cities along the gulf of Lorn. Men, women, children, peasants and merchants, common laborers and skilled guildsmen, sellswords and petty chevalier and brazen deserters, it did not matter who they were: all had been welcome to join Reynard, as long as they were willing to fight. Some Reynard had lured with gems, and promises of gold, and others merely with the offer of a full belly, but they had all come willingly.

There was a feast again that evening, in a clearing near the edge of the wood, and though the fare was nowhere near as magnificent as the food that Madam Slopecade had served them on the evening of Reynard's return to Maleperduys, it was a far more spectacular affair, for over two dozen priests and priestesses had joined their ranks- and while the Watcher's servants played on string and the priests of Fenix beat on drum the lovely women who worshipped the Lioness played their pipes and whirled and danced, their full skirts and gauzy scarves twirling with their every step.

The next day Reynard put his host to work. Those who knew how were set to build permanent shelters below the castle. There was plenty of timber for the work, and within a week the dozen or so frames had gone up. Meanwhile a team of stone masons, carpenters, and quarrymen that Reynard had hired from the fortified town of Goscinny began to survey the fortress of Maleperduys itself, to make plans for its repair- and, as there was certainly no shortage of free hands, the work began apace. The first thing they did was replace the warped and rotting main gates with a sturdy set of reinforced doors, which could be braced with a timber so heavy that it took three strong men to lift it.

As for the others, a full third, mostly those who had been farmers before they were fighters, were set to cultivating the land- clearing back the forest somewhat to make room for a fall planting. The rest were set to train day and night, and to keep watch over the camp. It was for this duty that Martin longed, and after a few entreaties to Reynard his wish had been granted.

Bruin had been the castle's master-of-arms when Martin had come to it, and he had seemed strict but fair . . . but Bruin was still with Tiecelin and the hundred or so riders that were harrying the Calvarians. Reynard had replaced Bruin with Isengrim, and his drills made Bruin's seem lackadaisical by comparison. Every morning Martin would crawl off of his pallet and make the walk down the causeway to the practice yard, where he'd be given a bit of pease porridge before being set to train with one of the pells that the Northerner had ordered set up, striking at the wooden targets with sword and axe until his arms were so weak that he could barely lift them. Only when the midday meal was ready would they break, and afterwards Isengrim would alternatively break them into pairs to spar with each other, or train with crossbow, sling, or spear. The unlucky ones would spar with Isengrim himself. Martin had been chosen only once, but he had gone to the evening supper so sore that he'd been forced to stand. Rukenaw had teased him mercilessly then, but he did not mind.

At least she had been paying attention to him.

Rukenaw might have grown more feminine in appearance, but her character had certainly not changed. She was still as willful as ever, always the one to bend or break the rules, and stubborn to boot. She seemed to have grown more fearsome as well- after all, it had been her, and not Martin, who had insisted that they wait to see if Reynard or any of the others had survived the battle of the Samara. They'd watched it from afar, and Martin could clearly remember the cold terror he'd felt in his gut as the Calvarians routed Nobel's army. He'd wanted to run, certainly, as had Tencendur, but Rukenaw had clawed and scratched and bit until the man had given up. Within moments Tiecelin had ridden up on an injured horse, and it wasn't long before the shrikes had reunited them with Bruin, Tybalt, and their men. If it had not been for Rukenaw, he and Tencendur might be as far away as Lazaward Tor by now, and he might have died never knowing what had become of Reynard.

After supper, on the days he was not set to patrol the edge of the forest, Rukenaw would lead him out of the castle, through the courtyard where they'd first met the Baron of Maleperduys, and then into the crumbling temple beyond. The laborers had cleared the courtyard of weeds and had cleaned the fountain, but the place still had a somber look to it, especially with the castle looming over them, its yawning doorway and red-litten windows above giving it the look of the maw of some heavy-lidded giant.

Once they were safe behind the temple walls Rukenaw would produce the pair of staves that she had hidden there and make Martin spar with her. She had asked Baron Reynard a dozen times to teach her how to fight, but he always refused her and Martin knew why- Hermeline had forbidden it. So instead of training with Martin in the yard Hermeline had her learning all manner of things: the names of healing herbs and deadly fungi, how willow bark, when chewed, could dull the pain of an injury, and how to dance. Martin could not help but wonder if she was learning the other aspects of Hermeline's profession, but he knew better than to ask. Still, he wondered, especially whenever he saw her speaking with one of the men during supper- he'd seen her flirting with Passecerf more than he'd care to. Sometimes, when the lights had gone out for the night, he'd think of her leading him back to the temple, only instead of revealing blunted swords she would slip out of her clothes and kiss him as she had kissed him that day in the woods.

She never did though. The lanky girl that he'd chased that day was gone, and she had been replaced by a fierce young woman who seemed to want to do nothing but fight, and so he sparred with her, no matter how tired he was.

She always won. Martin liked to think that it was exhaustion that hampered him, for he was certainly stronger than she was, but after the second week of finding himself flat on his back, disarmed and with a wooden butt pressing against his throat, he had to admit that she would have made a far better warrior than he ever would, no matter how long he trained.

The fact that he had next to no desire to hit her did not help either.

"It's not fair," he had once complained. "Isengrim is teaching us how to fight with swords, not sticks."

"Are they so different?" she'd laughed, and rapped him on the knuckles hard enough to break his skin.

Tonight was no different. They had hardly begun to fight before he found himself sucking on one of his injured fingers, and cursing at the pain.

"Isn't that white-faced bastard teaching you anything?" Rukenaw pouted. "You get worse every day."

"I'm not getting worse," Martin grumbled. *But you're getting better.*

He picked up his stave, and they met again. Rukenaw spun around his opening thrust and landed a blow across his back. He blocked her follow-up, but then she struck at his legs and knocked him off of his feet.

"You *are* getting worse," she said, tapping him in the forehead with her stave.

"Stop it," he growled and grabbed the stick with both hands. She tried to wrench it away from him, but he was stronger. He started to laugh as they struggled.

Suddenly Rukenaw shifted her weight, and slammed the end of the pole into Martin's face. The world seemed to flash white for a moment and then he was lying on his back.

"Martin," he could hear her saying. "Martin, I'm sorry, are you alright?"

When his vision cleared he could see that Rukenaw was hovering over him, her brow knit with worry. It made her look very pretty.

"I think I'm done sparring for the night," he said and reached to embrace her.

She wriggled out of his grip and stood. "Fine," she said. "I'll practice by myself."

"I meant," he said, swallowing down the lump that was beginning to form in his throat. "I thought that maybe we could, um-"

"Yes?" she said.

"I want to kiss you," he said.

"I know you do."

"And do you? Want to kiss me, I mean?"

"Not now," she said, and his heart sank.

"But you did? Before?"

"Maybe I did," she said, twirling her stave. "And maybe I didn't."

"I love you," he said. He hadn't meant to say it, but he had said it all the same.

"You don't love me, silly," she said. "You're too young."

His face felt flushed. "Don't say that."

"Say what?"

"That I don't love you."

"*Martin*," she said, her tone turning his very name into an admonition, "You don't know what you're saying. You don't love me. You just want what every man wants. Don't you?"

I do, he thought, his eyes wandering over her body, but still he said, "I love you."

She sighed. "You're not very good at *this* either. Do you want me or not?"

"I do," he said, his voice nearly cracking. "I want you."

"And maybe you can have me," she said, raising her staff. "But only if you win."

He fought Rukenaw harder than he ever might have thought possible that night, but still, he was always the loser. He was stronger, yes, but she was quicker, she was smarter, and she always fought to win.

"No more," he said at last. Her last strike had been against his ribs and it hurt now even to breathe.

"Too bad," she said, and leaned on her stave. "Still, you fought well enough for a kiss, I think. You still want to kiss me, don't you?"

He nodded and went to her. When their lips met she slipped her tongue into his mouth, and rubbed her palm against the front of his breeches, but when he reached for her left breast she pulled away.

"I didn't say you could touch me," she said by way of explanation, and went about hiding the practice staves. "It's time to call it a night."

"Rukenaw," he said, hoarsely, "Please, you can't just-"

"What? What can't I do?" she said, and smiled wickedly at him when he could not bring himself to answer. "Goodnight."

Then she slipped through the temple doors and was gone.

He wanted to go after her, to kiss her, to hit her, to knock her to the ground and make her his, but even the thought of forcing her made him ashamed, and so he sat down beneath the moldering statue of the three women and wept.

He nearly jumped when he felt the hand on his shoulder. He rubbed his eyes, cursing himself. *Gods*, he thought, *she'll never let me forget this*, but when he'd cleared his eyes it was Baron Reynard staring down at him, not his love.

"My lord," Martin blurted. "You frightened me."

"Force of habit," Reynard said. "My apologies."

Martin got to his feet. "I'm sorry if I disturbed you, I just- I wanted to-"

"It's alright, Martin, I know you and Rukenaw come here so that she can train. I promise I won't tell Hermeline."

"She's better than me," Martin said, unsure of what Reynard wished of him.

"She's strong-willed," Reynard replied. "I can see why you like her."

"I love her," Martin said, and he felt the tears beginning to well up again, but he fought them back. "But she doesn't love me."

"She may," Reynard said. "Someday."

"How?" he said, and he began to cry again. "How do I *make* her love me?"

"You cannot," Reynard said, patting him on the shoulder. "But you can still try to woo her."

"But how?"

"Walk with me awhile, and I'll tell you what I know."

Reynard led him out into the garden, and up the flight of steps where he'd caught his first glimpse of the hidden valley. The Watcher was full, and the sky was clear, and the lake below them seemed to glimmer like polished steel.

"My first advice, is this: never beg. It rarely works, and even when it does it makes you seem weak. In my experience most women are attracted to strength."

"Rukenaw is a better fighter than me," Martin said, rather glumly.

"There are many kinds of strength," Reynard said. "And that brings me to my second piece of advice: be excellent, and let her see it as often as you can."

"What do you mean?" Martin asked.

"Why do you think Rukenaw liked Tybalt?"

"I don't know," Martin said rather hotly, unable to hold back his anger. "He was a bastard."

"A *magnificent* bastard," Reynard said. "And many women swoon over men who are no good."

"I'm not Tybalt," Martin said.

"True, but what *are* you best at?"

Martin was at a loss for a moment.

"I am good with horses," he offered.

"Good," Reynard said. "Start with that. Teach her how to ride. I'll see that Hermeline allows it, and tell Isengrim to give you an afternoon or two off so you can be alone with her."

"And when she's learned to ride?"

"Go riding with her. There are worse ways to begin a courtship."

"Alright," Martin said.

"Now go get some rest," the Baron said, giving him another pat. "And try not to think of her too much. It doesn't help."

"I will," Martin said, but when he finally fell onto his pallet he could not help but think of the feel of her hand against his quick, and the smell of her hair in his nose.

"I love you," he whispered in the darkness. "I love you, I love you, I love you."

* * * * * * *

In Redmonth the leaves began to turn, and the trees of the valley seemed to be crowned in shades of amber and gold, and red- red as brilliant as fire and dark as blood. The skies were growing grayer with every passing day, and there was a pleasant crispness in the air that made food taste good and wine even better. The birds that had come with summer were slowly leaving, though there were still herons in the lake, and enough geese to keep the castle of Maleperduys well provided with game.

One morning Reynard awoke early to see that it had snowed during the night. He threw on a heavier coat and, leaving Hermeline slumbering in bed, crossed the breezeway and entered the shrikes' tower. Isengrim was not waiting for him, but he could hear him down below, working at the forge. The two of them had not dueled for some time now, for Isengrim trained his warriors by day, and worked at his forge morning and night. Reynard guessed that the man was nervous, and he did not blame him- in less than a month Hirsent's third child would come, and perhaps it was best that the Northerner did not think of it overmuch.

It was Sharpebeck that greeted him this morning, trading the message tied to her leg for one of the rats that still infested the catacombs below. Tiecelin's letter was much like his others: *Calvarians remain at Barca, though their fleet has retreated farther downriver. Men are growing restless. I await further instructions. T.*

Reynard folded the note up and slipped it into a pocket, then left the tower by the door that led to the courtyard.

Isengrim was shirtless, his muscular body glistening with sweat as he brought down his hammer again and again. Today it seemed he was making spearheads out of reforged steel. Yesterday it had been arrowheads, and the day before a sword.

The man will run out of ore if he keeps this up much longer, Reynard thought to himself as he sat down at their campraeden board and moved a contingent of soldiers out of the Glasir Forest and into the city of Lyfthelm, where a host of Isengrim's units awaited battle.

The lacquered game board and its gorgeous soapstone pieces had probably belonged to a *Heafodcarl* of the Seventeenth before Reynard had lifted it from one of the supply wagons they had raided. Isengrim had taught him how to play, and had won their first three games. Reynard had won every game since then.

Isengrim ceased his labor for a moment to toss his dice as his soldiers and archers attempted to defend his capital. It was hopeless, though- Reynard had three times as many men, and siege engines besides. The faux battle was a massacre, and when it was over Reynard's army held half of Midgard.

"Victory in eight turns," Reynard said as Isengrim removed his pieces from the board.

"Nine," Isengrim said.

"Do you concede?"

"No," Isengrim said, and played his turn, pulling soldiers back to defend the cities of the western coast. He always played the game until none of his pieces remained. By the end of the game, Isengrim's last provinces usually resembled islands surrounded by Reynard's forces.

"You always put up a good fight," Renyard said, as he moved his biggest fleet to counter.

"I should be winning," Isengrim said, and sent several units of cavalry to their doom. "I have played this game since I was six summers old."

"You play too cautiously," Reynard said, rolling the dice. "You try to defend everything, but you end up defending nothing. When you fight, fight to win. Three sixes."

"I can see the dice," Isengrim said, and removed his cavalry from the board.

Reynard's troops landed in the Hesperides and took Argadnel. Isengrim pulled more men back to stem the flow of Reynard's advance. Renyard's armies converged on Valholl and crushed its defenders. Isengrim moved the last of his units into Idavollr, attempting to break through Reynard's battle line. The dice were with him, and he lost only half of his pieces. Reynard closed his own trap then, bringing up all of his cavalry at once.

"I told you it would be eight," Reynard said as Isengrim returned his units to their box. "Another game?"

"Perhaps later," the Northerner said and returned to his anvil.

The sky above grew lighter. Madam Slopecade brought them both a bit of broth to break their fast, and the night watch descended from the walls.

"I suppose you must train the men," Reynard said as they finished their meal, and he got up and stretched.

"Yes," Isengrim said, wiping the sweat from his brow with a cloth. "But first I have a gift for you."

"It won't be Crowning until Spring," Reynard said, but he had to admit that he was curious.

"It would have been ready sooner," Isengrim said, opening a chest, and taking out a leather satchel that resembled Reynard's old roll of thieves' tools. "But I did not have a proper manual to refer to."

As Reynard could hardly open the thing with only one hand, Isengrim undid its clasps for him and pulled out what Reynard first took to be an iron gauntlet.

It was left-handed.

"Hold out your arm," Isengrim said. "And I will show you how to put it on."

Reynard felt his ghost-hand ache as Isengrim slipped the prosthetic over his stump and locked it into place with a series of straps. When he was done it looked as though Reynard was merely wearing a metal glove.

"Go ahead," Isengrim said. "Make a fist."

Reynard moved his ghost-hand and felt a smile cross his face as the metallic fingers curled into a fist. He repeated the action several times, turning the thing around to marvel at the way the muscles in his forearm controlled the fingers.

"This one is not strong enough to hold a blade," Isengrim said. "I will need to keep experimenting, but I have come up with a temporary solution. Make a fist again."

Reynard made a fist.

"Now tighten it, as hard you are able."

Reynard pictured his ghost-hand tightening in the prosthetic and suddenly a blade sprang from the hand, just above the wrist. When he loosened his grip it easily slid back into its housing.

"This- this," Reynard said, stammering slightly. "This is- I don't know what to say. Thank you."

"You are welcome," Isengrim said, throwing on his undershirt. "The next one will be better."

"What do you call it?" Reynard said.

"Left-Hand," Isengrim said, and smiled his faint smile.

* * * * * * *

Four days before Summer's End Hirsent went into labor.

Reynard was relieved. Hermeline had confined her to her own quarters for weeks previous, and the woman was growing quite quarrelsome. He'd offered to keep her company, and to help teach her the Southern tongue while Isengrim busied himself training their soldiers, and sometimes he wondered if he spent more time with her than even Hermeline, who would always say *soon, soon*, until Reynard thought that soon would never come.

It did though. It began in the morning, though Reynard could hardly tell that there was anything different about Hirsent. She had even insisted that Isengrim not be told immediately, yet as afternoon was wearing on Hermeline had ushered Reynard out of the room, called in Rukenaw, and bolted the door, and Reynard sent Turpin down to bring the news to Isengrim that his child was being born. Within the hour the Northerner had come cantering up the causeway on his black charger, and headed straight for the room that he shared with his wife.

Isengrim's pace slowed somewhat as he mounted the first steps up to the second level of the keep. Hirsent's cries were probably audible to the men on the walls, Reynard guessed.

"Don't worry," Reynard said to the man. "Hermeline will take care of her."

Isengrim nodded, and continued to climb.

He hesitated only a moment before knocking at the door.

"What is it?" Hermeline's voice called out. She did not sound as if she were in the most patient of moods.

"I wanted to know," Isengrim said, swallowing hard. "If there is anything I might do to help?"

"There is," Hermeline shouted. "Leave us alone!"

Hirsent called out then, and it took very little of Reynard's strength to pull Isengrim away.

"Is it hot in here?" the Northerner asked, glancing back towards the door.

"Why don't we go outside?" Reynard suggested. "It will be cooler."

Isengrim shook his head, and stood statue-like against the wall, listening to his wife curse and scream. Slowly his perfect posture loosened, until he nearly slouched, and finally he began to sink, until he was sitting with his arms folded over his knees.

Reynard left him there, and went to get a cask of wine.

Isengrim and he had drained their second bottle of Oscan white when a new cry joined those of Hirsent. As Isengrim scrambled to his feet the door opened and Hermeline appeared and said, "You have a son."

Isengrim pushed past Hermeline, and Reynard followed, returning the smile that his lover flashed him.

Hirsent was holding the child in her arms. He was a shiny red thing, wet and squalling. Hermeline had already cut his umbilical cord. Hirsent looked as though she had been bathing in her own sweat, and Rukenaw looked rather pale herself.

"*He lives*," Hirsent said to her husband. "*A boy and he lives.*"

Isengrim kissed Hirsent and, his normally steady hands shaking, took his child to his breast.

"*He is so small*," Isengrim said, and flinched suddenly. "*But his pinches already hurt.*"

"Considering whose son he is," Reynard said, "That hardly surprises me. Who knows, perhaps someday 'The Pincher' will ride with the Fox and Warg?"

Isengrim laughed, but winced again as his son's fingers nipped at a bit of his skin. "Pincher," he said. "*A fitting name, perhaps?*"

"*Yes, but I would not have my son wear a Calvarian name*," Hirsent said.

"I am not naming my son 'Pincher,'" Isengrim said.

"What about Pinsard?" Reynard suggested. "That is the old Aquilian."

"Pinsard," Isengrim said, and turned to Hirsent.

"Pinsard," she nodded.

"Pinsard Secondson,' Isengrim said, and kissed his son's shiny head.

"A good name," Hermeline said. "But now we must deliver her pouch. Rukenaw, help Isengrim clean the child, and keep him warm. Reynard . . . get me a cup of wine."

There were no complications, and within days Hirsent was up and out of bed, Pinsard always in her arms. The castle's women fawned on him, and the men slapped Isengrim on the back, and that evening, after they made their toast to Wulf, they toasted to the Warg and the She-Wolf's son. The servants of the Watcher took the child's birth as some sort of omen, for soon it was the last day of summer, and Wulf's Night drew nigh. Each of the village priests had brought their warg masks with them, and while the followers of the Firebird lit torches and lanterns along the edge of the forest, the servants of the Watcher prowled in the darkness, and sang their dreadful songs of murder and woe to all who had the stomach to listen. Finally they butchered one of the oxen, and laid its carcass on a stone far from the castle. That night Reynard could hear the howling of wargs, and by the morning the beast's body was gone, even the bones.

* * * * * * *

The next morning he found Rohart waiting for him in the shrikes' tower.

"Doom," the chimera had said, sounding for a moment remarkably like Tiecelin. The message he bore was far longer than the others.

Hermeline awoke with a start when she heard him scribbling at his desk. She sat up, wide awake, saw the look in his eyes. Midnight, who was lounging near the end of the bed, looked up at him as well with her pale yellow eyes.

"What is it?" Hermeline said. "What's wrong?"

"A Calvarian army is marching west out of Larsa," he said, not stopping to look up. "Another is making its way through the Erycinian Highlands to the south. Tiecelin can't be sure, but he believes that they are converging on us."

"Two armies?" Hermeline balked. "How many of them are there?"

"Fifteen thousand? Maybe more. The shrikes aren't very reliable when it comes to numbers."

"Then, we must leave here," she said, worry beginning to creep across her face. "Mustn't we?"

"We can't leave," Reynard said, scribbling faster. "A third army has landed to the west of us, in Landuc, less than a day's ride away."

"We're trapped."

XII

Reynard watched Rohart glide away from the tower, his wings flapping languidly as he rose higher into the air, and then the chimera passed over the rim of the valley and was gone.

By the time he returned to the great hall, the laborers had been assembled, as well as all of the men who knew the layout of the catacombs. Baldwin and the other village priests too were there, as well as Isengrim and Hirsent, who was nursing Pinsard, and Martin and Rukenaw stood by Hermeline, who was sitting at her place at the head table, Midnight curled up on her lap.

She did not look up when Reynard began to speak.

"The Calvarians are coming," he said. "Someone has betrayed us."

"We all know who," Hermeline said, her teeth clenched, but Reynard ignored her and continued.

"The forest will slow them, but it will not confound them forever, and we have precious little time to prepare. You all know they will offer us no mercy, so we have no choice but to fight. I had not expected to face them so soon, and we are not as ready as I might have hoped, but still we can make a stand that will long be remembered."

The men and women who filled the hall nodded, and murmured in agreement, but Reynard could see the desperation in their eyes.

"First, we must seal all of the passages that lead to the castle. Gaignun, Russet, and Tencendur will each lead a party into the tunnels, and each party will use the explosive powder we have stolen from the enemy to collapse them. It will not hold them for long, for they have sappers of their own, but it is possible that they will overlook the entrances to the catacombs. At any rate, it will buy us some time."

"What good will time do?" Baldwin asked. "With thousands upon thousands of the Northern demons closing in on us?"

"Perhaps none," Reynard answered. "But I have sent word to Tiecelin. I do not know if there is aught he can do for us, for his band is small, but at least we may hope."

"Aye," said the stout priest named Turpin, one of the first men to join Reynard's army. Isengrim had made him a war hammer to replace his smith's, and he hefted it now. "And I'll not go down without a fight."

Reynard gave the man a nod. "For the priests and priestesses, I would ask that you gather those too sick and old, or too young to fight, and bring them into the castle. Quarter them in the undercroft, or in the tunnels if you must, but bring them all. I would leave no one behind to die at the hands of the Northerners. And give them weapons as well- we have enough to spare. Should our defenses fail I would not have them face their killers unarmed."

Reynard turned to Hirsent. She met his eyes then and nodded.

"As for the warriors," Reynard went on, "I am placing them under the command of Isengrim."

Reynard waited for the objections, the murmurs of disapproval, the shock. There was none. All who had ridden with Reynard knew that the Warg had no love for his brethren.

"What are your orders?" Isengrim said.

"Assemble our best riders," Reynard answered, "and our best scouts, and buy us *time*."

Isengrim nodded.

"Those you do not take will stay with me, to see to the defense of the fortress," Reynard said. "That is all."

"I want to fight!"

Rukenaw's voice had cut through the hall like a whip crack. She was already advancing on Reynard, her brow furrowed and her fists clenched.

"I won't hide with the others," she said as she strode forward. "I won't."

"Neither will I," Martin said, coming around the other end of the table to stand by the girl. "I'm ready."

"No," Hermeline said, rising to her feet. "Reynard, speak sense to them."

"You are still young," Reynard said, looking into Rukenaw's eyes. "Both of you are."

"You promised you would let us fight," was Rukenaw's only response. "You *promised.*"

Reynard sighed.

"So be it," he said.

"No!" Hermeline cried out. "Martin perhaps, but Rukenaw-"

"Rukenaw fights better than many of the men," Reynard said, cutting her off. "And there are younger men and women who have fought for me already."

And died as well, he might have added, but he did not think it prudent. Eventually Hermeline lowered into her seat, and was silent.

A moment later all of the men headed for the tunnels cleared out of the hall, no doubt to retrieve their tools and the stout kegs of blasting powder. Isengrim bent over Hirsent, whispering something to her as they locked hands, and then he too swept from the room, his only farewell a brief nod in Reynard's direction.

The priests and priestesses too appeared to be ready to go about their duties, but they waited for Hermeline, who was still sitting at the table, her gaze turned to the uneaten plate of eggs that sat before her, her hands folded neatly on the table.

"Hermeline," Reynard said. "Please. The others are waiting."

"Is there any hope?" she said, looking up at him, her mouth tight. "Tell me. And do not lie."

Reynard knelt down beside her and put his living hand on top of her own and whispered, "I won't let you die."

She turned to him, her eyes suddenly wet, and she nodded.

* * * * * * *

Tybalt had smirked when he received word that Gerin had been shot and killed in one of Reynard's traps. The man had been leading a group of scouts when a hail of crossbow bolts erupted from the forest and had taken down a half dozen pale-faces as well as his fellow guide.

Drauglir would have to take care of his only Southerner now.

The Calvarian general had chosen Tybalt and Gerin to guide his army through the dense woods of Maleperduys, while Blanc and Sautperdu had been given to the one called Thrivaldi, and Jacquet and Gerier to the young one, Thrym. The twins had not been happy at being separated, but there had been nothing for it- according to Mosca, the translator, the Calvarians considered twins to be an ill omen, or bad luck, or simply extraneous. Tybalt didn't really understand, and frankly, he didn't give a piss what the reason for it was.

He just wanted the gold. And with Gerin dead, there was one less man to share it with.

He wondered how many of his boys would die in the woods. Certainly not as many as the Northerners. Every few hours they met with ambush from concealment, or with covered pits full of sharpened stakes that maimed their steeds, and false trails that led off into the parts of the forest where the chimera were more numerous. Reynard's men had felled trees as well, forcing the long column to come to a halt as the engineers cleared the way with axe and saw. And, of course, even the true path through the forest had to be widened to accommodate the siege engines and supply wagons. Tybalt had explained all of this several times to Drauglir, through the interpreter, but he could tell the man's patience was wearing thin. Once, when Tybalt had told the man that he should have expected their pace to be slow from the start, Drauglir had ordered the blood-guards to beat him for his insolence.

He'd taken the beating gladly. After all, it didn't matter. As long as he got the gold.

A hundred thousand crowns, he thought as he waited for another deadfall to be cleared. *A hundred thousand golden coins*. Tybalt would be the richest man in Arcasia, richer than any guild master or nobleman, richer even than Nobel himself. With such a sum he might buy a title, not in Arcasia, of course, no man would be like to welcome Tybalt the turncoat there, but perhaps in Frisia, where the size of a man's fortune would count for more than honor. And was it not said that the Princess Zara of Beria has no husband? With a ransom such as this he might marry her and become a prince. What care he if the rumors were true that she was so wanton as to lie with more men and women than a hundred priestesses of the Lioness combined? He could always have mistresses of his own- or perhaps they might share some together.

He would regret having to kill Blanc and Jacquet. They were both men after his own heart, and had stood by him time and again, Jacquet especially. The man had been the second of one of the bandit chieftains of the forest before Isengrim had chopped the man into mincemeat, and he did Tybalt's business with no questions asked. For a while he'd considered bringing Jacquet with him, but he knew it would not do. Tybalt would never agree to parting with even a sixth part of the gold, and he imagined that- when it came to it- Jacquet would have a blade of his own intended for Tybalt's heart.

A pity for him that I am quicker, he thought, and made one of his knives dance on his palm.

"The path is clear," one of the white-uniformed Calvarian scribes said to him eventually, and Tybalt sheathed his dagger. Drauglir had been forced to wait for months for enough men trained to speak his language to arrive before they set out. He was wise to have done so, too- three of them had already been shot dead. This one must have come from Solothurn, for he spoke in a peculiar Eastern accent.

"Come," the scribe said, and Tybalt followed him up the lines to where the path through the forest was now open.

Tybalt crept forward carefully, his eyes scanning the path, the trees, the rocks, and the escarpment that loomed over the southern side of the trail. Reynard's men were hard to spot, for they wore coats hung with the leaves of the forest, and underneath their cloaks were as gray as tree bark. But Tybalt could usually spot them, for he had come up with the idea himself, being no stranger to ambush.

"There are no pits, and if they are lying in wait I cannot see them," Tybalt said to the scribe when he returned. "Though be wary of the heights to the left. If it were me, that's where I would attack from."

The scribe nodded and translated his words to the Calvarian captain in command of the vanguard, a white-haired man with a cruel look to him. The captain delivered his orders in his quiet voice, and then the column of soldiers resumed their march. Several of the scouts detached from the column and nocked arrows, their gaze kept sharply on the edge of the escarpment.

Sure enough, the column had hardly gotten moving when the scouts let loose a flurry of shafts towards the shelf. A man screamed and tumbled forward, his body pierced by several shafts, narrowly missing one of the foot soldiers when he finally hit the ground. The fall had not served to kill the man either, despite shattering his leg, and now he howled piteously for mercy.

"Sorry friend," Tybalt said as one of the soldiers cut his throat, and then the column moved on.

It could hardly be called a march. The scouts were taking no chances as they advanced, and had spread out as far as the terrain allowed while still staying in sight of one another. Every dozen yards the column ground to a halt as they examined a suspicious bit of ground, or discovered another fork in the path. Then Tybalt would be forced to come up the line and point out the correct path- all the time hoping that a stray crossbow bolt would not streak out of the forest and put an end to him- and then they would move on. Less complicated were the caves and dolmens- those the engineers simply collapsed. Reynard would not be escaping that way.

At first, he had offered to draw the Calvarians a map, but he did not have to wait for Mosca to translate the general's words to know that Drauglir would have none of that. No, he wanted Tybalt and the others close, to ensure that they were not leading them into a trap, so he'd assigned them twenty scribes, a hundred scouts each as escort, and men and women to feed them and care for their horses. Once they'd been separated, Tybalt had gained a shadow, too: the honey blond youngest of the Seventeenth's blood-guards. Otr, he thought his name was, and he never left Tybalt's side now that Gerin was dead. He reminded Tybalt of Isengrim, somewhat, though he was stouter and broader of shoulder, and his eyes were olive green rather than the blue that was so common among the Northerners.

I'll soon be rid of you, Tybalt thought, grinning at Otr toothily. *I'll soon be rid of all of you, and rich besides. After all, we are almost there.*

The fifth ambush of the day came shortly before dusk, along one of the narrower tracks. Rather than aim for the soldiers, Reynard's men shot and killed two pairs of oxen, effectively blocking the path. By the time the carcasses had been butchered by the cooks and the wagons had been re-hitched it was growing too dark to continue. The engineers and half of the men made to pitch camp as best they could in the dense forest, felling trees and gathering up dead wood for the campfires.

As usual, once the camp was set, Tybalt and the scribes were summoned to report to Drauglir.

"How much farther must we travel?" Mosca asked him in his somber voice, his tone as emotionless as it had been the day Tybalt had offered to lead the Calvarians to Maleperduys. Tybalt wondered how long the man had been in the Calvarians' service; he almost seemed one of them.

"Not far," Tybalt answered. "We should reach the hidden valley by tomorrow evening at the latest."

Mosca translated his words and Drauglir nodded and dismissed Tybalt with a wave of his hand.

Tybalt had been provided with a humble tent that had been erected next to Mosca's, not far from the center of camp. He sat down on a nearby rock, took out his whetstone, and one by one he sharpened his knives. Otr stood at a short distance from him, his arms folded over one another. Eventually one of the cooks brought him his ration- a loaf of hardened bread, a bit of cheese, and several slices of sausage. He ate his meal slowly, bitterly wishing for a skin of wine.

"Not hungry?" Tybalt asked the blood-guard. "I haven't seen you eat a thing all day."

The man stared at him, and said nothing.

"It's not poor fare, this," Tybalt went on, spearing a sausage slice with his dagger. "Though I've had better. I've had worse as well. Wulf, there was a time when I had nothing for days on end. This would have been a feast to me then."

He put the sausage in his mouth, pulled it free from the blade, and chewed thoughtfully.

"I suppose you've never seen Engadlin, have you, my shadow? Beautiful country, it is. Dark earth, steady rains, plenty of sun . . . you could grow anything there. Suppose your kind will, too, when this war is done. You're welcome to it for all I care. As long as I get the gold."

He tore a hunk of bread off and ate it with the cheese.

"Don't know why anyone would choose to be a farmer when they could be a bandit," he managed to say between bites. "You work all day and night, trying to keep yourself and your family alive, and then one day some bastard chevalier comes and takes your head off with a sword, rapes your wife and daughters, takes your food and leaves your sons to starve. And what can they do? No way to live except by stealing and killing. Might as well have been bandits from the start, no?"

His ration finished, Tybalt went back to sharpening his knives.

"Men like to tell themselves that they are good, my shadow," he said, drawing his whetstone over his blade. "That they would not kill friend or family to survive. But you put two men who call each other 'friend' in a pit with only enough food to feed one, and you'll see what sort of friends they are before long. Me, I don't pretend to be any man's friend. But I guess your sort's like that too. It's better that way, right? Easier, at any rate."

Tybalt laid down his whetstone and ran his thumb lightly along the dagger's edge.

"Sharp enough to cut through a shadow," he judged, and smirked. "You had best be careful."

The blood-guard stared at him, and said nothing.

* * * * * * *

Rukenaw was training in the courtyard with a crossbow when Isengrim and his men returned. His arrival was heralded by the shouts of Gaignun, who was stationed atop the southeastern tower, and Rukenaw managed to beat the press of men making for the walls and she reached the parapet in time to see him and his riders tearing across the pasture that lay under the shadow of the castle.

Isengrim had left with nearly a fourth of their fighting men and women, some three hundred riders, but even without Tiecelin's sharp eyes Rukenaw could tell that they'd suffered numerous losses. Of those who had gone, perhaps half were returning, and as they neared the edge of the tilled fields a flight of arrows rose from the tree line and fell amongst the stragglers. The men and women who shared the wall with her let out a moan as a dozen riders fell from their steeds, some crushed beneath injured horses, others mortally pierced by steel-headed arrows.

Rukenaw squinted at the trees, and she could just make out the gray figures moving between them. Another flight erupted from the woods, but the shafts fell short.

"Martin," she said, her hands gripping the edge of the battlements. He had gone with Isengrim. Was he coming back, or was he lying dead somewhere in the forest, his body left to rot or be eaten by the wargs. *They should have taken me*, she had fumed the night that Martin had left, but Isengrim had said 'no,' she had not 'the sufficient training' to be considered useful. It wasn't her fault that she'd been previously forbidden to learn how to fire a crossbow, and had been unable to steal one from the armory.

But, no, Isengrim had taken Martin instead of her, and now he was returning with half of his warriors.

If he is dead because of you, she thought as the riders made their way up the causeway, *I will kill you. I swear it.*

But Rukenaw's fears for Martin were swiftly allayed, for he was amongst one of the first horsemen to pass through the castle's main gate, and though his hair was greasy and tousled, and his gear and face spattered with mud, he was not injured.

Rukenaw practically flew from the wall to greet him, catching only a glance of his face before she had caught him up in her arms and buried her head against his neck.

A moment later she felt his arms around her, holding her close.

"What was it like?" she asked when they finally parted. "Did you . . . kill any of them?"

"Three, I think," he said, sounding rather sober. "I hit them anyway."

"Good," she said, and gave him a kiss.

Rukenaw was surprised when he did not return it.

"Are you alright?" she asked.

"It was-" Martin said, hesitating. "Oh, Rukenaw, it was horrible. It wasn't . . . what I thought it would be. One of them- he couldn't have been much older than me. The bolt- my bolt- it hit him in the stomach. He didn't even scream- he just sat down, right there, and stared at it. Passecerf shot one of the men that was going to help him, and then- gods- then he started to cry . . . Rukenaw, he was so *young*."

"So was Eme," Rukenaw said, and Martin looked at her then as if he'd been slapped.

"I- I know," Martin said. "It just- I didn't think they would be . . . I don't know. I don't know what I'm even saying."

"It's alright," she said, and took his hand. "I understand."

The last of the riders were streaming into the courtyard, and the sound of horses whickering and neighing and men and women shouting at each other seemed like to drown out all, until finally Isengrim himself passed through the gate, and it was shut and barred behind him, the timber falling into place with a heavy thud.

The yard fell silent as Baron Reynard stepped out of the keep, and men and women made way to let him pass as he strode across to meet his captain.

"What news?" he said

"They are coming," the Northerner said as he dismounted. "The Seventeenth, the Second, and the Ninth bringing up the rear. They had guides to bring them through the maze. Tybalt, and his men, I would guess."

"I do not doubt it," Reynard said. "What are our losses?"

"A hundred and thirty of our riders are dead," Isengrim said. "But I made Drauglir pay dearly for the passage through the forest. I would guess we've slain some five hundred of the enemy, and gravely wounded at least a hundred more."

"Would that we only faced one army," Reynard said. "Still, you have gained us time."

"Is there any word from Tiecelin?" Isengrim asked.

"None."

Reynard spoke truly. They had not seen a shrike since the day that Rohart arrived with the news that they were being surrounded. Had Tiecelin deserted them? *If he has*, Rukenaw thought, a hot ball of anger welling within her, *then he is no better than Tybalt*. She would never abandon her companions, she knew, never, not if all the hosts of Calvaria stood between her and them.

"My Lord Reynard!" Gaignun called from his tower. "The enemy is moving!"

"Stay at your posts!" Reynard bellowed as the men and women of the castle surged towards the wall. "Riders, stable your horses and get some food inside of you. There is time yet to prepare."

Despite Reynard's words, Rukenaw found herself abandoning her crossbow practice and following- at a distance- the Baron of Maleperduys and Isengrim up one of the stairs that led to the battlements.

She had to sidle up between Russet and one of the sellswords that she did not know to get a good look at the valley below, but both men hardly seemed to notice her- their eyes were locked on the swarms of figures that were pouring out of the southern wood at a steady clip. Some were forming into tight squares, while others on horseback were fanning out across the valley, stabbing north around either side of the lake, heading directly towards the only other entrance to the valley- the one that led directly into the part of the forest thickest with wargs. 'Warg country' Reynard's men called it, and even Rukenaw had shied away from it. She could still remember the hot stink of the warg's breath against her face as it had ripped at her clothing. It was an experience she hoped never to relive, though she found herself hoping that an army of the monsters would erupt from the woods and fall on the Calvarians, even if it meant lying with a thousand of the beasts.

But if there were wargs waiting in the dark eaves of the forest they did not show themselves, and soon the scouts of the enemy had traversed the circumference of the bowl-shaped valley, having found nothing but the trees.

The sky grew dim as more and more Calvarians marched out of the woods, and Rukenaw felt her heart sink. There were thousands of them- over three times as many as had routed the King's army, and as their numbers increased they fanned out so as to encircle the fortress. On the right, the Calvarians marched beneath flags on which three silvery triangles were bound together, while on the left the emblem of the enemy was that of a rune-carved hammer, but in the center she recognized the banners of Drauglir: the wolf with the Firebird in its jaws. Behind this great host labored hundreds of others, some armed with axes and shovels felled trees and dug ditches, while others saw to the erection of tents and palisade. Calvarian riders wielding torches braved the archers and crossbowmen stationed on the walls and set fire to several of the wooden buildings that had taken them months to erect. The flames rose quickly and soon they had engulfed the rest of the little town and anything made of wood caught, even the trees. Plumes of black smoke rose into the sky, and Rukenaw's nose was full of the scent of burning.

"They will wait until nightfall to attack," Rukenaw heard Reynard say, and she turned. He was standing by Isengrim, the two of them watching the town go up in smoke with surprisingly calm faces. "It will be harder to spot them in the darkness, and they can bring up their engines while we shoot at their sappers."

"I fear you are right," Isengrim said. "Though Drauglir may yet choose to starve us out."

"He cannot afford to," Reynard replied, the fingers of his iron hand curling slightly as he spoke. "Every day he is forced to sit here and deal with us lends Nobel more time to rebuild his army. Besides, I doubt that Drauglir will be satisfied by anything less than a trial by combat after the bloody nose we've given him."

"Then it is far past time for us to begin preparations for the assault," Isengrim said.

"Indeed," Reynard said. "I will command the left."

"And I the right?"

"And you the right," the Baron said, and clapped his good hand on Isengrim's shoulder. "May the Watcher overlook you, my friend."

"And you," the Northerner replied, and clasped his hand to Reynard's wrist for a moment before turning to enter the gatehouse.

A moment later Reynard finally noticed Rukenaw, and he looked at her quizzically.

"What are you doing here?" he asked.

"I'm here to fight," she said.

"If you're going to fight," he said, cocking one of his eyebrows, "you might want to consider fetching your crossbow and armor."

"Oh," she said, having forgotten that she had left her weapon in the courtyard below, and wore little in the way of protection save for her leather jack and breeches.

"Run quickly," Reynard said. "And, if you like, bring Martin back with you. We'll need all the crossbowmen we can spare on the wall."

She nodded, and excused herself hurriedly, making for Hermeline's quarters.

When she and Martin had first come to the castle they'd both been quartered with Hermeline, and after that with Madam Slopecade and the kitchen maids. During their journey with Reynard and his men they'd slept together, often beneath the same blanket, sometimes holding onto each other, other times simply side by side, a bit of warmth at her back the only thing she needed to know that he was there. But now Martin slept in the barracks above the gatehouse, and she slept wherever it suited her fancy. A boy named Peregrine was her current lover, one of the many they'd picked up along the road back to Maleperduys- he was olive-skinned and curly-haired. She made certain not to let Martin catch them together, for she knew how much it would wound him to know how she spent her nights. After all, he still thought that she slept on a cot that Hermeline had set aside for her in an antechamber off the kitchen, where the priestess's herbs were hung to dry. To keep up appearances this was where she had stored the arms and armor she'd been given, and where she returned each morning for a few hours of sleep. She knew that Hermeline knew what she was about, but the older woman never asked where she had been, or what she had been doing, and for that, at least, she was very grateful.

Bring Martin back with you, she could hear Reynard saying as she slipped a coat of chain over her jack, *if you like*. As if the choice were up to her. Martin would follow her, whether she wanted him to or not. In fact, she guessed it was probably only a matter of time before he came looking for her.

Part of her wanted him to come. It would be good to have a friend at her side . . . yet another part of her wished that the boy was far away, where the Calvarians could not touch him.

Poor, dear, stupid Martin, she thought, and smiled. He was her only real friend, and he was kind, and he wanted her, she knew. It had felt good to be wanted by him, once, and she used to think that she wanted him too.

Now she could not look at him without remembering the sound that Eme's neck had made when the Calvarian dog snapped it, or the way Brunel, the miller's son, had spat up blood when one of the Northerners' arrows entered his back. And, sometimes, she looked at him and she could remember the songs at Crowning, or the dancing at the Midwinter festival, or the laughter of her mother and sister. That was worse somehow.

Martin was the only part of her old life left, and sometimes she hated him for it.

Sure enough, she was securing the flanged steel mace that Reynard himself had given her to her belt when Martin came blundering into the room.

"I thought I might find you here," he said. He looked less peaked than the last time she had seen him.

"The Baron wants us on the walls," she said to him. "That is, if you're ready to fight."

"I'm ready," he said.

His mock bravado might have been funny to her if things were not so grim. Yet she knew there were no words that could dissuade him from standing by her side, so she kissed him on the cheek and said, "Let's go."

* * * * * * *

The fires below them were beginning to go out when the assault began.

As a child, Rukenaw had delighted to hear the stories of Cassel, their village's servant of the Watcher, especially those of the Seven Heroes, but also of the fall of Old Aquilia, when great armies and noble houses contended with each other for the rule of the three kingdoms. In those stories there would be parlays before battle, or personal duels between chevalier that would decide the outcome. Men would meet beneath banners of truce, and offer mercy to the foe that yielded- it was said that even Basiliscus the Cruel of Glycon had afforded his enemies that choice before unleashing his dragon host . . . but it was not so with the Calvarians. A horn sounded once, twice, three times, and then the Northern army was on the advance, and the battle had begun.

True to Reynard's words the enemy had waited for the Firebird to set before making their first move. By that time their engineers had managed to construct a formidable camp ringed with sharpened stakes and ditches full of brambles and thorns. But the enemy had also been busy placing great wheel-mounted shields made of timber- mantlets she'd heard Reynard call them- and in the blue dusk Rukenaw could see them beginning to crawl across the fields towards them.

Behind them the siege engines sat, ready to spit forth smoke and death.

She shared her place on the wall with five others. Martin was there, of course, but also Passecerf, whom she had often guessed fancied her, and a pair of foreign sellswords whose names were so hard to pronounce that she'd given up trying. The sixth was a young woman named Hartnet, who might have been rather pretty if she still had a nose. She wore a veil over the lower half of her face to hide her deformity, but it barely helped: the veil hung weirdly, almost drawing more attention to the fact that there was nothing betwixt her dark eyes. Rukenaw shuddered to think of how she had lost it, and what other horrors she had been forced to endure.

"They come," she said as another horn echoed across the valley, and readied her crossbow. One of the mercenaries, the one she thought of as 'Patches' due to the state of his clothes, nodded at her words and lowered himself into a firing position.

"Archers!" a voice called out from the tower- Gaignun's she thought, but it was hard to tell. "Open fire!"

Interspersed along the walls and towers Reynard had stationed some two score bowmen- hunters, most of them, but also Southerners trained as archers- and they'd been supplied with arrows doused with pitch and a brazier to light them over. None of these men were Tiecelin's equal, but they did not have to be.

They were not, after all, aiming for men.

The flaming arrows fell amongst the mantlets, most of them sticking where they struck, though some had found human targets as well judging by the cries that rose from the field below. The archers sent a second flight streaking through the night, and then a third, and by the fourth volley, so many arrows had riddled the mantlets that they glowed like torches.

"Crossbows!" another voice yelled- it was undoubtedly Reynard. "Fire at will!"

Rukenaw hesitated, but only a moment. Her hands were sweaty beneath her gloves, and her heart was pounding wildly in her chest, but when she looked down the sight of her weapon she found a sort of calm take hold of her. She aimed at a figure that was attempting to clear the arrows from the mantlets, squeezed her trigger, and felt the brief shock of the bolt being loosed run up her arm.

She didn't wait to see if she'd struck her target, but ducked down behind the battlement and began to reload, her fingers shaking only a little as she redrew the whipcord. While she did Passecerf and the other sellsword took their turn at the wall, and then Martin and Hartnet. By the time Martin had gotten behind cover, she had a bolt ready. She let out a breath and popped up over the rampart just long enough to take aim and fire.

The Calvarians were returning fire by then. The first few volleys of arrows flew either too high or too low, and most clattered harmlessly against the stone walls, though some fell into the courtyard, and a least one or two of her fellow defenders were unlucky enough to be pierced by them. The enemy archers seemed to be finding their bearings quickly, however, and by her third turn at the wall she felt one whiz right by her head as she exposed herself to fire. It was growing so dark that she could hardly see the archers, and wondered if any of them were hitting anything as she sent a third bolt hurtling into the darkness.

She was reloading her fourth bolt when she heard a sound like a great door slamming- it was so loud that she could feel it inside her chest- and then the entire wall seemed to shake beneath her.

"What was that?" she said out loud, not wholly expecting an answer.

"Siege engines," Patches said to her. "Very bad. Keep reloading."

As she readied her quarrel, another war machine discharged with a *BOOM*, and then there was a sound like a strange animal shrieking as something flew overhead and smashed into the keep. Martin was holding his hands over his ears. She stood up. *BOOM BOOM BOOM*, the enemy weapons roared and the castle shook again. She looked down the sight and fired.

"They're testing our walls!" Passecerf yelled as he took her place, aimed, and fired.

An arrow flew out of the night and struck the other mercenary- the one she had not named- in the breast. He screamed and dropped his crossbow. *BOOM*. Part of the southeast tower blew apart, showering the men and women on the wall with tiny shards of stone. Martin and Hartnet stood, aimed, fired. Rukenaw felt blood trickling down her cheek and realized she'd been cut somehow. She stood, aimed, fired.

BOOM BOOM BOOM.

The castle shuddered, and she could hear the sounds of stone and mortar collapsing, and men and women screaming in fear as something large crashed to the earth behind her. She put it out of her mind and reloaded.

As the Calvarian war machines continued to belch forth their deadly shot, several volleys of flaming enemy arrows flew overhead and landed in the courtyard. Voices were crying out for water. She could hear horses screaming in terror.

The stables must be on fire, she thought, and stood, aimed, and fired.

She was reloading when she noticed that Patches was dead. He was sprawled over the rampart, an arrow lodged directly underneath one of his eyes.

"Keep reloading!" Passecerf shouted at her. The other mercenary was quivering, clutching at the shaft that was protruding from his breast.

She wondered why the thing had not killed him. There were only four of them now, so they did not fire in pairs. She went first, then Passecerf, then Martin, then Hartnet. There was plenty of time to reload.

How long they did this before the main gate was shattered Rukenaw could not have said. Hours it might have been, or mere moments. All she knew was the feel of the cold stone beneath her, the action of her crossbow as she pulled the ripcord taut, the brief sight of the enemy, their ranks shrouded by white plumes of smoke and the clouds above, hiding the Watcher from view. And always the terrible sounds of the war machines. She knew they were aiming at the gate, for she could hear wood splintering and groaning in the wake of every retort. Finally the engines fired as one, and the great beam that held the doors shut split.

They were breached.

Part of her wanted to take Martin by the hand and run, as they had the day the Calvarians had destroyed their village. By the look on his face, she could tell that he was thinking the same thing. *Perhaps we could hide in the catacombs*, Martin's eyes seemed to say, *perhaps they will not find us*.

Then she heard again her mother's screaming suddenly silenced by a Calvarian arrow. Brunel spitting up a mouthful of blood. Eme's neck snapping. The dog snarling in her face before Martin's axe split its skull.

She stood, aimed, and fired.

The siege engines were quiet, the thunderous sound of their voices replaced by the steady tramp of booted feet. When it was again her turn at the wall she saw that a column of enemy soldiers was marching up the causeway. She fired a bolt at the head of the line and was rewarded by the sight of her quarrel striking a man in the head. He staggered and tumbled over the edge, falling no doubt onto the sharp rocks below.

"Get down!" Passecerf shouted at her as he dragged her below the rampart.

"I hit one," she said.

"Good," Passecerf said, firing his own bolt. "Keep reloading!"

She nodded. Martin took his turn. She could hear Reynard yelling for men to hold the gate. Hartnet took her turn. An arrow sailed right over the woman's shoulder as she fired.

Rukenaw stood to fire. A moment later she was flat on her back. She had an arrow in her chest.

It did not hurt at first. She reached for the shaft to pull it out, thinking that perhaps it had caught in her mail, but as she did so she could feel the arrow tip twisting like a knife inside of her, and saw the hot blood streaming from the wound.

Martin was screaming something, but it was lost beneath the cry of the Calvarians as they charged up the last bit of causeway and met the men waiting for them. Steel met steel. Passecerf caught Martin and shouted something at him, and then the boy was lifting her up, using his arm to help support her, and they were half hobbling, half running towards the southeast tower.

Her wound made her dizzy with pain, but somehow she kept to her feet. "Hold on," Martin kept saying to her as they stepped over the bodies of the dead and dying. The air was thick now with arrows- one of them caught a man in the bowels as they passed by another knot of crossbowmen. She turned and saw that the shrikes' tower had entirely collapsed, and the breezeway that connected it to the main keep had fallen as well. The stables, the smithy, the barracks, all were on fire. Some of the horses had escaped the flames and were racing through the chaos in the yard, rearing and kicking as armed figures raced to join the press at the gate.

"Hold on," Martin said again, and then they were inside the tower. The second story was full of the wounded, and the enemy siege engines had blown a massive hole in one of the walls. Still, fighters wielding crossbows were firing at the Calvarians through the gap, or out of the narrow arrow slits. She could hear Reynard's voice echoing down the steps that led to the third story.

All this Rukenaw took in, and then they were making their way down the stairs, down a passage, through a door, and then into the courtyard.

The heat of the flames engulfing the barracks hit Rukenaw in the face like a slap- she could almost feel her eyebrows singeing as they took a few steps forward, and the smoke threatened to choke her.

It was no use. Martin dragged her backwards, into the tower. A moment later someone slammed the door to the courtyard, and barred it.

"Wait here," Martin said, propping her against the wall of the passage. "I'll go get help."

"No," she said, and took hold of him. "Don't go."

"I have to," he said. "You're bleeding to death! You need Hermeline."

"Don't go," she said again, and took his hand. "Please. You have to help me take the arrow out. I'd do it myself but I'm afraid I might pass out."

"Rukenaw, I can't," he said.

"Do you want me to die?"

"No, of course I don't," he replied, tears in his eyes. "But I don't know how!"

"Just do what I tell you!" she shouted at him. "And pull the arrow out!"

Martin gritted his teeth and took hold of the shaft as gently as he could. Rukenaw gripped onto him by the shoulders. Then he began to pull.

She'd watched Hirsent's face when she'd been delivering her child, had imagined the pain the woman had suffered. Was this any worse? She could not say. Did she scream as the arrowhead tore its way out of her flesh? She could not later recall. One moment Martin was pulling, and her fingers were digging into the leather jack he wore, deeper and deeper. Then the arrow freed itself, and a thick gout of her own blood painted Martin's face dark red, and she felt her legs go limp beneath her.

* * * * * * *

For a time there was nothing but a roaring in her ears. Then the earth lurched and quivered beneath her, and her eyes fluttered open.

She was still in the tower- on the second level now, with the rest of the wounded warriors. Someone had removed her armor and bound her chest in bandages. Martin was sitting beside her, her hand in his.

For some reason, men and women were cheering all around her.

"Have we," she asked, hissing slightly at the pain in her breast. "Have we won?"

"No," Martin said. "At least I don't think we have. I'm not sure what's going on."

Reynard loomed over her then.

"The enemy brought one of their engines up the causeway in order to blast a way into the main keep," he said. "Isengrim just destroyed it with a flaming arrow. They'll not risk losing another, I think."

"Then Hermeline is safe?"

"I would hardly call any of us safe," Reynard replied. "They've taken the gatehouse and the southwest tower, and soon they'll be coming for us. Still, we have gained some breathing room, if only a little."

"What time is it?" she asked. Through the hole in the tower she could see that the sky was gray.

"It is nearly morning," Reynard said. "You have been asleep for some time."

She tried to sit up, but Reynard pushed her back down with his cold iron hand and said, "Rest yet awhile. Sleep if you can. You will need your strength I think, before this day is through."

She nodded, and laid back. She gave Martin's hand a squeeze.

"And to think," she said to him. "That I was worried about you. My brave Martin."

He smiled at her words, and kissed her hand.

"I'm sorry that I tease you," she said.

"I liked being teased," he replied, grinning ever so slightly.

"No you don't."

"Shhh," he said. "Reynard said that you should rest."

She closed her eyes for a while, and tried to sleep, but it was impossible. The sounds of battle still raged all about them, from the shrieks of the dying to the steady sound of men pounding at the tower doors.

Finally she turned her head away from Martin and opened her eyes. She found she was facing one of the larger windows. It must have overlooked the lake, for Reynard and Isengrim were standing in front of it, speaking quietly to one another. Or, rather, Reynard was speaking and Isengrim was listening. There was something strange about the look on the Northerner's face, and the way that his bow hung loose in his hands. If she did not know better, she might have thought that the man was . . . sad.

She leaned towards them, and tried to hear what they were saying, but all she could make out were the last words that Isengrim uttered before they parted.

"I will do it."

XIII

Drauglir's eyes snapped open. He'd been sleeping in the saddle. Not long, he judged by the color of the sky, but still, he had fallen asleep.

I am getting old, he thought and rubbed his temple.

He had viewed the night battle from the rear of the lines, watched as the siege engines had made short work of the main gate, and Heafodcarl Byleist and his men had stormed the moldering fortress that The Fox called home. They were all dead now, as well as several companies from the Ninth and Second. The place was stronger than it looked, and its foundations were carved out of solid stone- the work of giants if he did not miss his guess. After the siege engine went up, slaying not only its crew but also two score of his soldiers and wounding dozens more, he was tempted to order the engineers to pound the place into dust.

But no, Drauglir thought. *That would not do. I must have his body.* If he thought it were possible he would have marched The Fox back to Dis in chains, but the risk of escape was too great. His corpse would have to do.

"*What are the night's losses?*" he asked Heafodcarl Skirnir, who, as usual, had the command of the early morning watch. The man had obviously been waiting some time to deliver his report.

"*One hundred twenty two archers dead*," the man answered. "*Thirty seven wounded, five dead of dysentery. One thousand one hundred and thirteen infantry confirmed dead, two hundred and sixty five wounded, thirty two dead of dysentery.*"

"*It's the lake water, no doubt. Order the engineers to dig up a proper system of wells,*" Drauglir said to the prafost who was on watch, and turned back to Skirnir. "*What of the enemy?*"

"*At least four hundred were slain during our main assault, by our best estimates. The rest have holed up in the towers and central keep. They seem well provisioned for a siege, and have repulsed several attacks on the towers.*"

"*I trust the Fox was not among the dead?*" Drauglir asked.

"*Not that the soldiers could identify, no,*" Skirnir said. "*Shall we send one of the Southerners in to examine the bodies?*"

"No," Drauglir said, glancing towards the four men who remained of the six turncoats. They were clustered together, with Otr No-Father and a dozen men guarding them. "*We can sort out the dead soon enough.*"

He was about to dismiss Skirnir and order Heafodcarl Andvari to lead the next attack when one of the soldiers from the Ninth rode up with a message from Latteowa Thrivaldi.

Drauglir read the message.

"*They . . . are sending out boats,*" Drauglir said, and called for his spyglass.

Sure enough, a tiny squadron of wide-bottomed row boats was launching from what appeared to be a crack in the base of the shelf upon which the castle sat, and each of them held at least a score of figures. They did not look much like warriors, though, but women and children. They were making for the northern shore of the lake.

"*Latteowa Thrivaldi requests orders, Latteowa,*" the soldier said. "*Shall he send out men to intercept them?*"

Drauglir lowered the spyglass, and squinted at the boats, the far shore of the lake, the castle above. It did not smell right to him.

"*What think you, Golden Arm?*" Drauglir addressed the man who was always by his side. "*Is this a trap or merely simple desperation?*"

Fafnir No-Father said nothing.

"*Send two companies of scouts,*" Drauglir decided. "*No more. Tell Thrivaldi I'm sending two of the turncoats as well. Mosca, inform the Prince of Cats that I have a scouting mission for him and one other of his fellow creatures.*"

Mosca seemed to sense that time was precious, for he merely bowed before striding over to the arrogant Southerner and translating Drauglir's command. The Prince of Cats replied in his usual acerbic tone, but jerked his head at one of the other Southerners and set his horse into a canter.

"*Otr,*" Drauglir said, catching the blood-guard's gaze with his own. "*Slay them both if they prove untrue.*"

"*As you wish,*" Otr No-Father replied and fell in after the messenger from the Ninth and the two Southern traitors.

"*Heafodcarl Skirnir you are dismissed,*" Drauglir said, and called for a messenger.

"*Your orders, Latteowa?*" the man said.

"*Inform Heafodcarl Andvari that the next assault is his. He will lead one of the veteran companies. Tell him I expect him to take the remaining towers by midday.*"

"*Yes, Latteowa,*" the messenger barked, and rode off towards the front lines.

It only took Andvari a moment to choose which company would follow him, and with a horn blast one hundred soldiers of the Seventeenth began the deadly march up the causeway that led to the fortress.

Drauglir had no eyes for them however. His gaze was instead locked on the tiny boats, and the soldiers who were riding out to meet them. He lifted his spyglass again, and peered at the receding figures rowing across the lake. If these were warriors in disguise, there were hardly enough of them to overpower the scouts- half of them would be shot down before they even reached the shoreline. If The Fox thought that he would spare the lives of the mongrels that followed him, then he was a fool who had misjudged Drauglir greatly.

But The Fox is no fool, Drauglir thought, shifting the glass towards the western shore. He could make out the Prince of Cats amongst the gray uniforms of the scouts, and Otr No-Father riding close behind him.

"*It is a message*," he said under his breath. *But what sort? And for whom? Perhaps he means to show his followers that we offer no mercy, even to the young and old . . . but no, we have taught the Southerners that lesson for over five hundred years. They do not need reminding. What then? What was the message? Who was it for?*

As he lowered the spyglass, something strange caught his attention. He thought he had seen a dark winged shape land in one of the trees that ringed the valley. For the past ten days the scouts had caught not a glimpse of either The Fox's tamed monsters or any other chimera for that matter, winged or otherwise. And yet the thing he had seen was too large to be a bird.

He trained his spyglass on the trees.

"*Call for battle formations!*" he bellowed as Southern warriors began to pour out of the forest on either side of the valley. The scouts were already wheeling their horses around. "*Reform to the rear!*"

Thrivaldi and Thrym were no doubt shouting the same, for horns were soon ringing throughout the valley. Suddenly one of his prafosts went slack in his saddle. A red-fletched arrow protruded from the back of his neck.

"*Archers on the heights!*" Drauglir yelled, kicking his horse into a gallop to get out of range. More arrows fell, hundreds now, many of them falling directly into their camp.

Out of the corner of his eye he could see that several of the turncoats had taken flight. More Southern warriors were erupting out of the woods. Battle had already been joined on the right. The arrows were falling thick around them.

"*Reform!*" he shouted again, and whipped his reins, making for the center of their lines. His bodyguards and staff followed suit.

Many thoughts spun through his mind as they charged across the trampled pasture.

How long did it take them all to scale the steep walls of the valley, and then climb down again? How long have they been waiting to attack? How could The Fox have summoned so many men in so little time?

Then he understood. The Fox had known they were coming. Somehow, he had known it before even Drauglir had. He had wanted their armies to come here.

To die.

More and more enemies were pressing in on the flanks. Drauglir could see the Second's lines bowing under the press of foes that were surrounding them. Thrivaldi still had the Ninth forming battle lines when the first wave of Southerners hit them. Even at this distance Drauglir could see that there were giants amongst the enemy. Then he and his retinue had reached the Seventeenth's own ranks. His soldiers had just reversed their ranks, forming a tight semicircle around the siege lines.

Heafodcarl Hervor rode up to meet him.

"Your orders?" she said as Drauglir brought his steed to a halt.

"We split in two," Drauglir replied, dismounting. "*You will reinforce the Ninth, Heafodcarl Managarm the Second.*"

"*And you, Latteowa?*"

"*I am going to kill The Fox,*" Drauglir replied, and made for the causeway.

* * * * * * *

Bruin roared and brought down his axe. The Northerner he faced brought up his sword to parry the blow and wound up with a shattered arm for all of his efforts. He swiped the man aside and moved on to the next.

It had been a while since he'd been in an honest fight. Reynard's ways were effective, there was no arguing with that, but sometimes they rankled Bruin all the same. He preferred to meet his enemies face to face with a belly full of liquor and an axe in his hand, as they had at the Samara. There was something simple about it that just felt right to him.

Still, he had far preferred their ambushes to the work that Reynard had set for him over the past three months, traveling across the breadth of the Southlands to drum up mercenaries. He'd wondered why Tiecelin had not been chosen for the job, but then he thought about the way the man hardly spoke save to his 'pets' and realized that he was probably the better choice.

And, granted, Reynard's instructions had been incredibly simple: *Hire mercenaries*, he'd written, according to Tiecelin. *As many mercenaries as you can find. The more the better. Don't haggle with them. Find out what their fee is and then offer them double. If that doesn't work, triple. There will be no payment up front. You must be at Cadwallon by Wulf's Night. Tiecelin will meet you there with further instructions.*

So, Bruin had spent all of Harvestmonth hiring mercenaries. He had the best luck at Lucra, for that Southern port saw trade from Frisia, Therimere, and Glycon. Some of the captains he met with had thought him mad, and had sent him away with curses and threats, but many others did not- even there they'd heard the stories of Lord Reynard, and the gold he was promising proved so tempting that he soon found himself swamped by sellswords seeking contracts. Skirmishes broke out between mercenary companies seeking to prove their worth to him, and men brought gifts to curry his favor: drink, exotic food, women. Sometimes all three. But there was hardly any reason to bribe him- he hired them all. He hired the Company of the Storm, the Southern Brotherhood, the Seventy Seven Shields (of which there were actually a hundred and thirteen), the Farstriders, the Steel Heels, the Ladykillers, and the Red Children. He hired the Iron Band, which a scar-faced warrior named Thierry had somehow reformed. He hired a company of tattooed Myrmidons, whose 'captain' was a perfumed dandy who wore silk slippers and a powdered wig. He hired a band whose leader was a giant, and a dozen giants who followed a man shorter even than Reynard. He hired a woman claiming to be the sister of the Prince of Therimere. He hired a hundred men who'd heard of the gold and had formed a company in order to serve- they hadn't even chosen officers, let alone a name. He'd hired them all.

By the time they'd reached Cadwallon, Bruin rode at the head of an army that might have rivaled Nobel's at the Samara. The city had closed its gates to them, fearing that they would sack the city- and for good reason. The mercenaries were impossible to control and seldom paid for the food they stole as they marched- but no matter, two days after Wulf's Night Tiecelin had appeared with his own riders, and had said that they were heading for Maleperduys. They marched across Lorn, and then into the wild wood. Finally Tiecelin had ordered the best climbers to scale one of the steep-edged hills and secure ropes to the strongest trees. Then it was the simple matter of some thirty thousand men climbing up one rope and down another.

It had taken all day, and most of the night, and they'd been forced to huddle, shivering beneath the trees for hours before Reynard sent out the signal to attack, but Bruin had a bottle to keep him warm, and the look on the faces of the Calvarian scouts as they charged out of the woods was well worth the wait.

The valley was ill-suited to the Calvarians' orderly formations, for it was strewn with boulders and thick shrubs, and here and there were dried-out creek beds that made it next to impossible to form any kind of unified front.

Bruin was one of the first to meet with the enemy, charging at the head of the Steel Heels and the giants. The Calvarian lines wavered almost immediately under their assault, and soon the front ranks of the Calvarians shattered and the fight became a free-for-all.

It hardly mattered to Bruin. He had his axe, and it was easy to tell the Calvos from the mercenaries, though he nearly took the head off of one of the Steel Heels when the man got in the way of his swing.

"Sorry," Bruin said, and kicked the man off the edge of Mauler.

Two men came at him. As he was hacking down one, the other landed a good hit on his shoulder, but the Calvarian's sword merely glanced off his thick armor. Bruin laughed and flattened the man with a backhand. Before he could get up, one of the giants stepped on him.

Finding himself momentarily surrounded by allies, Bruin paused to catch his breath. Ahead of him the Myrmidons were hacking away at the enemy, not even crying out as they were cut down. Their sort gave Bruin the chills- they reminded him too much of Ghul, with their tattoos and Glyconese armor- so he skirted around them and joined another melee.

He had just hacked down his third man when he saw a giant fall, crushing several of the mercenaries beneath it.

Its killer was a man in black. One of the blood-guard.

In the time it took Bruin to kill two more opponents, the Calvarian had cut down a dozen other mercenaries. When one of the Steel Heels fired a bolt at the man, he *caught* it.

Three more mercenaries went down, and then the blood-guard shifted, and focused his gaze on Bruin.

Bruin hefted his axe and charged.

His first swing would have chopped the man in half, if it had struck home, but the blood-guard merely leaned backwards, seeming almost to dance as he tested the strength of Bruin's plate with a series of slashing cuts.

He's fast, Bruin thought as he reversed his swing. Again, Mauler caught nothing but air. *Too fast.*

The blood-guard made a thrust then, and Bruin felt the cold bite of steel as the man's sword slipped underneath one of his besagues, but the blade barely penetrated the chain that he was wearing underneath his plate. He roared and brought his axe down in an arc meant to cut through the blood-guard's shoulder- the man didn't seem to be wearing any sort of armor- but the Calvarian was already moving before he'd started his swing, landing a hard blow to the back of Bruin's helmet as he maneuvered behind him.

Bruin wheeled to face his opponent, and caught a brief glimpse of the blood-guard's palm before it smashed into his nose.

The strike dazed him. Blood spurted from his nostrils and clogged his throat. He couldn't seem to focus his eyes.

He couldn't see the enemy.

Bruin began to swing his axe left and right, backpedaling as best he could. He nearly tripped over something, a rock maybe, or a corpse. There was blood in his mouth.

His vision was just beginning to clear when the blood-guard stabbed him.

The sword point had all of the man's force behind it, and it sheared through chain as the length of the blade slid underneath Bruin's breastplate and into his bowels.

Bruin made to grab for the blade, but he was too slow. The blood-guard pulled it free, and Bruin's lifeblood spurted freely from the wound.

Too much, Bruin thought vaugely, shaking his head as if to clear it. *Too much blood.*

I'm dying.

He sunk down to one knee. He felt his hands clutching at the wound, trying to stem the dark flow. When had he dropped his axe? The blood-guard had turned from him, his blade flashing red as he cut down another one of the Steel Heels. Bruin's vision was growing dim.

With a growl he picked himself up, and nearly fell over the Northerner as he wrapped his massive arms around him, and began to squeeze.

Bruin's armor was covered in spikes, and he crushed the man against them. The blood-guard battered him with his sword, but it was useless- he couldn't get his arms free enough to gain any momentum. He let go of the blade and began to tear at Bruin's neck. He might as well have tried to strangle a tree-trunk. Bruin tightened his hold. He could hear things beginning to pop inside of the man. He could hear himself laughing. The blood-guard lashed forward with his face and bit into Bruin's cheek. Bruin did not let go. Even when the man tore a chunk of his flesh off with his bare teeth, he did not let go.

The blood-guard's eyes were fluttering. His tongue was lolling in his mouth.

Bruin squeezed harder.

Bruin felt the man go limp in his arms before he died.

* * * * * * *

Reynard's soldiers shot down nine Calvarians before they reached the gatehouse. They could fire more freely now, as the archers below were now more concerned with the hordes of sellswords descending upon them, but Drauglir had sent some of the archers into the castle to reinforce their captured towers, and they were deadly accurate with their bows.

How many are there? Reynard wondered. *Two hundred? Three? And how many of us are there left? We must have lost at least five hundred men trying to hold the gate. Maybe another two hundred on the walls. Will all of us be enough?*

There was no use thinking about it. The time for thinking was over.

"Make ready to light the basement," he said to Gaignun. The old man had taken at least three arrows during the night, but he was still on his feet.

"Baron?" Gaignun said, confused. "Will we not hold this tower?"

Reynard shook his head. "We need to retake the gatehouse, and I can't afford for the enemy to gain any more ground. We're going to light the basement. Get everyone ready to follow me."

Gaignun nodded, and grabbed one of the lamps before plodding towards the steps that led down to the cellar. In preparation for the siege, Reynard had each of the tower's lowest levels filled with pitch and timber. A spark could set the whole thing blazing within moments.

"Better put this on," Reynard said to Isengrim, and tapped the man's helmet. The Northerner had taken it off to improve his aim as he fired at the Calvarians in the courtyard below. "Things are bound to get confusing in a moment, and some of the men know the Warg's face better than yours."

The Northerner nodded, and affixed the helm to his armor.

Reynard went to Martin then, who had taken a position by the hole in the tower. The boy had stopped firing for a moment, and was staring, wide-eyed, at the melee that was erupting in the valley below.

"We're saved," Martin said, not sounding as if he wholly believed his words. "Reynard, we're saved."

"Not just yet," Reynard said. "But soon, I think, if we are lucky. Come along now, follow me."

Martin stood, his eyes still locked on the sight of the mercenaries surrounding the Second Regiment. Reynard pulled him away, taking hold of his arm in his iron hand, and dragged him over to where Rukenaw had been propped up.

"Can you walk?" he asked the girl.

"Yes," she said, "I think so."

She began pushing herself from the floor, and despite a few pained winces, managed to gain her feet.

"Martin," Reynard said. "Stay by her and keep her safe."

"Where are we going?" Martin asked.

"To meet the enemy," he replied. "Be ready."

Martin stared at him, shocked, but nodded all the same.

When Reynard had finished signaling his intentions to the main keep, and after all were gathered on the first floor, Gaignun set the basement of the tower on fire. Within moments smoke was curling up through the floorboards, and gusting up the spiral stairs, and Reynard could feel the heat of it even through the floor.

"Now!" he yelled, and threw open the portal to the courtyard. The Calvarians manning the timber that had been hammering at the door were taken momentarily by surprise, and spent a second gaping before reaching for their weapons. It was a deadly mistake, for Isengrim was the first one amongst them, Reynard was the second, and behind them were some seventy odd warriors who were desperate to escape the tower before flames engulfed it from below. They fought like animals as they hacked and stabbed their way into the press of Northerners, some of them firing their crossbows at point blank range before taking up sword, axe, and mace. Reynard could not see them through the press, but he knew that all across the castle his warriors were sallying forth to meet the enemy head-on.

He ventured they outnumbered the Calvarians two-to-one.

Three-to-one, if we are lucky, he thought, and then he was fighting for his life.

If he had one advantage, it was his left hand. Isengrim had forged it, and it was sturdy enough to catch a blade without injuring him. Again and again an enemy would find their swords glancing off of the back of his iron palm before Cut-Throat found their necks. Other times an enemy would think himself safe up until the moment that hidden blade in his wrist plunged into their sides.

Isengrim had reforged Cut-Throat too, replacing inferior Southern ore with Calvarian steel, and now it was as strong as it was flexible. Isengrim himself stayed close to him, and several times Reynard found the man cutting down an opponent that he had not even seen until he was dying at the tall man's feet. Still, it was impossible to deflect every blow, and soon he was bruised and bleeding, and when one of the Calvarians struck his side with a longsword he could swear that he could hear one of his ribs snapping in spite of his breast plate. Arrows were raining down amongst them, and bolts as well, and the stones were growing slick with blood as men and women fell on one another.

It was beginning to snow.

He was finishing off one of the Calvarian officers, a prafost by the pips on his collar, when he saw Drauglir. He had only seen him once, himself hiding amongst the rocks so many months ago, but there was no mistaking the Calvarian general. He was holding the gate, along with a score of his men. One of them was a blood-guard, tall, and white-haired. As Reynard watched the man cut down Grandoyne and Valdabrun, two of his best, and then a half dozen others.

Soon there were only a handful of men between them.

"I will face the blood-guard," he heard Isengrim say.

Reynard nodded, and they began to make their way across the courtyard. Any Calvarians who stood in their way died.

Drauglir saw them coming, his eyes flashing at the sight of them. He motioned for his men to stand down, and drew his sword. Reynard would have needed both of his hands to wield it.

"*Kill the Warg,*" Drauglir said to the man in black by his side, his tone almost casual. The blood-guard nodded, and advanced on Isengrim, almost pacing as he shifted his footing back and forth. Then his sword flashed and the older man was pushing Isengrim back as they traded a half dozen blows. They paused, gauging each other for a moment, and then rejoined. Three strokes later Isengrim had taken a blow to the arm that had actually drawn blood.

The two were evenly matched.

Reynard forced himself to turn away. He had his own fight ahead of him, and he was already tired.

"*Fox,*" Drauglir said, bringing his sword up in a brief salute before lowering his helmet's visor.

"Drauglir," Reynard said, and planted his feet for his opening stance.

Drauglir was big. He was nearly as tall as Isengrim and as wide at the shoulder as Bruin. His cloak made him seem enormous. And he was wearing plate. A beautiful gorget protected his throat.

Reynard's only consolation was that the man had no shield.

Wear him down, Reynard thought. *That armor has to be heavy.*

Drauglir moved first, bringing his sword down in a simple vertical cut. Reynard parried, riposted, blocked a pair of Drauglir's follow up strikes, and then slid sideways, trying to gain some ground.

Drauglir swung at him as he turned, missed, blocked a swing that Reynard made at his legs, and then bulled into him, nearly knocking him down as he charged forward. Reynard twisted around the bigger man, but Drauglir was ready for this, and as he spun around he landed a blow on Reynard's right shoulder that might have carved through bone were he not wearing pauldrons. As it was, Reynard staggered backwards, and only just managed to bring his sword up in time to counter another blow.

Drauglir kicked Reynard in the midsection then, and sent him sprawling.

He rolled to one side as Drauglir brought his sword down in a cut that would have cleaved his skull open, and somehow gained his feet. Reynard let Drauglir take a few swings at him, ducking and dodging under the blows as the big man advanced, letting him over-extend himself before landing a blow of his own on his opponent's midsection. The edge of his sword scraped across the Northerner's armor, squealing, and then they parted.

The cut had left a faint scratch across the Drauglir's breastplate. He doubted that the man had even felt it.

Reynard was panting. If Drauglir was even winded, he could not tell. The entire southeast tower was burning now, and the courtyard was full of dead men, and the wailing wounded. Screams were rising from the keep- the enemy must have broken into it somehow. There was fierce fighting going on near the gate too, but his duel with Drauglir had taken them some distance from it, and he could not tell what was going on. He couldn't see Isengrim either.

"*Tired, Fox?*" Drauglir said, his voice muffled by the visor he wore.

"*Merely catching my breath,*" he replied, and then the Northerner was on him again.

Don't let him get too close, he thought, and let Drauglir push him back as they exchanged blows, their swords screaming against one another as they met again and again.

He had just sidestepped one of Drauglir's blows when he saw Rukenaw. The girl was racing across the courtyard, her mace clutched in her hands. And then he saw that Martin was chasing after her, screaming for her to stop.

I have to end this, he realized. *Now.*

He went on the attack, and aimed for Drauglir's legs and head. The Northerner seemed surprised by the change in tactics, but adjusted accordingly. On their sixth exchange Reynard knocked Drauglir's sword aside with his left hand, and slammed the hilt of his sword against the bigger man's helm.

Drauglir responded by backhanding him. He felt his own helmet fly from his head and heard it land somewhere amidst the corpses. Then he took another sword blow, this one to the back. His armor held, but the force of it knocked him to the ground. He spat a mouthful of blood onto the courtyard and turned, raising Cut-Throat as he did so.

Drauglir's armored foot stamped down on Reynard's right wrist. He let go of his sword reflexively.

It was over. He had lost.

"*You are a worthy opponent, Fox,*" the Northerner said, readying his blade for the killing stroke. "*But you are no Drauglir Seventhson.*"

Drauglir had just finished speaking those words when Rukenaw reached them. The girl smashed her mace against the Calvarian with as much strength as she could muster.

It wasn't enough.

Drauglir snarled, and grabbed the girl by the arm. She screamed and twisted in his grip, but he was far too strong for her. He raised his sword to hack her down.

Out of the corner of one eye, Reynard could see Martin racing towards them.

He squeezed his ghost hand as tight as he was able. The hidden blade sprung forth, and with all of his remaining strength he buried it into the thick of Drauglir's leg.

The Northerner grunted, stumbled backwards, and swung.

His blade cut straight through Martin's left arm, shearing through leather as it buried itself in the boy's side. For a moment both the Northerner and the boy did not seem to understand what had just happened. Then Martin's blood was showering them both, and the

Calvarian began to recover. The blade was so deeply planted in the boy's chest that for a moment Drauglir could not free it, and he had to use both hands to pull it loose.

Reynard stabbed Drauglir then, right between the eyes. Unlike a Calvarian sword, his blade fit perfectly into the gap between Drauglir's helmet and visor.

The Calvarian general let out a hollow gurgle, and died.

* * * * * * *

For a long while it seemed to Thrym that he was again defending the mountain pass against the chimera, the press of enemies was so thick, and their own numbers were so few by comparison. He half expected the Raveler to come loping out of the crowd of Southerners, whispering riddles as he raked men apart with his claws, but as the soldiers of the Seventeenth smashed into the enemy's right flank he returned to his senses, and he ordered his center to give ground while sending his best companies to strengthen the flanks.

Back and back the men and women holding the center let themselves be pushed, until the rear ranks were waist deep in the water of the lake. The enemy warriors swarmed forward, some of them trampling each other as they closed in for what they assumed would be an easy kill.

Then Thrym ordered the flanks to close inwards, and the Southerners found themselves surrounded on three sides. Still, they were ferocious, and several hundred of them died on the edge of Calvarian steel before they lost heart for the fight. Thousands broke ranks, and made for the pass between the hills that had brought the Calvarians through the forest, but the majority found themselves trapped in a ring of enemies from which Thrym knew there would be no escape.

The ring was tightening, and hundreds of foemen were dying, when Thrym saw that the fleeing Southerners were turning in their flight. Within mere moments he understood why.

A host of riders, some five hundred strong was charging out of the pass.

Thrym's spirits swelled. The cavalry and mounted scouts that Drauglir had set to watch their rear had returned in time to aid in the destruction of the enemy. When they had finished with this lot, they would turn on those the Ninth was dealing with, and their victory over The Fox would be assured.

"*Calvaria!*" he shouted, and drew his sword. "*Blood and honor!*"

"*Blood and honor!*" the men and women of the Second took up the cry, and threw themselves into the fray.

Thrym was making ready to do the same when he noticed that the riders were not joining the battle. Rather they were scattering across the valley, as if in flight.

Then he caught his first sight of the Southern cavalry as they flew through the pass themselves. At their head were banners bearing lion, leopard, and stag. More and more of them were coming. There were at least a thousand of them, and perhaps more besides, if they'd brought foot as well as horse. Already the routed Southern warriors were reforming, and any moment now the enemy cavalry would smash into Thrym's own lines.

Nobel. The man who called himself 'King' had come to the Fox's aid, and Thrym knew then that they were doomed.

"*Soldiers of the Second!*" he yelled over the din. "*To me! To me!*"

His personal guard pressed close to him, as well as the closest companies, and with great effort they cut a swath through the Southern host, taking nearly as many losses themselves as the enemy did, and yet finally he and several companies of his men broke through and found themselves racing north, leaving the Southerners to destroy what remained of the Second, the Ninth, and the Seventeenth.

Forgive me, my brothers, he silently asked as they made for the northern pass, *someone must survive to bring word of this defeat to Svartgard. Our people must be warned, no matter the shame.*

Of the five thousand men he had led into the forest, less than three hundred remained, and few of them were his old veterans. Fewer still had horses. Of his senior Heafodcarls, all were dead, or soon would be. Only one of his blood-guards was still alive, and he had taken a spear wound in the battle. Still, they should be enough to forge a way back to Svartgard, where the Fourteenth could be mobilized, and the remainder of the Second and Ninth could be called up to defend the city.

We must reach Svartgard, he thought as they marched at the quick step. *They must be warned.*

Once through the pass the forest grew close, the trees seeming to loom over them. The trail here was no more than a deer path, and in places they were forced to go single file. The falling snow, which was growing heavier as the day grew longer, made following any kind of pathway difficult, but Thrym urged his men to press on. He was glad of the snow. There was no telling when The Fox's warriors would come howling after them, and the thick clinging flakes that were gusting out of the sky would soon cover any sign of their passing.

Several times they encountered forks in the trail. Thrym ordered his advance scouts to always chose the right-hand way. In traveling to The Fox's castle, the left-hand way had often proven to be the correct one, though it had often felt wrong. Thrym only hoped that by doing the opposite they would escape this maze of a forest, with its tree-choked defiles, its narrow gulches, and sheer-edged ravines.

They had been traveling for some time through a shallow gorge when the column came to a sudden halt.

"*What is it?*" he said as one of the scouting party came sprinting back down the line.

"*The path ahead is blocked, Latteowa,*" the scout replied. "*An avalanche. There does not seem to be a way around it, sir.*"

Thrym ground his teeth together with annoyance.

"*Turn the column around,*" he barked to one of his prafosts. "*We've lost enough time as it is.*"

"*Yes, Latteowa,*" the prafost replied, and began to salute when his arm froze in midair, his eyes filling with sudden terror.

"*What is it?*" Thrym said, and then he saw them too, their lupine bodies dark against the falling snow.

The lips of the gorge were lined with wargs. There were at least a hundred of them.

"Tresspasserrrs," one of them said, its jaws slathering as it spoke.

Thrym had just time enough to draw his sword before the wargs fell on them.

* * * * * * *

The boy was dying. The girl had tied her own belt around what was left of his arm to stem the flow of blood, and held her hand over the wound in his side, but Reynard could see that it was no use. He'd lost far too much blood.

"Martin," she was saying, "Martin hold on. We'll get help. You'll see."

"Mother," Martin said, his brow furrowing. "Mother is that you?"

"No, Martin," the girl said, taking his hand in hers. "It's me. It's Rukenaw"

Martin's eyes opened, seemed to focus on the girl for a moment. His lips flickered, and then he closed his eyes again.

"I can't-" he said, and died.

Rukenaw lowered him to the ground, laying him in a pool of his own blood. She did not weep, but took up her mace and, silent, she walked over to where Drauglir lay, and began to strike him with it.

Again and again she brought the flanged head down on the Northerner's corpse, most of her blows landing on the man's chest and head. Her chest wound reopened, and her bandages grew dark with her own blood, but she did not seem to notice.

"That's enough," Reynard said at last, and took her by the arm.

She looked up at him. Her eyes were like two dark pools.

"It will never be enough," she said.

"Perhaps not," he said.

Finally, she lowered her arm.

"If I hadn't-" she said. "If I'd only-"

"I know," Reynard said, and kneeled down to unfasten Drauglir's fur-lined cloak.

"I killed him," she said. Her voice had grown very quiet.

"We all killed him," Reynard said, and then they laid the cloak over Martin's corpse.

"Come now," Reynard said. "There are still living enemies to fight."

There were not as many as Reynard might have guessed. The Calvarians still held the gate, but many others were surrounded by warriors wielding spears and crossbows, and as they crossed the courtyard they could see that it would not be long before there would be hardly a Northerner left within the castle. The two western towers had been set ablaze, and despite the snowfall and chill wind, it was quite hot.

Isengrim was not hard to spot. He and the blood-guard were still fighting in and around the charred ruins of the smithy, their swords dipping and bowing as they thrust and cut at one another. Isengrim had suffered a series of minor wounds, and Reynard was not surprised. The older man was as graceful as a cat, and his movements were as deadly as they were beautiful.

Reynard wrenched a crossbow away from one of his men and shot the blood-guard in the forehead.

"That was not honorable," Isengrim said as Reynard strode up to meet him, wrenching the warg helm from his head and casting it to the ground. There was true anger in his voice.

"I do not have time for honor," Reynard said. "And neither do you. Do you?"

Isengrim's mouth tightened, as did his grip on Right-hand, but finally he nodded.

"It will be over soon," Reynard said, and clapped the Northerner on the arm. Isengrim stalked off towards the fight at the gatehouse.

"My lord," a voice called to him. It belonged to Tencendur. The man was limping across the yard. He'd suffered a wound to the head, and half his face was wrapped in bandages. "My lord, Reynard!"

"What news?" Reynard asked.

"My lord, the enemy has been routed from the keep, but at great loss. They slew nearly all of the defenders before the last of them fell, and many of the wounded, for they forced their way into the undercroft."

"The priestesses-"

"Are all alive. Hirsent locked them and the children into the wine cellar and held the door herself with naught but a spear. If I had not seen it with my own eyes I would not have thought it possible that a woman could fight so fiercely!"

"I thought I ordered you to send her and her son out on one of the boats."

"She refused to go once she realized that there was not room for all and, well, my lord, you know what she is like. She did let Hermeline take Pinsard, however."

"Is she injured?"

"Not fatally, unless her wounds fester, though I doubt they will- the priestesses saw to her before any of the others."

"Good," Reynard said, and turned to the girl at his side. She was looking very pale, and was holding onto his arm for support. "Please, take Rukenaw to the priestesses as well, Tencendur. She took an arrow on the battlements and I fear that I am no expert when it comes to properly binding a wound."

"At once, my lord," Tencendur said, and scooped the girl into his arms.

When they were gone, Reynard climbed up the stairs of the northeast tower- the only one left that was not engulfed in smoke and fire- and made his way to the topmost turret. From here he could see the little figures in the valley below heaving and swaying against each other. He watched as the Ninth Regiment was torn apart by giants and sellswords, saw the Second nearly prevail over his mercenaries before Nobel's host arrived and swept the field of foes. Some fools from the Second broke free of the melee and plunged right into warg country. The Calvarian camp burned to the ground. The shrikes were already eating the dead.

When the battle was nearly over and done, he climbed back down the steps of the tower and went to greet his guests.

The first to arrive was Tiecelin. He rode through the gatehouse on his gray courser with a dozen or so riders at his back. The last of them had a rope tied to his saddle. Tybalt was at the end of it. The man had managed to keep his feet, but he was bruised and bloodied and clearly exhausted.

"I am glad to see you again, my friend," Reynard said as the Luxian dismounted.

"And I you, my Baron," Tiecelin replied, taking off his peaked cap as he bowed.

"Have you secured the Calvarian gold?" Reynard asked.

"I have," Tiecelin answered, producing a single bag of coins from his saddlebag for Reynard's inspection. "My most trusted men are ensuring that it is all accounted for, and are guarding it with their lives."

"See to it that the captains of the mercenaries are paid what they are owed for their efforts. Bruin should have the contracts."

"My lord," Tiecelin said, lowering his eyes somewhat. "I fear that Bruin is dead. The captain of the Steel Heels says that he saw him fall in battle to one of the blood-guard. My men are still looking for his body."

"He shouldn't be hard to find," Tybalt chuckled. One of Tiecelin's riders kicked him in the head.

"Ah," Reynard said. "Then, if that is so, see to it that he has his own funeral pyre, for this victory belongs to him in no little part, and he has always been a true and faithful friend to me."

"Indeed," Tiecelin said, turning then to regard Tybalt. "As for this one, we found him playing dead amongst the slain. What do you wish me to do with him?"

Reynard strode over to Tybalt. The man was still catching his breath, but at Reynard's approach he straightened, and attempted a smile.

"I like what you've done with the place," Tybalt said, gesturing to the courtyard full of corpses and the burning towers . . . but beneath his sour voice Reynard could hear fear, and he smiled.

"I'm glad you like it," Reynard said, and turned to Tiecelin. "Cut his bonds."

"My lord?" the Luxian said, looking nearly as puzzled by his words as Tybalt was.

"Cut his bonds," Reynard repeated. "After all, he played the part of my catspaw marvelously, have you not, Tybalt?"

"I-" Tybalt stammered, "I- why yes, I- I suppose I have."

"Who could have led the Calvarians to me, if not Tybalt? Who would they have taken for a baseborn traitor, if not Tybalt? Who could I rely on to do exactly as I planned, if not Tybalt?"

He directed the last question to Tybalt himself. The man swallowed and said, "No one."

"You see, that's exactly what I like about you, Tybalt," Reynard said. "You're so very *reliable*."

Tybalt was quiet as Tiecelin's men cut him free. The man rubbed his wrists where the bindings had cut into them.

"Return his weapons to him," Reynard said, "and let it be known that his men were acting under my orders. Should any of them be found alive, they are to be welcomed with open arms."

"As you command, my lord," Tiecelin said, and motioned for several of his men to ride back down the causeway. Another man returned Tybalt's short sword, and his bandolier of knives. Several were missing, Reynard noticed.

"One last thing," Reynard said, as the former brigand was strapping his sword to his side. He took hold of Tybalt's greasy hair with his iron hand and pulled him close.

"If you ever so much as dream of betraying me again," he whispered, "I will know of it. Turn on me again, and I promise you that I will personally carve you up, piece by piece, and make you watch as I have you fed to the shrikes. Do you understand?"

"Yes," Tybalt replied softly. "Yes, I understand, Reynard."

"*Baron* Reynard."

"Baron Reynard," Tybalt repeated. For once, there was no sarcasm in his tone.

"Good," Reynard said, and released him. "Have his wounds properly tended, and find him something to eat if he is hungry."

He'd directed these words to the man who had been Tybalt's keeper. The man nodded, and began to lead Tybalt across the yard to the keep.

They'd taken only a few dozen steps when Reynard called after them, "Tybalt! I almost forgot!"

The dark-eyed man flinched as Reynard tossed him the jingling pouch, and said, "What is this for?" as he opened the drawstrings and marveled at what he found inside.

"I promised you a bag of gold," Reynard said. "Remember?"

He didn't wait for Tybalt's response. The clatter of iron-shod hooves was heralding the arrival of his second guest, and this one he would need to meet before he reached the castle.

He passed through the gatehouse and stepped onto the causeway. Tiecelin and a handful of men followed. The gusting winds buffeted them, and the snow stung their ears and eyes, but they bore it. Riding up the gently curving ramp were a hundred heavily-armored chevalier bearing the emblem of the King.

Nobel was at the head of the column. He was riding Bayard.

The King brought his former steed to halt a few paces from where Reynard stood. He could not tell if the horse recognized him.

"Greetings, Your Majesty," Reynard said, and bowed. "I was beginning to wonder whether you had decided to accept my humble invitation."

"And I was beginning to wonder if your chimera were leading us in anything but circles, Lord Reynard," Nobel replied, lifting his aquiline visor.

"I am glad they did not," Reynard said.

"They were hardly necessary," Nobel said. "A child could have followed the path that the Calvarians left behind them."

"A pity I didn't have any children that I could spare," Reynard said, unsmilingly. "Or I might have sent them instead, Your Majesty."

"I see you haven't lost any of your charming wit," Nobel said, his eyes narrowing. "But I will forgive your impertinence for the moment. The Calvarian army is crippled, their general is dead, and our own losses have been minimal."

"Save for several thousand mercenaries."

"They were not Arcasians," Nobel said. "Their lives mean little to me."

"I did not think that they would," Reynard said, "Your Majesty."

"At any rate, I have won a great victory this day, and though it rankles me to say it, I have *you* to thank for it. Perhaps, Lord Reynard, I may have . . . misjudged you."

"Perhaps," Reynard said.

"We may speak more on this later," Nobel said. "For now, the day is growing long and I would be out of this cold. Come, lead on. I would see this 'hidden fortress' of yours first hand."

"Perhaps you should dismount, Your Majesty, and let me take your horse's reins," Reynard said, reaching out his right hand. "The causeway is growing icy, and Bayard knows me of old."

"I believe I can guide my own horse, Lord Reynard," Nobel said, and gently shook his reins.

The first arrow struck Reynard in the back, just shy of his spine. It sheared through his back plate and bit into his flesh through the leather padding he wore beneath. The force of the impact made him stumble.

The second arrow flew by his head, so close that he thought that he could feel the fletching on the arrow as it zipped past his ear, and struck Bayard in the eye- the only place he was not protected by metal barding.

The horse reared up, confused and screaming, and for a moment Reynard thought that he would be trampled. Then Bayard came down and staggered sideways, his hooves slipping on the slick causeway, and both he and Nobel went over the side.

Nobel did not let out any sound as he and his steed fell, though the drop was long. Reynard did not see them strike the sharp rocks below, either, but he heard it, and he knew without a doubt that the King was dead.

There was chaos on the causeway then. Men's voices were crying out, and horses were whinnying nervously as half of the men present attempted to dismount amidst the press, and the other half made to turn their mounts, though whether this was in order to see to the state of their liege, or to flee, Reynard could not have said.

"Assassin!" one of the king's bodyguards cried then, pointing to the battlements. "There!"

Every man present craned their heads. Sure enough, there was a Calvarian, one of the scouts, racing across the battlements, a bow in his hands and a quiver of arrows on his back. He seemed to be injured, and was limping as he ran.

A moment later Tiecelin had shot him through the throat.

"My lord," the Luxian said to Reynard. "You are injured."

"So it would seem," Reynard said, and allowed the man to escort him into the fortress, though he shrugged off the concern of his men as he walked, and finally urged Tiecelin to leave him be.

The main hall had become an abattoir. No one had yet had the time to see to the removal of the dead, and the bodies of Northerner and Southerner lay together in disordered heaps. The undercroft was little different, though fewer had been slain here, and Hirsent and the priestesses had cleared what space they could to care for the wounded.

At the sight of his wound, Hirsent waved the priestesses away. She snapped the shaft off, removed his armor as gently as she was able, cut through his clothes to expose the wound, and after making a few probes, pulled the head free.

"You are being lucky," she said when she had finished cleaning the wound with a bit of wine, and dressed it. "Arrow is very . . . what is the word?"

"Blunt?" Reynard ventured.

"Yes," Hirsent said, bustling off to wash her hands. "Arrow is very blunt. *No barbs.* Easy to be removing."

"The archer must have used one of our own," Isengrim said. He had entered the undercroft without Reynard seeing him. "A Calvarian arrow would have killed you."

Reynard looked up at his friend, and tried to smile.

"You know why it had to be done."

"I do," Isengrim said.

The Northerner set his bow down, and went to embrace his wife. The two of them kissed, and held each other for a long time, and when they finally parted Hirsent led Isengrim over to where Pinsard lay swaddled in Madam Slopecade's lap, his tiny hand held in hers.

Reynard found an open bottle of wine, and took it up to his quarters.

* * * * * * *

Hermeline came to him eventually. He knew that she would. He had finished the bottle by then, and was sitting by the fire he had started. The room still felt very cold.

"I saw Martin," she said. She was standing in the doorway. Her arms and clothes were slick with blood.

Reynard did not reply.

"You knew they were coming," she went on. "All of them. Didn't you?"

"Yes," he replied.

"Why didn't you tell us?"

"If I *had* told them," Reynard said, "do you think any of them would have stayed?"

Hermeline did not answer. A log snapped in two with a shower of sparks.

"There was no other way," he went on. "I needed them. All of them. Every single one."

"Even Martin?"

"Even Martin."

"Even though you knew he might die?" Hermeline asked.

"When I fight," Reynard said, and turned to face her. "I fight to win."

Hermeline met his gaze, and then she lowered her head and said, "I hope that you are happy with her."

"What do you mean?" Reynard asked, his voice flat.

"You think that I am stupid, don't you?" she said, not raising her head, her long hair covering her face like a dark veil. "You think I do not know what you write in your letters. You think I do not know. But I do. I always knew. And, always, I thought I could bear it. But now..."

"Is that what they died for?" she asked, her voice quavering only slightly. "For her?"

"Yes," he said, and his metal hand curled into a fist.

She looked at him, and finally seemed to see him as he truly was. There was hate in her eyes. He did not blame her.

"I am tired, Hermeline," he said. "Tired of pretending to be something that I am not."

"And what are you?"

"The Baron of Maleperduys," he said, and turned back to the fire.

"I am going now," she said. "Do not follow me."

He nodded, and watched the flames.

She did not take anything with her. He was not surprised. After all, there was nothing in the room that he had not given her.

EPILOGUE

Paquette was busy feeding the Prince when the bell rang.

The Queen wanted to see her child.

Paquette was glad to be back in the Duke's palace. Like her mother before her, and her mother before that, she had been born in the servants' quarters, and knew every nook and cranny of the seat of the Dukes of Arcas- even the King's chambers, for she had been a chambermaid before she had been a wet nurse. Her own daughter would probably be a chambermaid herself one day, perhaps even the head housekeeper, for Madam Epine would one day pass, and she had no children of her own to put forward for the position.

She had certainly hated the Southern fortress they'd been forced to flee to after the battle of the Samara- Carduel it was called, and it made her shudder. It was a vast place, cold and moldering, and even Madam Corte, who hardly believed in chimera, had agreed that it was surely haunted. After all, it was in its banquet hall that Queen Grisana was said to have held her infamous poison feast, and behind its walls the thirteen brothers of Carbonel the First had been entombed alive. There were older stories too about Carduel, some of them as old as the Telchines: tales of beheadings, and children eaten by unsuspecting parents, and worse.

So, when the news came that the siege of Calyx had been lifted, and that they would be heading back north, Paquette had cheered and danced with the other maids, and even let rough Master Arlequin give her a kiss and a squeeze without too much complaint. He'd always been a terror to her as a girl, and his interest had seemed only to swell along with the size of her breasts after she'd given birth. But he'd hardly had his hands on her long before Columbine had swooped in to save her, and she'd been so happy to be returning home that even she had managed to laugh at it.

She was not laughing now, however. Her own daughter had taken ill with the long cough, and in order to shield the Prince from the disease she had not been allowed near her for the last two weeks. The Queen, when she had finally discovered this fact, had been kind enough to request that another wet nurse be provided for the child, but it was cold comfort for Paquette. She was only thankful that the Prince had shown no symptoms himself. She shuddered to think what might become of herself or her child if the boy died because of them.

Prince Lionel was speaking more frequently of late, though Paquette was not certain that everything he said could be considered words in the strictest sense. He could walk as well, and climb stairs, though he still liked to be carried. From her own experience, she knew it would not be long now before he would begin to demand almost constant attention, and she expected that even Madam Corte might finally give in to Paquette's requests for a younger nurse maid to help care for the child.

For the moment though there was only Paquette and Madam Corte, and the older woman was not as swift on her feet. So, when Prince Lionel broke into a full run as they made for the Queen's salon, it was Paquette, not Corte, who caught the boy, taking him up in her arms against his protests.

"No," he shouted as she carried him through the door. "No, no, no, no, no, no!"

"I hope he has not been like this all day," the Queen said as she rose from her writing desk.

"He has not, Majesty," Paquette said, lowering her eyes.

"Mama!" Lionel squealed and ran into his mother's waiting grasp. Paquette was greatly relieved that the boy had finally understood that distinction. Their flight south, and the temporary breakdown of protocol that it had engendered, had at least done that much good.

"Are you being good?" the Queen asked.

"Yes," Lionel replied. Paquette smiled at that. The boy had few responsibilities beyond playing with blocks and dolls.

"Have you been fed?"

"Yes," the boy replied again.

"And are you driving your nanny to distraction?" the Queen asked.

"Yes." The boy already understood that the correct answer to his mother's questions was always 'yes.'

The Queen laughed, and kissed Lionel on the forehead. As if on cue, Madam Corte stormed into the room, her skirts swishing loudly as she crossed the carpet and leaned over the boy. A long strand of her hair, which was growing grayer every day, had fallen out of place.

"His Highness must not run," Corte chided, waggling her finger at the boy. "His Highness might trip and hurt himself!"

The Prince shrank under Corte's shadow, and clutched at the hem of his mother's dress.

"Oh, leave him be," the Queen said, "I'm certain that I did my fair share of running at his age."

"His Highness will be King one day," Madam Corte huffed. "He must be protected."

"Let us not protect him too much, Madam Corte," the Queen said, stroking Lionel to soothe him. "After all, even a King must learn how to fall, as well as how to pick himself up again. Is that not so?"

Corte bit her lip, obviously unconvinced, but said, "As Your Majesty wishes."

The Queen inquired after the Prince's activities, seeming to delight in the details of his play, and smiling at each of the new words he had learned, when the messenger arrived.

He was not one of the royal messengers, at least, not one of the few that Paquette had ever seen. His boots and the hem of his cloak were mud-stained, and he looked as if he had been riding for days without stop.

"I bear a message for the Queen," he said, removing his hat and bowing before producing a letter stamped with the royal seal.

It was a letter from the King.

Madam Corte accepted the message from the man, crossed the room, and handed it to the Queen.

The Queen broke the wax with her penknife, and began to read.

She was halfway through the letter when she said, "Madam Corte, will you please escort my son back to his quarters. I wish to be alone."

"As Your Majesty wishes," Corte answered. She did not need to tell Paquette to retrieve Lionel.

"Come along, Your Highness," the chambermaid said, "It is time for your nap."

"No," Lionel said, but he took Paquette's hand anyway.

As they were making to leave, the Queen addressed the messenger.

"Sir," she said. "Did you see it happen?"

"I did, Your Majesty," he replied.

"How did it happen?"

"A Calvarian shot his horse with an arrow," the man said.

"If you would . . . stay awhile with me, sir," the Queen said. "I would hear more."

"As Your Majesty wishes," the man said.

"You are dismissed Paquette," the Queen said. The maid had not realized that she had stopped in her tracks.

"Yes, Your Majesty," she said, curtsying by way of an apology before leading the Prince out into the hall.

They'd gotten halfway across the east wing when Lionel broke free from her. He giggled as he ran, and did not have a set of heavy skirts and undergarments to slow him down, so it was a long time before Paquette caught up to him. She was relieved too, for he'd come to a stop at the door to his mother's salon, and Paquette would not have to explain how a boy not yet three summers old had managed to escape from her.

As Paquette knelt down to scoop Lionel up she noticed that the door to the salon was partially open. She was not surprised, this part of the palace was in need of renovation, and many of the doors did not sit properly on their hinges.

What did surprise her was what she saw through the gap between the door and jamb.

The Queen was in the messenger's arms, weeping. Her head was buried in the man's shoulder, and he was holding her to him with his right hand.

She was backing away from the door, the Prince in her arms, when the man turned and saw her.

Paquette had once seen one of the old Duke's cats playing with a mouse. Again and again the cruel thing had let the mouse go, before pouncing on it, and batting it about with its claws. Paquette had finally put an end to it, and when she did so the cat had looked up at her in such a way as if to suggest that it wished that she were a mouse.

The look in the man's eyes was little different.

Paquette turned and fled.

It was not until that night, as she lay restless next to her husband- the news of the King's death still swirling through her head- that she realized that the man had not been looking at her.

He had been looking at the Prince.

Acknowledgements

I owe the completion of this novel to three people: my mother, and my friends Molly and Katie. My mother is an excellent proofreader, and probably my biggest fan. Molly served as the primary sounding board for this story long before I knew that I was going to turn it into a series of novels. Katie provided me with much-needed constructive criticism, and motivated me to consistently sit down in front of my computer and commit words to paper.

Thank you so much, all three of you. I hope to work with you again soon.